UNTAMED GLORY

"You mule-headed female!" Rafe snarled. "You could have been killed!"

"What about you?" Brenna demanded. "Standing there in full view! Are you crazy?"

"Better me for a target than a pea-brained witch!"

"You—you deliberately drew his fire from me?" Suddenly the enormity of what she had done hit her. Blackness threatened, and she swayed.

"Don't you dare faint on me now!" Rafe roared, shaking her hard.

"I—I'm not." She gulped, blinking away the darkness, then stared up into his gray eyes. "Why?" she whispered.

"Because . . . oh, hell! You ask too many damned female questions."

Then he took her lips, staking his possession of her senses with his kiss . . .

UNTAMED GLORY

SUZANNAH DAVIS

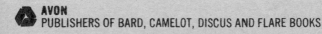

AVON
PUBLISHERS OF BARD, CAMELOT, DISCUS AND FLARE BOOKS

UNTAMED GLORY is an original publication of Avon Books. This work has never before appeared in book form. This work is a novel. Any similarity to actual persons or events is purely coincidental.

AVON BOOKS
A division of
The Hearst Corporation
105 Madison Avenue
New York, New York 10016

Copyright © 1988 by Suzannah Davis
Published by arrangement with the author
Library of Congress Catalog Card Number: 87-91679
ISBN: 0-380-75397-9

First Avon Books Printing: March 1988

In memory of Isabel Falvey Nelson,
my indomitable "Grandma Belle,"
who went to Marshall, too.

And for Diane Wicker Davis
with many thanks.

Chapter 1

1890

" 'If it 'tis done, then 'twere well it were done quickly!' "

Brenna Galloway's soft, dulcet tones held a note of urgency. She clutched a bundle to her breast, and her blue-green gaze stole furtive looks right then left down the long, deserted room. "Hurry, Annie, the blade!"

"The what?" Annie's flat, twangy Texan voice was puzzled. "Oh, you mean this!" She passed the curved, wooden-handled instrument to Brenna, then dropped an exaggerated curtsy, her warm brown eyes dancing with suppressed merriment.

"You're too, too kind," Brenna announced grandly. Brown paper crackled, and two young, feminine heads, one mousy brown, one glowing red-gold, bent over the intriguing package.

"Oh, ain't they fine!" Annie breathed.

Eagerly, Brenna picked up the glossy pair of brand-new high button shoes. The pungent odor of tanned leather and aromatic polish tickled her nostrils. With deft movements, she rid herself of her old, clumsy boots, and shoved her slim feet into the stylish footwear, stiff with newness. Wielding the buttonhook provided by Annie, she slipped the shiny black disks through their holes until they marched with military precision across her shapely ankles and insteps. Rising, she lifted her skirts and pirouetted.

"Will I do, Annie?"

"You'll be the belle of the ball, no doubt about it,"

1

the other girl answered confidently, a mischievous smile creasing her plump face.

"I shall dance all night," Brenna replied, her expression dreamy. She hummed a gay waltz under her breath and swayed gracefully. Happiness bubbled up inside her like a mountain spring, cool and refreshing after a long emotional drought. The room's dingy beams and fly-spattered walls disappeared, replaced momentarily by a shining vision of a brightly lit ballroom where elegantly dressed couples whirled to the music of violins.

Laughing, Annie lifted her skirts and bounced around in an energetic imitation of Brenna's movements. Crisp petticoats rustled in time to the lyrical tune, and happy smiles were the grace notes to their playful dance.

The deafening blast of a train whistle shattered the fragile illusion like the pop of a soap bubble. Both girls jumped guiltily. They gazed at each other for a long moment, listening as the vibration of wheels on iron tracks reached the upper levels of the building, shaking the rafters with a familiar litany.

"I think your carriage has arrived, my lady," Annie announced impishly. They dissolved into the threatening giggles, falling onto one of the narrow cots that lined the room, helpless with laughter. Arms clasped affectionately, they gasped and laughed and tried to contain their merriment.

"Oh, Annie! Your jokes make my sides hurt," Brenna accused, her cheeks pink.

Annie caught her breath and wiped tears from the corners of her eyes. "Honestly, I don't know how you do it, Brenna," she said admiringly. "I'd swear you was one of them grand English ladies living in a posh castle when you put on them hoity-toity airs. And quoting all that fancy stuff."

"It's just play acting," Brenna replied, her voice reverting to its usual lilting, faintly Irish cadences. "Like I did at home with my da before . . ." She paused, and a flicker chased across her face, robbing her pretty features of some of their gaiety. She gave a little shrug and smiled brightly at her friend. "Do you know your Shakespeare? Your part of lady's maid is a fine character piece. You'd be wonderful as Juliet's nurse. Perhaps we should join a drama company. Have you ever thought of going on the road?''

"Posh and nonsense!" Annie exclaimed, but she flushed with pleasure at the compliment.

The train's whistle sounded again, closer and louder, demanding attention. The blast rattled the windowpanes of the narrow garret dormitory that housed the twenty or so young women who worked in the Railway Depot Restaurant and Hotel in this small, bustling hub city of Marshall, Texas.

"For once, the one-ten is early," Brenna said. "We'd better hurry. Old Hudgins is probably looking for us."

"Can't be the one-ten," Annie said, frowning at the round gold watch pinned to her apron bib. "It must be that special Jimmy was talking about. Some bigwig from the East, he said. A private engine and everything."

"You and Jimmy have been seeing quite a bit of each other lately, haven't you?" Brenna teased. "The pay must be better in the rail yards than I thought."

Annie blushed, and for a moment her plain features were almost pretty. "We get along. But I worry about him being so active in the Knights of Labor. You know it don't pay to be involved in a labor organization right now." She glanced once around the dormitory to be certain they were still alone, then lowered her voice. "He says that our keeping our eyes and ears open around the depot is a big help to the brotherhood."

"I'm glad to do what I can, you know that," Brenna replied. "I just wish it were more." She glanced down, surprised to see that her hands were clenched tightly on her lap. She relaxed them with a conscious effort.

"I didn't mean to upset you," Annie said worriedly. "I know it's hard, about your brother and all."

"Sean's death is something I've had to accept," Brenna said quietly. "He chose to go out with the Knights during the Texas and Pacific strike four years ago, but it made no difference when Gould wouldn't even negotiate. He was a casualty of those riots, sure as if he'd gone to war. Those bloodsuckers in New York are still bleeding the wage earner dry. I'll do anything I can to destroy their power." Her voice was low but fierce.

"That's how we all feel," Annie agreed. She patted

Brenna's hand in an awkward gesture of comfort. "It's coming, too. Jimmy says they're having another secret meeting tonight. What would Mr. Gould say if he knew the Knights of Labor were meeting in his own roundhouse?"

"He'd die of apoplexy!" Brenna's wry expression sent Annie off in new peals of giggles. They rose and Brenna cast another admiring glance at her stylish footwear.

"Thanks for coming up with me, Annie. I couldn't wait to try on my new shoes."

"I can't blame you. It's not every day you get a Montgomery Ward mail-order package," Annie replied cheerfully. "You deserve something special, as hard as you've saved. You really oughtn't to send so much home, you know. You've hardly got enough for yourself, much less to pay for that college you want to attend! How do you ever expect to become a teacher at this rate?"

"I have to send enough for Maggie and Shannon. The nuns take good care of them, but it takes money, too. It's all up to me now." She broke off, shrugging and feeling a bit guilty about spending any money on herself, even for something as basic as shoes. The threadbare stocking she kept pinned to her petticoat bumped against her thigh with a reassuring weight of coins and bills. With a diligence that would have put Scrooge to shame, she scrimped and saved, knowing each day was a step toward independence and self-sufficiency, as well as her very survival. But she was entitled to something pretty once in a while, surely? She smiled confidently at Annie. "I don't mind being patient. I know I'll get to college one day."

"I just hope your sisters realize what you're doing for them," Annie sniffed. "It seems to me that that stepfather of yours—"

"No!"

Annie turned a surprised glance on Brenna, startled by the vehemence of her single word. Brenna shook her head.

"I'll never let them go back to that man—never!"

"But, Brenna, he was married to your mother," Annie said reasonably.

"It was living with him that killed her, too." Brenna's voice was acid with sudden bitterness. Behind the thick

line of her sooty lashes, her eyes were a turbulent green.
"No, none of us Galloways will go back to the O'Donnell house, not now, not ever!" Brenna raked her hands
through the luxuriant mass of her hair, automatically
tucking a stray, springy curl into the knot at her nape in
an effort to calm herself. She touched Annie's arm and
attempted a smile. "I'm sorry, I didn't mean to snap at
you."

"That's all right," Annie replied easily. "We'd better
go."

They crossed the room toward the steep flight of stairs
leading to the kitchens. Annie stuffed her mousy curls
haphazardly into her white frilly cap, then smoothed the
heavily starched white apron over the dark blue skirt and
long-sleeved white cotton waist worn by all the female
staff. "Would you see if my bow is straight?" she asked.

Brenna obligingly checked the recalcitrant bow, smiling
at its bunched and bedraggled appearance. She pulled
Annie's sash, then retied the offending bow into pert
perfection.

"Thanks, Brenna," Annie said, opening the staircase
door. "I don't know how I managed until you came to
work here. I can hardly believe it was only six months
ago."

"It was a godsend to me, too," Brenna said, and her
words were heartfelt.

Her mind touched upon the memory of the misery and
abuse she and her sisters suffered even before their
mother's death. It got worse after Bridget died and Sean
was forced to leave. The oldest at twenty, Brenna had
been able to take care of herself. But when fourteen-year-
old Maggie had come running to her, crying, her bodice
ripped from their stepbrother Padrick's brutish yet ineffectual advances, she'd known she couldn't protect either
Maggie or ten-year-old Shannon any longer.

The advertisement in the New Orleans newspaper for
young women "of good character" had promised little,
but the pittance of a salary and the long working hours
of a waitress in a railroad dining hall had seemed a kind
of salvation. Brenna shuddered to think of Malvin
O'Donnell's rage when he'd discovered their escape from
virtual bondage on his St. Francisville farm. Hiding the

girls with the nuns in the convent in New Orleans was a simple solution, but Brenna knew she'd never be able to find a job safely out of O'Donnell's way if she stayed in Louisiana. He'd not give up looking for them out of sheer Irish stubbornness, not to mention the matter of the small amount of money she had stolen from his strongbox to make their flight possible. She found a bit of grim humor imagining the red-faced fit O'Donnell had thrown at that audacity, but it was nothing compared to the price she would have liked him to pay for the way he'd slowly killed her mother.

"It seems we've always been friends," Annie rattled on. She paused at the top of the stairs. "Don't forget your cap."

"Oh!" Brenna brought her thoughts back to earth, then dug into her apron pocket and jammed the cap over her hair, grimacing while she pulled it low on her forehead. "I never feel comfortable in this thing," she muttered.

"You have to wear it. You know how particular Hudgins is about the uniforms," Annie said. "I guess he thinks it discourages flirting. After all, 'we are a respectable place of business.' " She mimicked their employer's stuffy formality and pompous tones, then grinned. "Anyway, you'd look beautiful in a feed sack! I'd give anything to look like you."

"Oh, Annie!" Brenna exclaimed in laughing dismay. "My nose is too small, my mouth is too large, and do you see these?" She pointed with absolute disgust at the bridge of her retroussé nose. "Freckles! Freckles that no amount of buttermilk will ever bleach out."

Annie studied Brenna's delicate coloring and high cheekbones. "Humph. I'd trade with you any day, freckles and all." Shaking her head, she preceded Brenna down the steep wooden stairs, their feet clattering noisily on the wooden treads. "Watch the landing. You don't want to slip. You probably should have roughened the soles of them shoes before you wore 'em."

"I'll be careful," Brenna promised, smiling fondly at the back of her friend's head.

She was unable to resist another admiring peek at the shiny tips of the new shoes visible under the edge of her long dark skirts. "Frailty, thy name is woman," she quoted inwardly, silently laughing at herself. The new leather creaked reassuringly, and Brenna wiggled her toes, testing the fit. The modish heel was a bit higher than she was accustomed to wearing, but the added height made her feel fashionable and ladylike, even though her hands rubbed down the rough plaster walls of the narrow stairwell for balance.

The smells of hot grease, roasting meat, and stewed collard greens wafted up from the kitchens to assault Brenna's nose. Annie pushed open the door at the base of the stairs and released the din of crashing cutlery, clinking dinnerware, and the shrill shouts of harried waitresses. The unseasonable October heat mixed with the steam of countless bubbling pots, making the atmosphere muggy and oppressive. Brenna walked through the hot, humid wall of air and instantly felt a sheen of moisture coat her upper lip and prickle beneath her arms. She wiped at the beads of perspiration on her temples, tucked a damp, strawberry-blond curl into the restraining band of her cap, and sighed, knowing the pristine, starched expanse of her apron would soon be a limp cotton rag.

"Where have you two been?" a strident voice snapped, halting both girls in mid-step.

"Had to visit the necessary room, Clara," Annie lied demurely.

"It was our break, anyway," Brenna added calmly, unwilling to let Annie take the full brunt of the head kitchen maid's ill temper. She watched Clara unflinchingly, secretly amused at the hostility that always surrounded the skinny woman. Rail thin and stringy, Clara always reminded Brenna of an undernourished Banty hen looking for a fight. Her sour, pinched mouth turned down at the corners. Brenna was certain it was because she laced her corset strings too tight, a garment Brenna flatly refused to wear to work, never mind Victorian standards of modesty. It infuriated Clara to no end that she couldn't intimidate Brenna as she did many of the other working girls. Brenna knew enough about bullies to stand her ground, do her job, and ignore Clara's surliness.

"The one-ten just unloaded four hundred hungry passengers, so get moving! Don't know why they hired girls as green as you two. Just asking for trouble," Clara grumbled. She fixed a beady eye on Brenna and Annie, who were listening patiently to her diatribe. "Well, what are you just standing there for? Get to work!"

"Yes, ma'am," Brenna and Annie said in unison. They turned, hiding smiles.

Brenna's new shoes clicked rhythmically across the hygienic ceramic-tiled floor. Annie dodged around a fast-moving waitress balancing a tray loaded with platters of fried steak and potatoes, beef stew, and chicken and gravy. When Brenna had first come to work, she often marveled at the apparent confusion in the kitchens; but now she paid scant notice to the near collisions as waitresses sailed back and forth, seemingly oblivious to anyone or anything in their paths. Just as Brenna and Annie paused by the swinging doors leading into the dining rooms and reached for order tablets and pencils, the door swung open beside them.

"Have you seen him yet?" Pollie, a frowzy brunette carrying an empty tray, asked in a low conspiratorial voice.

"Seen who?" Annie demanded.

"Why, Jay Gould, the richest man in America, that's who!" Pollie replied. "Rode his private car down from New York, he did. Fancy as a sultan's palace! Heard him tell old Hudgins myself."

"Jay Gould is here?" Brenna asked, her eyes wide and incredulous.

"What do you think he's doing in Marshall?" Annie demanded.

Pollie shrugged, moving away. "Who knows? He owns all these here railroads, don't he? Why don't you ask him yerself?" she suggested over her shoulder.

Brenna shot a sharp glance at Annie, a worried frown creasing the arch of her brows. "Did Jimmy say anything about this?"

Annie shook her head. "No, he didn't know it was Gould coming. Oh, Brenna!" she said in sudden anxiety. "Do you think Gould knows about the Knights' meeting? Has he come to cause trouble?"

"His kind don't do their dirty work themselves," Brenna said, her voice scathing and filled with loathing.

"But how can we be sure?" Annie wailed, fear for her beau raising her voice.

"Shh! We'll just have to find out what he's doing here," Brenna replied.

Annie relaxed at the calm determination in her friend's tone. "All right. I'll see what I can learn."

"No, let me." Brenna's voice was grim. "He's the one who wouldn't deal with the Knights four years ago. I want to see firsthand the man who murdered my brother."

Annie's brown eyes widened at the chill of hatred in Brenna's voice. "But how?"

Brenna thought rapidly, then her gaze lit on Pollie, returning with a laden tray. She nodded to Annie. "Like this."

In a matter of seconds, Brenna convinced Pollie to let her deliver the steaming contents of the tray to the dining room. "After all," she explained, "I want to see the richest man in America, too."

"Be my guest," Pollie offered gratefully. "This here stuff's for table twelve, and there's five screaming brats waitin' for it. Mr. Gould's sitting at the next table, there by the French doors."

"Thanks, Pollie." Brenna staggered momentarily under the weight of the tray, then she straightened and, giving Annie a wink, strode purposefully into the dining room.

Brenna concentrated on balancing the heavy tray as she crossed the crowded dining hall toward table twelve. Her lips pressed together with effort, she lifted her head to catch a glimpse of the men seated by the open French doors. There! Standing by the corpulent, checker-clad figure of Mr. Hudgins! Was the tall dark man with the mustache Jay Gould, the king of the robber barons and the man responsible for Sean's death? That man looked too young, perhaps only in his thirties. The other silver-haired man? No, wait! Hudgins bent deferentially toward a slight, bearded figure seated in the corner. Could that be Gould?

Brenna's wandering attention focused suddenly on the table of waiting customers. Two wilted parents were patently ignoring the antics of five hungry, cranky boys. The youngest, a child of three or four in a pleated frock, was dumping the contents of his water glass onto the floor. Brenna stifled a groan of irritation. Now she'd have to clean up that mess, and certainly get a dressing-down from Mr. Hudgins to boot!

She darted a glance in his direction. Good, he was still talking. Maybe he wouldn't notice it if she could just get the food down in front of those children. While she did that she could try to catch whatever it was they were discussing so intently. Jimmy and the Knights of Labor needed all the help they could get, especially against slick eels like Gould and his cronies!

She quickened her steps. The smooth leather soles of her new shoes hit the stream of water trailing across the tiles. Her right foot skidded awkwardly out in front. Brenna gasped, fighting to keep the tray balanced on her shoulder. Her left foot skidded sideways.

"Oh, *nooo!*"

Brenna's involuntary cry of dismay turned all heads in her direction. Stew sloshed from the bowls on the tray, scalding her fingers just as her treacherously stylish heel caught on the leg of a wooden chair. Up went the tray and all its contents. Down went Brenna, sliding on her rump to land beneath the table in an ignominious bundle of tumbled skirts and petticoats.

A rain of cutlery and food pelted down around her. Brenna's eyes widened in horror. A piece of greasy fried steak whizzed past her nose, then landed—plop!—on the tartan-plaid knee of a drummer's suit. Buttery yellow potatoes splattered against the lavender folds of a matron's best traveling gown, oozing through the feathered trimming like sickly albino worms. A spoon coated with rich brown gravy hit an itinerant preacher squarely in the chest, speckling his white clerical collar, then falling like a lost soul to the floor. Crisp chunks of corn bread dropped like hailstones, and the metal tray hit a table corner and vibrated with a drumlike thunder. A plate, now terrifyingly empty of its contents, hit the floor on its edge, then rolled like a cartwheel toward Brenna. Hypnotized, she watched it wobble, right itself, then wobble again, finally falling to its rim, rolling round and round, until at last its clattering stilled in the shocked, oppressive silence.

A titter of laughter rippled through the dining room, shattering the quiet. The little boy wailed loudly for his lunch, scattered now over most of the other customers. Brenna cringed and sucked the painful scald on her forefingers, too horrified to move. Checkered trousers and a spattered pair of shiny black patent-leather shoes pushed a path through bits of meat, soggy slices of potatoes, and rounds of orange carrots. Brenna tore her eyes from the one unbroken plate and looked up into Mr. Hudgins's beet-red face.

"Oh, I'm sorry, sir!" she gasped. Waves of hot color flooded her cheeks and her temples pounded. "I'll get it cleaned up right away!" She scrambled to her knees, averting her eyes from Hudgins's florid, purpling countenance. She hurriedly scraped the bits and pieces of the mess together, heedless of the sharp edges of the broken crockery. Humiliation and fear clogged her throat.

"You're dismissed!" Hudgins roared.

Brenna's head snapped up like a puppet on a string. Dismay parted her lips, and her blue-green eyes stared, saucer-wide. The blood drained out of her face. She couldn't lose this job. She couldn't! What would she do? Where would she go? What about her sisters? Suddenly, her hatred of Jay Gould paled in the face of a more immediate disaster.

"Oh, sir! It was an accident, please—"

Enraged, Hudgins swung his beefy fist, roaring like an inarticulate bull. Brenna ducked, years of conditioning enabling her to react instinctively. His blow glanced off her head, knocking the frilly cap aside and spilling her hair down her back in glorious red-gold disarray.

Polished boots stepped between Brenna and her angry employer. "That's enough, Hudgins," a deep masculine voice ordered curtly. Strong hands grasped Brenna's shoulders and lightly set her to her feet.

Bewildered, Brenna's gaze traveled up the long, buff-trousered legs, across the massive chest covered with the expensive wool of a tailored frock coat, and came to rest on the harsh, handsome face of her rescuer. He was the man who had been speaking with Hudgins earlier.

Up close, she could see the sensuous curve and mobility of his mouth, half hidden by the thick brush of his dark mustache. High cheekbones gave his face an aura of strength and purpose; the hollows beneath, a classical

handsomeness. His skin was dark and tanned. Hair and
sideburns as glossy and black as a raven's wing curled
slightly over the pristine white of his shirt collar. Despite
his conservative coat and trousers, Brenna felt a leashed
tension in his lean body that made him seem a man more
at home in rougher garb.

"Is the girl injured, Rafe?"

Brenna glanced in the direction of the soft voice. The
small, bearded man sitting at the table looked at them
inquiringly. His silver-haired companion passed a napkin
and he calmly wiped a dribble of brown gravy from his
trouser leg.

"It appears not, Mr. Gould," Rafe replied.

Startled, Brenna jumped. This little, inconsequential-
looking man with gravy stains on his pants was Jay
Gould! She could hardly believe her eyes. How could this
soft-spoken individual be responsible for so much misery?
For Sean's death? Her eyes darkened. What had Da
always said? "A rose by any other name can smell as
sweet—or as deadly." She wished in sudden hysteria that
she had thrown the whole damn tray at him.

The man holding her looked down at her abrupt
movement. She moved back a step, and his hands
dropped to his sides. Brenna licked dry lips and lifted her
chin. No matter what, she'd fight her own battles! She
knew this Rafe person was studying her expression with
an unnerving intensity. His unusual gray eyes noted the
defiant jut of her jaw, narrowing until they were mere
glints of silver. Brenna schooled her face into blandness,
shielding her eyes with the thick veil of her lashes.

"Surely we can avoid any more . . . unpleasantness,
Mr. Hudgins?" Gould asked.

Hudgins turned to the bearded man, his manner
obsequious. "I'm most terribly sorry, sir. We run a very
fine restaurant here. I assure you this incompetent slut will
be fired immediately."

"I hardly think that is necessary," Gould replied, his
bored voice as soft as a woman's. "What do you say,
Rafe?"

"Agreed. Especially when the accident was entirely my
fault," Rafe said. "I'm afraid my feet were in the way.

It would be unfair to dismiss the girl under the circumstances, not to mention an insult to Mr. Gould.''

Brenna's lips parted in complete astonishment. Why would this stranger come to her aid? It might be true that she had tumbled across his feet, but it was in the course of her fall, not the cause of it, as she well knew. Bewildered, yet with a growing glimmer of hope, she watched Hudgins stutter, backtracking at the very thought of insulting a millionaire of Gould's standing.

"Well, now, if you say so, Mr. Sinclair. I guess there's no harm done," Hudgins muttered, his porcine features twitching. He glanced at Brenna. "What are you waiting for, gal? Get this mess cleaned up!"

"Yes, sir." Brenna gulped. Rafe Sinclair's strong hand on her arm forestalled her.

"Are you sure you're all right?" he demanded.

"Yes. Thank you." She forced the words through stiff lips, galled that her reprieve should come at the hands of her hated enemies—Gould and his minions! She pulled away and dropped to her knees, determined to complete the cleanup swiftly and with as much pride as she could muster under such humiliating circumstances.

Pride. Rafe had to hand it to the girl, she had pluck. She hadn't shed a tear despite the nearly disastrous results of her fall. Any other female would have resorted to hysterics long ago, but this one held on to the scraps of her dignity with a fierceness that gave him pause.

Rafe watched her work on her knees, her spine stiff, scraping up the garbage from the tiles with the hem of her apron. He listened with half an ear as Jay Gould dismissed Hudgins, silencing that tiresome fellow's apologies with a cool nod and a penetrating stare. Rafe's lips twitched. Hudgins was no match for Gould. Rafe had seen him, with no more than a casual word, reduce the most powerful men on Wall Street to sniveling idiots.

The girl wiped congealing gravy off the floor with a soiled napkin. Rafe knew his feet were in her way, but he perversely stood his ground. She paused, her shoulders bent, the fall of strawberry hair hanging down her back, then she sat back on her heels and glared at him. Rafe nearly laughed out loud. The corners of his mustache lifted. Amusement filled him at the mixture of irritation, resentment, and downright hostility radiating from her smoky green eyes.

"Rafe?" Jay Gould's soft voice was insistent.

Rafe lifted a mocking eyebrow at the girl. Her cheeks went rosy with embarrassment—annoyance?—but she didn't glance away. Satisfied, the corner of his mouth twisting wryly, Rafe carefully stepped around her to take his place beside his employer. "Yes, sir?"

"Giovanni brings some rather alarming news."

Rafe glanced at Giovanni Rossini, Gould's confidential secretary for as long as Rafe had known them both. Indeed, it had been under Giovanni's supervision that Rafe had shed his slum upbringing, after being singled out by Gould himself during the Jim Fiske days at the Grand Opera House and tutored as a protégé in return for unquestioning loyalty. Rafe had repaid that investment a hundredfold, though there had never been any love lost between him and Rossini. Recent years had not been kind to Rossini, threading his black hair with silver although he wasn't much older than Gould's own middle years. His eyes were tired, dark and melancholy, but his mind was still astute, his influence with Gould undiluted, much to Rafe's irritation. Rafe looked at Rossini questioningly.

"Smitherson refuses to deal directly with us," Giovanni said sedately, steepling his long Italian fingers beneath his clean-shaven chin. His eyes were as opaque as black marbles. They spoke quietly, their voices not carrying far amid the renewed tumult of the crowded restaurant.

"We knew that was always a possibility," Rafe interjected.

"True. Yet now we must move to force his hand," Gould said. He stroked his long black beard with a pale hand. "To that end, Giovanni and I will journey by carriage shortly so that we can meet with Mahoney of the Santa Fe in Jefferson tomorrow."

"But, sir, Mahoney has no power to negotiate on the Santa Fe's behalf," Rafe protested.

"Ah, but Smitherson can't know that, and perhaps such news—carefully forwarded by Giovanni—will make him reconsider, allowing us to pursue our real target, the Southern Pacific."

Rafe pulled up a chair and sat down, leaning on his elbows. "Surely there's no reason for such precipitate action, sir," he began earnestly.

"Ah, Rafe!" Gould laughed softly, then glanced at Giovanni. "Only the young have the time for patience, am I not correct, old friend?" Rossini's faint half smile seemed to be the only answer he required. He turned again to Rafe. "I'm not a well man, and if I'm ever to control the southern routes as well as the northern lines west, then the time must be now. Especially since we hear rumblings of a new resurgence of the cursed Knights of Labor."

A muffled clatter of broken crockery brought Rafe's attention back to the girl still working on the floor beside their table. She tossed the dish shards onto her tray with a vengeance, but something about the tilt of her head suggested a listening attitude. He glanced at her averted profile and frowned. He supposed she could be considered pretty if one's taste ran to pale, thin women. Dark hair, smoldering eyes, and a voluptuous figure had always been more his style. He thrust the memory away. It did no good to long for what was forever beyond his reach. He noticed the girl's fingers were still shaking.

"Rafe, you will remain with the *Atalanta* until Plummer arrives," Gould continued.

"I had thought to accompany you," Rafe said, flicking a glance toward Rossini. He had no desire to cool his heels even in the luxury of Gould's private rail car. His jaw tightened at the bland look on the older man's inscrutable features. What game did his rival play this time?

"Nonsense. Giovanni and I are still capable of some things," Gould said with a soft laugh. "And it's time we laid our petty differences to rest. Don't you agree, Giovanni?"

"Mr. Sinclair is ever cordial to me, Mr. Gould," Rossini answered. He picked up a large leather satchel and fixed his liquid-black eyes on Rafe.

"Splendid! This makes for excellent business," his employer replied, a small smile on his thin lips. "You understand that we must have those securities, don't you, Rafe? We all stand or fall on the outcome of your negotiations with Plummer."

Rafe stifled his annoyance. "I won't let you down, sir."

"Good."

Gould scraped back his chair, and the three men rose together, moving to stand in the open doorway. Parallel lines of tracks stretched in opposite directions just beyond the wooden platform. A puffing locomotive waited on one end of the station, and the Doppler howl of a whistle indicated another impending arrival. While Rossini and Gould spoke briefly of their travel plans, Rafe let his glance trail back to the girl still working on her knees.

How many times had she wiped that particular section of the floor? Trained by early environment and inclination to be suspicious, Rafe's instincts flared into sudden arousal. She had been within earshot during their entire conversation. What had she heard?

She stood, lifted the groaning tray to balance on one hip, then pushed damp tendrils of red-gold hair out of her eyes. Gray eyes clashed with blue-green ones and the girl froze. Rafe let his gaze run insolently along the curve of her luscious mouth, down the soft thrust of her bosom to the incongruous tips of stylish shoes, and back up to her face. There was something appealing and vaguely familiar about that determined chin, the almond shape of those wide-set orbs.

She gasped, outrage tightening the delicately carved jaw, fury coloring her cheeks and setting the smattering of freckles across the bridge of her small nose into stark relief. She whirled with a flounce of her skirts and ran toward the kitchens, but not before Rafe saw the gleam of sheer hatred in her eyes. He followed Gould and Rossini out of the restaurant, his thoughts preoccupied. The girl should be grateful, yet she wasn't. Why?

There had to be a reason for the girl's interest in their conversation and the venom in her expression. Rafe's lips tightened and he jammed his hands into his trouser pockets. Whatever it was, his instincts told him he'd better find out if her enmity posed a threat to them—and find out fast!

Brenna rinsed yet another plate in the scalding water and sighed. The burn on her forefingers throbbed and her back ached from hours spent leaning over the steaming sink, but at least she still had her job—for the time being.

"You, miss," Hudgins had snarled upon her return to the kitchen, "made a damned lucky escape! Any other time, you'd be out in the streets, but I can't take a chance that Mr. Gould might ask after you again. Never know what them rich bastards'll do." He nudged a thick finger under Brenna's chin and forced her face up. It was all she could do to keep from flinching away, but a flicker of pride forced her to meet his look squarely.

"And you'll see to the dish washing from now on 'til I say different," Hudgins ranted. "Clara, you see she works extra until that broken crockery is paid for, too!"

Brenna risked a glance toward the kitchen maid. Clara's malicious satisfaction tightened her sour expression into a pucker that proclaimed Hudgins's decision a just punishment for all Brenna's offenses, real and imagined.

"And watch your step, girl," Hudgins warned, his eyes flat slits in his fleshy face. "Another episode like this and out you go, Gould or no Gould. Understand?"

"Yes, sir," Brenna replied, swallowing hard. She tried not to let her relief show. Any job, even the menial task of dish washing usually reserved for Mexican boys or Negroes, was better than none.

Hours later, she wasn't so sure. She wiped the beads of sweat from her forehead with a soapy forearm. Moisture trickled down her back, saturating her chemise. She was disheveled, her apron splattered, her skirt damp at the knees clear through to her petticoats. Her hair curled madly from the humidity, wisping in damp tendrils around her flushed face and escaping from the long rough plait that fell over one shoulder. Her feet hurt, too.

It was long after her regular working hours, but there were still mountains of dishes to wash from the day's meals. She could endure it, though, she thought wearily. What was this new catastrophe when compared to what she'd already survived? She just hoped that the names and information she'd been able to glean from Gould's conversation with his cohorts and then pass on in whispers to Annie had reached the Knights of Labor meeting tonight. What it all might mean was a mystery, but surely something useful could come of it? She remembered the cutting gray eyes and shuddered. Rafe Sinclair's penetrating stare had stripped her, robbed her of all her defenses in the blink of an eye, and sent her running like a coward. The thought of her undignified retreat made her hot all over again.

Suddenly, she knew she'd faint if she had to stand over this steaming sink a single minute more. She'd finish the job, but first she had to stop to get a breath of cool air.

Brenna pulled off her sodden apron, wrung out a towel in a pitcher of tepid water, and swabbed her face and neck, opening the top button of her blouse to the blessed coolness. Ignoring the frowning night cook, she poured herself a tall glass of water. She drank thirstily, sighing with pleasure when she set the empty glass down. The door leading into the alley behind the depot stood halfway open to admit any desultory breezes, and the thought of cool night air on her heated skin beckoned her forward.

The slim crescent of a harvest moon illuminated shadowy shapes of overflowing trash bins in the alley, touching with a dreamlike quality the piles of rough wooden cabbage crates and discarded burlap potato bags. The brick walls kept the day's hottest temperatures from penetrating the alley's gloom, and the air felt deliciously cool on Brenna's damp skin. The rancid smell of decaying garbage rose in a wave, and she wrinkled her nose in disgust. She walked to the entrance of the alley to escape the noisome odor, enticed further by the shape of trees and shrubbery that grew in the yard across the street.

It was only a few feet north from the alley's mouth to the rails and crossties of the tracks, busy even at this late hour with loaded freight cars. The workshops and round-house lay farther down the yard, and Brenna wondered again what Jimmy and his friends thought of Jay Gould's visit. Maybe they were still discussing his plans to acquire the Southern Pacific Railroad, and wondering what it would mean to the thousands of laborers who worked for the Gould system. She had done all she could, but for now it was enough simply to breathe in the scent of growing things and allow the quiet of the night to wash over her. She rested her back against the cool brick wall. Stretching and breathing deeply, she relaxed for the first time since the afternoon's fiasco.

It wouldn't matter if she had to wash dishes forever. The important thing was that she hadn't been fired immediately. She was so tired of fighting, she didn't think she would have had the heart to go on. No, of course she would. She'd do anything she had to. Her younger sisters must be protected, educated. She had to etch out a future for herself, too. Somehow, she'd find a way to become a teacher. She knew she was capable. Hadn't Sister Therese always said she had a mind too bright to waste and loaned her the books that made the drudgery bearable? Somehow, she'd get her teaching degree. With it, she could find a decent job and perhaps even be able to have the girls with her.

Bridget Sullivan Galloway O'Donnell's careworn visage rose in Brenna's imagination, every defeat and degradation lining her face with suffering. Her mother's failure had been in choosing the wrong men with whom to live her life. And such a life it had been! Old before her time, dead of neglect and hardship in what should have been her prime. Bridget was a bartered bride from the old country for Niall, and for all that Brenna had loved her father, she knew his dreaming and drunkenness had kept them on the point of starvation for so long that his death in a rain-swollen bayou was almost a relief. But then had come Malvin O'Donnell, seeking the hand of a respectable widow to raise his brood of screaming brats, and Bridget had had no choice but to accept him or see her own family starve on their rocky sharecropper's farm.

Brenna's lips firmed. She'd seen enough to know where marriage took a woman. That's why she was determined to find her own future, without being dependent on any man. No, she'd never repeat her mother's mistakes—never!

A sulphur match scraped against a rough brick, spluttering and fizzing golden sparks into the quiet darkness. Brenna stiffened, then stared—straight into the wicked depths of strange silver eyes. . . .

Chapter 2

The orange flare of the match cast the strong planes of Rafe Sinclair's face into black and yellow relief. Brenna's breathing stopped, then she sucked in a shaky gasp. The cool night air, pungent with sulphur, burned into her chest.

"Hello, Brenna."

She jumped. "How do you know my name?"

Rafe clamped a long black cheroot between his teeth, dropped its tip into the match's flame, and puffed silently. The sweet aroma of good tobacco tickled Brenna's nose. Rafe's quicksilver eyes narrowed slightly against the haze of smoke, then he fanned out the match, plunging the alley back into semidarkness.

"I asked."

Brenna shivered, a nebulous dread tightening her throat. A subtle, elusive danger emanated from this man. What did he want from her?

"Brenna Galloway," he murmured. "A good Irish name. Lots of them in New York. I may be part Irish myself."

"Don't you know?" The question slipped out before she realized.

His low laugh held an element of self-mockery. "The details of one's parentage matter little in the slums of New York. I was abandoned at birth, a foundling, raised in the bowels of Hell's Kitchen. You accept what you're given and don't ask questions. Even my name came from a stranger. Raphael Sinclair doesn't sound very Irish, but who knows?"

20

Brenna was shocked at the bitterness in his voice. "You've done well for yourself, then," she said.

"I've been . . . lucky." He studied the glowing tip of the cigar. "And I learned early how to survive. You use your wits, Brenna, and you listen when a little voice tells you all is not as it appears."

"I—I don't know what you mean." Brenna's heart raced and she licked dry lips.

He dropped the cigar and ground it under the heel of his boot. "A pretty girl like you must have lots of friends," he mused.

"I suppose so," she said, bewildered. She swallowed nervously. "I've got to get back to work."

"Lots of friends," he repeated. "Friends who work in the rail yards, in the shops. Friends who care what Jay Gould says and does."

"I've got to go." Brenna turned away, alarmed by the direction of Rafe Sinclair's words. Strong fingers dug into her wrist, whirled her around, pinned her between the rough brick wall and the broad expanse of a masculine chest. She cried out, struggling. "Let me go!"

"Not so fast, Red," Rafe said.

Brenna glared up at him, pitting her insignificant strength against his. Realizing she'd never pull free until he decided to let her, she stopped her undignified struggles. "Don't call me that," she ordered angrily, her teeth clenched.

"Red Irish and a temper to match." He chuckled and eased his grip. Brenna snatched her hand free, rubbing the red marks left by his fingers. Her mouth compressed into a resentful, mutinous line.

"I ask myself why a girl might be interested in the conversation of three gentlemen—"

"You're no gentleman!" Brenna snapped. In the dim light she saw the corner of his mouth quirk, but he continued relentlessly.

"So interested that she'd risk her job, her reputation, even fling a loaded tray at her own boss for the chance to listen in."

"That—that's crazy," Brenna spluttered. Her blood pounded in sudden panic. "It was all an accident! You saw it happen!"

"That's what I *thought* I saw. A simple accident. The reason I spoke to Hudgins. Only now . . ." A finger trailed down her shoulder, following the thick cord of her braid. His voice lowered ominously. "Now I'm not so sure."

Brenna slapped his hand away. "I'm sure you're insane!" she hissed. "I need my job. I'd never do anything like that on purpose." That, at least, was the truth, she thought. "I'm just a working girl. What's Mr. Gould got to do with me?"

"That's what I'd like to know."

"Nothing, that's what!" She pushed against his chest with both hands. "I've got to see to my work. Get out of my way!"

He caught her hands again, bringing her close so that he could peer into her face. His voice held a note of pure menace. "Just tell your friends that Gould knows—we all know—what's going on, and we won't stand for any labor troubles right now. Jay Gould crushed a railroad strike before. He can do it again, and this time everyone loses."

"I don't know what you're talking about," Brenna denied stubbornly. "Even if I did, I'd never carry messages for the likes of Jay Gould. Unlike you, I'll not sell my soul to the devil!"

"I thought I'd seen hate behind those big green eyes. Tell me the truth, Red. Why do you hate him?"

"For the same reason millions do!" Brenna cried, breathless with anger. Sean's lean, laughing face rose in her memory, but her brother's loss was too personal, too painful to share with this unsympathetic stranger. She tugged her hands, but Rafe held her fast. "He's starved his people, but it's work for him or die. He's evil!"

"Hardly!" Rafe laughed, a full sound from deep in his chest that denied her accusations. "He's merely a businessman, more successful than most, of course, but that's nothing I can complain about." His voice was wry and his long fingers curled around hers. He broke off, frowning. "Good God, what have you done to yourself?"

He examined the work-roughened skin of her hands. His thumb brushed the scalded place, and Brenna winced at the soreness of the rising blister. She clenched her hands into small, angry fists as humiliation washed over her. No lady of quality would have hands like hers, yet she was too proud to admit that his notice rankled.

"I work for my living. At least washing dishes is honest labor!" she ground out.

"Is that what Hudgins has you doing? You'd find it easier to make your living on your back like some of his other girls. Will you make me an offer, Red?"

Brenna looked blank for an instant, but then her confusion vanished. Her eyes widened and she snatched her hands free. She sucked a furious breath between her teeth and glared at him contemptuously. "I'd sooner lie with swine!"

A night train whisked toward the station, light from the passenger cars flicking parallel bands of brightness across Rafe's face. Brenna saw his jaw harden and his eyes turn smoky at her scathing words, but she was too angry and insulted to pay any heed. She turned on her heel, intent on leaving this odious man where he stood. Rough hands caught her shoulders, turned her, pinned her into the crook of a steel-sinewed arm.

"You play a perilous game, Red," Rafe warned, a dangerous edge to his deep voice.

Brenna's temper boiled over, rage and fury bubbling along her veins like molten lava. She was too angry to be afraid, even pressed so close to his hard muscular length. She smelled the starched, soapy freshness of his shirt and felt the warmth of his breath stirring the curls on her forehead. "Let me go or I'll scream the house down!"

"Then scream, for it's just as well to be hanged for a sheep as a goat," Rafe muttered. His eyes were hooded, his expression masked behind the thick fringe of his dark lashes, and his voice was suddenly husky. "And you, little lamb, are too tempting to resist."

He swooped, then fit his mouth expertly over Brenna's, using the pressure of his lips to subdue her. The shocking brush of his velvety mustache and the mobile persuasion of his hard mouth startled her into momentary acceptance. His hand moved up her rib cage, seeking the soft mound of her breast. His boldness brought forth the full weight of Brenna's wrath.

Sinking her nails into the back of his hand, she tore at

his flesh like a ravenous cat. Rafe grunted, and his mouth shifted just enough that she turned the attack to his lips, biting him sharply. He jerked back, and Brenna trod heavily on his booted instep, grinding the high heel of her shoe so hard he released her. She half fell, catching the brick wall for support, then faced him warily, her breathing harsh.

"Damn, you vixen!" Rafe scowled, touched the back of his hand to his lip, and brought it away bloody.

"You'll find worse than that if you ever touch me again!" Brenna cried, spitting out the words. She scrubbed her mouth with her sleeve to erase the loathsome taste of him. She straightened her shoulders, and her voice was heavy with scorn. "I'll be no fancy woman for Gould's lackey!"

"I'm no one's man but my own," he growled, stepping forward.

"Ha!" Brenna sneered, backing out of his reach, yet still spitting and ready to scratch. "Tell that to your master, Sinclair, then go lick his boots!"

"No one dares speak to me that way."

"Then you must surround yourself with imbeciles and cowards. For all your money and power, you'll never be free. Gould owns you. Satan tugs your leash and you hop like a lap dog. I wouldn't trade places with you for anything in the world."

"How fortunate for me," Rafe snapped, his jaw tight with anger. He folded his arms and looked down at her. "Very well, Red. Take your high sentiments and go back to your washtubs, but remember what I said. Tell your friends only fools will defy Gould again. No one tells him how to run his railroads. This time they won't just lose—they'll die!"

Brenna chewed her lip and worried. She wiped the last plate, set it on top of the tall stack of clean dishes, and threw down the cotton dish towel. The kitchen was quiet, the midnight stillness interrupted only by soft snoring from the corner where the night cook drowsed. Brenna placed her hands in the small of her back and arched her spine. Her muscles ached from hours of back-breaking labor at the sinks, but her mind was not on her physical discomforts.

What had Rafe Sinclair meant? "Tell your friends," he'd said. Had he known she was involved, even marginally, with the Knights of Labor? Or had it been a lucky guess? She didn't understand his warning, unless . . .

Her head lifted and she stared unseeingly at the gleaming assortment of spotless crockery. Yes, that had to be it! Excitement surged through her. If Jay Gould wanted to buy the Southern Pacific, the last thing he'd need now would be a labor strike on his Missouri-Pacific and Texas & Pacific lines. What better way for the Knights to thwart the plans of their evil nemesis? A unified, nationwide Gould railway network would only hurt the laborer by further reducing his bargaining power. And Gould didn't bargain, anyway. Everyone knew that.

Brenna let a small smile curve her lips. It wasn't much to go on, but it was a chance—a chance to sabotage Gould's plans and, in at least a small way, revenge Sean's death. It was a chance to cause trouble for Rafe Sinclair, too. Brenna's smile widened at that thought. Hateful, repulsive man! She would see his none-too-subtle warning backfire on him, or perish in the attempt.

She glanced up at the large pendulum clock on the kitchen wall. It wasn't really that late. Jimmy Teague and the rest of his friends often argued strategies well into the night. They would still be meeting in the shop at the rear of the rail yard. She'd tell them what she'd learned tonight. By tomorrow wheels could be turning to bring about the downfall of Gould and his railroad empire—and Rafe Sinclair with it.

Brenna fumbled impatiently with the knotted sash of her apron, drew it off, and tossed it aside. Her step was suddenly lighter, her fatigue forgotten. She picked up a red apple from the basket by the back door and polished it to ruby brightness on her sleeve. She'd have to hurry, but with a little luck she could be back in the dormitory and sound asleep within the hour, getting some well-earned rest before the four-thirty wake-up bell.

Brenna stepped out into the alley and looked around. She wanted no repetitions of her earlier encounter. The alley was deserted. Brenna moved around the stacked crates, hesitated a moment longer in the shadows, then walked briskly toward the rail yards.

Rocky chunks of gravel littered the yards and formed the foundations for the steel tracks that shone faintly silver in the moonlight. Pebbles bit through the bottoms of Brenna's shoes, but she walked purposefully between the tracks lined with waiting freight cars toward the dim outline of the shop buildings. From across the tracks, sounds of revelry spilled out of the busy honky-tonks and saloons. Merry strains from a tinkling piano set the rhythm for her steps.

Brenna sank her small white teeth into the firm flesh of her apple, savoring its tartness. Juice dribbled from the corner of her mouth down her chin. Laughing softly, she mopped the fluid daintily with her fingers as she walked. When she was finished, she tossed the core aside and wiped her sticky hand on her skirt. Now her belly wouldn't rumble while she told Jimmy about Rafe Sinclair. She increased her pace, eager to share her news.

Shadows moved between two boxcars. Brenna stopped, then peered carefully around the corner of the freight car. On the other side of the heavy metal coupling, two men stood silhouetted against the faint glow of distant gas lights. Tension made her cautious. Drunks often wandered through the yards on their way to the saloons. She heard the low murmur of their voices. One gestured sharply and the other bent forward, intent on his companion's words. Brenna breathed a sigh of relief. She could pass by and they'd never know she'd been anywhere near. She stepped forward quickly.

An agonized groan froze her in the open space between the cars. The two men struggled, and for a split second the unsteady light revealed the fierce, feral snarl of the taller man. Brenna's eyes widened. His lips were drawn back over yellow teeth framed by a long, drooping mustache, and one eye was covered by a rough black leather patch. He grabbed the smaller man's coat collar, turning him so Brenna saw a young man's fresh, clean-shaven face and the golden tint of curly hair. Light flashed off a steel blade. The one-eyed man lunged and buried the knife in his victim's chest.

Brenna gasped, pressing a hand to her mouth to hold

back her scream. Icy horror paralyzed her. The wounded man groaned again, emitted a horrible bubbling sound, and fell. The killer jerked the knife free, calmly wiped the blade on the dead man's cravat, then searched the body. It wasn't a wallet he removed, but a sheaf of papers that crackled loudly in the stillness. A river of crimson soaked into the gravel. Brenna whimpered behind her palm.

The killer looked up, pinning Brenna's motionless, horrified figure with his unwinking black eye. Her heart hammered into double time, but she couldn't move, caught in the grips of this chilling nightmare. The man's mustache lifted in a demonic grin. He stepped over the corpse toward her.

Brenna screamed, terror scattering her wits. The killer's smile disappeared. He jumped the coupling, and Brenna moved at last. She pivoted, grabbed up her skirts, and ran for her life. She headed for the safety of the depot, her breath rasping painfully, small, terrified sounds coming from her throat. Heavy boots pounded through the loose gravel behind her, closer, closer. . . .

Acting on instinct, Brenna swerved and ducked between two cars. She crossed the tracks, then jumped up and over the coupling between two flat cars loaded with lumber. Pointed rocks jabbed through her thin leather soles. She raced around the corner of a flat car and scrambled up onto the metal coupling. She crouched, heart pounding, breath shredding. Scrap lumber spilled from the car. She grabbed a pointed piece of board, splinters biting into the pads of her fingers.

She peeked around the corner of the car. The edge of a boot disappeared through the opening just ahead. Hope clutched her heart. She jumped and hit the gravel running. Pain shot up her legs. Only a few more cars, then she would be in the clear, in plain sight of the well-lit depot. Her fingers knotted convulsively on her makeshift weapon.

A rough hand caught in her hair, and pain ripped through her scalp as the man hauled her between two cars. Brenna shrieked, swung at him desperately. The plank's wooden point struck flesh with a sickening thud. Blood gushed from a jagged wound, splattering her

blouse. The killer howled, releasing her to grab his
forehead. She threw the board with all her strength and
ran.

Ragged sobs tore through her chest. Another rail car,
a long passenger car, loomed up before her. Frantic for
a place to hide, Brenna stormed up the metal steps. The
door was locked! She tried the windows in an agony of
fear. If she could just pry off one of the screens . . .

Gravel crunched nearby. She crouched, fingers tracing
the outline of the window screen. Here! Was it warped?
Her nails tore at the frame. Cold sweat prickled down her
back. Footsteps again. He was coming!

The window screen bent, and Brenna silently breathed
a paean of thanks. Gritting her teeth, she wrenched it
loose, slipped underneath, and fell headfirst inside. She
started up, fingers fumbling with the window sash, then
slipped the latch.

Boots rang on the metal steps. Brenna fell to her knees,
crawled swiftly through the parlor down the narrow
passageway. The door handle rattled quietly, then a
shadow materialized at the window. Gas lights from the
distant saloon cast a dim reflection on the glass. The
windows! Despite the unlighted interior, he would see her
through the line of uncovered windows. Panting softly,
she crawled forward again, the nap of plush carpet rasping
against her palms.

A narrow stateroom door stood half open, its interior
pitch-black. Here was her haven! She crawled over the
threshold, followed the cool paneled wall with blind
fingers, then crouched against it and listened. Every sense
reached out, trying to trace the path of the killer. Did he
know she was still inside the coach? Would he follow
her? Dared she hope she'd eluded him? Had he gone off
to lick his wounds? Brenna's heart beat erratically,
slowing, then racing at each new fearful thought. She
licked dry lips.

Minutes passed. Tired muscles quivered. She was so
scared, so exhausted. Should she try to leave this
sanctuary or wait until morning? What if that poor golden-
haired boy were still alive? How could she let him bleed
to death there in the gravel—if it wasn't already too late?
Nebulous questions whirled in her agitated brain.

A faint rustle jerked her drooping head upright. Fear rose like gorge, filling her with nauseating waves of terror while she crouched on the brink of hysteria. Had her search for refuge turned into a deathtrap? She clamped her teeth hard onto her lower lip to keep from crying out and tasted the sickly sweet essence of her own blood. Did the killer know she was here? Was she cornered, caught?

Again that silent whisper of movement. She surged to her feet. She had to get away! She had to run!

"One more move, and you're dead!"

Chapter 3

Brenna's scream strangled in her throat. Panic battered her senses. She threw herself toward the open door. Hard hands caught her, slamming her roughly against the wall. The silent flash of a blade moved menacingly through the darkness. She closed her eyes and prayed.

"What the hell? A woman?" It was a too-familiar voice, heavy with sleep, but instantly recognizable. Brenna's eyes flew open.

"Rafe!" His name leaped unbidden to her quivering lips.

"Who . . . ?" A hand cupped her cheek, traced the line of her up-tilted nose.

She shook with reaction, clinging weakly to his bare forearms. She tried to speak, but her mouth moved soundlessly, unable to express her horror.

"Edith?"

"No." The word was a breathless whisper in the darkness, but it was all she could manage. He didn't hear her. A strong arm caught her about the waist, then his mouth met hers.

Solace, comfort, human contact in the face of a chilling nightmare. Brenna's battered psyche responded. She pressed against Rafe's warmth, seeking after her brush with death to become one with the strong flame of life that burned within him.

His lips clung. His tongue probed boldly, tasted her sweet essence. Brenna gasped and her mind whirled. Her fingers curled into the soft furring on his bare chest, felt the hard thump of his heart against her palms. Relief and a strange elation melted through her like soft butter.

"You taste of apples," Rafe murmured, his lips moving over her upturned face.

The intrusion of reality shocked Brenna into awareness of time and circumstance. Her knees buckled and she sagged like an unloved rag doll. Rafe easily supported her weight with his arm.

"Oh, sweet Jesus!" she moaned. Shame and guilt heated her skin. How could she cling to this man of all people?

Rafe went suddenly still. His hands hardened, then released her. "What the . . . ?"

Curtains rustled and a window shade snapped up, spilling dim light into the tiny stateroom. Brenna jumped at the sound.

"Well, well. So you changed your mind, Red? You're to be commended for your ingenuity. Few are bold enough to board the *Atalanta* without an invitation." Gone was the drowsy, husky quality of Rafe's voice. A sharp, sardonic amusement replaced it.

Brenna stared wordlessly at Rafe Sinclair's cynical features. Her eyes flicked fearfully to the knife he held. He saw her glance and sheathed the long, wicked blade in a leather scabbard, tossing it on top of a built-in dresser. The bronzed muscles of his naked shoulders rippled, gleamed like satin. A thin silver chain and medallion winked from the dark nest of curls on his chest.

Brenna felt overwhelmed by his size in the shadowy confines of the tiny room with its rumpled bunk. The breadth of his shoulders and the muscular hardness of his thighs underneath the red wool of standard long-johns emphasized his strength and her vulnerability. He moved closer, slipped his hand under the tumbled remains of her braid to cup the nape of her neck.

"I can't say I'm disappointed, Red," he murmured. "We should have quite a romp, if you remember to sheathe your claws."

"Oh, please," Brenna gulped, trembling under his touch. "You've got to listen to me. I'm so afraid!"

Rafe's mocking expression changed, became somehow kinder. "Don't be frightened of me, Red. I won't hurt you."

"Not you! The one-eyed man! Oh . . ." Tears welled

over, spilled down her pale cheeks. Her breath clogged in her chest, and she sobbed pitifully as reaction took its toll, her head lolling forward like a daisy on its stem.

Rafe swore softly, his voice frankly puzzled. He gathered her against his chest, then eased them both down on the edge of the bunk. Brenna rested in the cradle of his arms, her fingers digging into the hard muscles of his shoulders. She gasped, sobbing incoherently while Rafe made little soothing sounds against her temple and smoothed the damp, springy curls back from her brow.

"Hush, now, Red," he ordered firmly. "You've got to tell me what's wrong. What's this all over you?" A fingertip touched the splatter on her bodice. "Is this blood? Are you hurt?"

"No, not me," Brenna mumbled. "I ran, but the one-eyed man almost caught me. I hit him with a stick." She felt Rafe start with surprise at her words and knew she wasn't making any sense. She took a deep breath, wiped at her runny nose with her sleeve, and hiccoughed. "We've got to help him. All that blood . . ." She shuddered uncontrollably, then stumbled on. "I saw it all. The one-eyed man stabbed him! He's dead, I know he is!"

"Who? Where?"

"A young man with yellow curls. Down there, in the rail yard, close to the shops."

"Yellow hair?" Rafe repeated, then frowned fiercely. "Oh, hell! Plummer!" He stood, jerked on a pair of trousers, and shoved his feet into tall boots. "He wasn't supposed to get here until tomorrow."

"Do you know him?" Brenna asked, her eyes wide.

Rafe's jaw clenched in a tight, hard line. "Probably," he said grimly, reaching for a shirt. A train's whistle screeched. Shouts and the rumble of men's voices floated across the rail yard.

"What's that?" Brenna's voice was high and anxious. She crawled across the bunk and peered out the stateroom window. "Someone's out there."

"They've found him, then. Stay here," Rafe ordered, moving to the door. He hesitated, then picked up his scabbard and jammed the knife into his boot top.

"I'm going with you," Brenna protested, a sudden lump of fear rising in her throat.

"No, you'll stay here where it's safe."

Anger replaced fear at Rafe's arrogant command. "You can't tell me what to do. I'll not stay here alone!" Her eyes glowed green with defiance.

"Don't be a fool!" he snapped harshly. "Do you want to run into that killer again? This time he'd slit your lovely throat for sure."

Brenna paled. Saliva puddled suddenly in her mouth, and she hastily swallowed a wave of nausea. "But—"

"Do as I say, Red," he growled, cutting off her objection, but his tone was not unkind. "You could get torn apart out there if things get ugly."

"You could, too. He's got a knife!" she said, swinging her feet to the floor and following him out of the state-room.

"So do I. But I've also got you. You're suddenly very important to me, Red. If it's really Plummer out there, then you've got to be around to help me find his killer. So don't move from here until I come back with the sheriff. Is that clear?"

Brenna nodded slowly and chewed anxiously on her lip. She understood his reasoning, but she couldn't help the rapid, nervous tattoo of her pulse, or the confusion that clouded her mind. For the moment, she and Rafe Sinclair were suddenly allies, whereas before they had been enemies. By sheer luck she had found a refuge in his strength, and a surprising tenderness in his comforting embrace. It didn't change anything, though. He still represented all she despised. It was just that for a brief moment she'd thought she'd caught a glimpse of a man one could admire. She must be more shocked than she realized.

"Lock the door after me," Rafe ordered. He touched her cheek briefly. "Don't worry. Everything will be all right."

Strangely, Brenna believed him.

Rafe vaulted off the coach's metal apron and took a last look over his shoulder. He could see the turbulent blue-green eyes, the gleam of red-gold hair through the window glass. If the girl had any sense at all, she'd stay put. There was no doubt that she'd been badly frightened, quivering in his arms like a wild bird. He felt an unexpected pang of protectiveness. She was such a tender little bit, he could snap her in two with one hand. And those lips, so sweet. Lord knew he was no monk, even for Edith's sake. He was more than a little disappointed that what had begun so auspiciously was fast turning into disaster. She was a plucky one, though. Pulled herself together well enough to give him the facts.

Damn! Had she really seen Plummer stabbed? The repercussions of such a heinous act would echo from California to New York.

Rafe strode rapidly across the rail yard, kicking rocks with the toes of his boots while his fingers moved down the buttons of his shirt. Gould would have his ass if the deal fell through now. Not to mention that most of Rafe's personal fortune was tied up in it, as well. A career as Gould's right arm had been profitable in more ways than one, but the ups and downs of railroad speculation meant that sometimes he didn't know from one minute to the next if he was a prince or a pauper.

Who could be responsible for this latest attempt at a coup? Gould had more than his share of enemies, men who stood to profit from his failure. It was up to Rafe to see that the situation didn't get any worse. He'd soon know for sure if that were possible. A group of about twenty men gathered near a boxcar, some running in and out, one or two bearing burning torches. Rafe's lips compressed into a thin line.

He pushed his way through the perimeter of the group, a scabrous bunch of laborers from the looks of them, wearing rough workmen's denims and stained, greasy shirts. They spoke quietly among themselves, words like *murder* and *sheriff* falling on his ears. Talk broke off as Rafe shouldered his way through the mass of bodies, and suspicious eyes raked him with open hostility. Rafe broke into the interior of the circle just as a burly fellow with a bristling black beard spoke.

"Anybody know who this 'ere fella be?"

Rafe approached the still body with a growing sense of dread. He leaned over and looked into Andrew Plummer's white face, handsome even in death. A line of crimson trickled from his mouth, but otherwise the young man's face was unmarked, a grotesque parody of life Anger surged through Rafe with a white-hot heat. Damned young fool! Wasted his life on a piece of foolhardiness. What was he doing coming in this time of night, alone?

"Hey, ye know this 'ere stiff?" the burly man asked, kicking Plummer's fashionable boots with the toe of his worn, scuffed brogans.

Rafe's eyes narrowed until they were mere glints of silver, and his gaze was glacial. He knelt and silently placed his hand on Plummer's face, closing the sightless eyes in a final act of decency.

"Yes, I know him. Andrew Plummer. He's an agent for the Southern Pacific." Rafe lifted the edges of Plummer's coat, the fabric sticky with blood, and examined his pockets.

"Here, there!" the burly man protested. "Leave him be, man! The sheriff is on his way."

"Good. This man had something that belonged to me. Whoever killed him stole it, as well," Rafe said. He rose and scanned the group. "Any of you see or hear anything?"

"It was screams I heard," a young sandy-haired man offered eagerly. "Could have sworn it was a woman's voice, though."

An icy hand tickled Rafe's spine, and his glance dropped to Plummer's body. Brenna could have been lying dead there, too, her life's blood trickling into the gravel to mingle with Plummer's.

"Say," someone muttered, "ain't that Sinclair?"

"That's right! That there's Gould's man!"

Rafe stiffened. He gave the group a look that old Pete Hooke always said could freeze the scales off a snake. Good old Pete. He'd have a good laugh if he could see what kind of fix Rafe had walked himself into. "Always cover your back," Pete would say in their Ranger days west of Waco. Rafe grimaced. Too bad he'd been too busy thinking about Gould and a green-eyed vixen to remember a basic rule.

"How'd he know this here fellow was dead, anyway?" demanded a voice.

A chorus of agreement surrounded Rafe, and harsh voices buffeted him with growing antagonism.

"I say we take him in ourselves—on suspicion of murder!" the burly leader announced.

"I wouldn't try it, friend," Rafe warned softly.

The bigger man laughed roundly through his bristly beard. "You hear that? Gould's man against all the Knights! We'll make you sorry you ever messed with us, you son of a bitch!"

Roaring this invective, the man charged toward Rafe with all the grace of a raging bull. Rafe held his ground until the last minute, balanced lightly on the balls of his feet. He sidestepped his opponent, clipping him sharply on the jaw as he passed. Rafe felt the jolt of the blow clear to his shoulder.

Adrenaline surged through his bloodstream, and the fire of battle filled his veins. Fists were his weapon, had been since the days when he was just a young street thug in the slums of New York. He grinned, oblivious to everything but taking his anger and frustration out on the nearest target.

The leader shook his head groggily, then rounded on Rafe again, the crowd shouting encouragement. This time, one of the man's meaty fists connected, snapping Rafe's head back so hard his ears rang. Rafe shot a blow into the pudgy fellow's midsection, satisfied at the groaned exhalation this produced. Two sharp left jabs and a right cross sent the fellow reeling backward. Rafe closed in for the kill. He'd disable the burly man before his superior weight and reach took its inevitable toll.

Rafe heard the swish before he felt the blow, a clout across the back of his head with a barrel stave that felled him like a giant timber. Gravel rose up to meet him, rocks gouged into his cheek and chin, fists and booted feet pummeled him.

Old Pete would really laugh, Rafe thought, then everything went black.

"I gotta rope!"

"We ain't gonna wait for the law, are we?"

"Gould'll buy him off. I say we hang him right now!"

Brenna stumbled after the churning mob, her ankles

twisting on the street's brick cobbles. Flickering torches and a handful of kerosene lanterns lit the way. "Wait!" she cried. "Listen to me!" But her words were drowned out by angry voices demanding vengeance. "Damn you, Rafe Sinclair!" she gasped, sobbing for breath. "You should have listened. You should have let me go with you."

Watching from the rear of the coach, Brenna had known the minute Rafe was in trouble. It took only a split second's deliberation to know that he'd be dead, too, unless she intervened and left her hiding place, killer or no killer. It wasn't a question of courage that sent her racing into the fray, but of justice. She wasn't a ninny to sit by idly, concerned about her own safety while a herd of rabble assaulted an innocent man—no matter that he might deserve it for other things! It wasn't a conscious decision. Brenna only knew that she didn't have any other choice.

But she hadn't reckoned with the frenzy, the sheer mob lunacy that worked emotions to a fever pitch, changing this group of laborers—mostly men she knew—into a pack of vicious, bloodthirsty animals intent on a lynching.

She caught a brief glimpse of Rafe near the front of the crowd, supported on sagging legs by two men who dragged him forward. Blood streamed down his face. They headed for the livery stable with its heavy protruding end beam, perfect for a hanging. She picked up her skirts and ran faster. She had to tell them they were trying to hang the wrong man. If they succeeded, all her friends would end up on the short end of a rope, too. She had to stop them for their sakes, as well as for Rafe Sinclair—innocent of this crime, at least!

Brenna reached the fringes of the shouting crowd just as a rough hemp rope flew up over the outstretched beam, the noose swinging back and forth with a manic rhythm.

"Let me through!" She pushed and squirmed, trying to worm her way through the writhing mass of bodies but to no avail. Rough hands pushed her away, ignoring her protests. Cheap, coarse boots trod on her toes. Shouted obscenities drowned out her pleas. Flaming torches cast grotesque shadows, lighting faces transformed from human to wild beast.

Winded, Brenna stepped back, searching frantically for some way to get to the front of the crowd. She had to make them listen before they made a terrible mistake. Suddenly she saw the back of a familiar sandy head.

"Jimmy! Jimmy Teague!"

Annie's beau turned at her call, then his homely face fell comically. "Brenna! What are you doing here? This is no place for a woman."

"Jimmy, listen to me!" Brenna cried, catching at the flannel lapels of his shirt with frantic fingers. Her hair, long freed of its braid, swirled madly about her shoulders, and she knew her eyes held a crazed light. "You've got to stop this! Sinclair didn't kill that man!"

"What? He had to! Kage even found the knife he did it with in his boot."

"No, no! You don't understand," Brenna screamed. She tugged Jimmy's slight form as if to shake some sense into him. "*I* saw it happen! Rafe Sinclair didn't kill that man—but I know who did! Jimmy, help me. Help me save him!"

"Are you sure?"

"Yes!" Her voice was shrill with despair. "I have no love for Gould's man, either, but he's innocent. I swear it!"

Jimmy hesitated, then accepted her story. "All right," he said grimly, his freckled face pale. "Let's go."

He placed an arm around her trembling shoulders, put his head down, and bulled his way into the mob. Judicious use of elbows, strategically placed heels, and within a minute or two they'd cleared a path straight to the center of the crowd, directly in front of the dangling noose.

Brenna stumbled, caught herself on Jimmy's arm, and stared at the hemp loop, horror widening her eyes into emerald saucers.

"Hold on there, Kage!" Jimmy shouted, dragging Brenna forward. A mountain of a man with a bristling black beard clamped a hand on Rafe's shoulder.

Brenna gasped. "Oh, my God!" Rafe's face was a bloody pulp, a purple lump on the side of his head swelling his right eye closed, his lip split. His hands were tied behind his back. Dried blood streaked his cheeks, matted his dark hair. His shoulders hunched forward favoring cracked ribs, and his breath wheezed through swollen lips. He staggered, shoved into position by his burly captor. Rough hands pulled the noose over his head, then tightened it snugly.

"No! Jimmy, tell them to stop!" she pleaded. She tore free of Jimmy's grasp and threw herself against Kage's massive form, her small fists beating as ineffectually as a gnat's attack.

"What the hell?" Kage roared.

Rafe lifted his head, and a silver eye pierced her. "Get out of here," he croaked.

"Let him go!" Brenna screamed. "He didn't do it!" Kage swept her aside with a blow of his massive fist, sending her sprawling headlong into the dirt.

"Listen to her, Kage!" Jimmy shouted. "You know Brenna. She works at the depot. She saw the real killer."

"Are you gonna stand there all night?" an angry voice demanded. "Get on with it!" A chorus of agreement sounded, furious and bloodthirsty.

Brenna scrambled to her feet. Hair tangled in her eyes and nose, and she thrust it back with a shaking hand. Her mouth tasted of dust and the sharp, metallic flavor of fear. It was happening too fast! Willing hands held the end of the rope. Kage stepped back and nodded.

"No!" she screamed. The rope tightened. Rafe jerked upright, dangling on his toes. Brenna started for the group of men at the end of the rope. She had to stop them! Just then she saw a black patch, one unwinking black eye. Breath slammed from her body. The one-eyed man! She shrieked in an agony of horrified impotence. "No!"

The deafening blast of a shotgun ripped into the night. Shocked silence fell over the mob. Three men on horseback plowed forward, splitting the crowd. Shiny metal stars glinted on their chests. The first held the smoking barrel of a shotgun level with Kage's head.

"Hold it right there, Hardesty. You men, drop that rope!"

Brenna sobbed with relief. The sheriff, at last! The rope slackened and Rafe dropped to his knees, his face contorted. Brenna moved swiftly. Her fingers tore at the scratchy cord digging into the tendons of Rafe's neck, cutting into his windpipe. She pulled it free, her fingers stained with his blood. Rafe bent forward, gasping hoarsely. Sweat poured from his brow and drenched his blood-stained shirt.

A bay horse approached. Brenna turned, flinging herself against the sheriff's leg in its stirrup. "Sheriff! Rafe didn't do it, I swear!" she cried wildly.

"Hold on, little lady," the sheriff said, swinging off the tall horse. "I ain't got no intention of having a lynching in my town."

"I saw it!" Brenna gulped, clasping her hands in agitation. "I saw it all. It wasn't Rafe. It was that man, there!" She swung around and pointed. "That one-eyed man. Don't let him get away!"

"What?" The sheriff followed her gesture, and his eyes narrowed shrewdly. "You, there!" The killer slunk backward out of the crowd. Men who had been his compatriots minutes earlier stared and backed away.

"You men! Stop that man!" the sheriff ordered. Three muscular journeymen moved to obey, cutting off the killer's retreat.

Hemmed in, the one-eyed man stopped, then walked boldly forward. Brenna shrank back.

"Is this the man you mean, miss?" the sheriff asked. He held Brenna's arm. Behind them, the horse whickered nervously.

"Yes," she said, shuddering.

"Ain't so, Sheriff Mobley," the one-eyed man denied. A bandanna formed a makeshift bandage around his head, covering his lank, greasy hair. He was so close Brenna could smell the pungent stink of unwashed skin. He fixed a baleful glare on her pale face, and she shivered at the deadly light in his single black orb. "She's just trying to protect her lover."

Brenna gasped. To one side, Rafe rose shakily to his feet. She jerked her arm free of Sheriff Mobley's clasp. Her lip curled in contempt and hatred. "Liar! I saw you stab that yellow-haired boy. Ask him about that gouge on his forehead, Sheriff. I did that to him when he tried to kill me."

"We'll get to the bottom of this, don't you worry,"

Sheriff Mobley said grimly. "I'm taking you all in. The rest of you men, go home."

The sheriff turned on this order. Swift as a striking snake, the killer pounced, seizing Brenna, pressing the cold metal barrel of a pistol against her chin. Brenna's breath squeezed out of her chest. Nerves stretched by too much terror refused to function, and she was paralyzed, motionless.

"Get out of my way," the killer growled.

"Let her go," Sheriff Mobley ordered. "You'll never get out of town alive."

The killer's laugh was low and guttural. "We'll see." He pushed Brenna forward, the gun barrel digging into the soft flesh at the juncture of her jawbone.

"God damn you! Let her go!" Rafe rasped. "Somebody cut me loose!"

"Don't anybody move!" the killer warned. His fist twisted into Brenna's hair, jerking her head up at an unnatural angle. She whimpered in pain.

Why don't I faint? she wondered, some part of her looking on in amazement. Surely fainting would be the ladylike thing to do at a time like this?

The one-eyed man sidled over to the sheriff's horse, dragging Brenna, his eye shifting warily over the silent, immobile crowd. He mounted the horse, swept an arm around her waist, and plunked her onto the saddle in front of him. The gun jabbed painfully into her right breast. He scratched one-handed for the reins, grabbed the leather straps, and wrapped them twice around his hand. The horse backed awkwardly under its unaccustomed load.

"I'll kill her, the first person I see following me," the one-eyed man warned. He dug his heels into the horse's flanks, wheeled it around, and galloped away from the mob.

Brenna held onto the saddle horn with both hands. The horse's hooves plunged underneath her, and the ground sped by in a blur. Before she could think, before she could plan, before she could even react, Marshall was far behind them.

Terrified, the musky odor of the horse mixing with the killer's stench, she held on, her only thought survival. Cold steel pressed into her side, but neither she nor her captor spoke. Darkness eked away, the horizon before her gradually giving birth to streaks of red and peach, a new dawn.

Brenna prayed that it wasn't the last one she'd ever see.

Chapter 4

The lowering sun was a hot yellow ball on the horizon. Brenna's tongue touched cracked, parched lips, dried by the wind and heat. Sweat trickled down her back. The killer continued to drive the tired horse across the rugged east Texas countryside. They hadn't stopped once, and she didn't know whether to be grateful or not.

Brenna clung numbly to the saddle horn. The bay's mouth foamed and its flanks were dark with sweat. Her captor slouched easily in the saddle behind her, his black hat pulled low over his bandaged forehead. He'd stuck his pistol into his belt under his black wool coat, and Brenna tensed each time he brushed against her. Each movement of the horse was an agony. She rode astride and her inner thighs were scraped raw. Every muscle ached with fatigue. She'd never been so tired, so thirsty, so afraid.

Why didn't he just kill her and get it over with?

They crossed a meadow, its waist-high grasses golden, and headed for a thicket of trees. The long stems whipped at Brenna's calves, tugged at the ragged hem of her skirt. All day long they'd ridden, avoiding roads and the occasional homestead, keeping to the backwoods. There was no way anyone could follow a trail like that, Brenna thought, despair crushing her feeble hopes. There was no guarantee that Sheriff Mobley had even tried to come after her, fearing that the one-eyed man would make good his threat to kill her. Brenna didn't know which was worse, facing such circumstances with at least the hope of rescue, or knowing that she was all on her own.

The bay picked its way into the thicket, and Brenna

sighed at the cool shady contrast to the sun's brilliance. A sultry silence blanketed the sylvan wilderness, and the slow crunch of the horse's hooves through the bracken seemed unnaturally loud to her ears.

"Get down."

Startled by this guttural order, Brenna froze and glanced fearfully over her shoulder. She hesitated too long. The killer shoved her and she fell, slipping off the horse and landing heavily in the prickly undergrowth. Stunned, she lay with the breath knocked out of her, her legs tingling painfully as the blood rushed back into circulation. The brown, resiny odor of crushed pine needles and rotting vegetation filled her nostrils. The scratches on her hands and forearms stung. As the man swung stiffly down from the saddle, the bay stood with its head down, sides heaving.

Brenna pulled herself shakily to her feet, glancing from side to side with wary eyes. Could she attempt an escape? On foot and unarmed? She almost smiled at the idea. Swallowing, she straightened her shoulders and ignored her fear. If she had any chance of surviving this at all, she'd have to keep her wits about her. She'd have to be ready when her opportunity came. She only hoped she recognized it.

"That's right, missy, don't get any ideas," the killer cackled. He motioned her forward, down a slight incline toward a narrow ditch. About an inch of water trickled down the shallow, gravel stream bed. "We'll water the horse here," he said.

Brenna drank as thirstily as the horse, cupping the dirty, tepid water in her hands and swallowing as if it were nectar. She splashed some on her hot face and rubbed her grimy neck. Ripping a bit of plain lace from the edge of her petticoat, she used it to tie back her hair at her nape. She felt better, almost hopeful, but jumped when the man rose from the stream, wiping his wet mouth on his coat sleeve. He dragged the tired horse around by the reins.

She stood, anxiously keeping her distance. "Where—where are you taking me?" she asked. If he had decided to kill her, he would have to catch her first.

The killer looked at her coldly, then began to explore

the contents of the saddle pouch. "You'll see," he answered, his voice gruff. "There's plenty of wild country 'tween here and the Sabine basin. Lots of places to hide a pretty filly like you." He grinned, showing his large yellow teeth.

Brenna hid a shudder. "You should let me go," she said. "I'm no threat to you now. You could travel a lot faster without me."

"Yeah, but you're my safe passage, missy. That's the only reason you're still alive. You ought not to have seen what you did, but it was right thoughtful of you to be so handy when I needed you. With you along, a posse won't dare get too close."

"What?" Brenna lifted her head wishfully. Could rescue be that near?

The killer laughed cruelly. "Oh, they're out there, all right. But it won't do you any good, so don't try anything. I can think of lots of ways to make you sorry you did." His one eye raked her from head to toe, a lustful gleam lighting the black orb when it rested on her bosom. "If I had a little more time, I'd show you what I mean. Pay you back for this knot on my head. Maybe later," he promised, shrugging.

Brenna shivered at his veiled threat. Was a choice between rape and death all she had to look forward to? Suddenly life was infinitely precious. She had so much to live for, so much she wanted to do yet. And who would look after her sisters? Brenna's resolve hardened. There had to be some way she could escape. She knew then that she'd do anything to get away—anything!

He gave a grunt and pulled a half-pint whiskey bottle and a small leather-wrapped bundle from the saddle pouch. "That sheriff's a stingy bastard," he said, his lips twisting. "Moldy jerky and rotgut is all the provisions he keeps."

"Maybe he wasn't planning a trip," Brenna remarked with a bravura she wasn't feeling. She knew firsthand from her stepfather that things went worse if you showed a bully your fear. Perhaps she could keep the killer off guard by pretending not to be afraid of him.

The man caught the cork in his yellow teeth, popped it out of the bottle, then swallowed several gulps of the amber liquor. He gave a wheeze of satisfaction and sucked air between his lips. He wiped the drooping ends of his mustache and offered Brenna the bottle. "Want some?"

"No."

He laughed, then tossed her a bit of the jerky. "Eat that, then."

Brenna looked suspiciously at the blackened chunk of dried beef, then nibbled delicately. Even though she was ravenous, it had the taste and consistency of old shoe leather. In fact, she thought with sour humor, a bite out of one of her new shoes would certainly be more appetizing. She shoved the morsel into her mouth and chewed determinedly. She had to keep her strength up if she wanted to escape this madman. She turned toward a line of trees.

"Where you think you're going?"

Brenna jerked to a halt. Her teeth ground together and her cheeks burned. "I have to relieve myself." She glared at him. "Unless, that is, you prefer to ride on a damp saddle!"

"You're a starchy one, ain't you, missy?" he said, laughing. "No farther than the other side of that tree, you hear? Might as well take care of things myself." He fumbled at the buttons on his pants, laughing again when Brenna whirled and marched smartly away.

The call of nature attended to, Brenna straightened her skirts. She toyed momentarily with making a break for it, but discarded the notion as too foolhardy—at least for the present. If she played along, pretending meekness, surely sooner or later she'd get her chance.

She brushed dirt from her skirts and felt a familiar heaviness bump against her thigh. Surprisingly, her money was still pinned securely in its stocking to her petticoat. If she could escape, at least she'd have the means to pay her way back to Marshall. She wished that she carried a knife in her garter like some of the heroines in the penny-dreadfuls Annie loved so well. Or a gun. Not that she'd know what to do with it if she had it. Sean had been the hunter those hungry years on the farm. Brenna had always done the gardening and harvesting. She'd gathered buckets of dewberries and spent many a winter night picking out hickory nuts. The memory made her mouth water. Even under these circumstances, the demands of body must be met. Lord, she was hungry!

Brenna looked up, shading her eyes against the dappled brilliance. A sprawling pecan tree stood side by side with hickory, sweet gum, and horse chestnut. Something crunched under her foot. She scanned the ground. Pecans! The earth was littered with wild nuts popping out of their drying outer covers. She reached eagerly for the pecan her heel had cracked, picked away the brittle shell, and popped the flavorful meat into her mouth. Heaven! She searched under the leaves, gathered up a double handful of the oval-shaped nuts, and cracked them between a protruding root and her heel.

"What the hell are you doing?"

Startled, Brenna swung around. Her skirt pockets bulged with nuts and she swallowed a mouthful guiltily. "I found these. I'm hungry."

"Give 'em here," he demanded.

"No! Get your own."

The one-eyed man slapped her hard across the mouth with the back of his hand. Brenna reeled backward, tears smarting from her eyes. She cupped her split, bloody lip with one hand and stared at him, impotent rage and hate glittering behind her lashes. "Now give 'em here," he repeated.

Silently, Brenna handed over the half handful of shelled nuts. The killer threw them into his mouth and chewed noisily.

"Not bad. Pick me out some more, missy. And none of your lip, neither."

Resentment smoldered, but she knew what Falstaff would have said about discretion and valor. Da's abortive career as a Shakespearean actor had given her a collection of pithy sayings to guide her life. She squatted down on her heels and began to shell the nuts into her lap.

Brenna licked the sticky-sweet taste of blood from her sore lip. Fingers flew, shelling the nuts. She reached into her pocket for another handful. A brown, thumb-sized nut joined the oval pecans in her palm. A buckeye. Not edible, as everyone knew. Poison, in fact. Sean would crush them, then throw them into the bayou to stun the fish for an easy catch. She picked it up to toss it away, then hesitated.

Dared she do it? She glanced anxiously at the waiting man. He took another pull from the whiskey bottle. She could mix the buckeye meat in with the pecans. At best, it would kill him; at worst, leave him unharmed. If it only made him sick, she still might be able to get away somehow. Should she risk it? What if he discovered what she was trying to do? Would he kill her outright? She took another look at his evil visage and shuddered, remembering the cold-blooded murder of the yellow-haired man. What choice did she have? He would kill her eventually anyway, she knew that without a doubt. And probably rape her first. She couldn't just wait passively for it to happen. She had to do something. Even if it were something as chancy as this.

She clamped her teeth together and hastily worked her nails into the stubborn shell. She broke the buckeye meat into tiny fragments and dropped it into the pile of pecans in her lap.

"What's taking you so long?" he demanded. He strode toward her, pulling his black hat low on his forehead. "We got to get goin'."

"Here." Brenna stood, thrusting the pile of nuts toward him. She watched him munch the mouthful, grimace, then wash it down with another slug of rotgut whiskey. She licked her lips and nervously wiped her sweaty palms on the side of her skirt. Disappointingly, there was no immediate reaction.

"Let's go." He mounted the horse and swung Brenna up in front of him again. She tried to repress a shudder at the touch of his hands. Her heart beat anxiously at the enormity of what she had done. What if it didn't work? What if it did? He clicked to the tired horse, and they cantered out of the thicket.

The flaming sun set behind them, plunging the rolling countryside into darkness. The weary bay moved slower under its double burden, but still the killer urged him forward under the starlit sky. Brenna wondered what star guided him as he carried them unerringly deeper and deeper into the wilderness on the border of Texas and

Louisiana. Her attempt at poison apparently wasn't working, and she was so tired her brain was numb.

The killer coughed harshly and spit into the grass. His hands were loose and slack on the reins, and he hadn't muttered more than a subdued curse in a long time. He swayed once, catching the reins up tight to keep his balance. The tired horse stopped and sidled backward at the pressure on the bridle.

"Damn. Giddup." The words were strangely weak and slurred. "Got to rest awhile."

Kicking the animal's sides, he urged it deeper into the concealing undergrowth of a heavily wooded patch. He pushed through thick bushes, then stopped in a small open space. The dim starlight provided only enough illumination for Brenna to see the black outlines of the trees. He dismounted, his movements awkward, then roughly pulled Brenna down from the saddle.

"Sit down."

He shoved her shoulder, forcing her down at the base of a tree. Brenna looked at him with apprehension marring her features. He ignored her expression, grabbing her wrists and tying them with a narrow strip of rawhide ripped from the saddle pouch. He tied the horse's bridle to a branch, then loosened the cinch and swung the saddle to the ground. His actions seemed jerky, as though they took some effort, and he staggered slightly.

Brenna blinked. Something was wrong with him. Could it be the buckeye's poison at work at last? She exhaled a shaky breath and tried to relax tense muscles. She lay back against the butt of the tree trunk. The rough bark poked through the thin cotton of her shirtwaist. A cool breeze came up, rustling through the undergrowth. The night was a mixture of sounds: chirping insects, hunting birds, the faraway scream of a bobcat. She let her eyes adjust to the differences of black and gray in the darkness, peering steadily at the man whose life was a threat to her own.

"Goddamn. I'm gettin' too old for this," he muttered. He sat down heavily, then stretched out, his movements as stiff as an old man's. His head rested on the saddle. Passing a trembling hand over his forehead, he sighed heavily. He patted his coat pocket, removed the whiskey bottle, and took a deep draft. When he replaced the bottle, he pulled a sheaf of papers from his pocket and flipped through them, satisfaction tugging at the drooping corners of his mustache.

"Won't matter none when that Wall Street bird gets these, though. Yes, sir, Edgar Larosse'll be sitting pretty for quite a while."

His laugh grated harshly on Brenna's nerves, and she swallowed. So the killer now had a name. She recognized the papers as the ones he'd taken from the dead man. What made them worth a man's life?

Larosse carefully folded the papers and replaced them in his coat. He groaned, grabbed his gut, rolled onto his side, and retched. "Goddamn rotgut whiskey!" he moaned.

Brenna's heart beat faster. This was it. It didn't matter if it was the buckeye or the whiskey that was making him sick, she had to make her move. She raised her bound wrists and gnawed at the knotted rawhide, tearing at the tough leather with her teeth. Larosse retched again, cursing and moaning. When the knot slipped, she pulled her wrists free from the constricting bindings.

Gathering her legs under her, she watched him carefully. Was he too sick to notice her? She glanced toward the horse and her tongue darted across her lips. Should she try to run now?

Larosse writhed in agony on the ground. He rolled toward Brenna, gasping. Spittle dripped from his mouth. "Oh, God, I'm dying!" he grunted, flailing wildly. "Help me!"

Brenna clasped a hand over her mouth to keep from crying out. His one black eye glared wide and unseeing, then rolled upward, showing the bloodshot white. He began to twitch convulsively, every muscle in his body contracting, jerking, in a St. Vitus dance of death. Saliva and vomit splattered the ground. Brenna gasped, horrified. Then he lay still. Night noises paused, then resumed their raucous chorus, sounding obscenely normal in Brenna's ears.

She'd done it. She'd killed him. She'd taken a human life. The knowledge made her sick. Her fingers dug into the bole of the tree, and she choked on a wave of nausea in her throat. No matter that he deserved to die, no matter that it was her own life at stake, Brenna quivered, conscience-stricken. She made the sign of the cross, but she couldn't pray for either herself or Larosse.

After a long minute, she took a deep breath and moved hesitantly forward. He had things—a knife, a gun, the papers—that might help her to get home. Her fingers trembled and she bit her lip. She didn't know whether or not she had the courage to bury him. All she wanted was to get on the horse and ride as far and as fast as she could away from what she'd done. She held a grip on her jangled nerves and forced herself to kneel beside Larosse. She reached for the gun stuck in his waistband.

A hand caught her around the throat, squeezing off her shriek of terror.

"What have you done to me, you bitch?" Larosse croaked. His fingers twisted into the cords of her neck.

Brenna gagged and clawed at his hand. She couldn't breathe. Her chest felt as though it were going to explode. She tried to roll away but he pressed harder, his hand clamped like a bulldog's jaws. A black fog clouded Brenna's vision, and her ears roared. Desperately, she reached for the gun in his belt.

They struggled for the gun, Larosse fumbling one-handed, Brenna tearing at the cold metal handle with a frantic strength. Larosse jerked, then went into a new spasm of uncontrollable twitching. The gun flipped out, falling to the ground. Abruptly, Larosse let her go.

Brenna gasped, choking, as air rushed into oxygen-starved lungs. She saw Larosse roll, grasp the gun. Oh, God! He'd kill her for certain now! She scrambled to her feet and plunged into the woods. A flash and the deafening roar of the pistol followed her. She rushed headlong through the brush, unmindful of the briars that whipped her face or the clutching tentacles of branches that tore at her garments. An erratic series of shots sent her crouching, moving even faster away—always away.

Air burned painfully into her chest, and her throat ached, but she was free! Free, at least, until Larosse caught up with her. This thought kept her moving, crashing through the woods. She hadn't killed him, after all. But surely he was too ill to track her down? Or had it been a trick? It didn't matter. She wouldn't stop until she dropped. Elation bubbled up inside her. She'd done it!

A stitch knifed into her side. Harsh gulps of air rasped painfully into her lungs. The shadowy outline of an ancient oak loomed in front of her. Brenna circled it, pressed her back into its knotty bole, and tried to control the pounding of her heart. She wiped the sweat of fear and exertion from her forehead and upper lip, panting shallowly, and listened. There was nothing except the nocturnal stirrings of the forest.

She sighed in relief and her body trembled. But she couldn't stop here, not this close to Larosse. He'd come after her, she knew it. She had to keep going and try not to wander around in circles. It would be too horrible to stumble back into his clutches by accident. Something skittered past her, rustling the leaves. Brenna gasped, her pulse hammering anew.

Calm down, she told herself firmly. It wouldn't do to panic now, just when the end of this ordeal was in sight. These woods were no different than the ones in which she and Sean had roamed as children. And there were no creatures in them she feared more than she did the one-eyed killer.

She started forward, moving more carefully now. As Sean had taught her, she lined up trees as well as she could in the enveloping darkness. Sticks and debris cracked under her feet and she brushed tangled vines aside, ducking under the natural arches. Occasionally, some small animal rustled past, disturbed by her passage, but Brenna plodded on, determined to set as much distance between herself and her foe as possible before dawn.

Fatigue made her stumble and clouded her brain until she wasn't a thinking human any longer, but a dumb animal moving on sheer instinct, self-preservation her only aim. Time lost all meaning. The flat floor of the forest changed, gradually becoming hilly, and she climbed without knowing she did.

Her foot caught on an exposed root. She fell heavily, then rolled down a steep embankment and lay, winded, on the muddy, fern-covered edge of a stream. The moving water gurgled and chuckled in its narrow bed. Brenna dragged her muddy skirts out of the muck and crawled forward, sinking her hands, wrist-deep, into the cool rushing water.

She splashed her face, gasping and coming fully conscious. She sipped the cool, delicious liquid from her cupped hands. Shaking her groggy head, she looked about in the moonlight. Steep banks rose on either side of the stream, darker shapes against the black sky. Trees overhung the brook, forming a lacy canopy. The breeze was cool and moist, and from a distance came the muted rumble of thunder.

With the fear of pursuit uppermost in her mind, Brenna tried to decide what to do next. Should she cross the stream or follow it? Up- or downstream? She looked at the high embankment and knew she was too tired to make the effort. That left following the stream. If she walked in the water, then her tracks would be washed away, leaving no trail for Larosse to follow. That seemed reasonable, but she wouldn't take the easy way; she'd go upstream instead.

Hiking up her skirts, Brenna stepped into the stream. Immediately, the cool water ran over her shoe tops, filling them. She squished stoically forward against the current, her legs and feet chilled and rapidly becoming numb with cold. Except for that, the walking was actually easier since she didn't have to push through thick undergrowth. Her only fear was that she might accidentally step into a snake hole along the stream, but she pushed that thought to the back of her mind.

She talked out loud, humming little ditties and lecturing herself firmly. She longed to stop, to rest, to lie down on the dry bank and sleep forever, but she knew that course was dangerous, perhaps even deadly. She made plans for when she returned to Marshall, how she and Annie would go shopping, maybe even stop for one of those new seltzer drinks or splurge on that velvet bonnet in Liberman's shop window. How worried Annie would be! Brenna hoped she was all right. And Jimmy, too. Had he been able to explain things to Sheriff Mobley? And what about Rafe Sinclair? She was sure he'd been badly hurt by that lynch mob. Poor man!

Tears of pity welled over in her eyes. Her emotions were dangerously near the surface, but she couldn't give way now. She slogged forward, splashing through the gravel-bottomed shallows. She stepped in a hole, abruptly plunging to her knees. Gasping, she struggled out, clawing at a low-hanging branch. Shaking and sobbing, she fell down on the bank amid her sodden skirts. Drops of water plopped loudly on the stream's surface and smacked her across the face. What had been a threatening thunderstorm now became a reality. Silver-fingered lightning crackled across the sky, and thunder boomed. Brenna cringed, shivering.

She was at the end of her tether and she knew it. All she wanted was to howl like a baby, but of course it wouldn't do any good. She was on her own, as always, with no one but herself to rely on.

She knuckled the tears out of her eyes and scraped back her damp hair. She had to find shelter. Another bolt of lightning split the sky. In that second of illumination, Brenna saw her sanctuary. The stream bank rose gently behind her, then jutted upward as part of a rocky outcropping. Under the edge was a small indention, a narrow shelf that might offer some protection from the elements. It would have to do. She was too tired, too weak from hunger to go another step. She would run to ground like an old, wily swamp fox, and pray that she'd outsmarted a predator, robbed him of his intended prey.

Squinting against the stinging spray, Brenna climbed carefully, painfully, up the small cliff. She found handholds in the clumps of coarse grass, toeholds among the lumps of sandstone and shale. Finally, she crawled, gasping, onto the overhanging shelf. She lay on her back for a minute, the rain soaking into her hair and garments. Every muscle in her body screamed for rest. She shivered violently. Rolling over, she crept back under the rough overhang as far as possible. The rain hadn't reached there, and the ground was dry and littered with dead, crackling leaves. Another flicker of lightning revealed that no other creatures shared her shelter.

With awkward fingers, Brenna unbuttoned her skirt and petticoats, then tugged off the drenched clothing. She twisted the fabric, wringing out as much moisture as possible, and spread them to one side. She pulled off her soaked and ruined shoes and rolled off her stockings. Finally, she took off her damp shirtwaist. She might feel chillier in just her chemise and ruffled drawers, but at least she wasn't soaking wet. She clasped her arms across her breasts and shivered. The rain fell in a shimmering curtain in front of her.

She pressed her back against the rocky wall, her knees pulled up to her chest. Leaves crackled under her, dry and still warm with the day's earlier heat. With nothing left to lose, Brenna scraped a blanket of leaves on top of her. At least they offered some relief from the damp breeze, though she might have to pay a price in chigger and tick bites later. Eyes itching, sandy with tiredness, Brenna yawned, and her head sank down on her folded arms. If she could just sleep for a while, just until dawn, then she could go on. . . .

Brenna's eyelids fluttered, resisting the tug of wakefulness that pulled her from the soothing, cottony depths of sleep. An insect buzzed softly near her ear, and from somewhere, the raucous, mocking shriek of a blue jay urged her awake. She lay on her side, curled into a fetal ball, her back pressed against the rocky wall. She blinked, squinting against the dappled sunlight spilling down through the leafy forest roof. She stretched, then stifled a moan at her aching, protesting muscles. Good Lord, she hurt all over!

A soft crunch of rocks and slide of gravel jerked her fully awake. What was that? Nerves tightened abruptly, and she bit her lower lip. Ignoring her stiffness, she slid from beneath her leafy covers with the stealth of a cat. She crawled cautiously forward, peering over the edge of the overhang.

She stopped breathing. She stared at the black crown of a man's felt hat! He had his back to her, and he led a bay horse by the bridle. She thought she'd emptied her well of fear, yet terror bubbled up in her brain like a artesian spring, endlessly replenishing itself. Her fingers clawed into the surface of a large jagged sandstone rock, but she was oblivious to her skinned hands. How had he found her so quickly? her mind shrieked. Would it never end?

She was frozen. Maybe there was still a chance if she remained completely still. He must not realize he'd almost found her. She prayed the rain had washed away all the marks of her climb. No! He stooped and examined a disturbed rock. He knew! Brenna's mind snapped. A murderous rage surged through her. A red haze of fury and hate clouded her vision. He'd never touch her again— never! Her hands closed on the rock and wrenched it up over her head.

Brenna shrieked and hurled the stone with all her strength. It struck the side of his head just as he turned toward the blood-curdling scream. He fell, pitching headlong down the bank. The horse shied, reared, then plunged off down the stream.

Teeth drawn back in a feral snarl, Brenna vaulted off the ledge, sliding down the bank toward the still body. She was a wild figure in her scanty drawers and chemise and tangled red-gold hair, a slim Amazon leaping to the attack. She scooped up another rock, panting. He meant to kill her, did he? Well, no more, she vowed. The buckeye poison hadn't been fatal, but if she were ever to have any peace she'd have to put a stop to his evil pursuit, even if she had to bash his brains out herself.

He lay sprawled on his side, face averted, unmoving. Was he dead? A pistol butt poked out of the holster strapped to his leg. Transferring the rock to her left hand, she jerked the gun free with her right. She'd show him! Her finger trembled on the trigger, and the blue steel barrel waved unsteadily at the still figure. Her jaw worked, clenched with effort. The sight refused to line up in the middle of his white-shirted back. Her lips tightened with determination.

She couldn't do it.

With a harsh cry, Brenna slung the gun away, sailed it over the creek and deep into the underbrush on the opposite side.

"Coward," she hissed at herself. "Fool!" She wasn't as tough as she thought. Tears prickled behind her eyes. What was she to do now?

The man groaned. Brenna bit her lip and clutched her rock tighter. What to do? Hit him again and hope it killed him this time? Tie him up? With what? Rock raised threateningly over her head, Brenna kicked his shoulder with her bare foot, flipping him over on his back.

The blood drained from her face, and the rock slipped out of her nerveless fingers. She sank to her knees, her lips suddenly twitching. Helpless, hysterical laughter burst from her throat.

It was Rafe Sinclair!

Chapter 5

Rafe groaned as he touched the aching place on the side of his head and drew his fingers away wet with blood. *His* blood. Damn! What happened?

He squinted, blinking to clear his hazy vision. Cat's eyes. Big green cat's eyes cloudy with concern, hovering over him. Hair a tumbled halo of red-gold. An angel, surely. He blinked again, wincing at the tug of the purple, swollen flesh around his black eye. The feminine vision fell into vivid focus. Brenna!

Memory jerked him into action. He tried to sit up, but gentle hands pushed him back.

"No, be still. You're hurt."

"I'm all right." This time he succeeded, pushing up to a sitting position despite the abominable pounding in his skull and the sharp protest of his bruised ribs. Jesus! That one-eyed bastard must have hit him from behind. But where the hell was he now? His hand automatically slapped at his holster, then came away empty. Christ! Got his gun, too. "Where is he?" Rafe demanded.

The girl dabbed at the side of his head with a wadded-up piece of cloth. She paused at his words, a puzzled expression on her dirty face. "I don't know."

She wiped at his wound again and Rafe grimaced. He couldn't understand her unconcern. He pushed her hand away in irritation. "Hell, woman! What do you mean you don't know?" he growled. He glanced quickly around, but they were alone beside the tranquil, tree-lined stream. "Don't tell me he just let you go after hitting me over the head?"

"Oh—ah, no." Her gaze flickered, and she fiddled

nervously with the cloth in her lap. "I'm sorry. I did that."

"What! How?"

"With a rock."

"Damnation!"

Her eyes behind their fringe of dark lashes were big and defensive. "Well, I thought you were Larosse!"

"Larosse?"

"The one-eyed man. He said his name was Edward—no, Edgar Larosse."

His eyes narrowed fractionally, and he felt the chilling fear and powerless rage return in full force, knifing into his gut just as it had when he'd watched her ride off in the clutches of that murderer while he was helpless to prevent it. Involuntarily, his hands roamed down her slim shoulders, feeling for himself that she was real, not an insubstantial figment of his imagination.

"Are you all right? He didn't hurt you?" he asked urgently.

Her eyes dropped from his, and a blush stole across her face. "I'm fine."

Rafe drew in a ragged sigh of relief. It was a surprising reaction, and one he didn't probe deeply. He shook his head, and his hand touched the throbbing bump. "That's more than I can say for myself."

"Well, I'm sorry! But all I could see was your hat. I thought he'd found me."

"Found you? You mean you got away from him?" Rafe asked in amazement.

She nodded. "Yes, last night."

"That explains why the trail split," Rafe said, frowning. "I'd been able to track it until the rain came. How did you manage to get free?"

"I—I poisoned him."

"You what!"

"With a buckeye. It made him sick, and I—I got away. I walked a long time. I don't know where he is now." She gave a little shrug.

Rafe stared at her, his jaw slack with surprise at her resourcefulness. Her hair was a tangled mass flowing over her shoulders. Her stained blouse was only halfway buttoned, revealing the dainty edge of her chemise. She wore no skirt, only petticoats that showed her shapely ankles and whose hems had been ripped in several places to provide the bandages she used. He realized that the dark bundle that had pillowed his head must be her skirt.

Dark circles lay under her eyes, making them seem even larger in her pale, dirt-streaked face. Purple bruises blossomed on her throat, and every portion of her skin not covered by clothes was crisscrossed with scratches and welts. Her lower lip was puffy and swollen around a red split.

She was battered, bruised, tired to death, but calm. Despite himself, Rafe was impressed. He'd known from the first time he'd seen her that this woman had pluck.

"You know, Red, this is damned embarrassing!" he admitted, more than a little chagrined. He rubbed the back of his neck, and his lips twisted in self-mocking humor. "I thought you might be in trouble, but if you can play Lucrezia Borgia and a bushwhacker at the same time, then it's clear you don't need my help!"

"Well—well, who asked for it, anyway?" Brenna huffed, rosy color staining her high cheekbones. "I'm sure the sheriff is quite capable. You didn't have to come after me. I can take care of myself."

Rafe's jaw hardened. Her evaluation of his character was less than flattering. "You think I'd let you save me from a lynching and then stand by idly without lifting a finger while some maniac drags you off to God-knows-what fate? And do you think I could count on that ham-fisted sheriff and his posse of sod-busters? You figure wrong, lady!"

Her color drained away, leaving milk-white skin stretched taut over her delicate bones, and that smattering of freckles on her pert nose standing out in stark relief, but she returned his gaze defiantly. "You don't owe me anything," she said, spitting out the words. "I'd have done the same for anyone, no matter how low-down!"

There it was again, that contempt in her eyes. He stirred uncomfortably, clenching his teeth in rising anger. Her scorn annoyed him—more than that, it made him furious! What gave this slip of a female the right to condemn him out of hand, to impugn his honor, his very manhood? He hadn't worked so hard and done the things he'd done merely for money or even power, but to prove to the world that the bastard child from Hell's Kitchen was as good as any man! Her contempt robbed him of his armor of respectability, yet he wasn't even sure why.

"I always pay my debts," he said, his voice cold. "I'll not be beholden to anyone."

"Well, consider this debt paid in full!" she snapped, outraged, and threw the cloth in his battered face. She struggled to her feet, her breasts heaving in indignation against the light cotton of her shirt.

Rafe gathered his feet under him, rising gingerly, and his head throbbed harder. The blood-stained cloth fell to their feet unnoticed, and they glared at each other. "Your gratitude is overwhelming," he said through clenched teeth, his voice laden with sarcasm. Never let her think it was her own safety that had set him on her trail. "Besides, there were other considerations at stake, including the small matter of those stolen papers."

"Larosse has your precious papers! He said he'd be sitting pretty because of them."

"No doubt he will," Rafe said darkly. He knew any number of Gould's enemies would pay handsomely for the means to destroy him. "And if an overzealous hellcat hadn't bashed me over the head, I might have had a chance to catch up with him and retrieve what's mine! Oh, hell, what's the difference? Let's get out of here." He looked around again, then turned a steely eye toward Brenna. "Where's my horse?"

"He ran away." Her jaw jutted upward at a belligerent angle.

"Really." He nodded slowly. "And what became of my pistol?"

Her lashes fanned down and she swallowed. When she answered, her voice was low. "I threw it away. Somewhere—" She gestured across the creek.

"Marvelous. So I can't even defend us if this Larosse turns up." He was gratified to see her eyes widen nervously.

"I didn't think of that," she admitted.

"If you had stopped to think, instead of behaving like a hellion, we'd be in a lot better shape right now. What kind of a lady attacks her rescuer with a rock?" His voice was scathing, his temper near exploding. "If I'd known I was going to get this kind of reception, I'd have stayed home," he roared. "Now, not only am I unarmed, but I haven't even got a horse."

"If I'd acted like a *lady*, I'd be dead right now!" Brenna shouted back defiantly. She picked up her dark skirt and jerked it on, fury written across her features. Her full lips compressed in a stubborn line, she turned and stalked upstream, her shoes making soft sucking noises in the mud.

Rafe watched her for a stunned moment, then clenched his jaw and strode after her. He caught her arm and whirled her around. "Just where the devil do you think you're going?" he demanded.

"Home," she bit out, struggling in his grip. Her eyes blazed emerald.

"You don't even know which direction home is!" Rafe snapped.

Brenna hesitated, nonplused, her movements stilled. "I'll find it without your help," she retorted bravely. "I don't need you or any man. I can take care of myself. Now let me go," she ordered, but her lower lip trembled uncontrollably.

Rafe felt something hard melt in his chest at her determined words, belied by her tired, smudged face and vulnerable mouth. The tension drained from his shoulders. "Oh, Red," he sighed. Shaking his head, he pulled her to him and watched her eyes fill with tears.

"Don't," she choked out, her small hands pushing against him.

Rafe ignored her, using his hand on the back of her head to settle her cheek against the hard wall of his chest, his other arm about her waist to draw her closer. "Poor baby. You've been through hell, haven't you?" he asked softly.

Her reply was a strangled sob. Rafe felt an unaccustomed stab of remorse. After all she had endured, he'd yelled at her just because his pride was a bit bruised. He felt like a cad.

"You're quite a woman, Red," he murmured into her hair.

Brenna's fist pounded weakly on his chest, and her

breath came in hiccoughing sobs. "Why do I always end up crying on your shoulder?" she demanded petulantly. "I hate you, you know. And don't call me Red!"

Rafe chuckled. Even reduced to tears, the flame of her spirit still burned brightly. "We'll talk about that later," he promised, smoothing the silky strands of red-gold hair back from her flushed forehead. He could feel the softness of her breasts pressing against him, and there was a stirring in his loins. She was slender, yet fit his embrace perfectly. Rafe gritted his teeth, forcing down the feelings of arousal. Even he, who took his pleasure as he found it, with scarce a thought for the woman afterward, wasn't so base as to take this girl now. He gently set her away. "Why don't you wash your face?" he suggested.

Brenna sniffed and wiped her wet cheeks with the back of her hand, a gesture that made her seem very young and defenseless. Avoiding his eyes, she moved to the edge of the stream and knelt, then splashed water on her hot cheeks.

Rafe watched her a moment before walking back to where he had lain unconscious on the bank. Stooping, he picked up the wad of bandages and his hat, which was mashed and rumpled by the blow and his tumble down the hill. He stood, then swayed slightly as a wave of dizziness darkened his vision. He blinked, forcing the blackness away. He couldn't afford any weakness now, not when it was up to him to get the two of them back to civilization. He joined Brenna at the water's edge.

Wringing out the bandage in the stream, he applied it to the swollen knot on the side of his head. He sucked in a sharp breath when the cold cloth touched the wound. Brenna shot him a wary glance.

"Does it hurt too bad?" she asked anxiously.

"I've had worse." He tugged at the bandanna twisted at his throat, pulled it loose, and soaked it in the stream. He heard Brenna's soft gasp and arched an eyebrow in silent inquiry.

One trembling finger traced the angry red welt that circled his throat. "That rope did you some damage," she said, her voice wavering.

"You're marked, too. We're quite a matched set." His eyes fastened on the purple bruises at the base of her slender neck, and his voice turned hard. "Did Larosse do that?"

Her hand jerked to her throat, then pressed carefully on the discolored skin. "I—I guess so. He tried to strangle me."

Rafe cursed softly and saw her shiver in the morning air, which was chilly after the storm's passing. "Now we both have reason to want to see him at the end of a hangman's noose."

"I suppose that's another of those 'considerations' you came after us for."

"Yeah." Rafe retied the wet bandanna around his neck. He thoughtfully smoothed his mustache with his knuckle. "Although I doubt your Knights of Labor friends would have been in such a hurry for a hanging if I hadn't been connected with Jay Gould."

"Maybe not," she admitted, glancing away. "But you can expect violence when men are caught in a situation not of their own making."

"We can argue about that later," Rafe replied, his voice curt. "Right now we've got to get going, or we'll never make it back to Marshall."

"Do—do you know the way?" she asked.

Rafe nearly laughed at the plaintive, hopeful tenor of her voice. Whether she liked it or not, at this moment she was dependent on him. "I think I can find the way out of these woods," he said laconically.

"But how? You're from the city. . . ." Her voice trailed off.

"I rode five years with the Texas Rangers."

"Oh."

"The question is, do we spend time looking for my gun, or should we try to find the horse?" Rafe examined the dense undergrowth across the stream, then looked at the lines of fatigue in Brenna's face. "The horse, I think. Which way did he run?"

"I'm not sure. That way, maybe," she said, pointing downstream.

Rafe squinted up at the sun to get his bearings. He dusted his battered hat on his knee and stood. "All right. Let's go, then."

"No, I can't." She stood up and rubbed her hands down the sides of her dusty skirt.

"Now, look here, Red," he growled

"I won't go that way," Brenna repeated stubbornly. She licked her lips and swallowed. "I came that way. If Larosse is following me, we'll run right into him."

"That might be the best thing," Rafe mused, remembering the stolen papers—invaluable securities and proxies necessary to the Southern Pacific deal.

"No! You do what you want to, but I'm not going back." Her fists clenched into the fabric of her skirt.

Rafe studied her for a moment, anger warring within him at her stubborn attitude. One look at her expression—a mixture of fear and resolution—and he knew he'd never convince her otherwise. And he knew that no matter how she provoked him, he wouldn't leave her alone again. He shot a look downstream, then shrugged. They'd probably never find the horse anyway.

"We'll have to go cross-country, then. And most probably walk all the way," he warned. "Do you think you're up to it?"

Her shoulders relaxed with her relief. "You won't have to worry about me."

Rafe made a low, noncommittal sound. That was part of the problem. He'd worried too damn much about this troublesome woman to stop now!

Brenna stumbled, caught herself again, then plodded on after Rafe. His pace was grueling as he led her across the rough east Texan landscape, which was rolling open land now, dotted every so often with clumps of stunted trees. She had no idea how far they'd walked, but she refused to complain, even though her feet were raw inside her shoes and her lungs burned. There was a knot of aching hunger deep in her middle, and every so often her stomach rumbled loudly in protest.

Harsh saw-tooth prairie grass clawed at her skirts, slowing her down, but she slogged determinedly forward. She wouldn't be caught lagging behind. The sun-warmed air caressed her heated cheeks and tossed her hair into her face. She was thirsty again, but dared not voice her need since it was at her insistence that they'd left the stream.

She would not listen to Rafe's derision on that account, no matter what it cost her.

When her toe hit a solid clump of grass, she tripped and fell heavily. Immediately, she struggled to her hands and knees.

"Are you all right?" Rafe's hand was on her upper arm, assisting her to her feet.

"Yes, yes," she answered breathlessly. Even with raw scrapes down his cheeks and his swollen, discolored eye, he was still a striking man, perhaps made even more attractive by his aura of unleashed ferocity. She felt light-headed, and blinked at him, as if from down a long tunnel. "Let's keep moving."

"In a minute." Rafe removed his dusty black hat and wiped his sweaty forehead with his sleeve. "I think we can take a short breather."

"Not on my account!" Brenna's voice was shrill and cracked.

"Then on mine," he said, throwing himself down on the rough grass. "That crack on the head took more out of me than I thought."

"Oh." She sank down in a billow of skirts. "I'm sorry."

"I'll live."

They rested in silence for a while, and Brenna's breathing gradually slowed to normal. "Do you know where we are?" she asked at last.

Rafe lay on his back, chewing a stem of grass. He turned his head to look at her. "I have a general idea. I know this country fairly well. There should be a branch of the river not too far from here where we can spend the night."

"No towns or farms?" Her fingers stripped a blade of grass, and she didn't look at him.

"There's not much around here except a few cattle ranches, and they're few and far between. We'll have to do the best we can on our own, at least for a while yet."

"Oh."

"What's the matter, Red?" he asked, and his wide white grin under the black brush of his mustache was wicked. "Don't you trust me?"

"Oh!" She surged to her feet and threw the piece of grass at him. "That's the last thing I'd do!"

Rafe laughed and jackknifed up beside her. "Then you'll just have to bear with me, won't you? Come on. I want to reach the river before sundown."

He helped her over a rugged bit of ground and set off again. Brenna followed, gritting her teeth. She didn't have the energy to fight him. Why did he find so much pleasure in baiting her, anyway? She touched her hair, then brushed it back over her shoulders. And her hair wasn't red! Not really.

The sun was nearly to the horizon when they came to the river. It was a small tributary, lined with scrub oaks and cottonwoods. They quenched their thirst, then followed it until they came to a bend in the river. A U-shaped curve cut into the bank, forming a pool whose smooth, untroubled surface indicated deeper water. Above and below the pool, the water moved faster, splashing past the gravel banks in a frothy frenzy.

"This'll do," Rafe muttered.

Brenna sighed in relief. She didn't think she was capable of going another step. She noticed that the lines in Rafe's face seemed more pronounced, and his cheeks were covered by the dark shadow of his beard, accentuating his haggard appearance. They were both tired.

Rafe reached into his boot top and took out his knife. He chopped several branches out of the undergrowth and tossed them out onto the bank.

"What are you doing?" Brenna asked.

"We'll use these to build a lean-to over there," he answered, indicating a small clump of spindly seedlings.

"Can I help?"

"Lay these across the framework I build. It won't be much of a roof, but it's better than nothing. Then gather some dry wood for a fire."

"Won't that attract attention?" Brenna asked in alarm. She threw a leafy branch across the skeleton of sticks Rafe had deftly constructed. "What if Larosse sees the smoke?"

"It isn't likely he'll be following us back to Marshall. And I don't know about you, but I'd like a hot meal." He grinned when he saw Brenna's look of surprise.

"You mean food? Something to eat?"

"Hungry, Red? How does a fish dinner sound?"

Brenna groaned. "Don't tease me, Rafe. I'm starving! But how? You haven't got a line or hook."

"We'll see if I can rig up a couple of fish traps like the Indians use." He swiftly cut and trimmed several limber branches. Sticking them in the sandy bank, he stripped out of his shirt and pulled off his boots. Brenna swallowed and glanced away from the tanned, muscular expanse of his bare chest, which was lightly sprigged with dark curls and marked here and there with bluish bruises. He wore a narrow chain and medallion around his neck. She hadn't realized how broad his shoulders were, nor how sharply delineated the hard muscles in his arms were. His movements were totally unselfconscious, yet Brenna's heart thumped harder when he looked at her again.

"Why don't you get the fire started? I'm going upstream a bit to try my luck, but you'll be safe here. There's not a soul within miles." He jammed his hand deep into his pants pocket and tossed her a tin container of matches, then retrieved the stakes and waded out into the water.

Brenna watched him for a moment, turning the tin over and over in her hands. She didn't think she'd ever understand Rafe. He was sometimes harsh, sometimes kind. He was an enigma she couldn't begin to fathom. Shaking her head, she began to gather wood for the fire.

Within a short time, she had a small blaze burning in a shallow pit she had scooped out of the gravel. Sean had taught her how, and she watched the fire crackle with some satisfaction. She hadn't seen or heard anything of Rafe since he waded around the turn of the river, but she was too tired, hungry, and uncomfortable to feel nervous. There was a dull ache at the base of her neck, and her throat felt raw.

She sat down on the bank and took off her shoes and stockings. She stuck her tired feet into the water and sighed with pleasure. How good the water felt! So cool and silky, almost a caress on her sticky skin. It would be sheer heaven to immerse herself in its liquid embrace. She bit her lip and shot a glance upstream. The temptation was great. It would be wonderful to wash away the grime and sweat, even for just a minute or two. Surely it would take Rafe that long to catch a few fish?

She studied the calm waters shimmering dully in the fading light, beckoning her. She couldn't stand it. She had to feel clean again, wash away the stench of fear and the stain of Larosse's touch. Her fingers fumbled with the buttons on her blouse. She hung her shirt, skirt, and petticoat on a nearby bush, then hesitated. It might be a sin to swim naked, but she'd only stay in a minute, she promised herself. With a furtive glance around, she slipped out of her chemise and drawers, rinsed them in the shallows and hung them to dry on another bush. The air was cooling, and she felt the goose flesh rise on her arms and thighs, puckering her nipples.

Stepping forward, she plunged into the river, diving shallowly as Sean had taught her, then stroking cleanly for the center of the pool. The first shock of the water temperature made her gasp, but she soon adjusted to it, reveling in the feel of the soft satiny fluid against her heated limbs. The sluggish current tugged at her feet, and Brenna let them drop. Her toes brushed the sandy bottom and she stood, chest high, in the middle of the pool.

She scrubbed hurriedly, using handfuls of sand to scour her skin until she tingled. Ducking her head, she rinsed the sweat and dirt from her hair, then let the current work the tangles from it. A splash from upstream jerked her head around. Rafe! She'd almost forgotten him in the luxurious sensation of bathing under the open sky.

Gliding silently, she raced for the bank, but she shot a glance behind her before leaving the relative safety of the water. Nothing. She drew a sigh of relief and gave a tiny half smile. She was jittery, but she knew that to stay in any longer was pressing her luck. The cool evening air chilled her damp skin as she climbed out of the water, but she felt refreshed and energetic, her headache receding. She wrung the moisture out of her waist-length hair, then tugged on her ruffled drawers. She reached for her chemise. A stick cracked. Brenna swung around, clutching the sheer garment to her bosom.

Rafe stared at her, his gray eyes molten steel. He carried a forked stick strung with half a dozen silvery fish. His gaze raked her, noting the small sandy bare feet, the way the damp fabric of her drawers clung to her thighs, the swell of milky skin above the defensively raised clump of fabric at her breasts. Brenna took a step back at the gleam in his dark expression.

"I—I'm bathing," she faltered. Hot color flushed her fair skin. "Kindly turn your back."

Rafe slowly set the fish aside and stepped closer. "No. Not this time."

Brenna's eyes widened, became more blue than green as the setting sun turned the sky and water to shimmering gold. Her voice was a whispered plea. "Rafe, please."

His large hands, wet and a bit sandy, clasped her shoulders and pulled her close. His mouth covered hers, his soft velvety mustache tickling her skin in a sensuous brush, the rasp of his beard on her sensitive skin a painful pleasure. His kiss was hard, demanding, and his tongue flicked the seam of her lips. Brenna gasped as if burned, and he plunged inside the depths of her mouth, seeking out all the sweetness there.

She tried to pull away, but her hands were knotted in the chemise, trapped against the massive wall of his chest. Her attempt was useless against Rafe's strength. Her mind whirled, dizzied by the untried sensations of his lips and tongue, exploring, penetrating. His hand dropped, slipped to her side to cup the lush fullness of her breast. His thumb stroked her nipple, rubbing it into pulsating life. Brenna whimpered deep in her throat.

Rafe lifted his head and looked down into her confused, bewildered eyes. His breathing was uneven, matching her ragged gasps. His hands were warm on her cool skin. "Brenna?" His voice was husky, persuasive, and seductive.

"No, please." She gulped, knowing he had no reason to honor her rejection, knowing she'd put herself in this position through her own foolhardiness, knowing the weakness in her knees and lethargy in her blood were reason enough for him to continue, yet hoping all the same.

The corner of his mouth twitched and his eyelids drooped, veiling his eyes. "You ask a lot," he growled.

Her chin dropped to her chest. "I'm sorry." She felt

the tension in his lean body and the effort it took when he unclasped his fingers, releasing her.

"You're either quite clever or else the stupidest woman I've ever known," Rafe said, his voice grating. Brenna's head jerked up at these harsh words, and she bit her lip. "In the future, if you aren't in the market for more trouble than you can handle, I suggest you keep your damn clothes on!" he snapped.

He turned his back, picked up the fish, and stalked toward the campfire. Brenna slumped with relief. She pulled on her chemise, shaking violently, and fumbled with the remainder of her clothing, buttoning her blouse to the top button. Humiliation filled her, coupled with self-reproach and a certain amount of dismay.

Maybe she was as stupid as he said. For a man as ruthless as she knew Rafe to be, he certainly had shown remarkable restraint. She was a fool to have put them both in such an awkward situation. Worse, she had responded to the consummate mastery of his kiss. Something deep inside had stirred at the excitement of his sure touch and had longed for more.

Where were her high ideals now? She was no more than flesh and blood, after all, for all her promises to keep herself inviolate, to give herself to no man since none could be trusted to deserve a woman's tender feelings. And Rafe was very much a man, one whose passions undoubtedly ran deep, deeper than her limited experience could even guess. Who was she to condemn him? Other men would have taken advantage of their good fortune, never mind her unwillingness. Why hadn't he?

She cast a glance at his back as he bent over the fire, tending the fish. He was dangerous, she knew that. Dangerous to her peace of mind, and a threat to plans and dreams she held dear to her heart. He represented a temptation that she must ignore, despite the tantalizing hints of hidden delights. He was her enemy, she reminded herself, linked to her beloved brother's death in all but actual fact, and she must never forget it. It didn't matter that he had been kind, in his own way. She must remember that it suited him to use her for his own ends. They'd been thrown together by a malicious fate, and short of setting out on her own again—an option that made her shudder—she must stay with him at least until they reached a town.

She drew her fingers through her damp hair, braided it in a long tail that fell over her shoulder, and tied it with another strip off her petticoat. She sighed at its ragged appearance. It was beyond salvage, and replacing it was just another expense she could ill afford. It meant less to send to Maggie and Shannon, less to save for college. Even a few days' lost wages were a hardship, and she had no idea when she would finally return to Marshall. The repercussions of this adventure were liable to haunt her for weeks, even months to come.

The tantalizing aroma of roasting fish drifted to her nostrils, and her mouth began to water. She had no choice. She had to depend on Rafe Sinclair to bring her home safely. She would keep her distance and offer him no further opportunities that might prove her undoing. She'd hold her tongue and her temper and do her best to ensure that the remainder of their journey together was uneventful. Then, when they reached Marshall, she could thank him kindly and say good-bye forever to the disturbing man whose lips and hands had shaken her very foundations.

Brenna took a steadying breath and straightened her shoulders, shivering in her damp clothes. She ignored the dull throbbing that had returned to her head. Resolutely, she walked toward the flickering campfire and the man crouched beside it.

Chapter 6

"More?"

"No. Thank you." Brenna shook her head at the fish Rafe offered her on a wide, flat leaf. He shrugged, his broad shoulders stretching the cotton of his shirt. Crossing his long legs, he sat down beside her at the campfire and proceeded to demolish the remaining fish.

Brenna licked a final morsel of the succulent white flesh from her fingertips then wiped her hands daintily on the edge of her skirt. Steamed on a bed of coals, with no seasoning but a sharp appetite, Rafe's fish was the best meal she had ever eaten. She clasped her arms around her upraised knees and sighed in contentment. Having a full stomach helped to put a lot of things into perspective.

She risked a glance at Rafe's profile, highlighted in the growing darkness by the rosy glow of the fire. The purple swelling of his eye was indistinguishable in this light. His harsh, masculine features were softer, more approachable somehow, but she knew that it was an illusion of the dimness. He'd made no further mention of their brief, flaming encounter, and for that she was grateful. Yet she sensed his tension, his inner fiber stretched taut as a bowstring despite the deceptive laziness of his movements. She cast an apprehensive eye toward the shadowy outline of the lean-to and asked the question that was foremost in her mind.

"How—how long do you think it will take us to get back?"

"Another couple of days, at least. Maybe a week on foot. Depends."

"On what?" She tried to hide the dismay in her voice.

Rafe threw the remains of his dinner into the fire, wiped his knife clean on his pants leg, and stuck it back into his boot. His response was low, careless. "If you can keep up the pace. If we run into someone who'll give us a ride. If Larosse catches up with us."

Brenna shuddered, catching her bottom lip between her teeth to keep from crying out at that thought. "Oh."

"Do you have anyone back in Marshall who'll be worried about you?"

"Just my friend, Annie. She won't know what's happened."

Rafe gave a short laugh. "Don't count on that. I'm sure the whole incident has been in the newspapers."

"I hadn't thought of that." Brenna swallowed, little beads of sweat breaking out on her forehead. What she'd experienced was bad enough. Did she have to face the possibility that she would be a notorious woman on her return? And how far abroad would the story be reported? As far as Louisiana? It was a frightening notion.

"I meant any family," Rafe persisted.

"No." She shook her head and let her gaze travel across the waters of the little river. "Only my two younger sisters. They're in convent school in New Orleans." Her voice became distant. "They're all I have."

"Hidden them from the wicked world, have you? And filling their heads with a bunch of religious drivel to boot," he added with a sneer.

"The nuns are kind to them," Brenna said defensively. "They'll get an education and learn to be ladies."

"They'll be so filled up with God and propriety they'll be no use to themselves, much less to any man," he snorted. "A couple of dried-up prigs."

Brenna gasped, outraged, and flounced to her feet. "At least they'll be safe from men like you!"

"Considering the provocation," Rafe drawled, "I think I've been more than a gentleman."

Brenna's cheeks flamed and her breath caught in her chest. Pressing her palms to her heated face, she whirled around, her slender back heaving as she struggled for air. Was she mad? She had promised herself not to provoke him again, and yet . . . She heard him come up behind her, and her spine stiffened.

"Wouldn't you agree?" he prodded.

Brenna swallowed. Her voice was small. "Yes. I'm sorry."

Hard hands caught her shoulders and turned her to face him, but she kept her face downcast, the picture of docility. His chuckle was derisive. "Careful, Red. I like you better when you're spitting at me."

Her chin jerked up and she glared at him. "And I don't like you at all! So leave my family out of it. What do you know, anyway?" She shrugged out of his grasp and went to the fire, squatting down on her heels and warming her trembling hands over the dying coals.

"Not damn near enough, it seems. Why aren't you with those sisters of yours, learning how to be a lady?"

"Someone has to support us," Brenna said sullenly. She was suddenly unutterably weary, conscious that every muscle in her body ached with fatigue.

"Quite a burden on those skinny shoulders of yours. What are you, anyway? Eighteen?"

"I'm twenty," she said with unconscious dignity. "And I don't intend to wait tables all my life, you know."

"Oh? What great plans cloud that pretty little head of yours? Going to invest in the stock market? I'll be sure to warn Mr. Gould," he added with light sarcasm.

"Not every ambition has to be as low as yours and your employer's," Brenna retorted sweetly. "If you must know, I want to be a teacher."

"What? No plans to marry a rich man? That would solve all your problems. No more slaving over a hot sink. No more dishpan hands."

She jerked her mistreated hands away from the fire, hiding them in her lap. "It's a small price to pay for freedom," she muttered resentfully. She laid her cheek against her knee and tried to stifle a yawn.

"A husband would have kept you out of all this trouble."

"A husband *is* trouble," Brenna retorted sleepily. "I don't need a man to run my life for me."

"Ah, a suffragette! So you prescribe to Mrs. Anthony's ideals?"

Brenna raised her head and glared at him. "If she advocates a woman living her own life, free of abusive men and the restrictions of unfair laws, yes!"

Rafe hunkered down on his heels across the fire from her. He broke a stick and added it to the blaze, a thoughtful frown creasing his brow.

"What do you know about abusive men?"

"Plenty. More now." Brenna's tone was contemptuous. "Certainly enough to know I'll never allow myself to be tied to one."

Rafe's knowing gaze raked her, and his mouth curled, lifting his mustache. "You'll never end up an old maid, Red. That would be like going against nature."

"Believe what you like," Brenna said, feigning boredom. She fought down the hot feeling of being mentally stripped naked by his glance, and buried her face in her arms.

Rafe rose and stretched. "Come on," he said. "We'd better get bedded down for the night. We have to make an early start in the morning."

Her head shot up, and she ran her fingers through her hair nervously. "You—you go ahead. I'm not sleepy."

"Liar. You're out on your feet, and with good reason."

"I'm all right," she repeated stubbornly. There was no way she was going to "bed down" in that little lean-to with Rafe Sinclair! Especially not when her nerve endings tingled with unwelcome awareness.

His laugh was mocking. "Scared, little lamb?"

"Of course not! I'm just not ready to sleep, that's all," she muttered uncomfortably.

Rafe studied her for a long second, then shrugged. "Suit yourself."

He sauntered over to the entrance of the lean-to, sat down, and began to remove his boots. Brenna ignored him, staring sightlessly into the dying embers of the fire. A cool breeze came across the water, and she shivered. Somewhere a dove cooed a mournful lullaby. Brenna's eyelids fluttered and she nodded, catching herself abruptly as she swayed. Rafe gave a low exclamation of impatience.

"You're a damned stubborn woman," he growled. He grabbed her arm, jerking her backward with a yank that deposited her unceremoniously on her backside beside him under the leafy bower. Brenna yelped in startled protest, punching at her flying skirts in an effort to maintain a semblance of modesty. He cut her railings short with a disgusted: "Shut up. I've never forced myself on a woman, and I'm not likely to start with someone so obviously immune to my charm."

"You're the most hateful man I've ever had the misfortune to know!" Brenna spluttered, her cheeks burning.

"And I'll have no use for someone who can't keep up tomorrow!" he snapped. "I've got important business in Marshall, but thanks to you we're both stuck out here. I want you where I can keep an eye on you, because you're more than an inconvenience, you're a damned nuisance!"

"All right!" She jerked her arm free and glared at him, but her eyes glittered with unshed tears and her lip trembled dangerously. Cut by the truth of his words, she was conscience-stricken, even though she'd come to this pass through little fault of her own. But she wouldn't cry, not again. Her jaw tightened, and her mouth clamped down in a mutinous line.

Pewter-gray eyes clashed with angry turquoise for a long, hostile moment. Finally, Rafe gave a thoroughly disgruntled snort and glanced away, rubbing his hand through his dark hair. She turned a haughty shoulder to him and unbuttoned her shoes, mentally giving a sigh for their squalid appearance. Again, her eyes prickled, but she refused to give into the release of tears. What right had she to cry over a pair of shoes when a man was dead?

"Ouch! Damn!" Rafe cursed under his breath. Brenna shot him a wary glance, only to find his words weren't directed at her this time. He grimaced as he inspected by touch alone the matted place on his scalp. Brenna's innate compassion and a sense of guilt at having been the cause of that particular injury made her speak up.

"Here, let me have a look."

Rafe glanced up, surprised. His mouth twisted. "Going to gloat over your handiwork?"

"You're a most unpleasant man, Mr. Sinclair," she retorted coolly. "But I have some knowledge of healing."

"Be my guest, then." There was challenge in his husky voice. Rafe leaned toward her, tilting his head for her inspection. Brenna instantly regretted her impulsive offer. Resolutely, she forced herself to touch him, gently parting his thick black hair with her fingertips. She *tsk*ed softly between her teeth.

"You've made it bleed again."

Rafe's reply had an edge to it. "Surely that proves I'm no monster, then, but a man whose blood runs red like any other."

Startled, Brenna frowned in confusion. Memory echoed his sentiment. Unbidden, a vision of Da as Shylock the Jew demanded, "If you prick us, do we not bleed?" Perhaps she was too harsh in her judgment of Rafe Sinclair. After all, he'd led their trek all day without complaint, and surely his wound made his head ache. "I'll make you a cool compress," she murmured.

She scrambled out of the lean-to. Sacrificing another strip of her bedraggled petticoat, she wet it at the water's edge and made her way back. Rafe, lounging on his elbow, watched her intently, but she ignored his regard, concentrating instead on cleaning away the clotted blood from the lump, gently releasing the thick strands of hair from the scab. The flickering light from the fire and the starless sky inhibited her efforts, and she had to bend closer than she would have liked to see what she was doing. She inhaled the disturbing male musk of his skin, felt the silky, vibrant texture of his hair, and had to remind herself sharply that this man was her enemy, a threat in more ways than one. Her thoughts betrayed her with unneeded vehemence.

"Ouch!"

"Hold still," she ordered crisply.

"Madam, must you add insult to injury?" he asked with heavy sarcasm, jerking away irritably.

"It will get infected if it's not kept clean," she muttered. Holding his chin between her fingers, she forced him to keep still and applied the cloth again.

"And that would never do."

Finished, she sat back on her heels and allowed herself a small smile. "No, for then who would guide me back to Marshall?"

"Then your attentions have a purely selfish motive?"

"Of course."

"And I was hoping your thoughts had softened toward me. Madam, I am devastated." His grin was a white slash under his dark mustache.

"I fail to see any humor in this, Mr. Sinclair," Brenna said crushingly. "Our precarious situation—a man dead, his murderer on the loose—no, there isn't anything funny, at all."

"Don't you know that you laugh when you cannot cry?" Rafe asked softly.

"Have you wept for that boy, that Plummer?" she demanded.

Rafe sat up, his face hardening. "He was no boy, but a man well versed in the ways of the world. He's dead because he made a crucial mistake, coming when he did, alone, and with invaluable documents."

"Was that worth a man's life? Your Mr. Gould demands a very high price of his business associates."

"Every powerful man has enemies, some known, some hidden. Those who choose to stand with him accept the risks." Rafe's brows lowered in a frown.

"Your loyalty to a man of Jay Gould's depravity is hardly a flattering reflection on you," she replied, her voice scathing.

"I owe him my life."

Brenna was startled by the steel in his words. "You can't mean that," she said shakily.

"He took a dead whore's whelp, a snotty-nosed rag picker well on his way to becoming a street thug, fed him, clothed him, educated him, then let him chose his own way."

"You?" The images his words evoked were too brutal, too sordid. A faint stirring of pity swelled deep in her heart.

"None other. Few better than I know the depths of Mr. Gould's generosity. He's a private man, a family man, devoted to his children. He grieves deeply for his dead wife. But he's also an astute businessman. A hostile press takes his accomplishments and twists them into gross caricatures of the true facts.''

''No,'' she said slowly, shaking her head. ''I can't believe that.''

''Why? It's the truth.''

''Only as you know it. You're on the receiving end of his kindness, such as it is. But you're a fool to trust in that Satan's spawn, and those who have felt the sting of his enmity can testify to that!'' she concluded bitterly.

Rafe's eyes narrowed. ''Your hatred is more personal, isn't it, Brenna? Not merely support for the Knights, or sympathy for the great unwashed masses. To you, Gould is an enemy, isn't he?'' He caught her wrists in a grip of iron. ''Tell me! Isn't he?''

''Yes,'' she flared, her eyes burning green with a savage light. ''Yes!''

''Why?'' His voice was hard. He shook her again. ''Why, damn you!''

''Sean's dead because of him. Gould killed him!'' She struggled wildly, but he controlled her easily, twisting her around to hold her still against the hard muscles of his chest. She gasped for breath, the sinewy bar of his arm clamped like a vise beneath her breasts.

''Who's Sean?'' he asked into her ear. She renewed her struggles, but he merely tightened his hold, squeezing her into submission. ''Who is Sean?'' he repeated.

Feeling a secret sense of betrayal, but dizzy from lack of air, she gasped, ''My brother.''

Rafe started in surprise, and his grip eased. ''How did he die?''

Brenna slumped, the fight going out of her. Her voice was dull. ''Shot to death during the T & P strike.''

''You blame that on Gould?''

''He wouldn't deal. He made them so desperate they had to fight.''

''It was their jackassed leaders, not Gould. Hotheaded fools, everyone of them. And you a bigger one to accept their lies!''

''How can you defend that devil!'' Brenna raged, wrenching free. Her face shadowed by the lean-to's roof, she scooted around on her knees, spitting her fury. ''He killed Sean, he and his henchmen. I hate him! I hate you!"

"Your hate blinds you to the truth," Rafe said. His silver gaze raked her quivering form, the clenched fists, the agitated rise and fall of her breasts. Some of the fierceness went out of his battered face. "It matters little at the moment, anyway."

"Maybe not to you," Brenna choked out. She pressed a hand against her lips to hold back a sob, the result of bone-grinding fatigue and overwrought emotions.

"Easy, Red," he soothed, laying a comforting hand on her shoulder. She flinched as though from the crack of a whip. He looked away from the fear and mistrust in her eyes, his hand dropping uselessly to his side. His voice was tired as he said, "We'd better try to get some rest."

He shuffled the stack of sweet-smelling dried grasses he'd placed on the floor of the lean-to earlier, then gestured an apprehensive Brenna inside. His voice held a familiar mocking tenor. "Your chamber awaits. I hope you'll find it comfortable."

Brenna swallowed, her tongue thick in her raw throat, and watched him, wide-eyed. He rose and went over to the fire, kicking sand onto the glowing coals. Brenna took advantage of the reprieve to settle into her bed, lying on her side as close to the inclined roof as possible with her back to the opening. The grass smelled of clean air and sunshine, and she tried not to groan with relief when her tired muscles finally relaxed. If only she could get warm. She tucked her skirts around her legs and curled into a ball, trying to contain her shivering.

The grass rustled as Rafe stealthily stretched his tall form out beside Brenna. There were no sounds except the soft whispers of breathing, the lap of water from the river, and the occasional call of a lone dove. Although Rafe didn't touch her, Brenna could feel the heat radiating from him. It made her shiver even harder.

"Are you cold?"

Brenna jumped at the husky question. Her answer was muffled. "No, I'm all right."

"I can hear your teeth chattering," he said. "Come here."

Brenna's head snapped around, and she stared apprehensively over her shoulder at him. He was a dark outline against the deeper blackness of the night sky. Her stomach tightened into a tight, cold ball and her voice was faint. "No."

"Oh, for God's sake, Brenna!" Exasperation laced his words. "I'm tired of your damned stubbornness!"

A strong arm seized her about the waist. Brenna squealed in protest, her fingers tugging at the immovable band of steel that pinned her against his long, lean length.

"Quiet, woman!" Rafe rasped. "I haven't got a blanket to offer you, so you'll have to make do with me, instead."

"Such chivalry!" she snapped nastily. Her heart beat like an Indian tom-tom. "Get your hands off me."

"Don't be a child," he ordered brusquely. He settled her head to rest against his arm and tucked her into the curve of his body. "You're chilled to the bone. There's no harm in sharing a little warmth."

"But . . ."

"Hush, Red. Go to sleep."

Sleep? Brenna wondered. How did he expect her to sleep pressed so intimately to such a man as he? She could feel the rise and fall of his chest against her back, feel the warmth of his breath as it stirred the tendrils of hair at her temples. Remembering, against her will, the mastery of his flaming kisses, she felt hot and cold at the same time, chills and fever raging in her bloodstream. His hand lightly clasped her wrist at her waist, and his touch was like a brand on her skin.

Was this an expression of kindness or merely a new way to torture her? she wondered hazily. She was so confused by this enigmatic man and more confused by her own reactions to him. How could she be attracted to someone she despised? How could she be so blazingly angry with him at one moment, and the next be at the mercy of his virile male magnetism? He wasn't a gentleman, yet he seemed to have a unique code by which he lived, something she couldn't begin to understand although she had experienced both his gallantry and his ruthlessness.

No, she couldn't understand him, and she was supremely conscious of the dangers of lying so close to him. His breathing was deep and even, and she thought he was sleeping already. Even so, she tried to hold herself slightly apart from him, but it was impossible. Her weary body kept relaxing against his warmth, until finally she couldn't fight it any longer and melted fully into his embrace. Her shivering subsided and, on the verge of sleep, she realized that for the first time since the nightmare began, she felt safe. Too tired to puzzle out that mystery, she gave a little sigh and gratefully sank into the realm of slumber.

Rafe knew the instant she was asleep. *Stubborn woman*, he thought and smiled into her hair. Then he, too, drifted off.

A shrill scream split the peace of the dawning day. Rafe dropped the fish trap. It hit the burbling waters and went under with a sucking sound, but Rafe was already running.

Brenna! He'd left her sleeping, the restless dreams of the night banished at last, looking as soft and sweet as a baby tucked in her cradle. Again the piercing cry of terror echoed across the water, startling a flock of sparrows into raucous flight.

Crashing through the undergrowth, heart pumping madly, alarm tearing through him with icy fingers, Rafe raced around the bend of the river. For a heart-stopping moment, he thought the area deserted, then he saw the huddled figure crouched beside the lean-to.

"Brenna! What is it?"

For answer, she flung herself at him, coming up hard against his chest and holding on to to him as if her very life depended on it. She shuddered violently, her garbled words made inarticulate by the harshness of her gasps. Surprised, Rafe caught her around the shoulders.

"Easy, Red, easy." His mouth quirked in a wry half smile. "Did you think I'd left you?"

"I saw him! He's over there!" she gasped, moaning in fear.

"What? Who?" Rafe demanded. He set her slightly from him so he could see her face, and his eyes narrowed, taking in her flushed face and her eyes, which were wide and green with fright.

"The one-eyed man! In the bushes! Watching me!" She pointed a quaking finger.

"Stay here. I'll have a look," Rafe ordered. Cautiously, he moved forward. In a few minutes he was back. "There's no one there "

"He was there, I tell you!" Brenna cried. She was still shaking. Her small fists clenched together so hard the knuckles showed white.

"Well, if he was, he's gone now," Rafe said.

"You don't believe me, do you?"

Rafe ran agitated fingers through his hair. Hell, he didn't know what to believe! "Maybe you were dreaming," he suggested.

"No! No . . ." She pressed her fingers to her temples and closed her eyes tightly, swaying where she stood.

Rafe caught her elbow to steady her, concerned at her high color and the uncontrollable shivering that seemed to rack her slender body in visible waves. She opened her eyes and stared at him, a wild light flickering within those changeable blue-green orbs.

"Oh, Rafe," she whispered. "Am I going crazy?"

His lips twitched, but he couldn't laugh at her, so real was her distress. He pulled her gently to him, shaking his head. "No, of course not. You've been through a lot, that's all."

She lay with her cheek on his chest, her small hand beside it. Rafe could feel her fingers trembling through his shirt. He wrapped his arms around her slim waist and rested his jaw on the top of her head, inhaling the sweet woman fragrance of her hair, and testing with his lips the texture of the wispy tendrils that curled at her temples and hairline.

"It seemed so real," she said faintly. "I'm sorry."

"I know. It's all right," he soothed. He gently kissed her forehead in comfort, reveling in the warm and womanly feel of her. Suddenly, he cupped her face with both hands, testing the temperature of her skin. He frowned. She felt too warm. Her lips were dry, her skin flushed with an unhealthy inner fire. "You've got a fever. That probably explains it."

"I do feel a little strange," she admitted huskily.

Rafe rubbed his jaw in consternation, his palm rasping

against the several days' growth of beard. Damnation! Now he had a sick woman on his hands. How was he ever going to get back to Marshall at this rate? "I suppose we could rest here another day," he said reluctantly.

"No! I'm fine, really," Brenna protested, an edge of desperation in her voice. "I'm just a little lightheaded right now, that's all, because of seeing . . . because of that dream. I want to go on."

"You're certain?" She drew herself up and nodded vigorously, causing her strawberry-blond braid to bounce. Rafe smiled to himself. She sure had pluck, a real woman's courage, even if she did look more like a frightened schoolgirl at the moment. "All right, then. The farther we get, the better. But you speak up if you start feeling poorly, is that understood?"

"Yes, Rafe."

Even though he was relieved that she had agreed to go on, he barely restrained a snort. He had no doubts that her amenability and willing obedience would last only as long as he didn't cross that spirited temper of hers. Well, he'd better make the best of it while it lasted.

They broke their fast on fish again, and while Rafe doused the fire, Brenna made her ablutions at the river's edge and tidied herself. Watching her carefully, Rafe decided she seemed fit enough to travel. They really didn't have any other choice.

The early morning air was still cool when they set off, following the river. They walked steadily, speaking little, pausing only when Rafe stopped to help Brenna over the rougher places. She did her best to keep up and—he had to hand it to her—never voiced a complaint. In fact, she became so quiet that he found himself wishing he could start another wrangle just to hear her voice.

Rafe pushed aside an overhanging branch in the woodsy thicket that lined the river and grinned to himself. He'd never found a woman he liked to fight with quite as well! And underneath all those prickles was a passionate little temptress. If they could ever get out of this damned wilderness, he'd like to try to tame the challenge he saw glittering in those big green eyes of hers.

Rafe broke into a clearing, came up short, and stared.

"Well, I'll be damned! Take a look at that." A tall bay horse stood hock high in the water at the river's edge.

"A horse," Brenna said blankly.

He grinned. "Not just any horse, *my* horse. Talk about lady luck smiling!"

"Oh, good." She sat down on an overgrown root, slowly, as though she were made of glass and might shatter with any false move. Her voice was faint. "I think I'll just rest here for a minute."

Rafe wasn't paying any attention. "Sure," he agreed absently as he moved slowly down the riverbank. He was damned if he was going to walk when he could ride. "Whoa, boy," he murmured.

The bay flicked his ears and gave his head a shake that jingled his bridle and made the leather of the saddle he still wore creak. Rafe caught the trailing leather reins and gave a sigh of relief and satisfaction.

"Well, boy, been seeing the sights, have you?" Rafe ran his hand affectionately down the bay's massive neck and slapped his withers. He led the bay out of the water, inspecting the animal for injuries, but it was the empty rifle holster that suddenly drew his attention.

He frowned. Something wasn't right. How could a horse lose a securely buckled rifle and yet retain the rest of the tackle? For that matter, why should a horse wander right into their laps? Things were a little too damned convenient.

Rafe swiftly checked the saddlebags, his mouth a grim, set line. The contents were jumbled, as though someone had sifted through them hastily. More alarming was the missing ammunition. In the bottom of the bag he found a pair of threadbare wool socks, still rolled into their untidy ball. Breath hissed from between his clenched teeth. Whoever had stolen the ammo had missed a vital item.

Eyes scanning the underbrush on each side of the bank, Rafe stealthily slipped the little two-shot derringer from its hiding place, sticking it into his shirt to rest like a lump of ice against his skin. Neck hairs prickling, he stuffed the socks back into the bag, then turned and led the horse toward the little copse of trees where Brenna waited.

He had the feeling he owed her an apology. Each second he was more convinced that she had been neither dreaming nor hallucinating this morning. It had the smell of a trap, and, virtually unarmed, all Rafe could hope to do was play it out. His jaw tightened. A patch of skin in the center of his spine itched, tensing in morbid anticipation, waiting for the deadly impact of a bullet to shatter bone and flesh. Yet, forewarned was forearmed. The trick would be to get the girl out of the arena.

"Brenna." Rafe spoke in a low, commanding tone, casually walking closer as if in no particular hurry. Her head rested against the bole of the tree, and at her name her eyelids flickered open. "Stay right where you are," he warned.

"What is it?"

Her voice was calm, but he knew she sensed his tension. Mentally saluting her for her perception and her lack of female hysterics, he explained what he wanted her to do.

"No."

Rafe cursed obscenely under his breath. "You'll do as I say, Red, or I swear I'll throttle you with my bare hands." Nearly even with her now, he wore a cocky grin that belied his threatening words.

"You're wasting time," Brenna retorted, coming shakily to her feet and stepping into the open. Her chin lifted at a belligerent angle. "I suggest we both get on this horse and—"

A rifle cracked, the screaming missile missing Brenna's head by mere inches. The tree trunk exploded into flying splinters.

"Son of a bitch!" Rafe roared. He grabbed Brenna and pitched her onto the horse, giving the animal's flank a mighty slap. "Ride, girl!"

The horse plunged into the thicket with Brenna hanging on for her life. A second shell slammed into the dirt between Rafe's boots. He dove into the underbrush, losing his hat in the mad scramble for cover. Another bullet whined over his head. His lips stretched over his teeth in a snarl of cold-blooded fury. With Brenna safe, the odds had just become even.

Chapter 7

Each rifle shot spurred the maddened bay forward, and renewed its determination to rid itself of the unwelcome passenger. Perched precariously astride, Brenna bounced in the saddle like a rubber ball. Her fingers knotted in the horse's mane in a desperate effort to keep her seat and avoid being swept off by the clinging underbrush.

A loose rein caught her across the cheek, momentarily stunning her, but she hung on doggedly. Rafe had given her this chance at the sacrifice of his own safety, perhaps his own survival. She couldn't let him down. Gritting her teeth, she grabbed the reins and, pulling back with all her strength, finally brought the runaway animal to a halt.

She bent over the quivering horse's neck, gasping for breath, her blood pounding in her ears, her mind reeling. Was it Larosse? Had he followed them, after all? Or was it merely another outlaw, out for easy pickings? What difference did it make? Rafe was back there alone!

Fool! she thought furiously. *The damn fool!* Without bothering to weigh her motives, she wrapped the reins around her hands and turned the blowing horse back the way it had come. She was too angry to be frightened. It was so like that damned arrogant man to order her about. She was no helpless ninny, as he well knew. And he was armed with only a derringer. Male pig-headedness was liable to get him killed. But not if she could help it! Her mouth firmed into a grim, determined line.

Caution seeped back into her consciousness the closer she got to the river. There were no more shots, just an ominous stillness. Very carefully, she allowed the horse to pick its way forward, stopping on the edge of the thicket where she had a clear view of the open riverbank.

At that minute, Rafe, crouched low, was running between two clumps of trees some distance ahead. Another figure stepped onto the riverbank, rifle at his shoulder, the end of the gun moving in a slow arc as he drew a deadly bead on Rafe's dark head.

Brenna screamed a warning, kicking and whipping the bay with the ends of the reins. Enraged at the sting of leather straps, the animal leaped forward, hooves churning. The rifleman swung around, and Brenna's throat clogged at the baleful one-eyed visage. Larosse raised the rifle barrel, grinning savagely. She heard Rafe's hoarse shout, but her only weapon was the horse, so she leaned against his neck and whipped even harder, sending the flashing, razor-sharp hooves flying straight at the gunman. She nearly laughed at the look of stark disbelief on Larosse's face. He pitched himself out of the horse's path, rolling across the muddy bank as she flew by.

"Rafe!" she screamed. Her eyes widened in horror. He stood in the open, a perfect target, completely at the mercy of the gunman. His face was a cold, blank mask, his eyes mere slits of silver. Brenna prayed Larosse wouldn't shoot Rafe down before she could get to him. A rifle shot whistled through the air, turning her prayers to dust in her mouth.

Calmly, Rafe raised his hand, the silver derringer glinting like a bright, winking eye, and he slowly squeezed off one shot. Another.

Brenna was upon him then, sawing madly at the bridle. With an agility that surprised her, Rafe grabbed the saddle horn and swung up behind her.

"Yah!" he shouted, heels digging into the horse's sides. Ears lying flat against its head, the bay carried them through the thicket and out of rifle range.

Brenna felt giddy with relief and gladly relinquished the reins to Rafe's control. He did not slow the bay's pace, and the ground flew by under its steady gallop. A wave of dizziness swept over Brenna, and for a terrifying instant memory slashed, and she was back on the horse with Larosse, reliving those frightening hours.

But no. The broad chest she leaned against was well-muscled, hard. The sharp pungency of his male sweat was familiar, enticing. The arm that encircled her waist held her firmly, almost possessively, but not painfully. Her breath sighed from her throat, and her head lolled back, rocking with the rhythm of the horse's movements. In a moment of total surrender, she placed her fate in Rafe's strong hands. An inexplicable contentment filled her.

Her reverie ended suddenly when Rafe abruptly reined in the horse, and she would have fallen but for the arm that steadied her. Brenna opened her eyes, fighting the lethargy that sapped her strength and will. They traveled through open country and crossed a road of sorts, little more than a cow track. Rafe turned the horse in circles, his eyes scouring the path while he muttered to himself. He swung down off the horse to examine markings in the dust.

Brenna watched him as though from a great distance. "Why—why have we stopped?"

"Riders passed this way, not too long ago." His tone was sardonic. "I suppose a posse's too much to hope for. At least it'll help cover our trail."

He wiped his sweaty brow with his shirt sleeve, his eyes narrowing against the bright sunshine. His silver gaze flicked over Brenna with her skirts bunched immodestly about her calves and her hair a wild tangle. His mouth hardened beneath his mustache, and without another word, he hauled her off the horse. Brenna gasped and staggered, her knees as soft as apple butter.

"You and I have got to get a few things straight before we go another step, woman!" Rafe snapped, his dark brows drawn together in a furious, formidable line. "Why the hell did you come back? I could have stalked him down if you hadn't interfered. You may have cost me my last chance of recovering those documents."

Dumbfounded, Brenna's mouth dropped open. After all that had happened, this was hardly a reaction she expected. Her temper began to smolder. "I was trying to save your rotten hide! You—you ungrateful wretch!" she spluttered, unable to think up a name vile enough to call him.

"You mule-headed female!" he snarled, catching her

upper arms and lifting her so that they glared at each other nose to nose. "You could have been killed!"

"What about you?" she demanded, her eyes spitting green fire. "Standing there in full view! Are you crazy?"

"Better me for a target than a pea-brained, red-haired witch!"

Her eyes widened and she blanched. "You—you deliberately drew his fire from me?"

Suddenly the enormity of what she had done hit her, crushing her breath from her lungs. Her impulsive actions had placed them both in jeopardy, and only by the grace of God had they survived. Blackness threatened and she swayed.

"Don't you dare faint on me now!" Rafe roared, shaking her hard.

"I—I'm not." She gulped, blinking away the darkness at the edges of her vision. She wouldn't allow herself to give way to weakness.

"That's better." He gave a small, rueful laugh and bent closer, his voice suddenly husky. "You looked like an avenging angel, high-tailing it out of those woods. God, Red, don't ever scare me like that again."

She stared up into his gray eyes, mesmerized by the light glittering in their depths. "Why?" she whispered.

"Because . . . oh, hell!" His vexed answer was a purely male growl. "You ask too many damned female questions."

Then he took her lips, staking his possession of her senses with his kiss and drawing her soul right out of her body. His mustache brushed sensually against her overheated skin. His tongue tantalized, thrusting into the sweet cavern of her mouth to taste each recess. Brenna's head was swimming when he finally lifted his lips from hers. Rafe's voice was tender-rough in her ear.

"You do exactly what I tell you from now on, or I swear to God, Red, I'll turn you over my knee. Is that clear?"

She nodded dumbly, too overcome and wobbly to risk a squeaky reply.

"Good." He drew a deep breath. "Do you think you can ride awhile? I'd rather not risk meeting up with our persistent friend again, at least until I can get my hands on another gun.''

"Will he follow us?" she asked anxiously.

"Who knows? If he were smart, he'd have cleared out of this part of the country by now, along with my securities. Being outwitted by a little twit of a girl must have made him pretty damned mad to risk everything by coming after you." Rafe grinned crookedly. "At least we gave that bastard something to think about."

"Did you hit him?"

"Not likely, at that range with such a small caliber. And two shots was all I had. If I had my pistol, I wouldn't mind meeting up with him again."

Brenna shuddered. The last thing she wanted was that! Her head pounded abominably, and she was horribly thirsty. She sighed. "I'm so tired."

"I know, Red. But you can't give up now." As badly as he wanted to retrieve the stolen securities, Rafe was no fool, and the girl swaying on her feet was his responsibility. After all, she'd risked her life for his more than once. "We can't rest just yet. We're still a long way from Marshall. And we're at Larosse's mercy, unarmed and riding double. He can pick us off at will. No doubt," he continued thoughtfully, "that's exactly what he expects to do. Maybe we ought not be so obliging."

"I don't care. I just want to go home." Her words wobbled, and to her horror a single tear slipped from the corner of her eye. Rafe caught the trickle of moisture with the callused pad of his thumb, gently rubbing it over the red welt on her cheekbone.

"You've got to trust me, Brenna."

Her lips trembled. "It's hard."

He smiled at her honesty. "Try anyway."

He squeezed her shoulder encouragingly, then picked her up and set her in the saddle. He climbed up behind her and clucked to the bay. Brenna was too weary and disheartened to protest when his arm circled her waist again, pulling her against his chest.

Rafe glanced down at the sagging girl, noting her shallow breathing, the illness and exhaustion written over her delicate features. It took him a few minutes to realize that she had slipped into a doze. Strange, he thought, how a man's protective instincts were aroused when he least expected, by a vulnerable mouth and the simple trust of a sleeping girl.

His jaw tightened and he prodded the horse into a canter, pressing Brenna to his heart. He had little choice. Brenna was in no condition to travel much farther, yet a killer with vengeance in his mind might well be hot on their trail. Gould was no doubt livid at Rafe's continued absence, and the Southern Pacific deal was as sour as week-old milk. But all that would have to wait. Larosse would expect them to continue north toward Marshall, but Rafe knew they'd be sitting ducks long before they reached any help.

Deliberately, Rafe turned the horse west. There was a place he knew that might offer some brief haven. Brenna wouldn't like it, but it couldn't be helped.

"Where are we?"

"A place I thought I'd never see again," Rafe answered, his voice stony.

Brenna tried to read his expression in the late afternoon shadows. The ride had taken on a nightmarish quality long ago, snatches of scenery, the bearded jawline of the man who held her, the swaying rhythm of the tired horse, all melding together as she faded in and out of sleep and consciousness. She gave a weary sigh. Was this new landscape a product of her feverish imaginings or reality? She did not know and, for the moment, cared less.

Once it had been a small ranch, tucked in the hollow of a low ridge. The sagging remains of a corral nestled beside a weathered gray barn and a decrepit bunkhouse. The modest main house was equally run-down, the steps leading to the front porch broken and the roof minus some shingles. It had at one time been painted white, but now had weathered to a mildew-streaked gray. An air of neglect was all about. But the windows were intact, although dirty and fly-specked, and the daub-and-waddle chimney rose unbroken on the side of the house. Tough weeds grew in clumps in the yard, and a couple of overgrown native privets hugged the sides of the house. There were no signs of life. No chickens scratched in the dirt yard. No dogs yelped a welcome. No people waited expectantly on the porch.

Rafe urged the horse forward into the yard. He dismounted and tied the reins around a porch post. Brenna watched him curiously for a moment, then let her gaze roam over her surroundings. Despite the fact that the place had obviously been deserted for some time, she could see that someone had once worked hard to make the ranch a prosperous, well-tended place. It was a pretty location, the low outline of the wooded ridge rising behind, the open grasslands of real cattle country spreading out in front. A small river cut a jade-green path across the distant prairie. The muted browns and golds of autumn made it seem somber at first, but Brenna could imagine it in springtime, with the first new green buds bursting forth from the trees and bluebells blooming on the grazing lands. In such a place, a man or woman willing to work could make a good life, provide for a family, grow old in peace and contentment. Once, this had been someone's home. What had happened?

"We'll rest here." Rafe reached up to help her down from the horse's back. She grimaced, biting her lips on a murmur of pain at her stiff, sore muscles.

"For how long? How much farther to Marshall?" She touched a temple, rubbing at the dull ache in her head.

"We aren't going to Marshall," he stated baldly.

"What? What do you mean?" she demanded, frowning in confusion and growing trepidation.

He stepped upon the porch. "Use your head, Red. We both could stand some food and rest. And I'm not going to let Larosse make an easy target of us again. In a couple of days he'll have given up, or been scared away. Sheriff Mobley's probably got men scattered all over this land. We'll head north after that."

"I don't want to wait. I want to go home now," Brenna said unsteadily.

Rafe's mouth quirked in a mocking smile. "It's a little late to worry about your virtue, isn't it?"

Brenna blushed. "If you had any decency . . ."

"I've never claimed to have any of that questionable quality." His voice was clipped, impatient. "What difference does it make if we're sleeping under the stars or under a roof? And who's to know, anyway? Come on, let's see what's here." He turned toward the door.

"How do you know about this place?" Brenna paused at the bottom step, shooting Rafe a suspicious glance. "Who owns it?"

"I do."

"You!"

"That's right." His voice held a sardonic quality. "The state paid off some of us Rangers in land. At one time I fancied myself quite a cattle baron." He tried the door, but it was stuck, so he set his shoulder against it and shoved. It opened with the shriek of warped wood.

Brenna licked her lips and gingerly climbed the broken steps. She peered past Rafe's broad shoulders into the dim interior of the house, then followed him slowly inside.

At first glance, the inside was as disappointing as the exterior. She gazed around in unconcealed dismay. The main room was empty except for a low bench facing the dirty fireplace. Behind this room lay a kitchen of sorts, containing only a rough-hewn table with a single chair and empty cupboards. Rotting calico curtains hung in tatters at the windows. Two smaller bedrooms paralleled the main portion of the house. The open door of one revealed a rope-strung homemade bedstead with a stained cotton tick mattress. Brenna wrinkled her nose. The place smelled musty. A layer of dirt covered everything.

As Brenna took another step forward, something scuttled past her ankles and streaked out the open door. She screamed shortly, grabbing up her ragged skirts.

"Just an old possum," Rafe said, grinning as Brenna blushed with embarrassment. He ran his hand over the wooden mantelpiece, and grimaced at the cloud of dust he raised. "Not much of a place, is it?"

"To some it would look like paradise," Brenna replied quietly. In her mind, she compared it to the sharecropper's cabin she'd been raised in and O'Donnell's farmhouse. The contrast was more than favorable, made overwhelmingly attractive by the mere fact of ownership. She'd never had a place that was her own. She was surprised at the stab of envy she felt. Wearily, she dropped onto the bench. "Why did you leave?" she asked curiously.

Rafe's gaze slid away from hers. "Mr. Gould needed me."

"And you gave this up, just like that?" she asked in amazement.

"I wasn't much of a cattleman anyway." His low chuckle was self-derisive.

"So you took the easy way out!" Brenna accused. She didn't know why she felt such hurt disappointment at his revelation. "Back to Gould, his lackey once again."

"I had a debt to pay." Rafe's features were carved in granite. "And it wasn't without its reward. I'm a rich man now, thanks to Gould. I make more in a day on the Exchange than I'd make in a year punching cows."

"You gave up something of your own to toady to a man like Gould!" she cried. "And for what? Money? Why'd you come to Texas in the first place if that's all you wanted?"

"That's none of your business, Red." Rafe's jaw hardened. Brenna's naive, scathing questions delved too deeply into memories he didn't care to examine. But even her face was a reminder, that little rounded chin so like another woman's that at one time had meant the world to him. But Rafe would never forget the night that world had shattered.

"Don't hate me, Rafe," Edith had pleaded, her dark eyes shimmering with tears. "I'm going to marry George."

"George Gould? That pup?" Rafe laughed his disbelief. "Old Jay will never agree to it."

"Much you know," Edith said airily, tears vanishing with an actress's ease. She turned to the large theatrical mirror to dust powder over her flawless face. All New York knew that Edith Kingdon, that beautiful young ingénue, was the theater's newest darling. She smoothed pomade over her lips and shot Rafe a sharp glance. "George's father has already given his approval. He says it's admirable that I'm willing to earn my own living." Her gay laughter tinkled in the little dressing room.

"You'll need Mrs. Gould's blessings, as well," Rafe said. "She's Murray Hill aristocracy through and through. She'll never allow her son to wed an actress." He stood behind her, tall and darkly distinguished in evening dress.

Pushing aside the neck of her satin dressing gown, he dropped a lingering kiss on one plump white shoulder. His voice was husky. "You'd do better to choose a man of your own social class, Edie. Somebody who thinks like you."

Edith shivered with sensuality, then irritably shrugged away from the hot questing of Rafe's lips. "You mustn't do that anymore, Rafe darling. You do understand, don't you? Why, I'm practically an engaged lady."

"You don't act engaged."

Edith whirled around on her low stool, her lower lip thrust out petulantly. "From now on I must. I really must thank you. It was too good of you to introduce me to George."

"I regret that already." A stain of red rushed up his neck. He'd never fancied himself in love until he'd met Edith. Enamored with her flashing brunette looks and the innate knowledge that they were both the same kind— alley cats clawing and scratching their way to the top— he'd risked his heart for the first time in his life, only to find it impaled on the talons of Edith's ambitions.

"I've enjoyed your company, darling, but you must see that George can offer me so much more. I'll make him a good wife."

"And help him spend Jay's millions," he rejoined sourly.

"But of course!" She laughed and, rising, came around the stool to run her fingers up the starched white expanse of Rafe's shirt. "You mustn't feel too badly, Rafe," she purred. "After all, later, if things work out and we are circumspect, perhaps we can resume our—friendship. You know I'll always care for you, darling."

Rafe's teeth gritted together. He'd known since birth that a woman was a faithless creature. What a fool he'd been to hope Edith would prove otherwise. Frost nipped the tender bud of love, sending that part of his heart into deepest winter, perhaps forever. His hands caught her wrists in shackles of iron, stilling the tempting dance her fingers played on his chest.

"How very generous of you, Edie. But I make it a practice never to become involved with a mercenary bitch. Especially a married one. So take George, and his father's money, and be damned!'' He let her go abruptly, as if her touch defiled him.

"There's no need to be coarse," Edith protested, rubbing her wrists. Then she smiled, a feline grin of satisfaction. "I'm sure I'll see you, either at the office or at some social round. After all, darling, your fortune and your future is as linked to the Goulds' as mine is.''

That taunt was what had decided him. He wouldn't moon after Miss Edith Kingdon, especially not when she became Mrs. George Gould. He owed Jay Gould that much.

Texas was the answer. When Rafe first finished his schooling, Rossini suggested he learn the ropes by working on one of Gould's railroad crews down in Texas. Later he set out on his own, joining up with old Pete Hooke to do some Rangering on the west Texas frontier. A boy had gone to Texas, but a man returned to New York after nearly five years, and was welcomed back into the Gould fold. He'd served well since then, but he knew that Gould wouldn't miss a junior clerk, even one who'd proved useful on occasion. After the Edith debacle, he decided to claim his Texas acreage and build a new life.

He'd been doing it, too, Rafe thought, looking around the shabby interior of the ranch house. He'd built it up by the sweat of his brow. But when his old master had called, he'd given it up. Not that he hadn't been torn. That's why he hadn't sold the place after all these years, and it wasn't like him to be overly sentimental. But he owed Gould and, by coming in during the Texas & Pacific strike, had played a valuable role in settling the matter, something Gould hadn't forgotten over the last four years as Rafe rose in prestige to become one of his most useful and successful lieutenants.

Rafe's lips thinned as his eyes lit on the weary girl. Yes, Brenna would really hate him if she knew he'd been involved in breaking the strike that killed her brother. He gave a snort of disgust. What the hell did he care, anyway? Once back to Marshall, he'd never see her again, his duty to her discharged. He'd be well shut of a trouble-making, hostile snip of a strawberry-haired wench, and the sooner the better!

"The pump and the privy are out back," he said, his voice curt. "I'll get the saddlebags."

Brenna watched him dumbly, too tired to move. When he came back into the house a few minutes later, he tossed the saddlebags and bedroll on the table in the kitchen.

"There's some beans and coffee in there. See what you can do." He turned on his heel.

"Where are you going?" Brenna dragged herself to her feet, slightly alarmed at the closed-off expression on his dark face. Had she antagonized him too far this time with her thoughtless words? Oh, when would she ever learn to hold her tongue?

"Hunting. A couple of rabbit snares might put meat on the table tonight. I won't be long."

"All right, Rafe," she said faintly. His gray gaze pierced her for a long moment, and Brenna saw the distance in his look. When he was gone, she felt more alone than she had in all her life.

An hour later, Brenna surveyed the results of her efforts with some satisfaction. Ignoring the fact that her headache was getting worse, she had doggedly explored the house as well as the meager contents of the saddle pouches. A small fire burned merrily in the hearth. Although the kitchen might have once had an iron stove, it was missing now, and she was forced to cook at the fireplace. A bent kettle she'd found discarded in a cupboard now hung over the coals, joined by Rafe's blackened coffeepot. The aroma of beans and coffee thickened the cool evening air that drifted in through the open doors and windows. A bundle of twigs had made a serviceable broom, and the faded calico curtain had been torn into rags and used to clean the dust and dirt from the table and window glasses. Brenna had even used Rafe's bar of shaving soap on herself. Feeling clean again was a great relief even if she did have to put on the same soiled shirtwaist and skirt.

With great temerity, she borrowed the comb from among Rafe's things and began the task of untangling her hair. It was tedious going and every so often she was forced to rest by strange bouts of weakness. She put it down to hunger and combatted it by taking tiny sips of strong black coffee from the tin cup she found in Rafe's supplies. The bitter brew made her stomach twist, but all the same, it was bracing, and would have to hold her until the beans were done.

The jingle of harness and steady *clop-clop* of a horse coming from the rear of the house alerted her to Rafe's return. She stood on the threshold at the back door, watching him ride up, the forgotten comb still in her hand, her hair spilling across her shoulders. He dismounted beside the pump, dragging two skinned rabbit carcasses across his saddle bow.

"You had good luck," Brenna said with a tentative smile.

Rafe's reply lodged in his throat at the picture she made with her hair loose and capturing in its depths the last rosy rays of the sun. He caught his breath. She was lovely and warm, waiting on the doorstep with welcome in her jewel-toned eyes. He could imagine she'd look at her lover with just that expression. Rafe's gut tightened and his lips thinned in annoyance. He shook his head to clear away the vision. Such dreams weren't for him.

"We'll eat tonight, at least," he muttered, turning away to wash the rabbits under the pump. That done, he brought them to Brenna, along with a bundle of willow withes he'd cut at the river's edge. "Use these to spit them on," he instructed. "I'll see to the horse."

Wordlessly, Brenna nodded and accepted the rabbits and withes, wondering what made Rafe look at her so queerly. Sighing, she realized that it was unlikely she'd ever understand even the remotest thing about him. Unreasonably, the thought made her sad.

The rabbits were sizzling over the fire when Rafe appeared at the back door. He looked around with surprise at the order and normalcy that Brenna had restored. "You certainly didn't waste any time making yourself at home," he said sourly.

Brenna glanced up from where she knelt at the hearth, bewilderment in her eyes. She wiped her hands on her skirts and stood. "If it's one thing I know, it's how to keep a house. Perhaps you prefer to dine with the dirt, Mr. Sinclair, but I do not."

"Indeed so, Miss Galloway," he drawled in a mocking tone. "Very well. Since we'll be *dining* this evening, perhaps I'd better make myself worthy of the occasion by shaving.''

"It makes no difference whatsoever," she said stiffly She watched him rummage through the saddlebags, then remembered the bar of soap drying on the windowsill. She handed it to him, blushing. "I borrowed your soap. I hope you don't mind.''

"Not at all.'' He caught a gleaming lock of her hair in his fingers, tugging gently, and his smile was slow and slumberous. "I find the fragrance of bay rum on a woman quite—tantalizing.''

Brenna jerked her hair from his grasp. "Then I will be certain never to use it again if it means I will be spared your further attentions!'' she snapped. To her astonishment, he laughed.

"Ah, Red,'' he said, chucking her underneath the chin, "what would I have done these past days without your sharp tongue to flay me? A very boring sojourn it would be, indeed!'' Chuckling to himself, he left her, heading for the pump.

Brenna clenched her fists in annoyance, biting back the words she longed to fling after him. Why did she always feel at a disadvantage with him? She watched him strip off his shirt, and her mouth went suddenly dry. He really was a magnificent male specimen, all bronzed, rippling muscle, his chest lightly dusted with crisp black hair. He quickly lathered his face and scraped away the stubble from his lean cheeks. Brenna peeked from the doorway, hypnotized by the masculine routine. Rafe caught her watching him and lifted a mocking eyebrow. Brenna gasped and turned away with a disdainful flounce of her skirts, but not before his laughter made her cheeks burn.

The meal they shared was a strangely intimate one. They ate the roasted rabbit and beans from a single plate. She used his spoon, he the knife. They were silent for the most part, intent on filling their bellies. The orange light from the flickering fire made a pool around them and cast their features into stark angles.

Brenna found it hard to keep her eyes off of Rafe's clean-shaven face. His black eye had faded to no more than a yellow bruise and the swelling was down. Gone was the rugged outlaw. In his place was the sophisticated businessman she'd first seen in the depot dining hall, a handsome, intimidating stranger whom she didn't know at all, and even feared at times. She shook her head slightly, chiding herself for being fanciful. Her thoughts danced along with the flames in the fire, and she felt unsettled and jumpy, her dinner a hard knot in her stomach. She lifted her eyes again to the man across the table, only to find him watching her, his eyes smoky.

"Do you want your coffee now?" she asked, rising from the table to escape his steady regard.

"Please."

She poured him a cup from the pot at the fireplace. As she bent, her hair formed a shimmering screen through which she watched him. Tossing the dangling skein over her shoulder, she placed the cup before him, then began to gather up the remains of the meal.

"Shall we share the cup?" Rafe suggested. He lounged low against the chair, looking at her over the rim of the tin mug.

She licked her lips at the husky intimacy of his words and shook her head. "I had some earlier."

His hand shot out, clamping hard on her wrist. "Leave it," he ordered tersely. "I've had all I can take of your charming display of domesticity."

Brenna was startled by the angry edge to his words, then irritation flooded her. "Release me. I'll not leave a mess just to please you!"

"You forget whose place this is."

"Why should it matter to you?" she demanded, wringing her hand free. "You don't care about it anymore. You gave it up for Gould!" Her face was flushed, but as she gestured at the modest room, her expression changed, became sad, almost wistful. Her words were low, a confession wrung from her depths. "I'd sell my soul for a place like this."

"You?" Rafe laughed harshly. "You'd starve to death the first winter!"

Brenna placed the tin plate on top of the kettle of beans and set it off the fire. She wiped the utensils with a damp cloth, her movements jerky. "You don't understand what it's like to be at the mercy of someone else," she muttered. "If we'd had a place to go, somewhere of our own after Da drowned, do you think Ma would have married *that man*? But you gave up something like this without a thought, Gould's man till the end. You're either a fool or a coward!''

Rafe came to his feet with a muttered oath. ''You go too far! I do what a man must do. What the hell do you know about the demands of honor or loyalty?''

''Loyalty!'' she cried hotly, flinging the spoon to the floor. It hit the hearth stones with a tinny clatter. ''Don't lecture me on loyalty. I could have left my mother and sisters, but I didn't. Who else could protect those poor wee lasses? And Ma killing herself slaving for O'Donnell's ungrateful brats. When he put his babe in her, did he think that it was like to kill her? No!''

Brenna's lips trembled and she looked at her hands with a frenetic, remembering light in her eyes, which made Rafe pause uncertainly.

''When the babe slipped,'' she whispered, ''I thought it was the blessing I'd prayed for. But the bleeding . . . I couldn't stop it. There was so much blood.'' She raised her face, so pale and tortured that Rafe took an involuntary step toward her. But Brenna backed away, spitting her scorn.

''Don't speak to me of loyalty! My hands ran crimson with my mother's blood! I buried her and my stillborn sister while that sotted brute of a husband drank himself senseless!''

''Brenna,'' Rafe said, reaching for her, shocked to his core by her naked revelations and alarmed at the unholy emerald gleam in her eyes.

She looked through him, her expression dazed, then stared in horror at her upraised hands.

''Have you ever seen so much blood?'' she whispered, and slid silently to the floor.

Chapter 8

Brenna's fever raged through the night, alternating periods of deep unconsciousness with bouts of delirium. At those times, it was all Rafe could do to keep her on the bed, ragged and filthy as it was, with only his bedroll for linens. She fought him, clawed him, cursed him, then pleaded with him, sobbing so pitifully he thought her heart would surely break. She was burning up and complained of the blanket he tucked around her, yet shook with chills that racked her slender form in giant waves.

Rafe sat in the chair he'd brought from the kitchen and mopped her face with a rag dipped in cool water, silently berating himself for pushing her too far with his harsh words. She moved restlessly, tossing her head from side to side and muttering, but she seemed quieter. Rafe raked a hand through his hair and studied her by the light of the candle stub he'd found. What if that meant she was growing weaker, getting worse?

He'd never seen such a fever, and all his efforts seemed for naught. He lifted her head, holding the tin cup to her lips, forcing her to drink again the willow bark tea. Pete Hooke had taught him to make it years ago, swearing about its ability to reduce a fever, but Rafe was bound to call him a liar after this night. Brenna choked and coughed, but he made her swallow some of the tisane. Her sooty eyelashes fluttered as he laid her back down, and she opened her eyes. There was no recognition in their depths.

"I can remember it, Da," she said. She frowned in

concentration, then began to sing in a high, sweet voice that curdled Rafe's blood. "Hey non nonny, nonny—"

"Brenna, wake up!"

"But I know it, I do!" she protested. "I can play Ophelia, and you the Prince of Denmark. I remember all the flowers." She plucked an imaginary blossom from an invisible bouquet. "There's pansies for thoughts, but rue for sorrow. I must give that to Ma. And violets, 'but they withered all when my father died.' Left us he did, drowned like poor, mad Ophelia." She gazed at Rafe kindly, then lowered her voice to share her secret. "You see, no man is trustworthy."

Rafe grasped her restless hands, disturbed by the fantasy in her mind. "Brenna, you're safe. Come out of it."

"I wonder if Da floated and sang? What a peaceful way to die. No blood at all." She frowned again. "I won't think about that, I won't! Just take the money and go! Damn O'Donnell to hell!"

Rafe felt the heat radiating from her skin and knew the fever soared. How long would it take to kill her at this rate? Dammit, he was no doctor! He should have known this was coming, picked up on the signs. Three days of terror and exposure would affect even the heartiest constitution, much less a slip of a girl with more heart than strength.

Having overspent herself with that outburst, Brenna lapsed back into muttered ravings, and Rafe knew he had to try something else to lower the fever. He unbuttoned her blouse and eased it off her shoulders, then removed her skirt and petticoat. He frowned at the heavy lump pinned within the slip's folds, then chuckled when he realized the stocking contained a small roll of bills and a few coins. Ever resilient and prepared, Brenna carried her life's savings with her. He shook his head over the pitifully small amount, then carefully replaced it.

Brenna mumbled incoherently as heat radiated from her. Rafe hesitated only a moment more before taking off her chemise and drawers, as well. For what he had in mind, it wouldn't do to get her only clothing soaked. Throwing the blanket over her, he left to find fresh cloths and more water.

When he returned, she had slipped back into insensibility, and for that he was grateful. Conscious, he had no doubt she'd fight him tooth and nail before she'd let him nurse her in this fashion. As it was, Rafe had only himself to fight as he bathed her slim limbs, trying to ignore the way his own body responded to the feminine beauty of her slender waist and hips, the small but perfect breasts with their rosy crests, the mysterious triangle of crisp golden hair at the top of her thighs.

Rafe ground his teeth and tried not to feel like a cad at the pleasure touching her gave him. But he couldn't help appreciating the cool, milky translucence of her skin, and he smiled at the light sprinkling of freckles that dusted her bosom and shoulders, the mark of a true redhead. He sponged her from brow to toes, then began again, repeating the procedure over and over, stopping just long enough to force more willow bark tea down her at intervals. She seemed cooler, but he couldn't be sure because she was still too hot, her skin drying nearly as fast as he bathed her. Rafe was scarcely aware that the eastern horizon was streaked with pink light when he raised the cup to her lips yet again.

"Drink it, Brenna," he urged.

Her throat moved, then a weak hand pushed the cup away. "Ugh. Nasty."

Rafe paused. That had sounded almost lucid. "You must drink some more."

"I don't like it." Her voice was faintly plaintive, like a child's. She blinked, gazing up at him with eyes that were puzzled and seemed too big for her pinched face. "Who . . . ?"

"It's Rafe."

"Rafe?" Her hand reached up and touched his cheek. She sighed and closed her eyes again. "Oh, good."

He pushed her gently back on the mattress, then picked up the cloth and ran it over her brow. He frowned, then rubbed his grainy eyes and looked again. A faint dew of perspiration filmed her upper lip. With rising hope, he dipped the cloth again and rubbed her neck and collarbone. Brenna stirred, pushing at his hand.

"Don't," she murmured. He could see the effort it took

to open her eyes, to focus on the concerned face bent over her. "What are you doing?"

Rafe laughed, a great feeling of relief and triumph flowing through him. "Just giving you a wash, love."

"What?" She was momentarily bemused, then she discovered her unclothed state. She gasped and reached for the edge of the blanket. "How could you? It isn't proper!"

A rare grin split Rafe's tired face. "Proper or not, I think it's done the trick. The fever's broken."

"Oh, my God!" she moaned, rolling her flaming, humiliated face into the mattress and curling into a ball of embarrassment. "Leave me alone!"

"Now don't take on so, Red," he drawled, sitting down beside her. "You have a beautiful body."

"Oh!"

"That I haven't laid a finger on—except in the line of duty," he added wickedly.

"Swine!"

Rafe could only laugh at her chagrin. A fine sheen of sweat covered her, and he knew the worst was over. "Come on, sweet, let me help you," he cajoled, supporting her into a sitting position. "You must feel as weak as a kitten."

"I'm all right," she insisted, trying to pull away.

He looked at her closely and nodded in satisfaction. "Yes, I think you are."

Ignoring her protests, Rafe tenderly blotted the purifying sweat from her limbs and helped her into the only clean garment between them, a shirt of his from the saddlebag. Her lips were pouty and her cheeks red with embarrassment, not fever, but she was limp and weak and had no choice but to submit. He made her drink some more tea, then rolled her in the blanket and tucked her back into bed. He was inordinately proud of his success as a physician.

"Try to sleep now, Red," he said, pushing the hair back from her temples. "You'll soon feel better."

"I'm sorry, Rafe," she whispered.

"For what?"

"I'm such a bother." She tried to stifle a yawn and failed.

"No bother. My pleasure, actually. Did you know that you've got a freckle shaped like a star on your—"

"Rafe!" Brenna blushed furiously.

His chuckle was low and husky. He pressed a chaste kiss on her forehead. "Never mind. Your secret is safe with me. Sleep now."

"Yes." Her breathing was slow and regular, and her voice was drowsy. "Rafe?"

"What is it?"

"Thank you."

He paused in the doorway, and a perplexed frown creased his brow. "Sure." He watched her drift off, a complexity of emotions tumbling through him. He shook his head and stretched, arching his back and groaning with stiffness.

He poked up the fire and heated the remains of the previous night's coffee. He drank it black and scalding on the porch while he watched morning creep across his land. He was tired and his muscles protested the lack of respite, but a strange restlessness kept him up. He watched the horizon grow brighter with each passing moment, but the vague feeling of emptiness and regret wouldn't leave him. He'd once had a dream here, and Brenna's sharp words had pricked him. What would his life be like now if he'd refused Gould's summons four years earlier? It was a useless question. His choices were made, had been made long ago when Rossini came to a hungry boy with Gould's offer of sustenance and work. He couldn't regret it.

Rafe spilled the remains of the bitter brew onto the ground and went back inside. Brenna slept peacefully. He smiled down at her, amazed anew at her courage and pluck. He'd been mean to tease her. It was just that he was so damn glad she was better. As a comrade-in-arms, she couldn't be faulted. Maybe they'd never be friends, but he'd come to appreciate her drive, her will to survive.

Poor kid! She'd had a rough time of it all her life, if what she'd revealed and what he guessed were even half true. Sure, he'd had hard times himself as a child, but then Gould had become his mentor. Besides, he didn't have the disadvantage of her sex to hinder him. She had a perfect right to be an embittered, sour-souled woman, but she was as sweet and appealing as a soft summer's night. He thrust such dangerous thoughts away. Brenna Galloway had already taken up too much of his time, too much of his life.

Fatigue weighed his eyelids. The thought of a few hour's shuteye was too tempting to resist. He turned away, then stopped. He'd be damned if he was gallant enough to sleep on the hard floor when he could share the dubious comforts of the old bed. Besides, Brenna was so deeply asleep she'd probably never even know he was there.

Rafe pulled off his shirt and boots and gingerly climbed into bed beside Brenna. Her deep breathing never faltered. Rafe gave a tired sigh and stretched out, his brain whirling. As soon as Brenna was able, they could head north again. No doubt Gould had gone back to New York by now. He'd have his hands full pulling loose ends together in the wake of Plummer's murder. Rafe just hoped that they wouldn't have to shelve indefinitely their assault on the Southern Pacific. If they could just find this Larosse and discover who he worked for, then maybe they'd know who their real enemies were.

At the thought of Larosse, Rafe's eyes narrowed and he glanced at the sleeping girl. A fierce protectiveness squeezed his chest. He had to find Larosse before the killer found Brenna again. Maybe he had given up his pursuit of the only witness to Plummer's murder, but something told Rafe a man obsessed enough to track her down once wouldn't give up that easily.

Rafe turned and gently eased his arm around Brenna, as if by doing so he could protect her from such dire ruminations. His nose rested against her springy strawberry-blond waves, and he smiled. She still smelled of bay rum soap.

Brenna snuggled beneath the scratchy blanket and tried to roll over, but something held her hair. She opened her eyes and her breath caught. Rafe was sound asleep next to her, his fingers twisted into her long tresses. Brenna tried to bring her leaping thoughts under control. Most of the night was a blur, dreams and nightmares blending in her memory, only Rafe's deep voice an anchor to reality. He had cared for her, she knew, and most tenderly. Small wonder he slept so deeply.

Her hand grazed the unfamiliar fabric of the garment she wore, and she remembered her protests when Rafe dressed her in his shirt. A rosy tide climbed up her neck. It was hardly proper to wear the shirt even though it came to her knees. And it was definitely scandalous to sleep in the same bed with the owner of said shirt!

She bit her lip, then tentatively tugged a lock of her hair, sighing as the silky strands slipped from his loose grasp. She had to get up. She pulled another portion free, then paused, gazing with interest at the sleeping man. His features were relaxed in slumber, and he looked much less formidable than he usually did. His lashes were thick, black, baby fine, and they cast long shadows on his high cheekbones. Even his mustache seemed less bristly and blatantly masculine; it appeared softer, like velvet, and she longed to run a finger along its length. She closed her eyes against such madness. She knew what kind of man Rafe Sinclair was—ruthless, a taker. And yet . . .

Yet he had been kind to her, in a way few men had ever been. She could not fit him neatly into the role of villain any longer. She opened her eyes in confusion, and this time her glance stole across the broad expanse of his chest, following the whorls of soft black hair that thickened and led down his flat middle to disappear beneath his waistband. His muscles were hard and perfect, the faint outline of blue veins marbling his arms. His was the strength she'd come to depend upon, and the notion left her strangely breathless, her heart stirring unevenly in her breast.

When had he become special to her? When had her emotions betrayed her by letting her care what became of this man? Their fates had intertwined, but only a fool would let her feelings get out of control. She mustn't long for what he could not give her, what must surely only be a fantasy brought on by the fantastic adventure they'd shared. She quivered with a sudden urge to run far, far away.

"Don't go," Rafe said.

Brenna jumped, her startled eyes flashing to Rafe's

sleepy face. He watched her from under his long lashes, and a smile crooked his finely carved lips.

"I can't. You're holding my hair," she pointed out breathlessly.

"So I am." He raised his hand, letting the strands flow through his fingers like gold dust. He played gently with the soft curls, and Brenna was fascinated by the contrast of her bright hair against his dark skin. "It's like silk," he said softly.

"Let go."

He might not have heard her for all the attention he paid. "How do you feel?"

"Fine." She was mildly astonished to find that it was true. She was a little stiff and sore, but she felt refreshed and rested.

"Good. You gave me quite a scare."

"I should get up," Brenna said, rather desperately.

"Hush, Red. Rest a few minutes more. The day is half gone anyway. Listen, can you hear it?"

"What?"

"The quiet. I'd forgotten how quiet it can be here. How big and empty. And lonely."

Brenna turned her head, listening now, as well. The faint sound of the breeze rustling through the grass and the desultory twitter of birds was all she heard. "It doesn't sound lonesome to me. It sounds peaceful."

"Perhaps. I suppose loneliness is a state of mind, not a place. Whatever, I've been there before."

"I understand," she murmured, touched by this unexpected revelation, this admission of vulnerability.

Rafe shifted so that he could look directly down into her eyes and continued to run his fingers through her hair. "Do you?"

Her mouth was a soft, sad line, a bittersweet testimony. "I know that an empty heart is the loneliest place of all," she whispered.

"Then, perhaps you do understand." His silver gaze examined her expression intently, then he lowered his head and his lips brushed hers softly, sweetly.

Brenna trembled. Her fingers pressed against the warm solidity of his chest. "Rafe, please. Let me up."

"Why don't you stay?"

"I—"

His warm lips trailed a path of fire down the cords of her neck, cutting off her words. His arms slipped around her, pulling her so close she could feel the steady beat of his heart through the thin cotton of the shirt. He felt warm and solid and secure, and a thrilling excitement began to burn low in her belly, melting her will. She'd been able to resist his lovemaking before, but this was different, a sweet wooing, a gentle seduction. Everything womanly in her longed to respond.

"You are so lovely, so delicate," he murmured, running his palm over the curve of her hip into the indentation of her waist.

"Rafe, I can't!" Her choked cry was more anguished than she realized.

He drew back, his eyes smoky with desire, yet questioning. "I know neither of us planned on this, but—" He broke off as Brenna sat up and slid away. She stood up shakily, her hand resting on the bedpost for support.

Rafe's voice was husky, and he studied her with eyes that burned. "Am I wrong? Am I the only one who feels it? I ache with wanting you, Brenna."

"You're not wrong," she admitted, swaying slightly with the force of her longing. She took a deep breath and squared her shoulders, tossing her hair back in a gesture of pride, which made him want her even more.

He lifted a questioning eyebrow. "You say you want no husband, and I require no wife. So if we fight the loneliness together, what harm is there?"

"What harm?" Her soft, unbelieving laugh was tremulous. "You should know better than I." She lifted her chin, and her gaze was straight and clear. "I've never been with a man before."

He slowly sat up on the edge of the sagging bed and frowned, pondering. "Then, if I ask you again to stay, am I being selfish?"

Brenna caught her breath. No moralistic arguments could restrain the desire she felt for this man. She was afraid, yet she knew it would be her choice. Her life was bound by convention and duty, and soon she'd take up that burden again. Suddenly, she knew she wanted to be able to look back and know that just once she'd done something solely for herself. Something exciting and forbidden and wonderful. Slowly she shook her head at Rafe's question.

"No more selfish than I—if I stayed."

He smiled at her, a look of amused tenderness that caught at her heart. His heated gaze swept the slender daintiness of her bare feet, moved up over the subtle hints of womanly curves covered by the enveloping shirt, to rest at last on the shimmering, expectant jade depths of her eyes. He offered her his hand and his voice was gruff. "Then stay," he urged softly.

Poised on the brink of something so wonderfully unknown that her heart thundered, Brenna could only trust in herself—and in him. Shyly, she laid her hand in his.

Rafe's warm hand curled around hers, tugging her forward to stand between his thighs. The pressure of his hand made her bend slightly and, understanding his intent, she dropped her lips to his, bestowing her first freely given kiss. It was soft, inexpert, a trembling prelude that was provocative by its very mixture of untried sensuality and maidenly innocence.

Rafe's arm circled her waist, settling her down on one iron-thewed thigh. When they pulled apart, he turned the hand he still held and placed a kiss within her palm, then held it to his jaw.

"Ah, Red," he said with a wry, self-derisive chuckle. "Was there ever a woman such as you? You should save your purity for a man who's worthy of it."

Brenna searched his face for signs of mockery but found none. "It's mine to give as I please."

"Yes, and I can't believe I hesitate even a moment over so precious a gift. Such concern is not normally part of my character."

"I've reason to doubt that. After all, you have been kind to me." She stroked the lean line of his jaw, testing the texture of his dark sideburn, liking the feel of it beneath her fingers.

"Kindness is not in my nature, either."

It was her turn to laugh, a soft evidence of her disbelief. "You must allow me to make my own judgment about that."

His expression darkened and he glanced away. "You

may not feel as friendly toward me in a while." He
caught her hand again to still her exploration of his face.
He looked at her hard, his eyes glinting with steel and
self-restraint. "That is why you must be certain, Brenna."

"I am."

"I don't want this to be something you've convinced
yourself to do out of some kind of damned sense of gratitude," he said hoarsely.

"No, Rafe."

"Are you sure?"

"Must you take all my shame and leave me with no
defenses?" she whispered, a blush coloring her cheeks.
"Will you call me whore if I confess that I long for you,
too? That I stay not for you, but for myself?"

His arm tightened on her waist, and his hand cupped
her chin, forcing her to look at him. "Never that. But an
honest woman? Dare I believe it? No, someday you'll
hate me for this."

"I'll remember the gentleman who let the choice be
mine." Boldly, she touched his lips with hers. "I will
live with that."

Rafe groaned and pulled her fiercely against him,
kissing her passionately, his palm holding the back of her
head. Brenna's hands stole around his neck, and she
returned his ardor, her lips softening, then parting at the
insistent thrust of his tongue. He explored the interior of
her mouth with breath-stealing thoroughness, as though
he would savor every molecule of her being. A need to
become a participant, not merely a passive observer, led
Brenna to meet the heat of his tongue with a tentative
touching of her own. The contact sent an electrical surge
to every nerve ending. Feeling Rafe tense, she drew back,
confused. Had her boldness shocked him? Perhaps a man
didn't want the woman to join in the play.

"No, darling, that's good," Rafe murmured in encouragement. "I want you to taste me, too."

Brenna relaxed, melting against him as he stroked with
his tongue, coaxing her to join in the mating of mouths.
She sighed, drinking in his hot breath, reveling in the
sweet sensations that sent all thought spinning from her
head. Rafe's large hand caressed her thigh, sliding underneath the hem of the shirt to massage the soft curve of

her bare hip. Brenna quivered, her excitement building. Rafe pulled his lips away, and they both gasped for breath.

"Oh, Red." He groaned, a half smile curving his lips. "You make me forget all my good intentions."

"Why?" she breathed.

He caught her face in both hands and kissed her eyes, her nose, the corners of her mouth. "You respond so sweetly, I almost forget your innocence. You make me want to hurry when there is need not to."

"I want you to hurry."

His laugh was a soft rebuke. "It will be better for you if I don't, so don't tempt me."

"Show me what I mustn't do to tempt you," she said, provoked by an imp of feminine instinct into teasing him. "Shouldn't I do this?" She leaned forward to nip at his earlobe. "Or this?" Her fingers rubbed the hard wall of his chest in provocative circles, her thumb slipping over the bronze coin of his male nipple. "Or perhaps not even this?" Her hand moved down his flat stomach to dally at the opening of his trousers.

"Witch!" He caught her wrist, forcing her hand under the waistband to cup his rising tumescence. "See what your little games do to me."

Brenna gasped in wonder. He felt so hard yet velvety smooth and alive against her palm. Was this what made a man? How strange that she knew she should be frightened, but all she felt was a surging excitement and an overwhelming curiosity. Rafe's eyes were hooded, and when she moved her fingers to test the resiliency of his flesh, he groaned with pleasure.

"Enough," he said, pulling her hand away, his tone wry. "Or our pleasure will be counted in seconds, not in measured moments as it should be."

Brenna buried her flushed, embarrassed face against his neck. "I'm sorry. I don't know how to please you."

"Ah, sweetheart, no need for that. You please me very well, indeed. But it's my turn to please you now."

His fingers worked skillfully at the top button of her shirt, moving down until the garment hung completely open. He slipped a hand inside its folds to caress the curve of her waist. Brenna trembled in his arms, and he kissed her again lingeringly. He moved his hand slowly, his fingers casually brushing the full underside of her breast. When he finally cupped the lushness in his palm, he could feel the muted thump of her heart racing double time. Bending backward, he gently placed Brenna on the lumpy mattress, then stretched out beside her with the rough blanket beneath them.

Brenna's eyes were misty, shadowed by passion as she watched him fold back each side of the shirt, revealing her fully to his silvery gaze.

"You're so very beautiful," he murmured.

"I'm too thin." Her voice was weak.

"You're perfect." He trailed a finger down her breast bone, then circled each globe in a lazy salute, laughing softly as her nipples puckered and budded. "And I love this freckle."

Rafe lowered his mouth to the upper swell of her breast, laving the little star-shaped mark with his tongue. Brenna gasped and arched, her eyes wide with surprise. Rafe's mustache tickled her sensitized skin, and his lips burned a path of pure delight across her breast, then covered the sensitive crest.

Brenna moaned. "Rafe!" Involuntarily, her hands clutched his head, her fingers twining through his thick hair to push him away, or pull him closer, she knew not which.

While Rafe gently teased the one nipple into throbbing, pulsating life with his tongue and lips, his thumb circled the other with exquisite expertise, plucking at her and playing her like a violin string until she vibrated to the very center of her being. When she did not think she could stand his splendid torture another instant, he dipped lower, kissing and nibbling her ribs, then teasing the shallow well of her navel.

Bombarded by a host of new and totally novel sensations, Brenna could only gasp, clutching at Rafe's broad shoulders as shudders of pleasure washed over her. She was melting into a molten pool, the sweet liquid rush of passion dewing her womanly folds. Rafe's mustache brushed the inside of her thigh, and she squealed and wiggled, unnerved.

Instantly, he was beside her again, soothing her with

his kisses, stroking her and praising her, his lips and tongue playing a skillful litany of desire that drowned out every thought of protest. Hesitantly, then with growing confidence, Brenna caressed Rafe's muscular shoulders, traced the tendons in his neck, and explored the valley of his spine.

Suddenly, Rafe pulled away, and Brenna gave a little cry of bewilderment. He stood beside the sagging bed, his fingers uncharacteristically clumsy as he fumbled with the buttons on his trousers, his eyes burning into her. He kicked free of his garments, and Brenna swallowed anxiously at the proof of his rampant maleness. He saw her uncertainty and came quickly back to her, easing her arms from her shirt and flinging it to the floor.

"Don't be afraid," he whispered, gathering her close.

"I—I'm not." Her head rested on his arm, and she gazed trustingly up into his face.

"I'll make it good for you," he promised. "Just touch me, and let me touch you."

The feelings of imminent discovery and excitement threatened to choke her, but Brenna placed her small hand to his chest, then moved lower. Rafe stroked her from breast to hip, murmuring endearments, and his fingers tangled in the crisp hair at the top of her thighs. Kissing her with utter gentleness, he tenderly parted the soft folds of flesh that protected her womanhood.

Brenna moaned at his touch, the burning heat and fullness deep within crying out for release. He opened her, his fingers exploring the sleek, wet tightness of her, bringing her to the brink of fulfillment, then subsiding again and again until she nearly wept with wanting. She caressed his throbbing manhood, almost frantic to feel the final consummation of his loving.

"Now, darling," Rafe said, his voice hoarse with strain. He slowly lowered himself over her, allowing her to become accustomed to the feel and weight of him. His knee spread her thighs, and he continued to kiss her while one hand massaged and caressed her. When the hot, velvety tip of him probed her outer petals, Brenna gasped.

Rafe made a move to pull away, but she clasped her arms around his waist and refused to let him go, arching against him in mute invitation. Rafe clenched his teeth, nearly overcome by the overwhelming urge to bury himself deep within her soft, womanly flesh. But he did not want to hurt her, so he held himself in iron restraint. Easing slowly forward, his finger caressed the delicate nodule of feminine pleasure until with a gasping cry she gave a giant shudder as the tremors of release swept through her.

With a deep groan, Rafe surged against her, plunging himself fully within her feminine mysteries. Blinded by the explosion of sensuality, and deaf to her own soft cries of ecstasy, Brenna paid scant attention to the flicker of pain that was quickly gone. As the spangles of light disappeared from behind her eyes, she became slowly aware of a number of things. She had never felt so light, so blissfully happy. She could hear Rafe's constricted breathing rasping in her ear. Her arms were wrapped tightly around his shoulders as though she would never let go. And their bodies—oh! Joined so intimately as he filled her up, casting out loneliness as she had never dreamed possible.

So, she thought, *this is love.*

Rafe lifted his head, supporting his weight on his arms, and looked deeply into her bemused eyes. The thin silver chain he wore dangled between them, catching the light in his eyes. She had not known she spoke her thoughts aloud until he smiled.

"Only a portion of love, sweet." He moved then, a slow stroking that set the harsh planes of his face into a grimace of pleasure.

"Oh!" She felt foolish, a selfish child who'd forgotten that another deserved to share in this delight, as well. As he pushed forward, she gasped, her eyes opening wide. Could she feel those wonderful stirrings again so soon? Rafe continued to thrust, slowly, methodically, building a new need within her, setting her on fire once again. She arched to meet him and heard his low, ragged groan, and forever cast off her innocence. She would be fully a woman for him, giving to him as he had given to her.

She circled her arms around his neck, pulling his head down for her kiss. Their lips met in a searing communion. Rafe's hands molded her breasts, then slipped to her hips, lifting her to him while she clung to his shoulders.

A film of perspiration covered their striving bodies. Faster and faster, each surge more powerful, each withdrawal an ache that had to be filled again and again. His medallion tapped against her collarbone in time to the rhythm of his lovemaking. Brenna felt herself reaching, reaching . . .

Their climax was upon them with such force that they were both caught unawares. Rafe gave a final groan, shuddering, finding peace deep within Brenna's body, and his tremors pushed her over the peak. Their mutual cries of ecstasy were a duet that echoed in the little room. Again, Brenna found that place where time lost all meaning, and Rafe was beside her, calling her name.

After a long time, when they could find air to fill their aching lungs, Rafe lifted his head. What he saw made him whisper a curse. Brenna's eyes were closed, but the betraying moisture of tears seeped from their corners, trickling down to dampen the hair at her temples.

"Dammit! I knew I'd hurt you. Dammit!"

Brenna's eyelids fluttered, and her mouth opened wordlessly. When he began to roll away, her hands clasped around his neck to forestall him.

"What is it?" she asked in breathless bewilderment. "You didn't hurt me."

"But you're crying!"

Brenna was still, then began to laugh softly. "Some women cry when they're happy."

"They do?" He frowned and she smoothed the crease in his brow with a fingertip.

"Sometimes. I never . . . it was . . ." She shook her head helplessly, unable to express her feelings of wonder in mere words. She could feel him relax.

Relieved, Rafe placed a light kiss on her pink, swollen lips and eased their bodies apart. He grinned, a satisfied, lazy smile of pure male ego.

"I once said we'd have quite a romp, and you didn't disappointment me, sweetheart."

Brenna blushed fiery red. "Nor you me!" she retorted tartly.

Rafe threw back his head and laughed his delight. With a sudden twist, he rolled over on his back, bringing her on top of him, still chuckling. She sighed and rested her cheek against his broad shoulder, content. Rafe held her in an affectionate embrace, his fingers gently playing over her. He spread her hair out across her back, stroking and smoothing the tangled mane, and occasionally his hand cupped possessively around the sweet curve of her bottom. Her fingers drew designs in the soft hair on his chest and tangled in the thin silver chain around his neck.

"What is this you wear?" she asked after a while.

His hands stilled on her and then he shrugged. "My birth certificate."

"I don't understand."

He picked up the medallion and held it between two fingers. The silver coin winked in the shadowed light of the room. "It belonged to my mother, whoever she was. She gave it to the nuns for my care the night she abandoned me. I suppose they couldn't bring themselves to sell it because it bears a cross."

Brenna was amazed at the bitterness in his voice. She rose up on her elbow to gaze into his face, but his expression was shuttered. She touched the medallion and he let her have it. She closely examined the small silver circle, which was no bigger than a dime, with a delicate filigree cross etched into one side. She turned it over.

"What's this on the back?"

"The inscription once said '1859' but it's too worn to read now."

"The year you were born?" she guessed.

"A year before. You needn't look so serious, Red. You can't glean its secrets anymore than I have these past thirty years. I'm not even sure why I stole it."

"Stole it?" she echoed.

"From the nuns when I ran away from the foundling home. I suppose 'stole it' isn't quite accurate since it was mine by right to begin with."

"You ran away? Why?"

"I was tired of the whippings." He grinned and his hands tightened on her. "Don't look so shocked. I deserved every one of them. They fostered me out for a while, but when that didn't work out, it seemed to me that I could do just as well on my own."

"How old were you?" she asked quietly.

"Eight."

"Eight! How did you live? What did you do? Did the nuns try to find you?"

"Odd jobs. Newsboy. Rag picker. When I got a little older I started hanging around the Opera House. Gould's people paid me to be a runner. And no one ever came looking, Red. New York City is a place running over with homeless children. If one disappears, there's always another to take its place."

"My God." Pity for the child he'd been choked her, and she buried her face against his neck.

"Hey, what's this? Feeling sorry for me?"

"Of course not," she denied, but her voice was strangely thick.

"That's better. Grow a tough hide over that tender heart. If you care, you'll only get hurt."

"No one knows that better than I do," she murmured.

He threaded his fingers through her hair and was silent for a moment. "If you feel up to it, we'll start for Marshall in the morning."

"Yes." Somehow she didn't want to think about that yet. To remember how and why she was here was an unwelcome intrusion of reality into this time out of time. For now, all that mattered was that Rafe had his arms around her.

"Are you hungry?"

She shook her head. "Not really. Are you?"

For answer he drew her up and nibbled at her lips. "Not for food."

Rafe came instantly awake, alerted by some inner sixth sense. Something disturbed the tranquility of the waning afternoon. He glanced down at the woman sleeping in his arms, and a curious softening eased the harsh lines beside his mouth. A perfect little wanton, she was, sweet and willing, all prickly thorns cast aside in a moment of abandonment.

Outside, a horse whinnied. He was up and stepping into his pants when the pounding started at the front door.

"Sinclair, is that you in there?" a voice demanded. "Come on out!"

Chapter 9

"Well, Sheriff," Rafe said, his mouth curved in a sardonic line, "this is an unexpected pleasure." He propped a casual arm against the door frame in an arrogant stance that held no welcome.

Sheriff Mobley, dusty and travel stained, eyed the bare-chested man before him with some irritation. A posse of four remained on their horses in the untidy yard, watching the sheriff on the porch.

"I remembered you had a place around this area," the sheriff said. He took off his Stetson and wiped his forehead on his sweat-stained sleeve. "Looks like you ain't had no better luck than us. We lost that killer's trail a ways back. Ain't no telling what he's done to that poor gal by now."

"I'm quite unharmed, Sheriff Mobley," Brenna said quietly, appearing like a wraith in the doorway behind Rafe. Her hair tumbled over her shoulders, but her shirtwaist was neatly tucked into her skirt, giving no evidence of the trembling haste with which she'd donned her clothes.

"Well, I'll be a son of a—pardon me, ma'am," the sheriff stammered. "Are you all right? What the hell are you doing here? With him?" he demanded bluntly.

Rafe stiffened, his displeasure plain in the downcurve of his mouth. "Miss Galloway used her wits to escape. Luckily, I happened upon her. It seemed reasonable to seek the nearest shelter when she became indisposed due to her ordeal."

"Well, ma'am, I sure am glad to see you safe, and that's a fact," Mobley said. His sharp eyes flicked from

Rafe to Brenna, trying to assess the truth of the matter. It was a unique situation to say the least, but he was not one to make harsh judgments over the impropriety of the girl's plight. It was enough that she appeared well and sane despite the hardships she must have suffered.

"Thank you, Sheriff." Brenna's face was very pale but composed, and no one could guess that she held fast to the tattered rags of her dignity with only the utmost effort. She hadn't expected reality to shatter her dream world quite so swiftly, waking her naked and vulnerable to face unexpectedly the consequences of her actions. She could hardly look at Rafe for fear that her face would flame, revealing to the sheriff's observant glance the exact nature of her degradation. Confusion raged within her. She no longer knew herself, could not comprehend the person she had become in just a few short hours. What on earth had possessed her to give herself to Rafe Sinclair? And who was the woman who had responded so ardently to his caresses?

"Are you able to travel, Miss Galloway?" the lawman asked. "I'm sure you're anxious to get home, and there are questions I need to ask about what's happened."

"Of course," Brenna murmured.

"Sheriff, Miss Galloway was delirious most of the night," Rafe objected. "You and your men look all in, as well, and you couldn't get far before dark at any rate. I'll be glad to offer my hospitality, meager as it is. We can leave tomorrow at first light."

Sheriff Mobley rubbed his stubbled jaw and nodded. "That makes sense, Sinclair. If it suits you, miss?"

"Oh, but –" She broke off her unbidden protest. It would do no good to give the sheriff something further to wonder about. "Yes, whatever you wish. Mr. Sinclair has been most kind."

In agreement then, the sheriff called for his men to dismount. Rafe directed them toward the barn, offering to put on fresh coffee for the group. He gave a quick summary of their situation, and they agreed to pool their resources for the evening meal. Brenna slipped back into the house, listening to Rafe's low murmurs to the sheriff. She heard the sheriff's booted tread leaving the wooden porch, and a deep trembling reaction began.

Hurrying to the bedroom, she swiftly straightened the rumpled blankets, hiding the damning evidence of her sin, her weakness, and trying to hold back the rising gorge that threatened to complete her total humiliation. Her complete vulnerability left her emotions raw and abraded and she was shamefully conscious of the sticky proof of her shattered innocence between her thighs. She heard Rafe pad on bare feet into the room, but she ignored him, double checking the alignment of the buttons on her shirt. It would be too embarrassing to find she'd cross-buttoned it in her haste!

"Brenna," Rafe began and touched her elbow. She jerked away as though stung. "What the hell's the matter with you?" he growled.

"Nothing." She could not meet his eyes. She grabbed up his shirt from the floor and thrust it at him. "Would you please put on your shirt?"

"Why, Red, not nursing a guilty conscience already, are you?" he drawled.

"Just get dressed!" she hissed. "I'd like to keep what remains of my shredded reputation, if I can."

"Why should you care what an old codger like Mobley thinks?" He slipped on the shirt but made no move to button it. "You know, sweet, you've got to keep these things in perspective. They're going to draw their own conclusions, like it or not. Should I pretend that nothing happened?"

"Yes!" she snapped, turning abruptly away, unnerved by the glimpse of chest tantalizingly revealed by the open vee of his shirt. "I—I'll go make the coffee."

He snatched her arm, holding her firmly as he gazed down into her agitated countenance. "But something did happen, didn't it, Brenna? Admit it."

"It meant nothing! Nothing at all to a man like you!" she cried, her lips suddenly trembling. "Please, let it be forgotten. I ask only that you allow me to keep what's left of my dignity and behave with decorum in the presence of the others."

"Why, you little hypocrite!" His expression was livid with anger and some vast pain she could not identify. "And I suppose you'll want me to sleep in the barn with our visitors?"

"I don't care where you sleep, as long as it's not with me!"

"You weren't complaining about the arrangements just a few minutes ago," he pointed out.

Brenna closed her eyes on a wave of confusion, regret, and shame. "I must have been mad," she whispered to herself.

Rafe gave her a little shake of impatience. "Come on, Red, I thought you were above all this self-recrimination. You've proved you make your own decisions and to hell with the rest of the world! Just because the sheriff is on the scene, why should that change anything between us?" His voice took on a husky tone. "You know what we have together is good—damn good!"

"I don't mean anything to you, so don't pretend that I do," she said angrily, glaring at him. "You have no claim on me just because . . . because . . ."

"Because I made love to you? Is that what you find so hard to say?"

"Love had nothing to do with it!"

His laugh was harsh, brutal. He let her go abruptly. "How right you are! It was pure animal lust, and I want you to remember how you begged for it, how you moved beneath me. You're right. It meant nothing, but try to deny it as you will, nothing will ever be that good for you again."

"You bastard!" she whispered, mortified and humiliated by the lurid visions his words painted. "I hate you!"

"Some things never change," he mocked, laughing at her. "Don't worry, Red. I'll gladly join the men in the barn tonight. Believe me, nothing could prevail on me to storm the bastions of your innocence again."

Brenna's fingers curled like talons, but she resisted the bloodthirsty impulse to scratch his eyes out. She would not sink to that level. Her features took on a haughty coolness, an elegance that cried out that he was the barbarian in this sordid scenario. He was her enemy, had been since the moment she'd laid eyes on him. She'd let him make a fool of her and use her for his own pleasure. That she had been a willing participant only made it worse. But her eyes were open once more, and she could see him as he was, not the tender dream lover, but the demon tempter, Gould's man to the end. He would not find her such easy prey again! Her eyes raked him with a scathing look of such virulent hatred a lesser man would have cringed, but Rafe merely laughed. He laughed harder still when she whirled on her heel and left him.

They rode away from Rafe's ranch at dawn the next day. The ride back to Marshall seemed interminable, although they made good time, especially after reaching a neighboring farm and acquiring a mount for Brenna. She was most relieved to be free of the hateful chore of riding double with Rafe. Hostility radiated from him in a palpable wave, and he was again the cold, hard stranger whose handsome face was a mask that hid his treacherous nature.

Brenna had told her story to Sheriff Mobley and he had listened with sympathy, telling her she was a "lucky girl." Brenna choked back a hysterical giggle and wondered if he meant to be funny. They agreed that Larosse must have been scared away by the presence of the posse and was probably deep in the wilds of the Sabine basin by now. Brenna noticed that Rafe did not adhere to this theory.

She stole a glance at Rafe riding just ahead of her. He sat on the horse with natural grace, almost one with the loping movements of the animal. Occasionally, he would exchange a word with one of the deputies, but he never spoke to her, never even acknowledged her presence with so much as a glance. It was as if she had ceased to exist for him now that he'd handed over his self-assumed responsibility for her to Sheriff Mobley. Brenna told herself that it suited her just fine.

She'd spent a restless night in the old rope bed, her heart full of self-reproach and guilt. She'd surrendered her virtue to the drive of sheer carnality, and she had no one but herself to blame. As the dawn streaked the sky with a new day's rosy light, she resolved to put that mistake behind her. There was nothing she could do now about the decision she'd made, except try to forget the moments of rapture in Rafe Sinclair's arms. That remembered pleasure was the seductive invitation to disaster, and she would not allow it to happen again. She refused to recall the intimacy of loneliness that had set two souls together down the path to mutual fulfillment. It was a fantasy, an illusion born of physical desire and nothing more. There had never been a man who could love a woman unselfishly, and Brenna had already resolved not to tie herself to a life of misery as a man's unwilling slave. Now that she knew the treacherous demands of her own body, she would be ever vigilant not to fall into that trap again. In an odd way she supposed she should be grateful to Rafe for teaching her that. It was small consolation.

It was almost dusk when they approached the outskirts of Marshall. Brenna felt she'd been away at least a century, not less than a week. So much had happened. She was ready for her life to become normal again, even if it meant washing dishes and putting up with Clara's carping. The frame homes and stores gave way to the more substantial brick outlines of the bank, the mercantile, the depot. A distant train whistle was a welcoming fanfare.

Brenna was so caught up in the relief and delight of being home that at first she didn't notice the attention that their stately procession attracted. They wove around wagons and buggies and other horsemen on the dusty streets, and loiterers and bystanders soon took up the call for news.

"Hey, Sheriff! You found her?"

"What about that murderer?"

"Any luck, Joe?"

"Did ya catch up with the filthy killer?"

"Why's Gould's man with you, Sheriff Mobley? You arrested him or something?"

"What happened to you, girlie?"

Brenna stared steadfastly ahead, trying to ignore the vapid, licentious interest but feeling increasingly naked and helpless. A small group of men hustled after them as the sheriff kept his leisurely pace toward the depot. He'd promised to escort Brenna there in exchange for her agreement to sign a statement as a witness to Plummer's murder the next day. Brenna drew a sigh of relief when they rounded the corner of the depot.

The noisy group piled around them, demanding answers from the sheriff. The doors of the depot opened, and more people stepped out on the board walkway to investigate the hubbub. Curious onlookers swarmed everywhere, and Brenna hesitated, too apprehensive to climb down into the small mob on her own. She bit her lip and gave a hurried glance around, disconcerted when she found Rafe's hard silver gaze resting on her. Sheriff Mobley swung down from his horse and walked calmly to Brenna's side, absently batting away the more persistent of the questioners as though they were pesky mosquitos.

"Well, now, little lady, let me help you down," the sheriff boomed. "You're home at last."

Brenna gratefully let him lift her from the horse's back, aware of her stiffness and her pitiful appearance.

"Here there! Let a fellow through!" a short man with a notebook shouted, worming through the crowd. He chomped a short cigar in the side of his mouth. "Hey, Sheriff, give us a report for the newspaper," he demanded. "Where's that killer? What unspeakable horror did he perpetrate—excuse me, ma'am—on the girl?"

"Shut up, Russell," Mobley ordered, pushing past the reporter with ill-concealed dislike. "Can't you see she's too tired to talk? Let me get her inside."

"I demand an interview!" Russell shrilled. "The public has a right to know the details." Chagrined when the sheriff turned his back, the reporter immediately collared one of the members of the posse, firing off questions and scribbling the answers in his notebook, glancing from Brenna to Rafe and nodding at the deputy's disclosures.

With the sheriff's arm supporting her, Brenna moved forward. The curious crowd fell back a pace, eyeing her with wonder and speculation. She felt uncomfortably like a prize cow on display at a county fair, and one up for auction at that! The depot's doors burst open and a rounded female figure barreled out.

"Brenna!" she shrieked.

"Annie! Oh, Annie!" Brenna hugged her friend and was hugged fiercely back.

"Oh, my God! I was afraid you was dead," Annie wailed.

"I'm all right, truly I am," Brenna reassured her. Then she took one look at Annie's kind, plain face and promptly burst into copious tears.

"Can you take care of her now, Miss Annie?" the sheriff asked.

"Yes, sir," Annie hiccuped, tears sliding down her plump cheeks, too. "I'll see to her. Praise the Lord, the prodigal is returned to us!"

"Bible verses, Annie?" Brenna teased through her tears.

Annie frowned ferociously. "I been praying a lot lately."

Brenna choked on a ragged sob. "Thank you, Annie."

"Now, you come on in here." Annie urged her forward into the gas-lit depot lobby. "We're gonna get you all fixed up. What do you want? Something to eat?"

"A bath," Brenna said firmly. "Oh, but I should thank the sheriff . . ." She paused, looking over her shoulder, but the sheriff and his men were moving off, and only Rafe Sinclair watched her, his steely eyes glinting and his face expressionless. For a frozen instant, their eyes clashed, and Brenna felt an exquisite, burning pain blossom like a rose within her, unfolding its petals of sorrow and regret and denial in perfect beauty to be savored for all her days. She knew it was good-bye, and despite everything, it hurt that he made no move to bid her farewell. When she turned away, it was like leaving behind a part of her own soul.

In a stupor of fatigue and inexplicable despair, Brenna allowed Annie to lead her through the brightly lit lobby, by-passing the massive burled wood staircase for the narrow corridor opening into business offices and the servant's stairs. The restaurant smells of fried chicken and coffee lay heavily on the air, but to Brenna it was a familiar and welcome perfume.

Annie kept up a nonstop stream of inconsequential chatter, and Brenna was grateful that none of it required an answer. She knew that she would never see Rafe again, but instead of rejoicing over her good fortune, it made her want to weep. She tried to tell herself it was a natural reaction to losing one's first lover, even if he were a cad, and reminded herself that it would surely seem different in the morning when she returned to the routine of hard work. The thought of her job lifted her spirits a bit. At least she still had that.

"Here now, girls, where do you think you're going?" Mr. Hudgins stood in the open door to his office in his checkered vest and shirt sleeves.

"Oh, Mr. Hudgins, sir!" Annie bubbled. "Ain't it grand? Brenna's come back to us safe and sound!"

"I'll be ready to start back to work first thing in the morning, sir," Brenna said faintly. The hard, oily stare her corpulent employer leveled at her made her distinctly uneasy.

"That's right funny, 'cause you don't work here anymore," Hudgins said flatly.

Brenna gasped. "What do you mean? I don't understand."

"You're all the whole damn town's been talking about. Look at those papers!" he ordered, pointing to the untidy piles of newsprint littering his desk. "You're a red-letter woman, and this depot only employs well-bred ladies. I can't have every curiosity seeker in five counties in my establishment sniffing after the likes of you!"

"But that's not fair!" Annie cried. "None of what happened was Brenna's fault."

"You watch your mouth," Hudgins snapped, pointing a stubby finger at Annie's nose, "or you'll be out on your duff, too. If for no other reason, I can dismiss little missy for being caught out after hours. She knew the rules."

"Please, Mr. Hudgins, I really need this job," Brenna said, swallowing her pride in desperation.

"You should have thought of that before you and that Plummer fellow got caught in your whorin' ways. This is a family place, a respectable business, and I ain't about to offend the sensibilities of my paying customers with a waitress that's ruined herself."

"It wasn't like that at all," Brenna protested.

"I don't give a crap. Just gather your stuff and make sure you're out of here first thing in the morning."

Brenna's weary shoulders slumped in dejection. "But I don't have anywhere to go," she murmured miserably.

Hudgins's black, piglike eyes squinted at her in speculation, gauging her from head to toe. "Well, now," he said slowly, "maybe I could arrange something."

"I—I'd be most grateful," Brenna said. "I'll do anything."

"Even cat for Mamie Ferguson? She's always looking for fresh talent. Maybe now you're more experienced than you look."

Brenna reeled back in stunned disbelief. Miss Mamie was the local madam. "No!"

Hudgins shrugged. "Take it or leave it. You ain't much good for nuthin' else."

"You panderer!" Brenna cried furiously. Her hands clenched into hard little fists. "I'll starve before I'll whore for you!"

Hudgins laughed. "Suit yourself. Just make sure you're out of here in the morning."

Brenna shot him a look of chilly disdain, and her lip curled, as if he were a particularly revolting smell. "Mr. Hudgins, nothing could induce me to spend even a single night more under your roof."

She marched away, her back ramrod straight, her bearing haughty as a queen. Annie scurried after her, wringing her hands in worry.

"Oh, Brenna, what will you do? Where will you go?"

Brenna paused at the foot of the stairs, lifting her tattered skirt with unconscious elegance. She smiled bravely, for Annie's sake, and for reassurance she touched the place beneath her skirt where her savings were still pinned. She was neither penniless nor helpless.

"I'm going to pack my things. Then I think I'll take a room at Mrs. Stratton's boarding house for tonight. I've always thought it was such a charming old place. It's not very late. I'm sure I can get a meal there and a lovely long soak."

"But what about tomorrow? You have no job! How can you not be worried?"

Brenna bit her lip and drew a steadying breath. "Tomorrow—well, tomorrow will have to take care of itself, that's all," she said, mounting the steep stairs.

"But then what?" Annie persisted.

In a frightened voice, Brenna whispered, "I don't know, Annie. I just don't know."

"It is utterly immoral what these journalists do to me! Have you seen this?" Jay Gould's normally soft voice was raised in agitation and echoed in the elegantly appointed parlor of the *Atalanta*. He tossed the folded newspaper on the table top with a soft slap.

Rafe Sinclair stood looking out of the rear door window of the moving railcar, his arms folded over his immaculately tailored frock coat. He'd caught up with Gould in Dallas, and now they were heading east again. In the three days since he'd last seen Brenna, he'd done his best to put the red-haired wench out of his mind. It hadn't been easy. Dragging his wandering attention back to his employer, Rafe gave a glance of mild surprise at Gould's unexpected vehemence. Unfolding his arms, Rafe reached for the offending newspaper. His lips twisted in derision, then he discarded the paper with a negligent gesture.

"Mere sensationalism."

"The press has decided that Plummer's murder and the girl's kidnapping are all part of a Jay Gould conspiracy! Oh, they don't say it in so many words, of course, but the conclusions couldn't be more damaging. And haven't you noticed that your name is mentioned prominently in that article?" Gould asked sourly, slumping into the confines of a leather armchair and pursing his lips behind his abundant black beard.

"It doesn't worry me."

"Being named the monster who ruined the spotless reputation of one of Texas's loveliest flowers means nothing to you?"

Rafe shrugged. "It will die down soon enough."

"Tell him!" Gould exploded. "Tell him, Giovanni."

The serious-eyed Italian grimaced distastefully. "The atmosphere is quite ugly. The Gould name has been connected with murder and possible rape in the press. Unless something can be done, we will have little chance of convincing our Texas associates that an alliance with us would be worthwhile, as our meetings in Dallas can testify. This adverse publicity will kill our chances as surely as this Larosse killed young Plummer." He sighed. "And, until an account can be made of those missing securities, our hands are virtually tied. Our venture toward the Southern Pacific will have to be postponed indefinitely."

"Not to mention that George has sent an urgent wire," Gould added. His smile was slow. "Mr. Adams of the

Union Pacific will face a crisis shortly. I must return to New York to pick up the pieces."

"I still say that ignoring the reports in the press is the best policy," Rafe said irritably. "There's not a half-truth in any of those overblown lies."

"And I say something must be done!" Gould replied heatedly. "I've had to take all sorts of unwarranted criticism before, but at least this time we might be able to do something about it."

"About what?" Rafe demanded.

"Well, to start with, your relationship with that Galloway girl. I suggest the usual method of reparation," Gould said smoothly.

"And that is?"

Gould met Giovanni Rossini's dark eyes across the room. Rafe followed that look, puzzled.

"Why, Mr. Sinclair," Giovanni said mildly, "you must marry her, of course."

"What!"

"By that simple act, you could redeem us in the eyes of the public. Exchange your role of villain for that of hero. They are a romantic people. It would be exceedingly easy to convince the press that yours was a love match when you return to Marshall to sweep Miss Galloway off her feet."

"You forget the lady in question may have an opinion regarding your fine plans," Rafe said irritably. "She detests me."

"My dear boy!" Gould laughed and waggled a blunt finger at him. "I know very well of your prowess with the feminine gender. I count on your skill to persuade her."

"And if I do not choose to marry?"

"You must make the grand gesture for me, Rafe," Gould admonished. "I know that you'll find the married estate quite satisfying when you give it a chance. Besides, Miss Galloway is very beautiful, I am told. It will scarcely be a hardship, will it not?"

Rafe frowned. If even Jay Gould assumed he had bedded Brenna Galloway on their wild adventure into the Texas hinterland, then what did the people who knew her and lived around her think? He knew well the Victorian intelligence. Perhaps he had abandoned her to a future worse than mere poverty. Brenna's valiant, feisty features rose in his mind to mock him, while the memory of her sweetness, her untouched ardor continued to torment him. He shook his head.

"No, it's no use. She'll never agree to such a thing."

"I rely on you to convince her otherwise. We will turn this disaster into a resounding success of popular opinion, with only a few words spoken before a minister. Then we will be able to concentrate on other matters." Gould smiled benignly and stroked his beard.

"It is too much to ask, even for you, Mr. Gould," Rafe said coldly. "Excuse me."

He went out the door to stand on the exterior platform. Gould and Rossini watched him through the glass, noting the stiffness with which he lit a cigar. He smoked it with agitated movements and stared sightlessly at the passing east Texan scenery.

"Rafe resists the idea," Rossini opined softly.

"Of course. I expected no less of him," Gould returned. "Still, he will find the merits of it quite expedient in time. It is his duty. And I have more than one reason to push him to end his bachelorhood."

"Your daughter-in-law?"

"Astute as always, old friend," Gould said, nodding.

"Have you reason to suspect . . . ?"

"None at all. Still, it is better to take no chances. Wed to the Galloway girl, Rafe becomes unavailable. Merely precautionary, but I take no risks with George's happiness. And as you know, I plan these things precisely."

"I doubt Rafe wishes to marry."

"But he will, Giovanni, he will."

"You can't give up," Annie said.

Brenna untied the black satin ribbons of her bonnet and wearily removed it. She stared at the slightly out-of-style tucked velvet and ruche creation for a moment, then set it down on the patchwork quilt that covered the bed in Mrs. Stratton's least expensive rented room.

"I've been everywhere in town. No one has a job of any sort—at least not for me," Brenna said. Her usually determined air was gone, replaced by discouragement and a growing sense of desperation. She slowly unbuttoned the fitted jacket of her best black wool albatross suit, the one she'd made herself under Sister Therese's watchful eye. But putting on a decent, sober appearance, complete with hated corset, hadn't impressed even one prospective employer over the past three days—and time was running out.

"I'm sure you'll find something soon," Annie said optimistically. She sat down on the edge of the bed and bounced on the squeaky springs. "I told Jimmy to ask around. We'll find you a job, somehow."

"I'll do anything, you know that. Scrub floors, milk cows, anything! But no one wants to take a chance on a ruined woman," Brenna said bitterly. She sat down beside her friend and her lip trembled. "It's as though I'm unclean. They act like I'm some kind of leper out of the Bible."

"Oh, Brenna, no! None of what happened was your doing."

"Perhaps not everything," Brenna said obliquely. She couldn't tell Annie what had happened between Rafe Sinclair and herself. Some things even a friend might not understand, especially when she couldn't even explain it to herself. But she couldn't blame all her present troubles on Rafe. Even if he hadn't come along, she was sure that things would be the same now. And without him, she might still be wandering the Texas wilderness—or worse. But it didn't pay to think about Rafe.

"They're all very sympathetic, of course," Brenna continued, "but no one wants a girl even old Hudgins won't have. And the men on the streets, the way their eyes follow me. . . ." She shuddered.

"There's got to be something you can do."

"I've got to face it, Annie. There's nothing for me in Marshall now. And I don't have enough money to stay here much longer. I've got to have enough for train fare to some place I can make a new start."

"I don't want you to go," Annie wailed. "Could you take in sewing? Maybe Mrs. Stratton will let you help out in exchange for your room."

Brenna shook her head. "She says she's got all the kitchen help she needs. I think the only reason she rented this room in the first place was because she was too surprised to say no. And I couldn't make enough to feed a cat on what my sewing would bring in.''

"I suppose it's the only way, then." Annie sighed in resignation. She settled her plump person and forced a smile. "Where do you want to go? I've got some money saved and—''

"Oh, Annie, I couldn't!''

"Yes, ma'am, you will!" Annie retorted. "Consider it a loan. I know I'll get it back. And don't tell me I can't help my best friend in the whole world if I want to.''

"Oh, Annie, I'm going to miss you!" Brenna tried to smile, but it was a lost cause. They hugged each other fiercely, eyes moist with emotion. After a minute, Annie cleared her throat.

"Well, now, let's make plans," she said briskly.

Before Brenna could reply, there was a tapping on her door. "Yes?" she called.

"You have a caller, Miss Galloway," the housemaid answered. "In the parlor.''

"Maybe one of the people you talked with has come to hire you," Annie said eagerly. "I've got to go anyway. I'll walk you down.''

Brenna nervously checked the pristine appearance of her high-necked shirtwaist in the mirror hanging over the wash basin and smoothed the rolled upswept topknot of her hair. The two women then hurried down the stairs together.

At the front door, Annie held up crossed fingers and nodded in the direction of Mrs. Stratton's overstuffed parlor. "Good luck.''

Brenna smoothed her black skirt and took a deep breath, then opened the frosted glass door into the parlor. Her breath caught in her throat.

"Hello, Brenna," Rafe said.

She stared, her mouth suddenly dry. He seemed taller and darker than she remembered. His expression was solemn, the black slash of his mustache making a grave statement over the straight line of his mouth. Conflicting emotions churned in Brenna's breast: surprise, uncertainty, even a little fear, and most astonishing, an unexpected pleasure that she tried hard to deny.

"What—what are you doing here?" she stammered.

Rafe came forward, his silver eyes never leaving her face. He pushed the door closed behind her and the latch clicked ominously.

"I've come to ask you to marry me."

For an instant, Brenna couldn't breathe, then her eyes blazed in outraged indignation. "I don't find this jest the least amusing, Mr. Sinclair."

"I've never been more serious in my life."

She turned on her heel. "I have nothing to say to you."

"Brenna, wait!" He caught her arm, stopping her before she could reach the door. "At least hear me out."

"Why should I?" She was breathing hard, her breasts rising and falling in agitation beneath the delicate lawn of her shirtwaist.

"We owe that much to each other, don't we?" he asked softly. "Please."

Brenna cast him a sullen look and lifted her chin. She sailed regally over to perch on Mrs. Stratton's carved rosewood settee. Its cherry-red upholstery matched the heavy gold-tasseled velvet drapes. She adjusted her skirt primly and then eyed Rafe, her gaze cold. "Well, go ahead."

Rafe cursed under his breath. He stalked after her, a handsome man in navy frock coat and fawn trousers, his dark masculinity a startling contrast to the crisp white cotton of his shirt. "You're not going to make this easy for me, are you?"

"Hardly," Brenna replied in a cutting tone. "I can't fathom why you'd put either of us through this further humiliation. If you plan to tell me you've fallen madly in love with me and can't live another moment without me, please save your breath. We both know that's a lie. So what other reason can you give me for this rather preposterous proposal?"

"Is it totally beyond belief that I could feel a genuine concern for your welfare?" he demanded. He threw himself down opposite Brenna on Mrs. Stratton's little cherry slipper chair, with fine disregard for its delicate dimensions, ignoring the creak of protest it made under his weight.

"Yes," she replied steadily, "I do find that hard to believe."

"Dammit, Brenna!" he exploded. "I was worried about you."

"Why? I'm perfectly fine."

His expression was thunderous. "Fine, are you? Is that why you lost your job?"

"I chose not to return to the depot for my own reasons," she lied.

"And have you found other employment?"

"I'm expecting a new position momentarily." Her expression was mulish. She would not confess her true circumstances, not for anything!

"You'd rather starve than admit you're in trouble, wouldn't you?" he asked furiously. "You and your damned pride! I'll bet this entire hick town is treating you like you've got a scarlet A embroidered on your chest. The only job you're going to find will be in a bordello. I only want to help you."

"Don't you dare offer me money, Rafe Sinclair!" Brenna gasped, infuriated that his words struck so near the truth. "Don't you dare!"

He sighed and shook his head. "Don't you understand? It's my name I'm offering."

"I don't want it."

"Not even if you're pregnant?"

She jumped to her feet. "I don't have to listen to this!"

Rafe was beside her, forestalling her furious flight with his massive bulk. "Are you?"

"Of course not!" she snapped, her face flaming.

"Are you certain?"

"The truth of the matter will be apparent in a few days," she said, her voice icy with embarrassment. "You needn't concern yourself."

"I won't abandon my child." Rafe's voice was tight.

"There is no child!" she cried, as though saying it with sufficient force would make it so. "Besides," she muttered, "I can't believe you propose to every woman who might be pregnant with your baby, so why start now?"

"Any previous liaisons were with women of experience, not girls of your tender innocence. I've told you before, I pay my debts. If not for you, I'd be the victim of a lynch mob.'' His voice gentled and he took her hand. ''Even if there is no baby, I'll not leave you to take the consequences of those unselfish actions that saved my life.''

''You don't owe me,'' she denied breathlessly. ''Surely marriage is too drastic a solution.''

''You tell me. Do you think you can survive on those few dollars you've pinned into your petticoat?'' He laughed softly at the blush that ran up her neck. ''Yes, I found it. And what about your sisters? How will you take care of them?''

''I—I'm leaving Marshall. I'll find a job somewhere else.''

''Come on, Red, why must you do everything the hard way?'' He raised her hand to his mouth, nibbling a small knuckle while his mustache tickled her skin. His voice was husky. ''Think, Brenna. What we have together physically is a good basis for a marriage, all notions of love aside. I promise to take care of you and your sisters.''

''I don't need a man to take care of me,'' she said faintly. She felt confused, disoriented. Rafe Sinclair wasn't the marrying kind. What prompted this change of heart?

He grinned, a slow, wicked smile that made her skin feel hot and cold. His arm went around her waist, drawing her close. ''You're being a stubborn wench, Red,'' he admonished softly.

''Stop, Rafe!'' Brenna's heart fluttered wildly, and her hands plucked vainly at his iron-thewed arms. She couldn't think when he was this close, when her traitorous body throbbed with the echoes of remembered ecstasy at his touch.

''Don't be foolish, darling,'' he said. His lips covered hers, and her heated reply died in her throat.

She was drowning, drowning in the sensual sea of his magic, and for a mad moment she longed to give in to the pull of the tides, to crash again on the distant shore to which only his loving could bring her. But old lessons were hard to forget. He offered her no more than her mother had been given, a union without love, based only on need—the *man's* need. There were no guarantees, and she would not give up her independence for that!

Brenna wrenched backward, pulling free so abruptly that Rafe had no chance to hold her. "Don't!" She backed another step, trembling fingers touching her lips. "I want you to go."

Rafe tried not to frown his displeasure. "Brenna, be reasonable. I promise you won't regret it."

"You can't promise that," she said, shaking her head. "And no, I won't marry you. I—I appreciate whatever impulse of conscience prompted you to make the offer, but I can't accept. It wouldn't work, Rafe, and you know it."

"Brenna, you're not thinking straight," Rafe began angrily. A knock on the door interrupted his frustrated rebuttal. Mrs. Stratton, the aging dowager owner of the boarding house, stuck her graying ringlets in through the door.

"Oh, there you are, Miss Galloway. She's in here, Sheriff Mobley," Mrs. Stratton called over her shoulder. She pushed open the door to admit the sheriff and another man. "You have visitors, dear."

Brenna blanched and gasped, and Rafe took an instinctive step toward her.

Malvin O'Donnell's voice boomed, filling the dainty parlor with his thick Irish brogue. "Well, daughter! Ain't ye going to kiss your papa hello?"

Chapter 10

"You're not my father!" Brenna gasped.

"A mere technicality," O'Donnell retorted jovially. "Why, ever since I married your sainted mother—God rest her soul—I've thought of ye as one of me own."

"Liar," she whispered, her voice thin with shock.

"See there, Sheriff Mobley, I told you she'd be pleased to see me." O'Donnell chuckled. "It's come to take you home, I have, me darling, after your terrible ordeal."

"No!" Brenna's irises dilated with horror so that only thin rings of blue-green circled the black centers.

"There, now, don't try to be brave," O'Donnell soothed, advancing on her, his great hulking belly hanging over his belt. A leer split his bumpy red countenance. "See what a pack of trouble all your gallavantin' has brung ye! There's plenty of duties to be seen to at home, and your brother Paddy misses you and your sisters dearly. Where are Maggie and wee Shannon?"

"Safe from you!" Brenna called out defiantly.

"Come now, darling, don't misbehave in front of these fine folks," her stepfather cajoled, but his bloodshot eyes held a malevolence that chilled Brenna's blood.

"Perhaps I can be of some assistance in sorting all this out, Sheriff," Rafe said. His arm slipped around Brenna's waist in a possessive gesture that made her jump but was not lost on her stepfather.

"And who are ye?" O'Donnell demanded belligerently.

"This is Rafe Sinclair," Sheriff Mobley said. "He rescued your daughter, Mr. O'Donnell."

O'Donnell relaxed slightly and stuck out his beefy paw.

"Well, in that case, it needs I should offer you my thanks." Rafe ignored his outstretched hand, and O'Donnell's face curled into a snarl. "I'll be thanking you to let Brenna go now, so's I can be taking her home with me."

"That's not going to be possible," Rafe replied steadily. Brenna stiffened at his words, and he tightened his hand at her waist, silently urging her to keep her peace.

"And in the name of all the saints, why not?" O'Donnell bellowed.

"Because I've proposed to your stepdaughter, and she's just agreed to become my wife."

Brenna gaped at Rafe. "Oh, but—" A firm squeeze silenced her protest.

"Is that a fact, now?" the corpulent Irishman asked mildly. "And what will you be saying, my fine Mr. Sinclair, if I remind you that she needs her guardian's consent to wed? No, my dear, it's out of the question. You're much too young, and we've things to settle between us at home." He reached for Brenna, who cringed away, seeking shelter within Rafe's comforting embrace.

"I'd say you're a reasonable man," Rafe interjected easily, "and will certainly reconsider under the circumstances." His casual, friendly tone did not match the leashed tension Brenna felt in his arms, nor the cool disdain in his steel-gray eyes.

O'Donnell's blunt features took on a murderous cast. "And what might they be, I'm asking?"

Rafe smiled. "She's carrying my child."

"You slut!" O'Donnell roared. His giant palm lashed out, striking Brenna's cheek and sending her sprawling nearly senseless to the floor. Mrs. Stratton squealed in fright.

O'Donnell reached for Brenna again, intent on meting out the punishment he felt she richly deserved, his face contorted with frustration and thwarted revenge. But he hadn't counted on Rafe Sinclair.

In a red rage, Rafe lunged forward, plunging his fist deep into the man's fat belly. O'Donnell grunted and wheezed, but Rafe gave no quarter, smashing the Irish-

man's bulbous nose with a bone-crunching punch that sent
him reeling backward to land on his backside. Bleeding,
O'Donnell reverted to type, screaming for the sheriff.

"Call him off, Sheriff! Throw him in jail! A man's got
a right to discipline his own children," O'Donnell
whined, fumbling with a handkerchief to staunch the flood
of crimson from his nose.

"You touch her again and I'll break you in half," Rafe
promised, his voice deadly. He turned away, kneeling
beside Brenna, who was trying to tell a solicitous Mrs.
Stratton she was all right.

"He threatened me! I'll press charges!" O'Donnell
blustered.

"Shut up, before I arrest you for assault," Sheriff
Mobley said coldly. "Is she hurt?"

"No," Brenna said, letting Rafe help her up. Her hand
cupped her cheek where the red imprint of O'Donnell's
fingers contrasted starkly with the pallor of her skin. She
swayed slightly. "I'm all right."

"Is what you said the truth?" the sheriff asked Rafe.
"Is the little gal in the family way?"

"Yes, sir. And I intend to marry her, despite anything
that brute says," Rafe growled. He supported Brenna on
his arm.

Sheriff Mobley's jaw tightened and he nodded. "All
right, son, I'll fix it with the judge." He looked at
Brenna's stricken face. "Isn't that what you want, little
lady?"

Brenna regarded the malevolent, blood-streaked face of
Malvin O'Donnell and shuddered violently. Slowly she
looked up into Rafe's eyes, but surprisingly, they had lost
their steel. Instead, they were a soft, smoky gray that
beckoned her into the unknown. She swallowed, quivering
like a fledgling taking wing for the first time.

"Yes," she said in a voice so low that the sheriff had
to lean forward to hear her words. "Yes, I'll marry
Rafe."

"There now, dearie," Mrs. Stratton said, fluttering.
"You two have a nice cup of tea. It'll calm your nerves
after so much excitement." She poured the hot amber
liquid into a fluted china cup with ugly pink rosebuds

embellished on its rim. She passed it to Brenna, who sat on the velvet settee. "Cup for you, Mr. Sinclair?"

Rafe dropped the drapes down over the parlor window through which he'd been staring and turned to the older woman. "Perhaps later, Mrs. Stratton. You're most kind."

"Well, in that case," she simpered, "I'll leave you two lovebirds alone. I know you have so much to discuss. It's so romantic." She sighed, then bustled out, pulling the frosted glass door shut behind her.

Rafe watched Brenna take a cautious sip of the tea, but when she set the cup on the saucer it rattled, revealing the tremors of reaction that still shook her. Her head was bent as she studied her hands tensely clasped in her lap. The soft red-gold of her shining topknot was a bright note in the heavily appointed room. He flexed his right hand, grimacing at the tenderness of his knuckles. He hoped he'd broken that damned O'Donnell's nose.

"You're very subdued," Rafe said, suddenly irritated by Brenna's silence. "Surely an engagement is reason for rejoicing?"

"You can't really mean to go through with it," she replied, lifting her gaze at last. He saw the struggle she fought for calm in the stormy turquoise depths of her eyes. The smattering of freckles he found so charming stood out across the bridge of her pert nose, for her face was still too pale.

"Perhaps you'd prefer to accompany your stepfather back to Louisiana?" Rafe asked shortly. "I'm sure we can catch the train Sheriff Mobley promised to put him on if we hurry."

She shuddered. "No."

"Then concede graciously. You'll be a bride before another day is through."

"But why? Why are you so insistent? You told me you had no need for a wife," she said, a hint of her desperation revealed in the throaty timbre of her voice.

"Things change," he said abruptly. He reached into his coat pocket, lit a thin cigar, and began to pace up and down the Oriental carpet. "I find the idea of a child much to my liking."

"But there may not be a child! If you'd only be patient,

the truth will be known in a matter of time. Then you could go about your business conscience-free."

He stopped and stared at her, and felt a familiar tightening in his loins. God, he wanted her! The thought of their last time together tormented him, made him hungry to feel her flesh, to know her touch once again. He'd let her get under his skin, become almost an obsession, something that hadn't happened since Edith. Never mind that Gould considered this marriage expedient, the perfect answer to a touchy situation; Rafe knew he was willing to accept those bonds for no other reason than to bind Brenna to him so that she was forever and without question his. It made him angry with himself to feel that way, he who had always been able to maintain his aloofness with any woman. It also made him more determined to take her despite her resistance. Of course, the flame of desire that flared between them would no doubt burn itself out as it had with every other woman he'd known, but he needed a respectable wife and family. They were an asset in the eyes of polite New York society. And he would see that she had no cause for complaint. He shook his head, then ground the cigar out in an enameled dish.

"You do not understand me, Brenna. This entire affair has been a disaster from start to finish, yet I have always been able to pluck some small success out of even the darkest moment. I'd not thought of marrying until now, but a presentable wife and heirs would not come amiss at this time in my life, and I find that you suit me very well, regardless of whether you carry my child at this moment or not. That will come soon enough."

"You'd really make me do this, even though you know I come to you unwillingly?" she asked in a low voice, swallowing hard.

"My dear, I use whatever devices come to hand to have my way, and if I must threaten to turn you over to that monster of a stepfather to sway you, then I will."

"I see." Her words were tiny stones cast into the chasm of his indifference. "I must give up everything I ever dreamed of to suit your plans."

He sat down beside her and took one of her cold hands, lacing her fingers through his. "Your dreams could become mine. It doesn't have to begin in bitterness, Brenna.''

"If you do not release me from this madness, there can be no other outcome," she replied, her anger rising. She pulled her hand from his and reached for the cup of tepid tea.

Rafe leaned back, his elbows resting on the carved back of the sofa, admiring the slim delicacy of her neck and the way the little golden hairs curled at her nape. His words were lazy. "You'll find that life in New York as my wife can be very pleasant."

"New York?" Her surprise jerked her head around, and she unsteadily set her cup aside.

"Of course. That's where I live. What else did you think?"

"I don't know, I didn't . . ." She faltered to a stop. New York was so far away from everything she knew and understood.

"I own a very comfortable townhouse not far from the Goulds. I've had little time for socializing, but as my wife you can change that. Theater, parties, soirees, and of course, the shopping is excellent."

"I wanted to be a teacher," she said, her voice distant.

"That will be out of the question, of course. Your duties as wife and hostess will take up all of your time," he replied brusquely. "Now, give me the details of your sisters' location. It would be wise to discuss their future." Startled, Brenna provided Rafe with the information he wanted. "I will see to their needs," he said. "Are you satisfied at present with these arrangements?"

Brenna nodded uncertainly. "They write to say they are very happy. Would—would it be possible to let them stay there, at least for a while?"

"Of a certainty." He paused, watching the chase of emotions across her face. "You miss them very much, don't you?"

"Yes." She drew a shaky breath.

"Would you like to visit them on our way north?"

Her head spun. He was taking so much for granted, yet now she realized he was not only accepting the responsibility for a wife, but also for her family. She couldn't understand him at all. Mutely, she nodded.

"I think we can arrange a quick trip to New Orleans," he said, his agile brain already moving on to other plans. "Now, as far as the wedding itself, I think something quiet in the judge's chambers—"

"I'm a Catholic," Brenna protested. "If I'm to be married, I want a priest to bless it."

His expression clouded over. "No. I had enough of priests and the church as a boy. My experiences deny the presence of their loving God."

Her lip trembled and wetness glistened in her eyes. "So I'm to be denied even that comfort, too?"

"Look to me for your comfort from now on. I'll make the arrangements. Invite anyone you wish, of course."

"What kindness!" she sneered, suddenly uncontrollably furious with him, with herself, with the fate that had brought her to such a predicament. "I hate you, Rafe Sinclair! If you force this farce through to its end, then I swear I'll make you pay!"

"Well said, my dear!" Rafe laughed, liking the return of her spirited resistance far better than her subdued acceptance. He caught her chin between his fingers, smiling at her mutinous countenance. "Do your damnedest, Red," he invited softly. "We strike sparks so well together during the day that I know without doubt our nights will be the better for it. By this time tomorrow, you'll know where your duties to your husband lie."

"I won't do it!" she insisted.

"Yes, you will," he said, holding her chin firmly, his lips only a breath above her trembling mouth. "Because you've no other place to run."

His kiss dammed up her denial, blocking the words unspoken in her throat, casting them adrift on a sensual whirlwind. His tongue probed, staking his claim with authority, robbing her of her will, stealing her identity, leaving her dizzy and drained.

He rose to his feet, and Brenna followed his movements with dazed eyes.

"I'll see to the necessary arrangements and return later this evening. Put on something pretty and I'll take you to supper," he added, stroking her cheek with his knuckle. His mouth quirked upward in a grin that was almost indulgent.

"Rafe, please." Her voice wavered as he moved toward the door.

"Don't fight it, Red," he advised, not unkindly. "This time, it's bigger than both of us." He smiled wickedly. "And if you find you can't stand being married to me, then there's always poison or a handy rock to put an end to it."

He ducked through the door just as the china teacup she hurled exploded against the ornate molding. Pink rosebud shards danced in time with his distant, mocking laughter.

The soft glow of the oil lamp made a halo of yellow light that clashed with the cherry velvet of Mrs. Stratton's upholstery. Brenna knew she'd never be able to look at red velvet again without thinking of this parlor and the changes in her life that had occurred here. She paced across the Oriental rug just as Rafe had done earlier, pausing only when Annie's twangy voice broke into her raging thoughts.

"Maybe," Annie began tentatively, "maybe it will be all right, if you just give it a chance. There are lots of women who'd think marrying a man as rich and good-looking as Mr. Sinclair was a wonderful thing."

"I'm not one of them!" Brenna declared. She worried the edge of a fingernail with her teeth, then glanced down in disgust. She hadn't done that since she was a child. Tucking her hands into the side pockets of her cream-colored lawn frock, she appealed to the sandy-haired young man at Annie's side.

"You understand, don't you, Jimmy? He doesn't care about me the way you do about Annie."

Jimmy Teague's Adam's apple bobbled in his scrawny throat, and his homely face pinkened, starting with the tips of his ears. "Well, now, er—"

"Lots of people get married who aren't in love," Annie interrupted. "Not everyone is as lucky as Jimmy and me. These things take time. You could grow to care for Mr. Sinclair, and he can certainly provide for you."

"Yes, because he's Gould's man!" Brenna said bitterly. "You haven't forgotten that, have you? The

Knights have no love for either Gould or Rafe Sinclair, and I can't forget what they did to Sean and the others."

"Brenna," Jimmy said slowly, a fierce frown puckering his sandy brow, "maybe you can help the cause by going through with it."

"What?" Brenna was startled.

"I mean, look at the possibilities," Jimmy continued with growing excitement.

"Jimmy Teague, what are you talking about?" Annie demanded.

"If Brenna marries this Sinclair fellow, she can be a bigger service to the Knights than anyone."

"I don't understand," Brenna said, shaking her head. She wanted her friends to help her figure out a way to avoid this marriage, not give her reasons to go ahead with it.

"What better revenge could you take than to supply the Knights with direct information about Gould's doings? And how easy it would be for you as practically part of his household." Jimmy's light blue eyes took on the glow of fanaticism, and his voice became deep and persuasive. "If you go to New York, you could pass on all sorts of important news about his plans to our people there."

"Jimmy, I'm ashamed of you!" Annie scolded.

"No," Brenna said thoughtfully, "there is something to what he says. If I can't avoid this marriage, at least I can make Mr. Rafe Sinclair regret every single day of it for the rest of his life."

"Brenna, that ain't the way to get along with a husband," Annie admonished. "You know what the Bible says about a wife being obedient and humble. You'll only make yourself miserable."

"I don't think Rafe believes in God," Brenna murmured.

"What?" Annie was genuinely shocked. Everyone believed in God, at least in Texas.

The parlor door opened, and Rafe stood silhouetted for a moment within its outline, a massive Mephistopheles, all flowing dark hair and burning eyes. Annie stifled a gasp.

"Good evening, my dear," Rafe said, stepping forward

to take Brenna's hand. "Will you introduce me to your friends?"

Brenna did as he asked, her teeth gritted at the proprietary air with which he held her hand and pressed a kiss to her brow. He was at his most charming, plying Annie with extravagant compliments and thanking her for her friendship with Brenna.

He shook hands with Jimmy, assessing the younger man with narrowed eyes. "I remember you from the night of the murder. I believe I owe you my thanks."

"I was helping Brenna," Jimmy said through stiff lips, reluctant to entertain any overtures from an avowed enemy of the Brotherhood.

"Will you be our guests tomorrow?" Rafe asked smoothly. "The wedding ceremony is set for eleven o'clock, with a luncheon afterward at the McDade Hotel. I'll collect you, Brenna, shortly before that time."

"Annie has agreed to stand up for me," Brenna ventured.

"Very good. Might I suggest she meet you here?"

"That would be very nice, Mr. Sinclair," Annie answered, casting a quick glance at Brenna's stony expression.

"Please, call me Rafe." He laughed. "We must all get to be good friends. Could you join us for dinner?"

"No, th-thanks, I—I'm sorry, we can't," Jimmy stuttered. "I'm seeing Annie home. Excuse us." He hauled Annie out by her elbow.

"I'll see you in the morning, Brenna," Annie called, then disappeared through the doorway.

Brenna glanced nervously at Rafe, trying to judge the speculative tilt of his head as he watched them leave. He turned his attention to her, and she bristled under his leisurely inspection.

"The yellow suits you," he said, his index finger flipping the girlish ruffle at the dress's high-necked yoke, "but don't you have something a bit more . . . daring?"

Brenna stiffened. "I've never had a need or the means for an evening dress. I'm sorry if my meager wardrobe offends you."

He frowned. "What do you intend to wear tomorrow?"

"I have only my black wool suit."

"I suppose it will have to do," he said. "Although the color is depressing."

"It will suit my mood well enough," she said, a bit snippish at his obvious disapproval. It was too bad, for it was the only garment she had worthy of such an occasion as her own wedding.

"What did young Teague want?" Rafe asked, changing the subject so abruptly that Brenna stared.

"Just to wish me—us—well," she stammered.

He frowned. "You'll have no more to do with your friends in the Knights of Labor. Those troublemakers will lose no opportunity to interfere with the rightful business of the Gould lines. I won't have you becoming an unsuspecting pawn in their schemes."

"I'll see whomever I please!" Brenna cried, incensed at the astuteness of his guess about Jimmy but unwilling to confirm it by her words. "I don't know what you mean about the Knights. Jimmy's my friend. You won't tell me what to do!"

"Did you never hear that obedience is a quality all wives must give to their husbands?" he said. "I demand your loyalty above all else."

"That is something that must be earned," she said coldly.

"It is what a wife pledges to her husband. And you will be guided by me in this and all matters."

"You have no right!" Brenna choked, chilled to the core by his words. He would subjugate her free will already!

Rafe's expression was hard. "I protect what is mine."

"That I'll never be, no matter what words a judge reads over us." Brenna spit her rebellion and defiance at him, her heart racing in her chest at her temerity.

"You were mine from the first moment I saw you," he said, catching her shoulders in his large hands. He lowered his head. "And tomorrow you will know it for certain."

Brenna fought his kiss, but he would have none of it, claiming her mouth and holding her pressed against him until she could no longer breathe or do anything but submit. She whimpered at the fierceness of his mouth, frightened yet exhilarated by the unleashed passion that rippled beneath his civilized veneer. She sensed the savagery he was capable of, yet somewhere in her feminine nature, she knew that she had the power to both temper and inflame it. The question was: did she dare?

Rafe released her by sheer force of will, more than a little appalled at the violence this woman evoked in him with her defiance. He put a little distance between them, aware that he was treading dangerous ground with his impatience for her. They'd not said their vows yet. He could still scare her into bolting if he wasn't careful. And despite his threats, he knew he'd never turn her over to Malvin O'Donnell, even if her stepfather was able to find her.

"You try my patience sorely, Red," he said, by way of the only apology she was likely to get. "I don't want to hurt you."

"Then don't do this thing," she whispered, biting her lip to force back the sting of shaming tears.

"You know as well as I that it's too late to go back, for too many reasons," he said, his voice weary. "Come along, we'll go to dinner now."

"I—I don't have any appetite," Brenna said, faltering. "Would you excuse me?"

He studied her for a long moment, then nodded. "Very well."

"Thank you." She spoke with a quiet dignity that made him feel very small, indeed, yet did not diminish his desire for her one whit. He walked her out of the parlor to the bottom of the staircase, then caught her wrist to detain her.

"I'll be here for you and Annie in the morning," he reminded her.

"Yes." She did not look at him.

"You can't run away from this."

"I know." She turned and faced him squarely, their eyes even as she stood on the step. "I'll be ready."

He relaxed imperceptibly, then kissed her forehead, inhaling the sweet fragrance of her skin. She accepted his attentions submissively, and he bit back a sigh, then chided himself for his impatience. It would take time, he knew, before she accepted him fully again and allowed her resentment to fade. But passion would be the catalyst, for she could not deny her nature. Had he not felt her quiver with reluctant sensuality within his embrace? He smiled to himself as he thought of their wedding night to come. "Good night, Red."

On her last night as her own woman, Brenna lay under the patchwork quilt on Mrs. Stratton's bed and cried herself to sleep. She cried for the loss of a freedom she had only recently begun to cherish, and she cried with a singular sadness for a dead dream. And she cried hardest of all because she knew in her heart that, even though she and Rafe would be husband and wife, they would never again be friends.

Brenna was pale but composed the next morning. With Annie's help, she arranged her hair in a sedate knot at her nape that showed off the elegance of her profile. She dressed with exacting care, her mind far from Annie's incessant chatter. Her suit jacket of dark wool was primly buttoned, the high lacy collar of her best blouse starched and stiff. Gloves and reticule waited beside her bonnet on the bed. Her meager belongings were neatly packed. She stood at the lace-curtained window, a slim figure of understated loveliness, the faint circles under her eyes only adding to the porcelain fragility of her complexion.

The breeze stirred the sheer curtain, and the coolness in the clear air revealed the presence of autumn. Brenna let her gaze roam down the quiet street. The oaks and cottonwoods glistened with brilliant yellow and scarlet hues. Soon a frost would blast the countryside and the leaves would wither and die, but today there was only beauty.

She waited patiently, only faintly surprised at her resignation and acceptance. She had awakened with it, after wrestling all night with her problems. Given the choices available, she understood now that marrying Rafe was the only way out of a situation that had long since gone totally out of her control. She considered the child she perhaps carried. It was only right that she should pay the price of this marriage to give her child a name and expiate the sin that accompanied its conception. And if there was no child, Rafe had made it clear that he desired her and would provide for her. Her notoriety precluded her finding honest work, yet she could not allow the law to send her and her sisters back into her abusive stepfather's clutches.

It gnawed at her that she would be trading—no, selling—herself to Rafe in exchange for mere survival. Was it really any different in principle from selling herself to many men at Miss Mamie's whorehouse? She shrugged. At least Rafe's name would give her the veneer of respectability. She had run out of options. For Maggie's sake, for Shannon's sake, for the sake of the child she might be carrying, she had to set aside her dreams and aspirations and sacrifice herself. She was being swept along by currents of destiny she could not command, to a fate flooded with uncertainty. She shivered uncontrollably. She would be Rafe's wife soon, but what of her soul and identity? What would become of her?

A handsome buggy pulled up to the front of the house and stopped under the window. "He's here," Brenna murmured, watching Rafe climb down from the seat.

His suit was properly somber, yet it could not conceal the broad masculinity of his wide shoulders, nor the lean strength of his long legs. In the brilliant October sunshine, his black hair glinted with the blue highlights of a raven's wing. He raised his head, as if feeling her eyes on him, and she hastily stepped back from the window.

"I'll take your bag down for you," Annie offered. "Are you ready?"

"I'll get my things," Brenna murmured, reaching for her gloves.

Annie tied the ribbons on her pie-plate bonnet with its ruffles and cherries, and picked up Brenna's worn valise. She hesitated, then gave Brenna a fierce hug. "We'll always be friends, won't we?"

"Always, Annie," Brenna promised, swallowing a sudden thickness in her throat. "Go ahead, I won't be a minute."

Annie left and Brenna pulled on a glove, drifting back to the window as she smoothed it over her trembling hand. The other glove lay forgotten between her fingers as she stared outside, trying to control the quiver in her bottom lip.

"Brenna?" Rafe's deep voice was low and questioning. He saw her at the window, a slim silhouette lost in thought. He approached her, and his breath caught at her loveliness. She was a cameo carved by a master craftsman, but rather than creating a cool, hard shell, her maker had fashioned her with fire and an unquenchable spirit. "It's time," he said.

She raised her eyes, luminous with doubt, and Rafe felt a shaft of raw regret. Not for what he did, for he *would* have her, but for how he had gone about it. Silently, he held out a lavish bouquet of white roses. Just as silently, she accepted them, and the heady, sweet fragrance rushed through her nose in dizzying cascades.

"I wish I had sweet words to say to you that would calm your fears," he said gruffly. "I'm not an easy man, but I swear I will try to make you happy."

Brenna touched a velvet white rose petal and felt a great weight lift from her shoulders. Deep in her heart, a tiny flicker of hope sprang to life. No one, *no one,* had ever promised her that. She drew a ragged breath.

"I cannot ask for more."

Rafe searched her face with sudden intensity, then with a hesitancy alien to his nature, carefully folded her into his arms, cradling her like a precious, fragile blossom. He held her gently, and she laid her cheek on his chest in a gesture of trust, the bouquet and glove dangling from her fingers. Tenderness, and a softness he was surprised to find within himself, welled over in his soul.

"Ready now?" he murmured at last.

"Yes," she said. Suddenly the future did not seem quite so bleak.

The sweet perfume of the roses, the strength of Rafe's arm—these things bracketed Brenna's memories of the wedding ceremony. Hope was a golden cocoon that protected her, but too soon it faded away and reality intruded.

She wondered at the assortment of unfamiliar faces that lined the walls of Judge Daniel Thornton's chambers. She shied away from their curious stares, holding Rafe's arm like a lifeline. The judge, portly and beaming, welcomed them warmly.

"My best wishes to you, Miss Galloway," Judge Thornton boomed, pressing Brenna's hand with a politician's long practice. "You're a fortunate young woman to win a fine hero like Rafe here for a husband. Yes, indeed, Texas owes this man a debt of gratitude. In eighty-six he quelled those Ft. Worth strikers almost single-handedly. But I needn't expound upon Rafe's abilities to you. It gives me real pleasure to unite the two of you after such a harrowing adventure and make it a real happy ending.''

"Strike? Ft. Worth?" Brenna echoed faintly. She looked to Rafe for some word of reassurance, but he did not meet her eyes, and his jaw hardened imperceptibly. Brenna's head whirled. What had Rafe to do with that strike? What hadn't he told her? A terrible foreboding gripped her, but her brain would not cooperate, could not give credence to the creeping suspicion that Rafe had somehow been involved in Sean's death.

"If you're ready, Judge," Rafe prompted.

The judge made some joking remark about an eager bridegroom, and Rafe passed Brenna to a beaming Sheriff Mobley. She clung to the lawman, taking comfort in his fatherly assistance as he prepared to give her away. When the sheriff moved her into position before the judge, Annie stood as her only attendant, and to Brenna's shock, the frail, dark-bearded figure of Jay Gould stood at Rafe's side as best man.

Brenna murmured her responses as though in a dream, until the cold weight of the gold band Rafe placed on her finger jarred her fully awake. Rafe's face was very solemn, his voice low, and Brenna fought the panicky feeling that he was suddenly a stranger. Where was the warm, caring man who had held her so sweetly a short time before?

Judge Thornton pronounced them man and wife, but Rafe's kiss was perfunctory before the roomful of strangers. Then everyone crowded in upon them, offering congratulations. Brenna turned from being heartily squeezed by Annie to find Jay Gould shaking Rafe's hand.

"Look at those reporters lapping this up," Gould said in a low voice, his smile secretive and calculating. "I told you so, my boy. Your marrying the girl was the best idea I ever had."

Brenna's startled eyes flew to Rafe, but his ominous

expression offered no explanation, no denial. She struggled to comprehend Gould's words, nearly gasping with the piercing pain of betrayal. The golden shell shattered, and the burgeoning bud of hope withered under the cold, harsh truth. Rafe had forced her into marriage on Gould's orders!

Rafe drew her hand into the crook of his arm, and the glint in his eyes was one of warning. Her new ring dug into her finger, but that pain was nothing to compare to the searing agony in her heart. She'd given herself to this man once before, knowing she had no reason to trust him. Now, foolishly, she'd done it again, and he had used her for some nefarious purpose only he and his evil employer understood.

Only shock kept her from screaming. Only pride kept her from weeping. And only Rafe's strong arm kept her from running away. But there was no place left to run, anyway. She knew this mistake would haunt her for the rest of her life.

Chapter 11

The honeymoon suite at the McDade Hotel consisted of a small sitting room joining two lavishly appointed bedrooms. Any other time Brenna might have enjoyed the splendid furnishings, the softly patterned carpets, the brocade drapes that fell from the corners of the huge tester bed in her room, the vases of fresh flowers. But she was mercifully numb, and these things made no more than a passing impression on her.

Her bridal luncheon lay like a hard lump in her stomach. A blushing Annie had caught her bouquet, but the sweet odor of crushed roses still clung to Brenna's fingertips, making her feel faintly sick. Otherwise, nothing impinged on her frozen emotions, nothing except the realization that she had been taken advantage of unmercifully. That conclusion made her next decision an inevitable one.

Brenna glided into the room, outwardly calm, yet inside anything but serene. Rafe tipped the boy who'd shown them upstairs, then pocketed the key and closed the door. Brenna sat down on the striped satin loveseat and began to draw off her gloves. With a little sigh, she untied the ribbons of her bonnet and drew out the hatpin, setting the hat, gloves, and her reticule down beside her.

"Well, Mrs. Sinclair, have you nothing to say about the accommodations?" Rafe asked. He leaned against the door, one ankle carelessly crossed over the other, his arms folded. A slight grin of satisfaction creased his lean cheek.

She glanced up in surprise, almost as though she had

forgotten his presence. Her voice was distant. "Very nice. I'm sure you'll enjoy them."

Rafe's eyes narrowed. "What do you mean by that?"

"Really, Rafe!" Brenna allowed a certain amount of well-bred annoyance to show. "Must we go on pretending? You've gotten what you wanted."

His eyes glittered. "Not yet."

A sensual charge shot through her and exploded low in her belly. Shaken to the core, she sucked a tight breath between her teeth and fought for composure. Despite her screaming nerves, her gaze was cool and disdainful.

"Save your crude innuendo for someone else. I may be naive, but I'm not stupid." She gave a brittle laugh. "Now that I understand why you forced this marriage on me, I can appreciate the cleverness of the plan. Give the newspapers a happy ending and all's well that ends well within the Gould empire. A brilliant move, really."

"I'm so glad you approve," Rafe retorted sarcastically, glowering at her.

"I admire any well-trained lap dog. You jump to his bidding so well, Rafe," she said in a voice that dripped venom. "But your mongrel blood still shows, and I won't live with a cur!"

"Woman, you go too far," Rafe snarled, coming at her, his fists clenched.

"Not as far as I intend to go—away from you!" She jumped to her feet. The numbness was wearing off, and she was angrier than she'd ever been in her life.

"You're not going anywhere, except to New York with me tomorrow, Mrs. Sinclair," Rafe said. "No matter what you think you know, or guess, you're my wife now."

"Yes, I know." Her laugh tinkled like breaking glass. "I suppose I should thank you for that. By satisfying your master, you've made me a respectable woman." She held up her left hand, and the gold ring glinted dully. "This will take me anywhere I want to go."

"But only at my side."

"There's no reason to carry this farce any further. I've served my purpose. If you had only explained from the start, I wouldn't have been so difficult. Now you can go your way and I'll go mine." She reached for her bonnet.

"A most satisfactory arrangement on both parts, wouldn't you say?"

He ripped the bonnet from her hands with a savage curse and sent it hurtling across the room. His hands were hard on her shoulders and his voice was low like thunder rolling across the plains. "If you think you're going to walk out on me, you're sadly mistaken."

"What choice do you have?" she asked with a calmness that only infuriated him more. "That's exactly what I'm going to do."

"You'll take your rightful place as my wife if I have to hogtie you and carry you aboard the train over my shoulder."

"What a pretty picture that would make for your precious reporters." Brenna laughed. "A man who can't even control his own wife. My, my, whatever will Mr. Gould say?"

"This is between us," Rafe said darkly. His gaze raked her and settled on the soft fullness of her mouth. He smiled with lazy confidence. "You'll see reason soon enough."

"Don't count on it," she snapped. "I won't be wife to Gould's harlot, do you hear? Try it and I promise you'll regret it."

"And how do you propose to do that? Do you plan to drop a boulder on me this time?" he mocked.

She flushed angrily. "I'm not a puppet whose string you can pull. You think I'll act the doting wife simply because you wish it? Force me to this, and I swear I'll do my best to ruin you. I'll spy and lie and cheat and steal every secret you have and sell them to your enemies. And then where will you be?" She arched her eyebrows in defiant inquiry, and her eyes looked as green as sea water and as clear with purpose.

"I'll wring your pretty neck before I let you get away with that," he said mildly. He studied her closely. "But this is more than piqued pride, isn't it? More than a prissy attempt to slap my wrist for daring to marry you at Gould's suggestion. I admit he came up with the notion, but I had reasons of my own to see it through, and I'll not be thwarted by a temper tantrum."

"Temper tantrum? Don't you know raw hate when you

see it?'' Her breasts heaved and she struggled in his grasp, but he held her firmly. "You were there at Ft. Worth, weren't you? Were you the one who put a bullet through my brother's heart?''

"So that's it," he said grimly. "All right, then. I was part of Jim Courtright's duly deputized posse. The strikers ambushed that train. It was a dastardly, cowardly attempt to stop a lawful enterprise. If your brother was there, then he got what he deserved.''

"Liar!" Brenna screamed, slashing at Rafe's cheek with her palm. He caught her wrist and twisted it behind her back, subduing her easily.

"A lot of men died that day on both sides," he said between clenched teeth. "For God's sake, give it a rest. It was four years ago."

"Sean didn't deserve to die! I'll never forgive you. Never!"

"It doesn't matter. Add it to the list of reasons you hate my guts. But it changes nothing," he replied forbiddingly. "You're my wife."

He jerked her to him, and his mouth covered hers in a hungry, devouring kiss that shocked and demanded.

"No!" Brenna twisted away, staggering backward. Her hand touched lips that burned and trembled.

Rafe cursed, his face a furious mask. He worked his tie loose with deft purpose. "Hate all you like, Red, but you're mine. And, by God, it's time you learned it!"

"Damn you, no!" She picked up a vase of chrysanthemums and pitched it at his head, then turned for the door and freedom. The ceramic vase crashed against the wall, but she never reached the door. Rafe caught her in one stride, lifting her under knees and shoulders so that she kicked and flailed uselessly against the air.

"Put me down!" she railed.

"All in good time, my dear." He strode with her in his arms through the open door of her bedroom, and suddenly Brenna was truly afraid. His eyes were hard silver slits, and his lips were bared over his straight white teeth. She shuddered and began to struggle in earnest. "Patience, Red, patience," he said, dropping her feet to the floor.

His hands caught in her hair, and he pulled her roughly

to him, capturing her lips in a searing, angry kiss. He plunged his tongue between her lips, probing deeply and making her legs wobble and her breath come forth in ragged bursts. He held her still with one hand and with the other picked out her hairpins one by one until the knot at her nape slipped and her fiery-gold locks tumbled to her waist.

Brenna pushed at him, but she could not evade his demanding mouth, sucking and nibbling and robbing her of breath and thought. He pulled away, his hot tongue licking at her earlobe and down the cords of her neck. She gasped for breath, waves of dizziness and fear washing over her. His hand found her breast but moved restlessly over the layers of clothing. He began to unfasten her jacket, then lost patience, snatching at the last few buttons so that they snapped from their threads and flew across the room, bouncing and spinning on the carpet like half-mad June bugs. He wrenched the jacket down from her shoulders and tossed it away.

"Stop, damn you, stop," she moaned, her fists beating ineffectually on his chest. Her scalp ached from the pressure of his hand tugging her hair, and her skin felt scalded where his lips trailed. His large hand worked at the tiny buttons down the front of her blouse, but they stymied his best efforts. With a savage oath, he caught the neckline and ripped the soft lawn fabric, opening the garment to the waist.

Brenna cried out in alarm, clutching the edges of the blouse, her eyes wide with fright. Rafe growled low in his throat, hardly seeming human in that moment. He pushed her, throwing her backward onto the large bed, shedding his coat and covering her with his body in one movement.

"Why do you women insist on wearing these infernal contraptions?" he demanded, running a hand over the stiff spines of bone in her corset. He slipped large fingers under the strap of her chemise and reached under the edge of the corset, rubbing the rounded flesh of her breast, lightly pinching the nubby crest of her nipple. She moaned, beating at his shoulders and turning her head from side to side in a feverish denial. "Where are the tapes?" he muttered. He released the button on her skirt and petticoat, pushing them down and off, then he reached under her into the small of her back. He grunted in satisfaction as his fingers found the strings and pulled, loosening the constricting garment.

"Leave me be!" Brenna gasped, her lungs inflating fully. "You—"

His mouth caught her insult before she could hurl it at him, and she felt she was being eaten alive, his tongue tasting every hidden recess of her mouth, his hands moving with certainty across her body. She kicked, tried to roll from beneath him, tried to bite him, fighting with losing strength. She was aware of the hard ridge of him against the vulnerable inside of her thigh and shuddered. His lips found the rising swell of her breast, and his fingers cupped her flesh, pushing it up over the edge of the corset so that he could suckle at the rosy nipple, moistening it through the sheer cotton chemise. Against her will, Brenna felt the tug of sensation strum through her belly to the very core of her femininity.

She went totally still, shocked at her own willingness. *No!* she screamed in her head. She would not give him that. If she allowed herself to respond to his pleasuring, he would strip her of everything, including all self-respect. She knew she could not withstand him physically; his strength was far superior. Yet, she could withhold this triumph from him. She must!

She willed herself to go limp, all struggle seeping from her, her hands falling defenselessly beside her averted head. It took him a minute to realize the change in her, and he raised his head, frowning.

"What the hell . . . ?" He caught her chin, forcing her to look at him. "Giving up so easily, Red?"

"I haven't your strength. Since you'll take what you want no matter what I do, I'll save some bruises," she said, trying to put ice in her shaky voice.

"I always knew you were a smart woman," he murmured. He dipped his head. "Here, kiss me back, Red."

"No."

"Don't be stubborn. I don't want a dead fish in my marriage bed. It's time you gave your husband his rights."

"Rights!" she spat, contemptuous and haughty despite her position. "It's rape! So get on with it and be damned. What else could I expect from a whore's spawn? You've spent your life in the gutter, and you'll never be able to climb out of it!"

He stiffened, and she felt his desire wane. His jaw hardened and he rolled off her with a jerk, his breath harsh in his throat. She dared not move. He levered himself up, his eyes locked on her half-naked and defenseless pose. His face was a tight mask that hid his feelings.

"You have a tongue sharper than a Saracen's blade," he said slowly. She swallowed uneasily and he laughed, a strange harsh sound. "Don't worry, Red. Your talent has stood you in good stead—this time. And you've given me much to think on."

He picked up his coat from the floor and shrugged it on. "You've had an arduous day, dear wife. I suggest you rest in bed for the remainder of it. I'll tell the staff you don't wish to be disturbed."

Brenna raised herself up on one elbow, her look blank and puzzled. Rafe studied her with an intensity that seared her soul, then he shook his head slowly and left the room. Brenna sat up, her heart pounding, listening as he crossed the sitting room, opened the door into the hall, and went out. Was he really leaving her here alone? Perhaps she could . . . Her thoughts scattered at the scrape of a key in the lock.

She flew to the sitting room door, holding the bits and pieces of her clothes together—the loose corset, tattered blouse, sagging drawers. Her hand grasped the knob, but it refused to budge. She slumped, then kicked the door in frustration. He'd locked her in!

Rafe's soft laughter floated from the other side of the door. "Enjoy your rest, my sweet. And don't bother to call out. We're the only ones on this floor."

"You bastard!" Brenna raged. She pounded on the door with her fist.

"While I'm gone, contemplate your wifely duties. A few hours' meditation should do you a world of good. Try counting your blessings." His mocking laughter faded away, and Brenna cursed and called him every name she could think of.

She ground her teeth and tried to think. She hurried to the windows but found no help there. Their suite was three stories up, and the sheer brick façade offered no hope of her climbing down. Angry, scared, and defiant, she prowled around the rooms and swore that this would be the last time she let Rafe Sinclair take advantage of her.

After a while, she pulled her skirt back on and put on another blouse, sadly folding the ruined shirtwaist and tucking it into her valise. She gathered up her jacket and spent several minutes on her hands and knees looking for the lost buttons. Another space of time was spent reattaching them, using supplies from her sewing case.

The shadows lengthened, but Rafe did not reappear. Suppertime came and went, and although cooking smells wafted upward from the kitchens, no one appeared with a tray for her. When the growls in her stomach could no longer be ignored, she made do with a couple of apples out of the fruit basket the management had provided. She lit the gas jet and tried to read the flowery poetry she found in the little book on her bedside table, but contemplating the words of love and romance was like trying to decipher a foreign language. Pacing passed more time, but eventually the lateness of the hour, the nervous fatigue of her wedding day, and boredom drove her to bed.

She was mildly surprised to find that her door, too, possessed a lock and key, and she wondered if its presence expressed the hotel's philosophy regarding newlyweds. Perhaps the manager and maids had heard arguments and breaking glass on many previous occasions. At any rate, she was able to don her nightgown with a bit more confidence after locking her bedroom door to assure her privacy. She climbed into the enormous bed, letting her tired body luxuriate in the soft mattress and plump feather pillows. She rolled to her side, her ears attuned to the slightest sound. Perhaps Rafe did not intend to return tonight. Perhaps he didn't intend to return, at all. The thought cheered her. She would shout the house down first thing in the morning to secure her release from this opulent prison. She drifted to sleep with a smile on her lips, imagining the commotion she would make.

The outer door banged open. Brenna jerked upright out of a deep sleep, her heart in her throat. The room was dark, but her eyes were adjusted to the dimness, and she could see the outline of her closed door. She heard muttered cursing and the screech of a chair scraping across the floor. Rafe. She sank back down into the sanctuary of the pillows and stared at the locked door, swallowing apprehensively.

The doorknob rattled, then a heavy fist pounded on the panels, making the entire door frame quiver.

"Brenna! Open this door!" Rafe ordered, his words thick and strangely slurred. Brenna curled lower in the bed, the covers pulled up to her chin, and said nothing.

"Dammit, Red! Get your butt up outta that bed and open this door!"

"Go away. I'm sleeping," Brenna called.

The door exploded inward with his sharp kick, bolt and lock shrieking, hinges protesting. Brenna gasped and burrowed deeper in the covers. Rafe stood silhouetted against the soft glow of gas light, his hair mussed, his collar askew, a dark bottle dangling from his fingertips.

"Well, well, well," he mumbled and took a pull out of the whiskey bottle. He exhaled harshly. "My lovely bride."

Brenna could smell the sharp odor of alcohol surrounding him like a cloud. "You're drunk."

Memories of her father rose up to choke her. How often had she seen him in such a state, intoxicated just enough to be dangerous. She could never tell with Da, and she couldn't guess with Rafe. Would he be melancholy, or jovial, or out for murder?

"Very astute, my dear," Rafe slurred. "I'm *very* drunk."

"Well, go sleep it off," she ordered crisply. "I'm tired."

"Oh, ho!" He laughed and swayed on his feet. "Now you're beginning to sound like a wife. But that privilege comes only after you've begun acting like one."

Brenna cringed at the ominous threat in his words, and her heart thumped painfully. But she knew a show of weakness would only be her undoing. "There's no reasoning with a drunkard," she retorted, her voice tart. "Get out of my room."

Rafe threw back his head and laughed again, but his amusement sent cold shivers of uncertainty down her spine. Still laughing, he walked unsteadily to the bedside.

"Damn if you're not the plucky one. I think that's what I admire most about you. Even backed into a corner, you still spit and scratch." He carefully set the bottle down on the small, doily-topped table next to the bed.

Brenna's lips compressed angrily. "I certainly don't find anything admirable about your being stinking drunk."

"Just celebrating our nuptials, my dear." He trailed a finger across her cheek, then touched a curl that rested on her breast. He tested its springy texture between his fingers and Brenna stared coolly up at him, hiding her apprehension behind an implacable expression. The gas light from the sitting room provided just enough illumination to see Rafe's mustache twitch, and she wondered if he knew that her pulse was pounding in her throat. He began to wind the lock of hair around his fingers, bending as he did so, and Brenna's eyes grew wide.

The tether of her hair held her firmly, but she did not attempt to turn away. Rafe lowered his mouth, kissing her softly. He tasted, not unpleasantly, of potent whiskey and man. She quivered, holding herself stiff and still with difficulty and bracing to resist the treacherous pull of sensuality that emanated from his lips. He straightened, releasing her hair.

"Good night, Red."

Brenna stared in total bewilderment at his retreating back. Her lips tingled from the brush of his lips and mustache, and her mind tumbled, puzzled and confused. He had only to press his advantage and she would have been powerless to prevent him from finishing what he had begun earlier. Yet he did not. Why?

Baffled, she listened to him cross the sitting room, then heard the creak of the bedframe and the rustle of linens as he threw himself across the bed in the other room. She heard a long sigh, then the rumble of deep breathing, and finally a soft snore. Only then did she relax again, but her brain continued to reel in turmoil. She didn't understand Rafe Sinclair at all. It was a long time before sleep claimed her.

She dreamed of running, of flight from some powerful but unseen beast. A rough hand shook her, and she came upright in the bed with a gasp.

"Get up," Rafe said.

"What?" She shook her bemused head. It wasn't even daylight outside, yet Rafe stood fully dressed in boots, denim trousers, and leather vest over a white shirt.

"Wear something to ride in. We're leaving in ten minutes. Be ready or I'll dress you myself."

Brenna gaped after him, but something in his voice brooked no opposition. Groaning, she crawled out of bed. She didn't own a riding skirt, split for the purpose of riding astride, so she donned a serviceable old linsey-woolsey skirt and her shirtwaist. The hated corset remained packed in the bottom of her valise. She had braided her hair and was securing it at the nape of her neck when Rafe strode back into the room.

"Eat." He handed her a steaming mug of black coffee and a chunk of cold cornbread smeared with plum jam.

"What is it?" Brenna asked, mumbling around a mouthful of cornbread. She took a sip of the coffee to wash down the dry crumbs, grimacing at the bitter taste.

Rafe picked up her cotton nightgown from the foot of the bed. The garment was still warm from her body, and his large hands knotted in it. His mouth hardened, then he stuffed the gown into her valise and glanced around the room. "Is this all you have?" he demanded.

"Yes." She set down the mug. "Will you please tell me—"

"Come along. I haven't got time for your female chatter. Have you got a bonnet? We've got a long ride ahead of us."

"Yes, but . . ." Brenna's chin lifted stubbornly and she dug her heels in. "I refuse to go anywhere until I know what's going on. I told you yesterday I wouldn't go to New York with you."

"Fine, because we're not going to New York."

"What? Then where are we going?" she demanded in exasperation.

"You'll find out soon enough. And save your breath,

Red, because I'm not giving you a choice." He thrust her bonnet into her startled hands, grabbed the valise, and took her arm, hustling her out of the room and down the stairs without another word.

The street was growing lighter by the minute, but what waited for them took Brenna by surprise. Standing along with Rafe's bay and a dainty dapple-gray mare outfitted with a sidesaddle, was a loaded wagon with a team of four, an assortment of men, and a woman. Rafe put Brenna's case in the wagon and made perfunctory introductions.

"Brenna, this is Matt, Kelly, and Ned, your hired hands. Boys, Mrs. Sinclair." The three grizzled cowpokes doffed their dusty hats, and Brenna nodded back. He continued, indicating the plump Mexican woman with a sullen mouth. "And this is Juanita Alvarez. She's the cook."

"*Señora.*" Juanita's greeting held a touch of insolence.

"All right, let's get going," Rafe said. Matt tied his horse to the back of the wagon, and he and Juanita climbed up on the high seat while the other men mounted up. Rafe set Brenna on the gray, giving her no opportunity to protest. She fought for balance, hooking her right knee around the horn of the sidesaddle and settling her skirt. Rafe slipped her foot into the stirrup and adjusted the strap.

"What are you doing?" she demanded, leaning down to speak next to his ear. "Who are these people? Where are we going?"

Rafe gave her foot a comforting pat and grinned up at her, a wicked light in his gray eyes. "Simple, my dear. I'm taking you home."

It was dusk when their motley party reached Rafe's ranch. It looked just the same, neglected and empty. Brenna had not been able to glean any further information about this sudden decision of Rafe's, and it made her uneasy and apprehensive. What was going on in his head? She couldn't fathom his thinking, and she entered the deserted house with no small trepidation. There were too many memories here.

Rafe gave swift orders. Feed and tackle and tools went

into the barn. Supplies were stacked in the kitchen, and the new cast iron stove was assembled and a fire built. Ned chopped kindling in the back yard. Kelly saw to the horses. Juanita sang softly to herself in Spanish and stirred an aromatic mixture of food on the new stove. Matt cleaned out the bunkhouse.

Brenna worked with the rest of them, carrying in new blankets, bolts of cloth, dishes, and pots and crocks. A cot was set up in the second bedroom for Juanita, and a new feather tick mattress replaced the old one on the rope bed. Boxes of assorted household implements and staples sat in rows on the floor. It looked as if Rafe had come to stay. Brenna was mystified, but Rafe brushed all her questions aside, and she hesitated to make a scene in front of the others.

They ate spicy stew off new tin plates and drank coffee. Juanita took blankets and more coffee to the bunkhouse while Brenna washed the dishes, thankful for the simple, mundane task. It was an anchor of normalcy in a day that had been anything but normal. A kerosene lamp glowed in the bunkhouse, and Juanita's high giggle carried on the cool breeze through the open back door. Brenna dried the last plate on a new square of red-checked toweling just as Rafe entered the kitchen.

"Any of that coffee left?" he asked, taking off his hat and tossing it onto a peg beside the door. He threw himself down in the single chair at the table.

"Yes," she murmured. "I'll get it." Using the hem of her skirt as a potholder, Brenna poured the black brew from a blue splatterware pot into a thick crockery mug. She placed the cup down on the table in front of Rafe, then silently took a seat on the neighboring bench. A kerosene lamp sat in the middle between them, and she reached out to adjust the wick, then slid it to one side so she could see Rafe's face. He studied her over the rim of his cup, and silence stretched between them until Brenna thought she would scream. She clasped her hands together under the table to control their trembling.

"Shouldn't you tell me now why we're here?" she asked at last.

"A smart woman like you should be able to figure it out on her own."

Brenna shrugged. "I never said I was smart. Somehow I ended up married to you."

"Exactly." He took a final swig of the coffee and pushed the cup aside. "I have to leave for California in the morning."

"California? But yesterday you said New York!"

"A change of plans. I've got to try to salvage what I can of our Southern Pacific negotiations, and now's as good a time as any. Plummer made a mess of things."

"I'm sure Mr. Plummer would be sorry to hear that," she said with heavy sarcasm. "Too bad he's dead."

"We both could call him to account. Anyway, I can't take you with me, and our little discussion yesterday gave me cause to reflect. You know, Red, you should never reveal your trump card."

"I don't know anything about cards." She stirred uneasily on the narrow bench.

"If you'd held your peace, you might have had a chance to get your revenge, but I can't let you use your position as my wife to hurt Mr. Gould or myself. You won't be able to help your friends in the Knights of Labor very much out here. I hope you like country life."

"I'm to stay here? You wouldn't allow me to go my own way, but now you're dumping me on the edge of nowhere like so much excess baggage? How gallant!" Shock, anger, and frustration made her voice shake.

"I'm making you a gift of this place. Call it a wedding present, if you like. You've got help, and I've arranged for the start of a cattle herd to be sent. I'll leave you some cash to use. Get the boys to fix things up, check the fences, get ready for winter. And there's even Juanita as a companion and chaperone."

"Guard, you mean!" Brenna spat.

He shrugged. "Just don't try to leave. You'll be safe enough here, and maybe you'll be able to even keep yourself out of trouble. I'll be back. I'm on the road a lot between New York and Ft. Worth anyway, and I expect I'll have to go back to California more than once. You'll probably see me more than if I installed you in New York. I expect my bride to greet me every time I get a chance to visit, especially if you're carrying my child."

"That again! I told you—"

"Just don't get any ideas," he interrupted. "Your sisters will be the ones to pay the price."

She subsided abruptly, a glimmer of tears in her eyes. "You're despicable, the lowest—"

"What are you complaining about? Isn't a place of your own what you've always wanted? So make something of it." He pushed the chair back with a loud scrape and stood glowering at her.

"All right, I will," she snapped with a return of her old spirit. She stood and faced him with a growing sense of relief.

Thank God, he was going, leaving her in peace and giving her control over the ranch. She could regain at least a portion of the independence he had stripped from her with the marriage ceremony. She would make the best of the situation. As long as he made no demands on her, she might even be able to pretend he didn't exist at all. She lifted her chin and gave him a haughty stare.

"I'm sure you'll be on your way before I arise in the morning so I'll wish you a safe journey, but not a speedy return. Good night, Mr. Sinclair."

She swept past him with a flip of her skirts, but his arm snaked out, stopping her. She glared a question up into his face, then gasped at the savage, hungry fire that burned in his gray eyes. He caught her to him, flattening her soft breasts against the hard wall of his chest, holding her pressed tightly against him.

"You once said you'd sell your soul for this place," he said hoarsely. "I'm offering you a bargain, Brenna. All I want in return is your body."

His lips captured hers, seeking and draining, demanding everything. He plundered her mouth until she sagged helplessly, bereft of breath and coherent thought and the will to resist. Sinking into a morass of pure sensation, she was powerless in her limited experience to withstand the sensual onslaught of Rafe's virility and magnetism. He gave her no time to erect defenses, and when he carried her to the newly made-up bed, she was soft and pliant in his arms. . . .

And when he left her at dawn, she sobbed into her pillow, but not because he had hurt her. No, he'd been skillful and gentle, giving more than he took. She cried because she had lost everything to him, all her hopes and dreams of an independent life. He'd even thwarted her plans for revenge. But worst of all was the knowledge that she had not been able to withhold even the tiniest portion of herself from him, that her wholehearted response had been taken from her without her volition, and that her traitorous body had paid Rafe the highest accolades while betraying her utterly.

Chapter 12

"The *señora* did not sleep well?" Juanita set a steaming mug down on the kitchen table and gestured Brenna to the chair. "Come, sit down. Drink your coffee."

"Thank you, Juanita." Brenna pulled the edges of her crocheted fascinator over her shoulders and sat down. She sipped the hot, aromatic brew and blinked her heavy red eyelids, gazing listlessly off into nothingness. A dark cloud of depression covered her soul.

"You will feel better soon. When your man leaves, there is always sadness. And when you are newly wedded, and it is *such* a man . . ." Juanita shrugged her plump shoulders in silent eloquence, and her smile was a bit sly. "Señor Sinclair, he is very strong, very *macho*. I hear in the night, the way he says *adios*. It is right to cry with missing a man who loves with such power."

Brenna felt her face grow hot. She wanted only to forget last night. It was too utterly humiliating to know that there had been a witness to her wanton abandonment. She and Rafe had never stopped to consider their lack of privacy. Not that it would have changed anything. Rafe would not have been forestalled by such a trifling matter. His passion had been undeniable and unavoidable, and he had drawn her out of herself until she cried out with need and pleasure. Brenna's cheeks burned even hotter at that memory.

"I don't wish to discuss Mr. Sinclair," she said stiffly. She didn't like the knowing look in Juanita's bright black eyes.

Brenna rose, taking her empty cup to the dishpan. She

cast a doubtful glance around the cluttered kitchen, the littered cupboards, the enamel pan full of dirty dishes. Juanita's skill as a cook did not appear to extend to basic cleanliness. Since the thought of food held no appeal, she said abruptly, "I'm going for a walk."

Brenna stepped off the back porch and sniffed the air. There was a hint of autumn on the cool breeze, yet the sun still glowed with unseasonable warmth. She strolled aimlessly around the house, a frown making a pleat in her brow. There was no sign of the men, no evidence of work going on. Evidently their industry matched Juanita's. She shrugged irritably. What concern of hers was that?

For all that she'd accepted Rafe's challenge to make something of this ranch, it didn't seem important after last night's humiliation. Her fists bunched angrily. Did he think he could use her physically, then abandon her, keeping her like some slave on this isolated ranch, strictly for his pleasure and at his convenience? Rafe Sinclair had a lot to learn!

Her mind shied away from the memory of his expertise in bed. She was more shaken than she was willing to admit by her lack of control. Every time she succumbed to his lovemaking, she lost a little more of her independence. No matter how fulfilling she found him physically, she had to maintain an emotional distance for her own protection and self-preservation. What if she came to depend on him? She shuddered. He would certainly fail her, and perhaps even destroy her. No, she couldn't allow that to happen. Men were untrustworthy as a breed, and Rafe proved the rule. Just because he was her husband didn't give him complete rights over her mind and soul, and she must see to it that he never forgot it.

She paused at the corner of the house, plucking furiously at the old privet hedge. The small teardrop leaves fell in a pool at her feet, but she was hardly conscious of her agitated stripping of the slender branches. Did he think she was so spineless? After all, what was to keep her from leaving here—merely his orders? Ha! She'd show him. It would be a small matter to take a horse, elude Juanita, and make her way back to town. Her mutinous thoughts soon wound down, slowed, as did her fingers on the denuded bush.

Go back to what? She swallowed. Nothing had changed. She would still be that notorious woman, and no employment would drop in her lap. And what about Shannon and Maggie? At least with the nuns, her sisters were safe, and Rafe would continue to support them if she played the docile wife. She could not jeopardize their safekeeping by running away, at least not until she had the means to resume their care.

Brenna chewed her lip, thinking furiously. The nuns. Sister Therese. Of course! Maybe there was a way out for her, if she could prevail on the aged nun for help. With Rafe gone, there was no need to rush away from the ranch, to allow her emotional upheaval to force her into acting on impulse. There was time to formulate a plan.

She could write to Sister Therese and beg her to find some kind of teaching position for her. Surely there was a family somewhere with the need for a competent governess or nanny. Why, good Catholic families applied to the Sisters of Charity all the time for such respectable young women. Brenna frowned, and her fingers went back to stripping the greenery. She couldn't tell the good sister she was married, of course, but that couldn't be helped. Deserting a husband who deserted you wasn't much of a sin, was it? She had worse to confess than that.

Her lips twitched, a reluctant smile creeping over her face at the delicious irony of living on Rafe's largess only long enough to outwit him. Oh, he'd be furious to find her gone! And she'd cover her tracks well. It would give her the greatest pleasure to thwart his plans for her. With any luck, she could be safely ensconced at a new post by Christmas. With a bit more luck, Rafe's work would keep him away until it was too late, and perhaps she'd never have to see the wretched scoundrel again. She threw down the bare twig and turned away, her steps determined, her chin firm with confidence.

She inspected the yard, the ranch house, the assorted outbuildings with new interest. It wasn't really such a bad place to wait, after all. And with a little effort, things could be quite comfortable. She held back a laugh. The least she could do to repay Rafe's "generosity" was to prove herself a good steward, even though she'd be long gone before he could show his appreciation.

That protected, sunny area in the lee of the barn would make a perfect garden spot, she thought. Perhaps there would be time to get in a fall garden of greens before the first frost. Brenna's mind began to spin with the myriad of things that would need to be done to prepare for winter. She wasn't exactly sure what went in to cattle ranching, but she did know a lot about running a farm and a household. And it was time to test her mettle.

She crossed the back yard and ambled toward the barn. Peering into the dim, odorous interior, she heard a faint murmur of voices. She pushed open the door and walked past stalls crammed with piles of feed and equipment. She paused to stroke the dapple mare's nose, frowning at a box of jumbled garden seed thrown carelessly on the ground. Mice and insects would soon make short work of it, damaging if not destroying the precious seeds. Brenna had never been one to condone waste in any form, and the sheer neglect of this made her angry. She followed the voices.

She found Ned and Kelly just inside the small back door, sitting on twin kegs of nails, passing a plug of chewing tobacco back and forth.

"Good morning," she said pleasantly. "Taking a break?"

"Yes'm, we're about caught up, wouldn't you say, Ned?" Kelly asked his grizzled friend.

Ned leisurely spit a brown stream of tobacco juice into the dirty straw at his feet. "Yup."

Brenna fought back an unsettled feeling. She didn't know much about giving orders, but she was sure Rafe wouldn't stand for idleness. For that matter, she wouldn't either!

"Mr. Sinclair left instructions to have everything in readiness for the cattle he is sending. I want you two to start on the corral. It's practically falling down. Where is Matt?"

"He had a little too much of Juanita's tequila last night," Ned replied. "He's sleeping it off."

Brenna gritted her teeth and glared at the man. "Well, go wake him up! I expect a day's work for a day's wages.

Have fun on your own time, or you'll have more time on your hands than you want.'' She forced strength into her voice and gave them her coldest, haughtiest stare. ''Do I make myself clear, gentlemen?''

The two cowpokes glanced at each other, then shuffled to their feet. ''Yes'm,'' they chorused, dipping their heads respectfully. Brenna watched them leave with a growing sense of accomplishment. Maybe all that was needed here was some leadership. She walked back through the barn, her expression thoughtful.

Brenna stopped at the seed box and spent the next half hour sorting through it, separating the little cloth sacks of seed. She picked out the bags of collard and turnip seed to start right away, then packed up the rest of the corn, tomato, cucumber, and other various seeds for a spring garden. Even though she wouldn't be here to plant them next season, it went against her grain to ignore the need to store them in a place safe from hungry field mice. Brenna went to the nail keg and stuck a handful of nails in her skirt pocket. She would hang the little bags behind the kitchen stove as her mother had. They would be dry and out of the way until needed in the spring.

She carried her precious supply out of the barn, stooping to retrieve an empty cotton cloth feed sack. Its printed floral design was new and garish against the old straw, and she gave a little cluck of disapproval. She would have to remind the men to save these sacks. There was always a use for the fabric, and every penny saved was a penny earned when running a farm. Brenna felt a growing excitement and her spirits lifted. She'd show Rafe Sinclair! She'd make this ranch work. She'd have something to show him when he came back, make him eat his hateful words . . .

Her thoughts ground to a halt. She wouldn't be here when he came back. She had to remember that, had to keep her resolve fixed firmly. Pausing to watch the three ranch hands begin work on the rickety corral, she tried to sort out her confused emotions. What did it matter whether she proved anything to Rafe or not? What was important was survival and escape.

Brenna stepped into the kitchen with this thought in mind, but her words died on her tongue. Nothing had been moved in the kitchen. Not one dish had been washed, nor one box of supplies unloaded.

She caught Juanita eyeing her with a certain insolence and knew intuitively that things had to be settled between them now. She set the little bags of seed down on the littered table.

"Juanita, how badly do you need this job?" Brenna demanded suddenly.

The plump cook shrugged. "It is a job, that is all. No different than any other."

"I'm glad you feel that way," Brenna replied sweetly. "Because I've discovered that I don't require your services, after all. I'll have one of the men drive you back to Marshall in the morning."

"But, Mr. Sinclair, he said—"

"As you may have noticed, Mr. Sinclair is no longer here. And if I can expect no better than this"—Brenna gestured to the dirty kitchen—"well, I'll not fight you, but I don't have to put up with you either."

"Oh, but *señora* . . ." Juanita gulped, a panicky light in her dark eyes.

"I'll pay you for your time, of course. I'm glad we could resolve this so easily."

"Señora Sinclair, please!" Juanita launched into a torrent of Spanish and broken English, the gist of which Brenna understood. This job was indeed important to the Mexican woman, who begged for another chance.

Brenna was taken aback by the honest anguish in the woman's voice. "You—you have no place to go? No family?"

"No one." Juanita shook her head, her expression strained and anxious. "It is so difficult for a woman alone. . . ."

Brenna hesitated, and her anger faded. "Yes, I know." She sighed, searching the repentant woman's face for signs of sincerity. "All right, Juanita," she said slowly. "You may stay, but I want it clearly understood that this is *my* kitchen. You'll follow my instructions and with a good will, or you'll be on your way, no matter what."

"Yes, Señora Sinclair," Juanita agreed breathlessly. "Whatever you wish."

"I wish us to be friends," Brenna replied. "Try to

understand that, and remember that I will not stand for my kindness to be repaid with disrespect. Now, to begin, I suggest you wash those dishes, then organize the cupboards. Agreed?''

Juanita looked at her mistress with eyes that held a bit of wariness and also a growing respect. *"Si, señora."*

"Very good." Brenna dug in her pocket for a nail and picked up a small block of firewood. She hammered several nails into the wall behind the stove while Juanita watched curiously. When she was finished, she carefully hung each sack of seeds on a nail and then stood back to admire her handiwork.

Maybe things weren't going to be as easy as she had hoped, but she'd taken the first steps toward establishing herself as mistress of the house. Already, those little seed sacks made the place feel like a home to her, and even though this home was only temporary, she could still take pride in her accomplishments. Maybe Rafe had placed her in this situation for his own reasons, but she had the strength to make the most of it to suit her needs. The next step was up to her.

"I'll be back to help you in a minute, Juanita," Brenna said, determination sounding in her voice. "But first I have a very important letter to write."

Brenna didn't have long to worry or wonder how she was going to mail the letter. Two afternoons later, the jingle of harness buckles and the clang of iron wheels caught her attention. She put down the rag she'd been using to wash windows and went out on the porch just as a wagon loaded with children of all shapes and sizes pulled to a stop.

"Howdy! Whoa, Mabel, Shirley." The woman who spoke set the wagon brake and vaulted out of the seat, surprising Brenna with her energy and ability despite her roly-poly figure. "How do? Miz Sinclair, ain't it? I'm Sarie Henigan and this here's my young'uns. Me and my man, Paul, live acrost that ridge, 'bout five miles as the crow flies thataway."

"Pleased to meet you, Mrs. Henigan," Brenna said. "Won't you come in? I haven't had much time to get settled yet, but . . ."

"That's right kindly of you, but we can only stay a

minute. I just wanted to say 'howdy, neighbor' and let you know you ain't the only dern fool out here!'' Sarie laughed.

Brenna responded instantly to the woman's robust friendliness. She was in the company of strangers, more alone than she had realized was possible. At night, loneliness preyed on her, and already she missed Annie fiercely. Sarie Henigan's friendly face was more than welcome.

"Please, let me offer you' and the children a cool drink," Brenna said.

"Pump in the back? All right, you kids, go 'round and get a swaller, but come right back," Sarie ordered. She pulled off her bonnet and fanned her flushed, freckled cheeks, grinning brightly at Brenna. "We's just on our way over to Johnston's Crossroads. Them young'uns always get clear besides themselves on the day I trade my eggs and pick up the mail. They love those red licorice whips, and that's a fact."

"I didn't realize there was a crossroads near," Brenna said, and her agile mind had already picked up on the words that were most important to her. "Mrs. Henigan, could I impose on you to post a letter for me?"

"Why, that'd be no trouble a-tall."

"Wait, please!" Brenna said excitedly. She raced into the house, grabbed her carefully penned missive to Sister Therese and a few of her hoarded coins. She wouldn't use Rafe's money for this letter! She returned, breathless. "Here you are. How can I thank you?"

Sarie took the letter, peering nearsightedly at the curved writing. "You write a mighty fine hand," she said admiringly. "Always wished the children had the chance to learn such as that. I ain't much good at book learning myself. Maybe sometime you could see your way clear to helping the older ones with setting out their names? I can't, and Paul ain't got the patience."

"Well, ah, I did want to teach once," Brenna admitted. "But I'm hardly moved in here." *And I won't be here much longer,* her mind cheered. "Maybe sometime later?"

"Of course, you're right. Here, Junior, you hand Miz Sinclair down that sack of eggs."

Brenna accepted the rough hemp sack gingerly and gratefully. "How thoughtful of you, Mrs. Henigan. I was just thinking this morning how much I was craving eggs. Do you have any biddies for sale? I'd like to get my own flock started."

Sarie nodded. "Ought to in a couple more weeks." The two women dickered for a moment, then settled on a price that satisfied them both. "I'll bring 'em by the next time we pass," Sarie promised, shooing her brood back into the wagon like one of her own mother hens.

Brenna waved to them until they disappeared from sight, a bright smile on her face. She sent a silent prayer heavenward that Sister Therese would respond soon with the solution she so desperately wanted.

Waiting for an answer to her letter kept Brenna as edgy as a cat. To compensate, she worked herself unmercifully, scrubbing and cleaning, hoeing and carrying water to the little garden she'd planted with collards, turnips, and onions. She stitched squares of calico for curtains, gathering them on willow withes and hanging them over nails. With Juanita's help, the ranch house took on a sparkle that belied its humble appearance.

Brenna ended each evening with a bath in the large wooden tub in the kitchen. Then she fell into bed, exhausted, her muscles screaming from overexertion, only to rise again the next morning to plunge again into the unending chores. By the end of three weeks, she had dark circles of fatigue under her eyes, but the yard and house, as well as the outbuildings and barn, showed much improvement.

She was on her hands and knees, scrubbing the front porch with a corn shuck brush the morning the cattle arrived. At first, she couldn't be sure that the grayish-yellow cloud on the horizon was anything more than a storm brewing. Then the faint bawling of cows carried to her ears. She stood up, shading her eyes and absently rubbing the recurring ache in her lower back. After a while, the dark outline of a rider and horse materialized out of the bubbling yellow cloud.

Brenna's breath caught, and there was a sudden tightness in her chest. She strained to see. Was it Rafe? She smoothed back the damp tendrils of hair from her face

and straightened her skirts, her heart beating in anticipation and something more. Was she actually glad to
see him? What madness provoked such an unreasonable
surge of emotion? Confusion made her lips quiver, and
she pressed them together tightly to still their trembling.

The rider moved closer, and Brenna's unexpected surge
of disappointment was real and palpable. It wasn't Rafe
but, rather, an older, weathered cowboy. Brenna pushed
her reaction to the back of her mind. It was something
she'd have to examine later—much later. She waited on
the top porch step until the rider drew his mount to a halt
in front of the house.

"Ma'am," he said, politely touching the brim of his
dusty, dun-colored hat. "I'm looking for Miz Rafe
Sinclair."

"I'm Mrs. Sinclair," Brenna said. The words gave her
a little jolt, and she realized that it was the first time she'd
actually accepted it as fact. "What can I do for you,
Mr. . . . ?"

"Hooke, ma'am. Pete Hooke." He swung off the
horse with a slouchy grace and stood at the bottom
step. Unbuttoning the pocket on his blue chambray shirt,
he withdrew a much-folded envelope. "I brung you
this."

Brenna accepted the letter and studied Pete Hooke. He
could have been anywhere from forty to sixty, of medium
build and stature, but he moved with a lazy strength and
hard fitness that would have left many younger men
envious. His chin was sprinkled with gray stubble, and
when he removed his hat, his thinning brown hair held
streaks of gray. Years of outdoor living had etched lines
into his brown, leathery face. Deep crow's feet caused by
squinting into sunny distances radiated from the corners
of his faded blue eyes. Sharp creases, the evidence of a
lifetime of easy grins, fell from his nose and were lost
in his mousy mustache. His rounded cheeks had a rosy
tint under his tan, and his expression was expectant and
quietly friendly. Brenna decided his was a good face
and liked him in that instant. She smiled, then tore
open the missive. The bold black scrawl leaped off the
page:

Brenna,

This is brought to you by Pete Hooke, a good friend of mine. Treat him well, anyway. I return to New York at Gould's urgent word. Trouble there means I do not know when I will return to Texas, but I'm sure this pleases you. Rely on Pete.

It was signed simply, "Rafe."

Brenna folded the letter and stuck it in her apron pocket. She tried to ignore the lump of hurt in her chest. Rafe's letter was just like him, mocking and infuriating. But what else had she expected? And what was she to make of Pete Hooke? Was he Rafe's spy, sent to keep an eye on her? She swallowed her suspicion and went down the steps, her hand extended. "Well, Mr. Hooke. Rafe says I must rely on you."

Pete hastily took off his worn leather glove and shook hands with her, his callused paw gentle, as if she were made of the daintiest porcelain. "Call me Pete, ma'am. I don't answer to that Mr. Hooke stuff."

Brenna laughed. "And I'm Brenna. Have you known Rafe long?"

"Long enough, I 'spect. He weren't no more than a green kid when we first hitched up together. But he learned fast, especially for a city boy, and growed up fast, too. We had us some good years riding for the Rangers."

"Oh, of course," she murmured. "I didn't realize."

"You could've knocked me over with a feather when he shows up telling me he's done got hisself married. But now that I see you, ma'am, I'm not surprised. He's a mighty lucky man."

"Thank you, Pete." Brenna flushed. "But I'm not sure Rafe would agree with you. Our courtship was hardly conventional."

"Yes, ma'am, I heard all about it. You're a brave woman, and that's a fact. Rafe was plum put out having to head north again. Right worried about you alone out here, too. 'Pete,' he says, 'you just gotta see about my wife for me.' He picked out sixty prime head in Dallas and asked if I'd get them down here to his place."

"I hope it hasn't inconvenienced you," she said, her voice faint. Rafe concerned about her? It was too much to imagine. Worried that she had run away, perhaps, was more like it. She shook her head. No, it was merely a polite fiction to induce Pete's help. Rafe didn't care two pins for her. He'd proved that the way he'd left her here.

"I was kinda at loose ends, anyway," Pete was saying. "And Rafe thought you might need a foreman, like."

"Well, I have to admit I'd be glad of some help with the men," she admitted with a rueful sigh. "Maybe it's because I'm young, or a woman, but it's like pulling hen's teeth to get them to do what I want."

"Miz Sinclair, you look the kind of lady who could do just about anything you set your mind to. I'd be right proud to help out." Pete grinned and slapped his hat back into place.

"I did get the men to fix the corral," Brenna ventured, a portion of her self-confidence re-emerging under Pete's warm admiration. "We'll get a meal ready for you and your drovers. And there's room in the bunkhouse."

"Thank you kindly, ma'am," Pete said. He touched his hat brim again and climbed upon his horse. "It'll be a real treat for an old cowpoke like me who's only used to beans in his belly and stars over my head."

"You're very welcome." Brenna laughed, liking Pete more and more with each passing minute.

Brenna fed the drovers and cowhands that night on crispy fried rabbit, navy beans flavored with syrup and bacon, a salad of the first tender blades of collards, a pone of corn bread, and deep-dish apple cobbler. The compliments she and Juanita received from the grateful men were highly extravagant and made them blush.

Brenna invited Pete, as her new foreman, to join her at the table inside, and afterward, they dragged the chair and bench out on the front porch to enjoy the evening air. In the twilight, Brenna's initial suspicion melted. Pete was genuine, a soft-spoken Texan with the gift of easy humor and penetrating observation. They soon became fast friends.

This end-of-the-day conversation became the routine as the weeks passed, even when the weather grew colder and they were forced to seek the warmth of the fireplace. They played checkers and talked until fatigue from the day's chores and bouts of irresistible drowsiness drove

Brenna to seek her bed. Some evenings she would read aloud from one of her few treasured books while Pete busily whittled with the little pocketknife he always carried. Sometimes he worked at a stick until it was gone. Other times, the blocks of wood took on fanciful shapes—camels and woodpeckers and Trojan horses. Brenna soon became accustomed to finding the little curls of wood everywhere.

The signs of strain disappeared from Brenna's face as acceptance and a tenuous contentment formed within her. With Pete's help, a new working relationship had developed with the hired men. She wondered how she would have gotten along without Pete's friendship and thoughtfulness. One of the nicest surprises was the milk cow he had brought in with the herd. Now they had milk and Juanita's freshly churned butter, and Brenna frequently could indulge her newly acquired taste for buttermilk. The growing harmony of the ranch lulled her anxieties. Sometimes she almost forgot she awaited word from Sister Therese.

Often while he whittled, Pete told stories about his adventures on the Texan frontier, about a young Rafe, about life as a Ranger. Brenna listened to Pete's tales about his and Rafe's experiences in undisguised fascination. It was hard to see the picture Pete drew with his laconic words of Rafe as an enthusiastic, likable young man, not particularly skilled in woods lore and scouting at first, but growing more adept under Pete's tutelage.

She thought at times that it was like a secret Chinese puzzle. If she could just put the pieces together—all the things Pete told her, all the things she knew firsthand about her husband—then maybe she could begin to understand Rafe Sinclair and gain an inkling into what drove him. Then she would dismiss these musings with an angry shrug. She didn't have to understand Rafe. He and Gould had used her to their ends and discarded her, if Rafe's lack of communication was any indication. And this suited Brenna just fine. All she wanted now was to be left in peace until she could find a way to leave the ranch.

When Sarie Henigan appeared again on a blustery day near the end of November, she brought Brenna a letter, a package, and two laying hens. Brenna found it hard to ignore the letter burning a hole in her apron pocket and engage in charming civilities, but she plied Sarie with hot coffee and Juanita's fried cinnamon cakes and laughed and talked until the other woman took her brood home. Then she shut herself in her bedroom and tore open Sister Therese's letter. What she read with avid eyes made her breath catch.

A wealthy New Orleans family needed a new nurse-governess in January. But did Brenna have a working knowledge of the subjects required? Sister Therese had taken the liberty of sending several texts for Brenna to study. If, on perusal, Brenna thought she could handle the job, then Sister Therese would recommend her.

Brenna hastily unwrapped the bulky package of books, biting her lips and examining each one in turn. Geography, English literature, history—these she knew well. Then she groaned. Advanced mathematics—oh, no! She flipped through the text, gasping at the complex columns of figures. Mathematics had never been her strong point, but if she studied . . . Yes! That was it. She would study diligently and pray she could absorb enough to satisfy the New Orleans family. This was her way out, at last. She would not lose this chance.

Brenna's evenings took on a different character. She sat at the kitchen table or at the new settle Pete had built for her and poured over the books, scratching arithmetic problems on scraps of brown wrapping paper. Guiltily, she told Pete the reason for her industry was merely self-improvement, a long-time goal since her marriage had ended her dreams of attending normal college. Pete found this admirable and encouraged her.

An obliging Sarie Henigan passed by again, and Brenna sent off letters to Maggie and Shannon. Brenna didn't tell Pete about the letter to Sister Therese applying for the position of governess. She hated to deceive Pete. Sometime in the past weeks, she'd found in him a friend, a confidant, and even, in part, a father. He was the one man she knew whose basic integrity and goodness made her feel comfortable with him. She longed to confide in him, to ask his advice, but dared not, knowing that even though they shared a bond of growing affection, he was first Rafe's friend, not hers.

This deception and the anxiety she felt waiting for Sister Therese's reply kept her on edge, and unaccountably nervous. Her appetite waned, and she grew so tense her own body seemed unfamiliar, tender in unexpected places and prone to sudden attacks of tears whenever she pondered her dilemma.

The weather deteriorated into a wet and dismal December and still no word came. Finally, out of frustration, Brenna asked Pete to take her Christmas packages of small, homemade items for her sisters over to Johnston's Crossroads to post. She was crossing the back yard, holding two nest-warm eggs she had to search high and low to find, when Pete returned. She hurried after him into the barn, holding her crocheted shawl around her head as protection against the brisk, clammy wind that pushed the ominous dark clouds across the gray sky.

"Did you get the packages posted all right, Pete?" she asked breathlessly. "Was—was there anything for me?"

Pete's faded blue eyes were solemn as he reached inside his shearling jacket. "Yes, but nothing from Rafe, little gal. I'm sorry."

Brenna nearly laughed, feeling slightly hysterical. Was Pete actually feeling sorry for her because of Rafe's neglect? If he only knew! She tried to force a suitable tone of disappointment into her voice. "Oh. Was—was there anything else?"

"Just these."

Brenna snatched the letters from him, juggling eggs in one hand while she flipped through the letters with the other. Shannon's round childish scrawl, Maggie's more sophisticated hand, and here! Sister Therese's spidery script. In her eagerness, Brenna ripped open the letter and lost her grip on the eggs. They fell to the hard-packed ground, cracking and oozing at her feet. But Brenna concentrated on making sense of the close-set lines. The job was hers! She was to come immediately! She could have wept with elation, and suddenly she felt dizzy, lightheaded.

"Aw, too bad," Pete muttered. "Them eggs broke."

Brenna dragged her attention back to the old grizzled Ranger at her side. "What?"

She glanced down. Dark yellow yolks, thick and sticky,

swirled slowly through viscous, glistening whites, mingling with the matted straw and dirt in a lumpy pool of cracked shell. The warm, yeasty odor assaulted Brenna's nose and she gasped, her stomach heaving. Gorge rose in her throat. She clapped her hand over her mouth and lurched from the barn. She barely made it to the privy in time.

Afterward, she walked to the pump, her legs weak and shaky. She pushed the handle and caught the trickle of icy water in her palm. She rinsed out her sour mouth and patted the moisture to her hot temples.

"You all right?" Pete stood beside her, concern etching deeper lines into his weathered cheeks.

Brenna gave a weak smile. "I must be sickening for something."

Pete snorted. "Hmmph."

"What?" she demanded. She touched the crumpled letters in her skirt pocket, then pulled her shawl around her shoulders, shivering.

"You can lie to me, but don't try to fool yourself. You got that look. You're breeding, for sure."

"No!" she protested. But deep in her heart, the knowledge that she had tried to deny, to wish away, sprang into being. The fatigue, the irritability, the unaccountable cravings, the tenderness of her bosom—there was only one reason for that. And the calendar didn't lie. "No," she whispered frantically, "not now!"

She turned and bolted toward the house, but she couldn't outrun the fact she carried with her.

Brenna looked up from the books open before her on the kitchen table. The soft golden halo of the coal oil lamp made her hair gleam, and her complexion glowed like a peach, giving no hint of her earlier indisposition. Supper was finished, and Juanita had gone to her room. In a gesture of denial, Brenna studied furiously, certain that Pete was mistaken in his assumption. She was not pregnant. She couldn't be!

The back door opened, and Pete came out of the black night, shaking the icy drizzle from his shoulders like a puppy. He carried a small cedar tree set in a bucket. Brenna's expression was startled.

"Figured you'd want a tree, it being so close to Christmas and all," Pete said gruffly. "Might cheer you up."

Brenna's reaction was listless. "Thank you. Put it in the other room. I'll see about some bows and such later, if I feel like it."

Pete chewed his mustache worriedly, went to say something, but thought better of it. He did as she asked, but on his way out, he paused uncertainly beside the table, shifting his weight from foot to foot like a small boy called on to recite. Finally, he reached into his pocket and set a small object on top of her open book. "Here," he said, his voice as rough as gravel. Then he stomped outside.

Brenna stared at the whittled object, and her heart fell. The small carved cradle rocked slightly on its rounded bottom. The indented outline of a tiny form filled the little bed. Angrily, she set it aside, but her eyes wouldn't focus on her book, and she closed it with a snap.

Despair rose in her throat, threatening to choke her. She knew she carried Rafe's child, and the cruelty of the celestial joke pierced her like a knife. She was truly trapped, caught in a vast web with no hope of escape. She couldn't go to Sister Therese now, not in this condition. What family wanted a pregnant governess? Rafe had foiled her plans long before she'd even set them in motion.

As she pulled Sister Therese's letter from her pocket and re-read it, a tear trickled from the corner of her eye. Irritably, she wiped it away, hating herself, hating Rafe, even hating the unborn life that kept her tied to a man who didn't care for her. This ranch wasn't just a home. It was her prison.

She stuck the letter between the pages of the book and shut it with a snap, bitterness like gall in her mouth. Her jerky movements started the miniature cradle rocking again, and she grabbed it, intent on hurling the tiny, accusing toy across the room to vent her rage and frustration. But something stopped her. Maybe it was the warmth of the soft pine against her hand, or maybe it was the love with which Pete had crafted the tiny object. Still, she hesitated.

The sharp, pungent evergreen smell of the cedar tree tickled her nostrils. She traced the outline in the cradle with a trembling fingertip. Maybe Pete hadn't meant this to be just any baby. A wrenching remorse gripped her, contorted her soft mouth with a single sob. How could she hate the life growing within her, now, in this season of all seasons? No matter how, or who, or why, how could she feel anything but love for the life of an innocent, a child as sacred and holy in God's eyes as the Christ child himself?

Reverently, she set the little cradle on top of the stack of closed books. She sat silent for a long moment, then with a little sigh, rose and gathered her sewing things and several washed cotton feed sacks. Within minutes she had snipped out the pieces for a tiny shirt. Her smile was crooked and a bit rueful. She knew that the cloth sacks would come in handy, but this particular use was one that hadn't occurred to her. She held the front of the little garment up to admire, and suddenly her eyes filled with tears. She crushed it to her cheek and sobbed brokenly.

The back door swung open. A tall figure in dripping black oilskins paused in the opening. Brenna gasped, surging to her feet in shock. Rafe's dark, sardonic voice filled the room like the cold wind he brought in behind him.

"Why, Red! Have you been pining for me? Dry your eyes, sweet, your husband has come home to you!"

Chapter 13

Rafe swept off his sopping hat and took two steps forward, catching his wife about the waist and pulling her hard against his streaming wet slicker. Bending his head, he caught her little gasp of surprise with his mouth. He kissed her with an ardor that startled even himself.

God, she tasted wonderful! The rain water on his lips mingled with the salt of her tears, and he drank of her with all the thirsty haste of a desert traveler parched for the cool water of an oasis. Everything—the tense meetings, the fevered re-organization of the Union Pacific, the endless and countless details that ran the Gould empire, even the wretched, soggy ride to the ranch—was worth it for this moment.

He was tired, soaked through, and anxious for Brenna. Trying to deal with Wall Street as Gould's agent had wrung him out. He'd practically had to move heaven and hell both to be able to come here now. Gould hadn't wanted to send him back to California, especially now when things were just beginning to seem normal again after his masterful Union Pacific takeover. But Rafe had been adamant, and he had wrangled the assignment to seek Smitherman out. Gould still had not given up the idea of a southern route, even though he now controlled the northern one, at least to Ogden, but the juggling involved in packaging such a deal was mind-boggling. And there was still the problem of the stolen securities to deal with. They hadn't been recovered, and Rafe had been forced to cover their value out of his private funds.

But all this faded to insignificance as Rafe's fingers tangled in Brenna's shining hair and his tongue stroked and tasted her. All he wanted was to forget everything for the few days he could spare. He hoped Brenna had softened toward him in his absence, hoped her desire for revenge for their forced marriage and every other slight had run its bloodthirsty course. The soft delight of her mouth made him dizzy, and his resolve hardened. No matter what she thought, she was his wife and he would seek his comfort in her bed tonight.

He reached out, cupping the heavy lushness of her breast, staking his claim to her sweet flesh. Feeling her flinch, he frowned. Pulling back slightly, he stared at the moisture slipping from under the spiky dark lashes and wondered at last at the cause of her tears. His hand stayed at her breast, testing and weighing gently, finding her fuller, more womanly than he remembered.

"You're different," he murmured. Realization struck him like the blow of a hard fist to the stomach. "What news, Red? Has time proved the truth of my lie to O'Donnell? Do you carry my child?"

"Only because I have no choice," Brenna muttered, opening her eyes to glare her hatred. She pushed against him. "Let go! You're wetting me!"

Rafe laughed, releasing her. She spun away, wiping her damp cheeks with the bit of rag in her hand. He shrugged out of his oilskins without taking his eyes off her and hung them on the peg by the stove.

"By God, Red, but I've missed your evil tongue!" He chuckled. His eyes narrowed appreciatively on the damp, clinging front of her shirtwaist, and he noticed her skirt showed no signs of bulging yet. A primitive male pride spurred his ego. A child! *His* child, growing within that enticing female form. His loins burned with the memory of her beneath him in that act of creation.

"Well, I've not missed a single part of you!" she spat. "What are you doing here? Has Gould loosed your leash?"

Rafe shook the moisture from his hair, then raked long fingers through it. His voice mocking, he said, "If I didn't know you, I might suspect your delicate condition as the reason for such shrewishness. Unfortunately, it appears to be part of your nature. Let us sincerely hope it's not a quality that can be passed to one's offspring."

"Oh!" She gritted her teeth and her fists clenched.

"And as for what I'm doing here—isn't it a husband's duty to visit his wife?"

"I would as lief you neglected that duty."

"Perhaps I should call it a pleasure," he murmured. He reached for her, but she backed away.

"Leave me be!"

He lifted an eyebrow and folded his arms, stretching the woven wool of his rough shirt. "No need to play the modest maiden with me. The babe will be born despite any display of virtue, so there's no harm in taking what pleasure we can."

"Oh, yes," she said bitterly, "the baby will indeed come in full time, and that I cannot stop, but I will not lie again with you, for I despise you and all you've brought me to! You don't own me, and I won't roll onto my back at your convenience like some whore!"

Rafe frowned, his jaw clenching at her stubbornness, and his desire shriveling at her acid denunciation. "Your country existence hasn't taught you anything, I see," he said, biting off his words. "I thought the simple life might temper your lust for vengeance."

"Never! How could I forget, especially when your seed starts to swell in my belly? The proof of your perfidy will be always before me. So take your pleasure elsewhere, for I swear I'll not submit to you again."

His pride piqued, a deep burning anger flamed in Rafe. "And I swear, madam, that I will not touch a woman who finds my attentions so abhorrent." His voice was cold, expressionless. "But let me remind you that you're still my wife, and as such, under my direction. So curb your tongue."

"Or what? Would you beat your pregnant wife?" she said with a sneer. "What else could you do to me you haven't done already?"

"Do you dare to find out?" His voice was silky, and he felt a grim satisfaction when he saw her shiver. So much for the warm welcome he'd envisioned, he thought bitterly. He turned away, stopping at the table. "What's this? Schoolbooks?"

He missed the flash of panic that crossed her face. She hurried forward. "Give me that!"

He held them out of her reach, reading the titles with a taunting lift of his mustache. "Improving yourself, Red?"

"I—I'm going to teach Mrs. Henigan's children," she improvised, her rounded chin tilted belligerently.

"Sarie and Paul's kids?"

"Yes. We haven't worked it all out yet, so I've been . . . reviewing." She swallowed uneasily.

"Very commendable, I'm sure." He shrugged and dropped the books. "Clear the rest of this trash, will you? Get me something to eat." He hooked the rung of the chair with the toe of his boot, dragged it out, and dropped into it, feeling old and tired.

"That's not trash," Brenna muttered, her mouth twisted into a mutinous line. She snatched at the scraps of fabric. "Your child must have something to wear."

"What?" His hand clamped hard on her wrist, and he pried the garish sprigged cloth from her stiff fingers. "What the hell! You'd clothe my child in sackcloth?" he roared, coming to his feet and shaking the offending bits in her stricken face. "I can provide more than these rags. Dammit, woman, you go too far in your lust for revenge!"

"I was only—"

"God damn you! Are you that perverted? Despise me as you will, but when you punish an innocent child . . ." Livid with anger, Rafe raised his hand.

"Rafe, for God's sake, man! What's the matter with you?" Pete Hooke hurtled through the door and caught Rafe's shoulder in a clamp of iron.

"I'd never hurt my baby!" Brenna sobbed brokenly. "It's nice stuff, soft. . . . It was all I had." She buried her face in her hands and ran out of the kitchen. The bedroom door slammed, but it couldn't drown out the muffled sounds of her weeping.

The red curtain of rage retreated from Rafe's vision. Sanity came slowly, and he shook his head to clear his fury.

"By God, I ought to horsewhip you, boy!" Pete said from between clenched teeth. His hand fell from the younger man's shoulder in disgust.

Rafe passed a hand over his eyes, staggering slightly

under the crashing wave of self-reproach. "I must have misunderstood," he muttered weakly.

"You're damn right! You ain't got no cause to be raising your hand against that little gal. And her with child! You try it again and I'll thrash you good!"

Rafe swallowed harshly. His anger tasted like ashes, but his remorse was an overwhelming bitterness. Why had he done it? He'd known from their first meeting that someone had abused her, and he had witnessed firsthand O'Donnell's brutality. Now he stooped to the same vile tactics, damning himself in Brenna's eyes, naming him no better that her vicious stepfather. He felt a self-disgust that turned his stomach.

"It won't happen again," he vowed quietly.

"Damn right it won't!" Pete snapped. He cocked his head, listening. "Lordy, she's crying hard. She'll make herself sick. Maybe I should send Juanita in to her."

"No," Rafe said heavily. "I'll see to her." His mouth tightened at Pete's skeptical appraisal. "I've a right to apologize to my own wife, haven't I?"

Rafe went softly to the bedroom, carrying a coal oil lamp. Something twisted deep inside him at the sight of the crumpled, weeping woman on the bed. She'd thrown off her damp dress and now wore a faded flannel gown. Her shoulders heaved under the blankets, and Rafe swallowed miserably. He never wanted to reduce her to this. Sitting on the edge of the mattress, he stretched out a tentative hand.

"Brenna?"

"Go away!" Her face was averted, her small fist an ineffectual stopper to the sobs that wrenched her slender form with convulsive shudders.

He set the lamp aside and brushed the tangled, damp tendrils of hair back from her temple, then rubbed his hand down the flannel-covered valley of her spine. "Brenna, I'm sorry."

His touch made her stiffen, and her voice was muffled in the pillow. "Go away and leave me alone."

"Not until we've straightened this out." He listened to her rough hiccups as she struggled for breath, and his own throat thickened. "I made a mistake. I know you wouldn't intentionally hurt the baby, no matter how much you hate me."

"Then why'd you say such hor-horrible things?" she asked, gasping.

His hand hesitated in its up and down path on her backbone. "I'm a damn fool. And I was angry. Stop crying now, please? You'll make yourself ill."

"You're just worried about the baby," she accused, overcome by a fresh series of sobs.

"Not just the baby." He cupped her shoulder and rolled her over on her back so that he could see her features—puffy, streaming, red eyes; blotched cheeks; tremulous, vulnerable mouth. Glancing around the bare room, he saw the small pitcher and bowl in the corner. He rose, dipped his handkerchief in the cool water, and returned to bathe her face.

"You give me plenty to worry about, too, Brenna," he muttered, dabbing at her brow. "I want to take you back to New York with me."

"No!" she cried, shivering. She pushed his hand away and tried to control her erratic breathing. "I don't belong in that world. I'm happy here on the ranch." Her eyes, more green than blue now, told him more than her words. He saw the mistrust, the suspicion, the fear, and he knew he had no one to blame but himself.

"Are you?" He frowned, searching for the words he needed. "I was hoping this separation would prepare you to take your place as my wife. There's so much to tell you. Now that Gould is back in control of the Union Pacific, things are moving fast. You had heard that?" She shook her head blankly. "The old fox swooped down and snapped it out of Adams's hands, just like the old days." He chuckled. "Now he plans to tour the Richmond Terminal System, and there's new talk of a rail empire. I hope to be named the president of the Santa Fe System, should we gain control of that line. I'm too pressed to allow our marriage to continue like this. I want you close, especially now."

"What about what I want?" Her eyes filled with fresh tears. "You brought me here to make a life, and I've done it. I can't leave now, even if I wanted."

He wondered at the strange, bitter twist of her lips. "I can see the work that's been done, but—"

"But you promised," she interrupted, her tone shrill. "You promised to try to make me happy."

Rafe's jaw clenched. Damned stubborn woman! He sighed. "Oh, hell, so I did. I've botched it so far, haven't I?"

The strangled sound she made was half sob, half laugh. He offered her the sodden handkerchief, and she accepted it, her eyes wide in her pale face. Regret was a heavy weight that only increased his fatigue. He was too weary to fight her any longer. He let out a long, resigned breath.

"All right, Red, you win. Move over." He tugged off his boots and reached out to douse the lamp. In the dark, he stripped out of shirt and trousers and lay down beside her. She scrambled away, alarmed. "For God's sake, Brenna," he grumbled. "I said I wouldn't force my attentions on you, and I won't. But that doesn't mean I intend to sleep on the floor while I'm here."

He crossed his arms behind his head and stared at the murky shadows of the rough plank ceiling. He felt Brenna move cautiously, but she was boxed in by the wall on one side and him on the other.

"Does that mean I can stay?" she ventured in a low voice.

"It's what you want, isn't it? At least with Pete here, I'll know you're safe. You've acquired quite a champion in that old man."

"I like Pete."

"That may be the first thing we've ever agreed upon."

"Perhaps not quite the first thing," she quavered softly, her voice ripe with tears.

"Oh, hell, don't start that again." He uncurled an arm, reaching for her, pulling her against him. When she protested, he hushed her. "Relax, Red. It's not the first time we've shared warmth. Just pretend you're back in the lean-to. Now go to sleep. The baby needs a mother who's well and rested."

Rafe closed his eyes and let the tension drain from his tired muscles. After a long while, he felt Brenna give in to an exhausted slumber. He liked the slight weight of her on his arm, the feminine fragrance of her skin and hair close to him. Surprisingly, passion was missing, or at least dampered, and in its place was a surging tenderness and a vast regret for the pain he had caused her.

Why had things between them always been so complicated? They had started out all wrong, with murder, fear, old hatred and new bitterness between them. If only the past could be erased and everything forgotten except the attraction they felt for each other. He desired her with a force that left him drained and hungry, and he could guess by the way she trembled when he touched her that she was not indifferent to him.

A straightforward physical relationship based on pure animal need would simplify matters exceedingly, he thought with a wry twist to his mouth. Except that it was their physical attraction that had brought them to this point in the first place. Now they were truly joined by the life growing in Brenna's womb. Rafe knew firsthand the bitterness of a childhood without loving parents, and he vowed his child would not suffer that same unkind fate.

Rafe moved restlessly, remembering the sweetness of their first joining in this very bed. What magic had possessed them? They had been in complete communion, with no dishonesty between them. Perhaps if he had been more yielding, more concerned with her tender feelings afterward, they might have stood a chance of sustaining that newborn rapport. But at the time, neither of them had wanted that. And now? Now that circumstances and fate had woven their lives into a single destiny? Could he recapture that newborn understanding, smooth the rough edges of this shaky marriage into a partnership, which, if not based in love, still would bring satisfaction and contentment?

He knew one thing: he could not play the eunuch husband for long. Still, he was willing to curb his sexual hunger for a time if it would give Brenna a chance to learn to trust him and depend on him. His arm tightened around her shoulder, and she murmured softly in her sleep. Yes, it would be a sacrifice, but the rewards would be many. Was he not a man who had overcome other, more insurmountable obstacles? But in this, the winning of Brenna, he dared not fail, for now the price was not two people's happiness, but three, and that unborn child deserved everything Rafe could provide.

Rafe left on Christmas Day, after a very subdued and strained holiday dinner. Brenna stood on the porch as he prepared to leave and thanked him dutifully for the lace-trimmed handkerchiefs he had given her, feeling vaguely guilty that she had nothing for him.

"I'll settle for a kiss," he told her, taking her hands in his. "A Christmas kiss to keep me warm all the way to California."

Brenna looked at her husband uncertainly. She couldn't fathom his mood. He'd made no demands, in fact, had almost ignored her during the past few days. He and Pete had discussed the ranch, the cattle, the improvements, but he had addressed only the most necessary comments to her, even though he continued to share her bed. They revolved in elliptical orbits, coming near but never making contact. She looked down at their joined hands and bit her lip.

"Come now, Red. Not scared, are you?" he murmured.

Her chin jerked up. "Of course not!"

He bent, and his voice was husky. "Then kiss me good-bye."

His lips felt warm against hers, and the soft black hair of his mustache heated her cool skin. It was a soft, tender kiss that made no demands of her and was quickly over.

"Take care of yourself, Brenna," Rafe said. "I'll be back from California in about a month."

She watched him ride away, pulling her shawl around her shoulders against the chilly air, and wondering what tactic he plied now. She was beginning to think that Rafe's association with Gould had made him as devious as his employer. His constant chameleon changes kept her off balance, and she knew she must tread warily or she might disappear into a quagmire of intrigue, never to know independence or self-sufficiency again.

"Don't worry about him, Brenna," Pete said, appearing from the direction of the barn. His pale blue eyes followed Rafe's retreating silhouette. "He'll be back."

She shrugged. "It doesn't matter. He doesn't really care about what happens here. I'm no more than a nuisance in his life."

"Tain't so, little gal," Pete said sternly. "You listen to me. He takes his responsibilities seriously. That's the reason he's got to go, 'cause of the work he does. He wants to make a success for you and that baby."

"Success is all he loves. And what a price he pays for it—selling himself to a monster like Jay Gould! He might want a child, but not to love, only to show to the world as another measure of his worth, another asset to total." Brenna shook her head sadly. "I don't think he's capable of loving anyone."

Pete sighed. "You're being too hard on him. There weren't much soft in his life early on, but even a man like Rafe can come to crave it. And as far as that baby goes, why, that's *life* growing in you. Yours and his. You can't tell me a man don't feel *that!*"

"You don't know how things are between us. How can I bring a child into the world when its future is so uncertain?" She turned away abruptly, one hand unconsciously pressed to her abdomen. She noticed Pete's reproving expression, and her heart twisted.

"Don't look at me like that, Pete," she begged, her voice choking. "I'd never do anything to hurt this baby. I couldn't. God sent him to me, and I promise I'll do everything in my power to bear him, to raise him right, and to love him."

"Would that you could do that much for his father," Pete muttered. "You'd be good for him. You've been through a lot together. You must feel something for the man."

"I don't know what I feel," Brenna said. A single crystal tear appeared on her dark lashes, then spilled down her cheek. "I know you love Rafe like a son. I—I wish things could be that simple for me, but Rafe didn't marry me for love any more than I did him. There's so much bad blood between us. And now . . . and now . . ."

Pete patted her shoulder awkwardly. "Hush now, gal. Ain't no use crying. Things have a way of working out for the best."

She took a shaky breath. "I hope so, Pete, I hope so."

* * *

Brenna found that if she took each day as it came, it was easier to get on with her life. The letter to Sister Therese turning down the governess position was the hardest she'd ever had to write, but recriminations and worrying were fruitless endeavors. She would not allow herself to sink into a morass of self-pity. There was too much to be done

True to her impulsive words, she began to teach the Henigan children, traveling the five miles "as the crow flies" over the ridge a couple of days a week when the weather was fine. Brenna confided her condition to Sarie, who offered her service as midwife, but it was hard for Brenna to think that far ahead, especially since she hadn't felt the baby move yet.

She threw herself into the task of teaching the seven little Henigans the basics of reading and writing, and found much pleasure in the bright faces and inquisitive minds. The children were always ready for a story or a game, but were just as diligent in their lessons. As the weeks passed, Brenna was gratified by the progress they made and a little sad that this would likely be the closest thing she would experience to being a real teacher.

Brenna enjoyed these trips to the Henigans' modest spread, riding the dapple-gray mare or sometimes allowing Pete to take her in the wagon the "long way around." She relished the fresh air and exercise and was troubled less and less by morning queasiness as her girth began to increase. The happy socialization at the Henigans' was a sop to loneliness. Pete was a wonderful friend, but there were some things a woman just couldn't talk about to a man, and Juanita was more interested in keeping company with Matt, who, surprisingly, had taken up the role as her suitor.

Often, when the need to be alone with her thoughts became urgent, Brenna went walking, ignoring the January chill and exploring the ridge behind the ranch. It was during one of these walks that she found herself drawn to an old blasted tree near the crest of the ridge directly above the ranch house. In an introspective mood, she ambled toward it, the solitariness of it appealing to her. On reaching the old tree trunk, she was surprised to discover a small, sagging shack set back from it in a clump of bushes.

Curious, she peeked inside, pushing open the rickety door on its old leather hinges. The one-room cabin was constructed of rough planks weathered to a silver-gray. It had a hard-packed dirt floor, two windows covered only by wooden shutters, and a small fireplace. Surprisingly, it was dry inside, and Brenna was glad to get out of the crisp wind for a bit.

She wondered what purpose the building had served— line camp for some cattle outfit, or shelter for a trapper or hunter? Despite its age, the frame was still sturdy. She smiled to herself, pleased by the quiet and the privacy. She felt like a child discovering the perfect hiding place, and after that, she often found herself climbing up to the hut just to sit and think. She didn't question the inner need for a sanctuary.

A package arrived from Rafe containing fancy materials and laces, soft cotton sheeting, yarns and threads, as well as an assortment of small luxuries—scented soap, lump sugar, and copies of *Harper's Bazaar* and recent newspapers. Brenna guessed it was Rafe's way of making amends. The fabrics were fine enough for a baby's wardrobe, and there was enough cloth for dozens of diapers. Brenna soon found most of her free time spent with a needle, constructing the small garments that her son or daughter would need. As her fingers made the tiny stitches and the pile of infant's clothes grew, more often than not she found herself thinking about her child's father, wondering where he was, what he was doing, and most importantly and alarmingly, when he would return.

Although her emotions were still confused when she thought of Rafe, she came to a fatalistic acceptance of her situation, conceding to herself that until her child was born, she could do little or nothing to change her circumstances. It was a time of waiting, of accepting the changes that were taking place within, of seeking an inner peace and serenity that would carry her through the unknown time to come. She was sure she had almost achieved that state—until late February when Rafe returned.

Again, he gave no warning, simply burst back into her life, causing upheaval as he came, this time storming into the kitchen just as she sank into the wooden bathtub for her nightly ritual.

"Have you lost your mind, woman?" he roared, slinging off his hat and slamming the door behind him.

"Rafe!" she gasped. The small wooden tub didn't provide much room, but she drew her knees up and crossed her arms over her bare breasts in an instinctive move that splashed sudsy water onto the planks in front of the stove. Her hair was tied back with a ribbon, and a flood of crimson stained her cheeks.

"My God, Red! What do you mean gallivanting across the country by yourself? I can't believe Pete allowed it. Don't you have the sense God gave a field mouse?" He shrugged out of his heavy wool coat and glared at her, seemingly oblivious to her naked state.

"I—you—" Brenna gulped. She took a deep breath and shouted, "Get out! Can't you see I'm taking a bath?"

Rafe's lips twitched, and one mocking eyebrow lifted. "I can see plenty from here."

"Ohh!" She let fly her soapy washcloth, hitting him squarely in the chest. "Get out!" she shrieked.

He caught the sopping cloth, then leaned over her menacingly, his hands braced on both sides of the tub. "Not until I get an explanation," he growled. "I want to know why the hell my wife rides unescorted and walks unprotected!"

"What difference does it make?" she retorted, her breath spurting with embarrassment and defiance. "It's just to the Henigans', or down to the river or up to the ridge. I like to walk. Now get out of here so I can finish in peace!"

"The difference is that Larosse is still on the loose."

Brenna started, her lips parting and her eyes widening. "Oh."

Rafe's laugh was harsh. "Is that all you can say?"

"No! I say, even so, I won't hole up in this house like some kind of—of prisoner!"

"My God! Don't I have enough trouble without adding a pea-brained wife to the list?" Rafe groaned. He looked at her fiercely, his gray eyes like steel. "Nothing I say will make you stop, will it?"

"No." Her chin firmed stubbornly.

"Damn." He rubbed his jaw, then jabbed his index finger at her nose. "All right, so be it. But the first thing in the morning, I'm teaching you to use a gun. And no arguments!"

Brenna frowned and swallowed, knowing that now was not the time to attempt any sort of negotiations. She'd won this concession from him; she'd agree to his demand. She nodded. "All right."

Rafe relaxed. He came down on one knee beside the tub, and one hand dipped into the warm bath water. "Too bad there's not room enough in that for two," he murmured. "I could stand to wash off the smell of horse."

"Y-you can have it as soon as I get through," she stammered, sinking lower in the water. "If you would just please wait outside . . ."

"The view here is much better." He touched her shoulder, his lips tickling the delicate shell of her ear.

Brenna strained away, clutching her arms over her chest in acute embarrassment. Her heart beat like a frantic butterfly in her throat, and she felt her nipples pucker shamefully. Her reaction to him was totally involuntary, but her uncertainty and doubt cooled her blood faster than his touch inflamed it.

"Don't shy away, Red," Rafe urged gently. "You're my wife."

"But I . . . Oh!" Brenna's eyes rounded and she went utterly still.

"What is it?" Rafe pulled back, puzzled at her wonder-struck face. She slowly looked down at herself and the sudsy water that lapped at the rim of the tub.

"The baby . . . I felt it move." She said it in a whisper, almost as though she listened to some inner voices, and her smile was pure and beautiful.

Rafe caught his breath. He slipped his hand under the water, ignoring his wet cuff, seeking the rounded part of her that carried a part of him. "Let me feel."

She jerked, startled into awareness, half rising from the tub, but his arm around her shoulders and his palm on the swell of her abdomen held her steady. "Rafe, stop!"

"Shh, Red. Ah, there! Was that it?"

"Y-yes." She couldn't tear her eyes away from his face, so strong, yet in that moment so vulnerable.

"My God. A miracle." His voice shook and his eyes glowed. He measured her flushed face, the white rounded globes of her breasts peeking above the water. "A beautiful miracle."

"Rafe . . ."

"Brenna, lovely, Brenna," he murmured. "The child accepts me. When will you?"

"I—" She couldn't speak.

"Never mind, sweetheart." He rose, a rueful smile curving his carved lips. "Finish your bath. But the child knows his sire, and sooner or later, you will, too."

Chapter 14

If all the world were a stage, then as spring advanced on the Texas countryside, Rafe entered and exited Brenna's life with the unpredictability of Puck himself. His visits lasted as long as a few days, as little as a few hours, and Brenna had cause to think hers was by far the strangest marriage on the face of the earth.

True to his word, he made no move to renew their physical relationship, even though they shared the same bed. Little by little, Brenna realized that he could be trusted to keep his promise, at least in this. It did not mean, however, that he ignored her. Rather, it seemed that he found excuses to touch her. When she passed a dish at supper, his fingers met hers. When he helped her mount her mare, his hands lingered a moment too long at her waist. When she sat sewing, sometimes he'd drop an absent-minded kiss on the nape of her bent neck. In the dark of night, his lean body curled against hers. She had not known how warm and comforting the simple act of touching could be. She discovered she missed him when he left and found herself looking forward to his next visit. It was all very unsettling.

Rafe made a real effort to find common ground between them, and she was surprised at the range of topics he discussed with her. He forced her to learn to shoot a pistol, though she loathed it. Once she pointed out acidly that if she had been able to use a gun last fall, she might have shot him, thinking he was Larosse. He just grinned and insisted that he trusted her with a gun more than a rock.

Pete oversaw the everyday chores on the ranch, but he

deferred to Rafe's suggestions. Brenna was a bit envious of their easy relationship. She and Pete kept their initial closeness, and as her girth rapidly enlarged and she was forced to abandon her shirtwaists and skirts for the flowing and waistless "wrapper" or "Mother Hubbard," he was as overprotective of her as a mother hen. She gave up riding the mare and settled for a once-a-week journey via wagon to the Henigans' place, but she continued her long walks, enjoying the bursting forth of spring and her own robust good health. Her twenty-first birthday came and went with little fanfare, and she reflected on the changes a year had made in her life and wondered what the next year would bring.

She directed the establishing of a large vegetable garden, laughing at the men's grumblings that they weren't "sodbusters." She reminded them that they, too, would enjoy the peas, corn, tomatoes, and squash when it came time to harvest.

But all this activity was merely a way of filling time between Rafe's visits. She never felt more alive than when he was near, and her confused emotions kept her in a continual state of bewilderment, trying to understand her husband and herself. As the weather warmed, Rafe's preoccupation with his work grew apparent. She wondered what made him frown so when he poured over the stacks of papers he sometimes brought to the ranch in a carpetbag.

She watched him one evening working at one end of the kitchen table. Pete had beaten her soundly at checkers at the other end, and now made his good-nights, chiding her in his gentle way for her "wool gathering."

"I'll give you a better game next time," Brenna promised with a smile. She picked up her sewing basket. "I'm a little tired, I guess."

"Best be gettin' to bed early, then," Pete advised. "'Night, Rafe."

"See you in the morning, partner." Rafe set down a sheaf of papers and waited until Pete was gone. His gaze swung over to Brenna, sitting primly at the table in a blue-figured calico wrapper, its voluminous folds falling from a front yoke to effectively hide her rounded figure. She still appeared graceful and dainty, and now her bright hair hung down her back, making her seem remarkably girlish and appealing. Her fingers flew as she hemmed a square of cotton, another diaper to add to the growing stack. He'd seen her count that stack again and again, and smiled to himself. When would she think she had enough?

"Are you feeling all right?" he asked.

She glanced up and gave a little smile. "Of course. I'm disgustingly healthy. I'm continually hungry, and I'm getting as fat as an old sow."

He frowned, struck by a sudden thought. "Is the baby too big? Will you have trouble, I mean?"

She laughed. "Why should I? And as far as the baby's size goes, that can't be helped. After all, his father is a big man."

"Yes, but . . ." A flicker of doubt crossed his face.

"There's nothing to worry about, Rafe," she said gently, touched at his intimate concern. She changed the subject. "What have you been working on so hard tonight?"

He sat back in his chair and stretched, hands over head, a bit surprised. It was the first time she had ever asked about his work. "Had to go over these pledges. Since Gould recovered the Union Pacific, seems we're always scraping about to cover the road's obligations." He shrugged. "But he wants to hold on to it this time, no matter what the cost, and I have to give the old fox credit, he seems to come up with the money, sometimes right out of thin air."

"Sound suspicious, if you ask me," she said with a sniff.

Rafe barked with laughter. "But, then, you're not exactly an impartial observer, are you, Red?"

"What about the Santa Fe? Didn't he promise you that presidency?"

"Nothing's come of it," he replied shortly. He stroked his chin, pondering.

Talk of empire had receded, and now Gould was back on tour again, this time out west to the Iron Mountain, Missouri Pacific, and Union Pacific. Dr. Munn assured him it was a salubrious environment, and Gould almost always regained much of his old energy after such a trip. He had always been frail, and in recent years physical weakness had become more evident, especially after the death of his wife. Still, the old fox had many good years left, and his enemies would need to take care. Rafe shrugged away these musings, his glance returning to Brenna.

"I may try to acquire main interest in the Santa Fe myself," he admitted. "That would give me a strong bargaining position should Gould's plans for the Southern Pacific materialize."

"And Mr. Plummer's murderer still hasn't been brought to justice?"

"We have Pinkerton agents at work on it. The Texas authorities have no leads."

Brenna dropped her hands to her lap and shuddered. "It frightens me to think Larosse is still free."

"Don't fret. We'll get the bastard, sooner or later," he said gruffly. He placed a hand on the pile of papers. "By the way, you'll be happy to know that I'm being sent to meet with representatives of your old friends, the Knights."

"What? Why? I thought Mr. Gould refused to deal with them. After all he's done to the workers, what new indignities does he plan to heap on them?"

Rafe sighed. "Don't get your feathers ruffled, Red. I know things aren't good for the common laborer."

"You do?" She lifted her eyebrows in mock surprise. "Will wonders never cease!"

"There's nothing wrong with making conditions better, or raising wages, either, but unless a railroad is making a profit, none of that can happen. So when the Knights cripple the road with a strike, everybody suffers."

"But how else can they let their grievances be known?"

"By meetings like the one I'm going to. You have to face it. After the violence and the long T & P strike over four years ago, public sentiment is running high against the labor unions. Powderly and his crew cut their own throats. It will take a lot of hard work and time before unions are accepted by big business as a viable channel of communication between labor and industry. I wish there was an easy answer, but at least we're trying."

"Yes," Brenna said slowly, with new understanding.

Rafe's sympathy for the laborer was more magnanimous than she expected. Perhaps there was hope for the future if men like him could approach the problems of labor and management fairly. She nodded. "At least there's that."

Thoughtfully, she picked up her sewing and took a few stitches, her mind filled with memories of Sean. If only he had been willing to listen to such reasoning, and not have gotten caught up in the hot blood and fever of the strike. For the first time, she realized that Sean had not been totally innocent. Choosing to throw his lot in with men who advocated violence had been his decision, and although she deeply grieved over his death, she could not wholly blame it on someone else. Not even the peace officers who were trying to do their duty. She hesitated, biting her lip. Could she admit that to Rafe? Would he understand her change of heart?

She raised her eyes and found Rafe's gaze steady upon her, but his expression was far away, distracted. The silver light in his eyes seemed to burn right through her, and she shivered apprehensively.

"Why do you look at me so strangely?" she asked in a whisper, hardly knowing the words slipped out.

Rafe blinked, passed his hand over his eyes and looked away. "You remind me of someone."

"Edith?" She pressed fingers to her mouth in astonishment over her own temerity.

Rafe scowled blackly. "How do you know about her?"

"You called me by that name once, that awful night on the railcar." She gulped. "I'm sorry, I didn't—"

"It's a name that doesn't mean anything anymore, at least not to me." His tone was unaccountably sharp and, as if recognizing that, he modulated his voice. "Edith Kingdon Gould. I introduced her to Jay's son, George."

"Oh. Am I like her?" Brenna's voice trembled. She watched Rafe rise and move to her side. He caught her chin between his thumb and forefinger, lifting her face and staring down into her troubled countenance.

"Your chin. I've always thought you had the same stubborn chin. Maybe the shape of your eyes is similar, too. But she's dark and you are fair—exceedingly fair." He studied her intently. "No, you're not at all alike."

He knew that it was true. Where Edith had been false,

Brenna was constant. Whatever their disagreements, she did not deceive him, but gave him the truth of her feelings in a frank and candid manner. She was not grasping and acquisitive. Indeed, she had hardly asked for anything for herself, yet had made the modest ranch house a warm and cozy home and brought the first blush of returning prosperity back to the place. There was a basic goodness to her nature, spiced with a redhead's temper. When she cared about something, it was passionately, with all the loyalty and devotion a man could want.

And selfishly, Rafe knew he wanted those things from her. Had her attitude toward him softened? Were his tactics beginning to work? He smiled to himself and let his thumb glide across the tender underside of her jaw. He sensed with growing satisfaction the soft tremors that claimed her at his touch. Perhaps it was time to press his cause.

"Why did you want to know?" he asked mildly.

Brenna flushed, but his fingers held her chin firmly, and she could not pull away. Her limpid blue-green gaze was direct, though her words faltered. "I—I thought perhaps . . . she was important to you."

"At one time. But she made other choices." He shrugged. "She was an actress."

And now she's a millionaire's wife, Brenna thought, sensing almost instinctively a certain vulnerability, a point of weakness in Rafe's emotional armor. So this was another woman who had hurt him. Brenna was surprised at a sudden stab of anger toward the unknown Edith, and astonished by a surge of pure jealousy. What a fool this Edith must have been, to turn her back on a man like Rafe for mere money!

"My father was an actor," she blurted out to cover her discomfiture.

Rafe grinned and let her go. "Shakespeare, wasn't it?"

"Y-yes. How did you know?"

He patted his waistcoat, removed a thin cheroot, then rattled the stove lid and lit it on a glowing coal. The blue, aromatic smoke curled around his dark head. "You gave quite a performance the night you were delirious."

"I did?" she asked, aghast.

"Ophelia, as I recall. It was quite chilling, considering the state you were in."

"Oh. Well, I've known all the parts since I was small." She smiled and a soft laugh escaped her. "Being an actress must be marvelous. Annie and I even talked about joining a touring company, although I've never seen any of the plays on stage."

He puffed thoughtfully. "We'll have to rectify that when we get to New York."

She didn't know what to say to that, so she hastily reapplied her attention to her stitching.

"You never saw your father perform?" he asked.

"No. It was before I was born, back in Ireland before he decided to emigrate. But whenever he was in his cups, and that was most of the time, he liked to quote the great roles."

"An interesting life."

"It made it hard," she murmured, the corners of her shapely mouth turning down. "Da was always dreaming while his children went to bed hungry." She shook her head and was quiet. The coals shifted in the stove, but otherwise silence reigned in the kitchen.

Rafe rolled the ash off his cigar, and his jaw tightened. So, she had a weakling for a father, a drunkard who failed to provide for his family. Just another reason for her antipathy to men in general. Add an abusive stepfather, and no wonder she had been adamant in her decision never to marry. Top it with a husband who bullied her into a marriage she didn't want, and gave her a child to boot, and you had a woman with more reason than most to be bitter. He quashed a sudden sense of guilty remorse. The deed was done, and they'd both better learn to make the best of it. He tossed the butt of the cigar into the stove's grate.

"Why don't you leave that for tonight?" he asked. He came up behind her and rested both hands along the curve of her neck, gently massaging the tightness he found there.

"I'm nearly finished."

He tangled his fingers in her loose curls, inhaling the flowery scent of her soap and admiring the coppery tresses. "Glorious," he muttered. "Even the Bard would be hard pressed to laud your fairness, bright angel."

She looked over her shoulder at him, her lips parted in astonishment. She knew he was educated, but his literary allusion was a pleasant surprise. He pushed aside a heavy lock and kissed the tender hollow behind her ear.

"What say thou, Juliet? Will you take a husband to your bed?"

A sensual shiver tripped down her nerve endings, and she gave a little gasp. "Rafe, please . . ."

He drew her to her feet, catching her face between his hard palms and feathering light kisses across her cheekbones, her eyelids, her mouth. "It's been so long, Brenna. And I've been far more patient than Romeo."

"But we're as star-crossed as those lovers," she replied unhappily, catching his strong wrists with her hands, feeling the crisp sprinkling of dark hairs with her fingertips. "I—I'm just beginning to think I know you. Don't spoil that now."

"Soon you'll be too far along to risk loving. Will you use that excuse the next time?"

"I have no excuse, only your promise."

He dropped his hands to her shoulders and sighed, a long, ragged breath that hinted at the depths of his self-control. "I've stewed in my juices long enough to deeply regret that promise," he said huskily, with a hint of self-derisive laughter. "I've made my own purgatory, so I'll do my penance without complaining, Red. Kiss me, angel, then go to bed."

Without quite knowing why, Brenna smiled. He requested where he could have taken by right of law and God. Again he let her make the choice. He charmed her, and charmed, she began to trust. And trusting, she relaxed and let a flirtatious impulse she scarcely recognized guide her actions.

Lifting up on tiptoes, she pressed her lips to his, boldly brushing back and forth to enjoy the velvety texture of his mustache, tasting his smoky mouth. "A most honorable husband," she murmured before pulling back.

"Begone, wench, before I change my mind," he growled, running his hand down over her burgeoning stomach.

"I merely protect you from yourself," she teased, dancing away. "Should you see my swollen form without benefit of concealing garb, your passion would surely wane. I would spare you such embarrassment."

"You count your charms too lightly, angel." Rafe crossed his arms and eyed her thoroughly, a rakish grin slanting his mouth and creasing his tanned cheek. "And if you want me to prove it, simply continue this argument!"

"I am not so reckless." She laughed. "Good night, Rafe."

She lay on the edge of sleep for a long time, wondering if Rafe delayed joining her in an effort to cool his ardor. Knowing he desired her despite her misshapen bulk made a warmth grow within her, a tingling of physical awareness and emotional yearning. The development of their relationship encouraged her and sent shivers of hope through her bloodstream. Perhaps he might learn to care for her, as well as desire her. And what of herself? When had the lust for revenge faded, the hatred she nurtured withered and died? No longer did these things seem so important.

They said having a baby made a woman turn inward, she mused, and she supposed it was true. Now what mattered was the child, and the child's father. Every mother wanted a happy family, and Brenna found that she was no different. She examined her heart and found the hard core of it softening, forgiveness swelling within, and the small bud of affection she'd once thought dead now quickened with life even as her own body quickened. Was she falling in love with Rafe? The notion made her blood race, but caution was too ingrained for her to embrace it wholeheartedly. Besides, love could not be rushed.

She was vaguely aware when Rafe came to bed. She smiled as his lips touched her forehead and his low words seeped quietly into her dreams.

"Sleep well, angel. I'm glad at least one of us can."

Frustration was a continual state for Rafe after that. Desire for his beautiful wife warred with irritation at the state of their marriage, and the stress of constant traveling on Gould's behalf left him weary and snappish. A warm

April steamed into a torrid May, and by June the entire South was caught in a heat wave that foretold an unbearable summer.

Staring out the window of his second-story room in the Cattleman's Hotel and down on the busy evening traffic of Dallas, Texas, Rafe wondered how Brenna was bearing up under the heat now that the end of her term was drawing near. He discarded his black sack coat and rolled up the cuffs of his sweat-soaked shirt. Though the sun had set an hour earlier, beads of moisture still trickled under his armpits, and the evening air hung hot and thick with dust.

He frowned. There'd been blue circles of fatigue under Brenna's eyes during his last visit. Despite her protests of good health, he felt it was time to get her to a proper doctor. She was too isolated out there for him to remain complacent any longer. And hadn't he felt her attitude softening toward him at last? Patience on his part would have its rewards, he had no doubt.

His self-imposed chastity rubbed raw at times, but he couldn't bring himself to make use of the local ladies of the evening, not when all he could think of was a strawberry-haired witch whose sorcery held him spellbound. Gould had other lieutenants who could act as his western emissary, and Rafe had neglected his own interests in New York long enough. As soon as he cleared away the last details in Dallas, then he was going back to the ranch to insist they go north together, as was proper. This time, he'd stand for none of her arguments!

He dumped the last inch of tepid water from the cutglass carafe into a matching tumbler and splashed a finger of bourbon in with it. He sipped it slowly, grimacing as the sharp flavor set his teeth on edge. A soft knock sounded at the door.

"Come in," Rafe said. He recognized his visitor and lifted his drink in mocking salute. "Rossini."

Giovanni Rossini removed the sedate beaver from his silver-streaked head and closed the door behind him. He carried a silver-headed ebony cane, and his dress, as always, was impeccably correct, shirt spotless, tie knotted in the latest style, trousers sharply creased.

"Good evening, Rafe." Though Rossini's voice was

melodious with the remnants of his Italian accent, he was brisk and all business. "May I have your report on the labor negotiations? Mr. Gould was quite explicit that I bring him the latest information when I return to New York."

"Tell him—hell, there's nothing new to tell." Rafe drained his glass and glared at the older man irritably. "I've never been involved with a group of more stubborn, thick-headed, half-wits!"

"Then there is no progress to report?"

"What do you think?" Rafe growled. He slammed the empty glass down on the dresser.

He'd never liked Rossini, he thought. The damned supercilious nit-picker! Maybe it was because he had been the one in direct authority over Rafe's education and had supervised his apprenticeship in the Gould organization when Rafe grew older. Maybe the resentment was natural, like a colt chafing under a bit, Rafe mused. Although they had worked as equals for some years now, it was with a certain wariness and a bit of rivalry as Rafe's influence with Gould began to supersede Rossini's. At times, Rafe was acutely irritated by Rossini's continental formality, and at other times, the Italian condemned Rafe's aggressive and, to his way of thinking, impulsive actions. They weren't friends but, rather, a balance of business philosophies finely tuned by Gould's hand to serve him well. To that end, they could tolerate each other—barely.

"Mr. Gould will not be pleased," Rossini said now. He loosened the button on his coat and gingerly sat down on the edge of a straight chair. Removing a linen handkerchief from his pocket, he blotted his face.

"Dammit, Giovanni, just tell him I'm doing the best I can!" Rafe exploded. He took a deep breath, and his mouth twisted ruefully. "Sorry," he muttered shortly. "Must be this damn heat."

"It is rather, ah, debilitating," the older man admitted.

Rafe looked at him curiously, noting the tired lines radiating from the Italian's dark, melancholy eyes. Why had Rafe never noticed that hint of sadness behind those liquid orbs? Maybe because he'd been too wrapped up in his own survival, his own ambition, to give Giovanni

Rossini, the man, more than cursory notice. This reflection made him temper his answer.

"Look," Rafe said, "just tell Mr. Gould that the Knights are making overtures. That's something. And by the way, I finally met with Smitherman. It will take a lot to capture the Southern Pacific away from Huntington, although I have a feeling Smitherman might throw in with us if the price were right."

"Ah." Rossini nodded. "Even with the absent securities?"

"I made those good, didn't I? And at quite a cost to myself, I might add. It ties my hands in a number of ways, and it's damned awkward, especially now that I'm trying to make a raid on Santa Fe stock."

"Any success?"

"Not much." Rafe rubbed the stubble on his jaw. "You're going to think I'm losing my touch, Giovanni, but every move I make is being countered by one faction or another."

"Much as our move toward the Southern Pacific," Giovanni replied softly. He folded his hands on the top of his cane and leaned forward expectantly. "So? What do your instincts tell you?"

"Instincts?" Rafe snorted. "Hell, my nose tells me there's something rotten in all this. Almost as if there was a conspiracy at work. . . ." He trailed off, looking hard at the other man.

"I am forced to agree."

"I can deal with the vagaries of the market, but if someone's making a deliberate effort to ruin us, then I want to know who," Rafe said. "What do we tell Mr. Gould?"

"What, indeed? We have no hard evidence and he is not well, as you know."

"Then I guess it's up to us," Rafe said reluctantly. "We'll have to sniff around ourselves and see what we can turn up."

"A prudent plan. With facts in hand, then we can go to Mr. Gould."

"I'll turn the Pinkertons loose on it."

"That reminds me," Giovanni said. He removed a single folded page from his breast pocket and handed it to Rafe. "As you know, our agents were able to trail the killer, Larosse, as far as New York. He seems to have been there sometime this past January, but then dropped out of sight."

"Yes, I know," Rafe said impatiently. He glanced again at the name written on the paper. "Who is this Sully Heinz?"

"According to our sources, you'll find him at a certain saloon near the cattle pens, and for a price, he says he can tell you where Larosse is."

"What?" Rafe looked again at the name, and a slow grin split his face. "Well, well." He clapped the older man on the back. "Giovanni, I can tell it's going to be a pleasure working with you. Now, what would you like to drink?"

Edgar Larosse pulled his dusty hat lower over his forehead and sank deeper into the shadows of the dark office building across the street from the Cattleman's Hotel. He tugged his steel railroad watch out of the slit in his soiled waistcoat, grunted, then lobbed it back into place. Looking up, he could see the lights burning in several windows of the hotel, and he mentally retraced his earlier steps, the striped carpet, the long deserted hall, the door with its flimsy lock. His one good eye focused on the glowing window he knew to be Rafe Sinclair's.

Damn Sinclair's hide! he thought viciously. Hounding a man, setting his old buddies—the Pinkertons themselves—on his tail, never giving a man a minute's peace! Spreading all his money around, buying his information, bribing a man's friends. Even Sully. Good ole Sully.

Larosse fingered the long, thin, evil shaft of the knife inside his coat. His yellow teeth shone briefly in the gaslight. Yeah, Sully had blabbed, but Sully wouldn't talk anymore, not now, not ever.

But that damn Sinclair was getting too close. Larosse remembered what the old fox had said, that day in that fancy garden house, when the man had taken Larosse in for the first time.

"Under no circumstances must our connection become

known. Is that clear, Mr. Larosse? There's too much at
stake.''

"Yes, sir," Larosse had said, staring deferentially at
the tidy hands that idly stroked an exotic blossom with
creamy petals and a blood-red heart.

"Take any precautions necessary, but know that if you
fail, it will be *you* who pays.''

Larosse shivered even now at the scaly menace in that
soft threat, and he knew he wasn't taking any chances.
That's why he stood and watched that window and from
time to time glanced at his pocket watch. Yeah, he'd
learned a lot from the Pinkertons, and one rule of thumb
was that a man didn't have to be on the scene to do
murder.

At exactly 9:21 P.M., the window he watched
exploded. Flames and broken glass spewed out into the
street. Larosse didn't flinch, not even when the screams
began. He lit a cigar and sauntered with great unconcern
down the board walkway, moving against the flow of the
frantic and panicky crowd. For the first time in months,
Edgar Larosse felt like a free man, and he didn't care who
saw him.

Chapter 15

"The Lord was watchin' after you, mister." The chambermaid dabbed at the cut on Rafe's cheekbone with a towel. "Just think, if you and that Italian feller hadn't decided to step out for a drink . . ."

"Yeah. Thanks," Rafe said, accepting the towel. The maid smiled and moved on to another dazed victim.

Volunteer firemen swarmed around them. Bewildered guests milled about in the littered street. Haggard hotel personnel shouted and tried to restore order out of the chaos. Unbelievably, no one had been killed, and only a handful of people had injuries. The outcome would have been vastly different if Rafe and Giovanni had been inside that room when the bomb went off.

Rafe turned to his companion. "Are you all right, Giovanni?"

The silver-haired man sat beside Rafe on the curb in front of the Cattleman's Hotel. His shirt was splattered and his tie was askew, but he nodded sedately. "No more than a few bruises, thanks to you, my young friend. I was spared because you took the brunt of that explosion."

"We were both lucky," Rafe answered grimly. He flexed sore shoulders, but knew he'd suffer no lasting damage from the explosion that had flung him over Rossini as they'd walked down the hotel corridor. What concerned him more was who had planted the explosive, and why?

"I guess you can go now, Sinclair," Marshal Otis Terry said. A balding, thick-set officer of the law, he was an oasis of calm, far from pleased at the disruption of law and order in his town tonight. His wild-eyed deputy fairly hopped at his side.

"Ain't never seen nuthin' like it, Marshal!" the deputy exclaimed. "All hell breakin' loose, and that one-eyed man, walking the other way like he was out for a Sunday stroll without a care in the world!"

"It ain't against the law to take a walk, Collis," the marshal growled. "So shut up."

"Wait a minute." Rafe tossed down the towel and stood up. "Did you say a one-eyed man? Wears a patch and a long mustache?"

"Yeah, that's the one. You know him?"

Rafe glanced at Rossini. "Larosse."

Giovanni struggled to his feet, looked around vaguely for his hat, then realized it was gone. Tightening his grip on the cane he'd managed to hold on to throughout everything, he nodded at Rafe's conclusion. "That may be your man, Marshal."

Rafe gave the marshal a terse explanation, including everything he knew about Edgar Larosse. His anger built with each word.

"We'll get him," Marshal Terry promised. "In the meantime, maybe you ought to lay low awhile, Sinclair, in case it was somebody else besides this Larosse that was after you."

"My sentiments exactly," Giovanni said.

"Maybe I wasn't the only target," Rafe replied. He gave Giovanni a meaningful look. "Being associates of Mr. Gould has always had its dangers."

"Awful lot of crackpots in this world," the marshal agreed.

"This is no ordinary madman," Giovanni said. His hand closed over Rafe's arm. "His failure here will only infuriate him further. Rafe, your wife . . ."

"God, you're right!" Rafe swallowed harshly as Giovanni's warning struck home. He'd never questioned his own courage, but the thought of Brenna helpless against that killer terrified him. He had to get to her!

"Take no chances, son," Giovanni advised.

Rafe's expression hardened with an implacable ferocity. "That's a promise."

* * *

Two days later, Rafe urged his mount through the tall grass toward the banks of the little river near the ranch. The sun blazed down on him, and the air was hot and breathless. Pete had been surprised to see Rafe galloping in, and more astonished still at his abrupt demand to know where Brenna was. She'd gone walking, he'd been told—something about gathering cattails at the river—but Rafe hadn't stayed to listen to the rest.

Damn her saucy hide! She was alone, unprotected, and heavily pregnant. What the hell was that woman thinking about? Rafe raged inwardly. His jaw clenched furiously and the weight of the Colt on his leg was reassuring.

He caught a flash of blue calico out of the corner of his eye and nudged the horse forward. The garment hung neatly over a sapling growing near the water's edge, with shoes and stockings in a pile beneath. He dismounted and ground-tied the horse, tugging the soft calico wrapper from the branch. His boots made deep prints in the soggy ground as he followed the sounds of splashing and a woman's soft humming.

Brenna stood thigh-deep in the green water with her back to him. Her thin chemise and drawers were wet and translucent, and Rafe sucked in a silent breath at the sudden throbbing of his loins. From this angle, she was still as slender and curvaceous as when he'd first seen her, and his mind instantly conjured up the memory of that time at another river when he'd held her cool, wet body so close against his own. She squatted, turning slightly, and he saw the rounded shape of her belly. He was suddenly blazingly angry—angry at his burning response; angrier at her foolhardiness for placing herself in such a vulnerable, compromising position; and angriest of all because he couldn't take advantage of it.

"Madam, I did not bargain for a shameless wife."

Brenna gasped, her arms crossing over her breasts. "Oh! Oh, Rafe!" In her surprise, she sat down completely in the water. Her face turned crimson.

"You take too great a risk with *my* child!" he shouted. "Anything could happen out here. What if someone other than your husband found you?"

"It's the heat," she offered weakly, chagrined. "I've grown so big and—"

"Enough of your excuses, woman! Come out, right now!"

"Turn your back."

"What!" His laugh was incredulous.

"And leave my clothes on the tree," she ordered.

"Don't be ridiculous! Come here!"

"Please, Rafe!"

He ground his teeth and threw her dress over his shoulder. "All right, Red, since you can't act sensibly, I'll just take this with me and you can make your way back to the house in your altogethers."

"You wouldn't!"

He turned and stamped off, his mustache twitching at her shriek. There was a violent splashing behind him.

"All right! I'm coming!"

He turned, his fist hitched to his hip, and couldn't repress a grin at her furious, red-faced expression. The grin slipped at her awkward, heavy progress, the full volume of her distended womb and rounded, blue-veined breasts visible through the wet lawn chemise. He caught her arm to steady her as she picked her way carefully through the mud, and he realized she could scarcely see her own feet, so great was her burden.

"Give me that," she said, reaching for her wrapper.

Ignoring her incensed face, he forestalled her hand, making a leisurely examination of her swollen form. This was the results of their pleasure, and the knowledge made his anger evaporate and left him strangely sobered.

"Don't look at me," she muttered resentfully. "I can't help being big and ugly and—"

"You talk too much, Red," Rafe interrupted. "If the changes I find weigh on you, know that I accept my part in them and still find you beautiful." He bent and kissed her softly on her cool, damp mouth.

"Oh." She blinked, her lips parted in amazement.

"Besides," he added wickedly, tugging on a strand of red-gold hair that tumbled from her topknot, "not everything has changed."

"What?"

"My favorite freckle remains the same." He swiftly ducked his head, and his lips and tongue found and worshiped the star-shaped freckle on the swell of her breast. He heard her surprised sigh and felt her fingertips caress the nape of his neck. Her voluntary touch pleased him. He straightened to kiss her again lightly and urged her up the bank. "Come, we must get back."

"Why? What's happened?"

"Nothing." Rafe lifted the wrapper and dropped it over her head, then helped with her shoes and stockings. He decided to make no mention of the attempt on his life. Brenna had enough to worry about.

"Then why are you here?" she asked.

"I've come to take you back with me," Rafe said shortly. He lifted his wife and set her on the back of the horse before she could protest. "And none of your sass, either, Red. I want you close to a doctor. You're coming with me this time, and no arguments."

"But Rafe, I can't go! The garden is coming in. Who'll harvest and put up for the winter? And Mrs. Henigan is a good midwife. Why, she's got seven children herself. I had to stop visiting for lessons because the ride is too tiring, but I promised to start up again after the baby's born, and—"

"Juanita and Pete and the boys can take care of everything here. There's no use arguing about this, Brenna. My mind is made up." Rafe walked the horse back toward the house.

"But . . ."

"I expect you're nervous about the birth. Would you feel better if Annie were with you?"

"Well, yes, but how . . . ?"

"We'll hire her to come with us to New York. I'll bet she'll jump at the chance. You won't feel alone then."

"I—I'd like to have Annie," she ventured. Her head was spinning.

"Good. That's settled, then. I'll have Juanita start packing for you as soon as we get back. We'll take the trip in easy stages, and I'll get us a sleeping car for most of the way."

"You won't have to come back to Texas, or go to California again?" Brenna asked.

"No, not for a while." His lips thinned. "There are—circumstances—that warrant my attention in New York. And, of course, I'll stay until the baby comes."

"Rafe, are you sure . . ." An apprehensive frown creased her brow and she bit her lip.

"Trust me, Brenna. It's past time we were together as a family." Rafe covered her hands on the pommel with one of his and squeezed encouragingly. He wanted her to feel his strength, to sense his unspoken promise to protect her, and to lose that frightened light in her green eyes.

Brenna looked down at their joined hands and felt courage and a caring warmth flow from his skin into hers. She'd known their relationship couldn't remain in limbo forever. Slowly she nodded.

"Yes, Rafe, I'll trust you."

There wasn't very much to pack. Juanita helped wash Brenna's few things and heated the flat irons to press her traveling clothes. Rafe decreed an early start the next morning, so Brenna pulled out the tub and took a cool bath and washed her hair. Rafe kept tactfully out of the house and, while she rinsed her hair, she heard the steady thud of an ax as he worked at the woodpile.

Refreshed and dressed in a clean wrapper, Brenna checked the bubbling stew pot on the stove, then went to call her husband in and offer him the use of the tub before supper. She was unprepared for the sight of Rafe, shirtless, his bronzed muscles glistening with sweat and rippling as he swung the ax to split a chunk of stove wood. His medallion glistened in the dark nest of curling chest hair, winking in the late afternoon sunshine. Brenna stammered her offer, then quickly withdrew, unnerved and surprised by the involuntary spark of attraction she felt even in her advanced state of pregnancy.

When he came inside to make use of the tub, she retreated to the bedroom, chiding herself for her awareness of his male physical perfection. The baby kicked, as if to remind her that she would be a mother within a few weeks and to demand more decorum. She smiled to herself and rubbed her distended stomach to ease the tension she felt gathering there, then set her carefully stitched infant's gowns and the stack of neatly hemmed diapers in her old valise. Her own things she placed in a small wooden box Pete had built her. She heard Rafe dragging the tub across the kitchen floor to dump it out at the back door and breathed a sigh of relief. She added her stack of schoolbooks to the top of the box, then carefully lifted it and carried it out to the kitchen.

"What the hell!" Rafe yelped, grabbing the loaded box. Books slid off the top and hit the floor, along with Brenna's trinkets and a ruffled petticoat she could no longer wear. He set the box on the table and glared at her. "Don't you have a grain of sense? You shouldn't be carrying anything this heavy."

"It wasn't heavy. Now look what you made me do," she complained, dropping awkwardly to one knee and reaching for the spilled books. She didn't know what irritated her more—his cavalier insistence on treating her as though she were helpless, or the fact that he was clean and freshly shaven, and that the smell of bay rum surrounding him made her dizzy.

"Here, let me do that," Rafe said, batting her hands away. He stuffed the petticoat into the box and reached for a book. A folded letter fluttered to the floor. "I'll do this. Go sit down."

"I can help—" Brenna's breath stopped. Rafe picked up the letter and glanced idly at it. Panic punched the air from her lungs. It was Sister Therese's letter! Why hadn't she discarded that piece of damning evidence long ago? Rafe would never understand. "Never mind. I'll get it," she spoke too hastily, snatching at the letter.

"Wait a damn minute," he said, rising. His expression grew thunderous as his eyes scanned the spidery writing. "What the hell's the meaning of this?"

"It's nothing," Brenna said nervously. She pulled herself clumsily to her feet, her hand extended in supplication. "It's not important any longer."

"Nothing? You call this nothing!" he roared. "By God, woman, I call leaving your husband *something!* Is this why you begged so prettily to stay on here at the ranch? Was it easier to plan from here? You deceitful liar! Looking like butter wouldn't melt in your mouth as you promised to trust me!"

"No, Rafe, you don't understand," she protested guiltily.

What could she say? But for the babe, she would have carried out her original plan. Yet she had to make him see that things had changed since the day she'd been so full of anger and vengeful plans. Her feelings had mellowed and so, she had reason to hope, had his. Shaken by his anger and his unwillingness to listen, she realized this discovery touched him in a most vulnerable spot, making her seem as faithless as the mother who had abandoned him at birth.

"Let me explain," she pleaded.

"There's nothing to explain!" he shouted furiously. His hand closed around her arm in a grip that made her wince. "It's all right here! And I'm not so foolish as to believe any more of your convenient lies. You were going to leave me and take my child! But I'll be damned if I'll let that happen, do you understand? You're mine and so is that child, and you'll never be free of me—never!"

Rage at her betrayal surged through his blood like molten lead, reducing his aspirations to ashes. She was as treacherous as all women and disloyal, but hadn't he known that from the start? Wasn't that why he'd settled her in the wilds where she could do him no harm in her quest for revenge?

Why then did his chest ache with the evidence of her rejection, and his heart pound with the savage urge to wound her as he was wounded? He'd let her get too close to him with her soft, winning ways, forgetting her false female nature. The fault was his.

Brenna saw the massive struggle for control in his contorted face, and for an infinitesimal second she felt real fear. Then he thrust her from him in revulsion.

"For the love of God, Rafe, listen to me!" she cried. Scalding tears splashed her white cheeks. "It's not what you think, not now."

"Neither God nor love has anything to do with it," he said harshly. "You and that damned nun, conspiring against me. Just like when I was a kid! Don't try to convince me it's got anything to do with mercy or love or kindness. I know better!" He turned and stormed out the back door.

"Rafe, wait!" Her voice was choked with sobs of despair. The fragile framework of their relationship lay shattered at her feet. Devastation and despair flooded her soul, tore at her heart. She didn't want him to hurt so.

Rafe had been so good to her of late. He didn't deserve this pain as his repayment. "I can explain," she choked. "Where are you going?"

He strode toward the barn, his every move punctuating his anger. He made a gesture of disgust but didn't look back. "I need a drink!"

With growing dismay, Brenna watched him disappear inside the barn. A minute later, he spurred the big bay horse out of the yard. She sank down on the chair at the kitchen table and cried into her palms.

"*Señora?* Can I help?" Juanita asked at her side.

Brenna shook her head and wept brokenly.

"Brenna! Little gal, what is it?" Pete demanded, bursting through the back door. "That loco boy rode outta here like he got a burr under his saddle blanket. Said something about getting drunk."

"Pete!" Brenna threw herself against the old Ranger's chest and poured out her anguish. "He found the letter and we had a fight, but he didn't understand, he wouldn't listen. Oh, Pete, you've got to go after him. Make him come back so I can tell him how sorry I am!"

Pete awkwardly patted her shoulder. "All right, all right. If that's what you want. He's probably just gone to cool off. He's hotheaded, you know. Always has been."

"Please, Pete!" she begged.

"I'm going." He shot a significant glance at Juanita.

"Come, *señora*, it is not good for the little one for you to cry so. Such an upset can bring it too soon," Juanita said. She urged a distraught Brenna toward her bedroom.

"Pete! Find him!" Brenna sobbed.

"I'll do it for you, little gal," he promised.

"You planning on riding all the way to Marshall for a drink?" Pete asked, reining his horse in beside Rafe's trotting bay some time later. Rafe gave his old partner a surly look out of the corner of his eye but didn't slow his pace.

"You're getting old, Pete," he said. "I've known it was you back there for the past mile."

"Figured you needed a bit of time to yourself," Pete replied laconically.

"You were right. So why the hell did you follow me?"

"Brenna."

Rafe grunted. "She's wrapped you around her little finger, too, has she?"

"She was some broken up. Wailing something awful. Tain't good for the baby when its mama gets so worked up."

"Stop trying to blackmail me. I need to think."

"All right. But why don't we get that drink of yours over at Johnston's Crossroads? It's a sight closer than Marshall and Old Man Johnston usually has a quiet corner and a bottle he don't mind selling."

Rafe shrugged. "Suits me."

When they got to the Crossroads, Pete led the way into the dimly lit room attached to the side of the Johnston homestead that served as trading post, general store, and on occasions such as this, saloon. Pete shared a laugh with Old Man Johnston, passed him a coin, and got two tin cups and a bottle of something fiery and potent in return. He and Rafe sat down at one of the scarred tables near the back. They sipped in silence, Rafe brooding darkly, and Pete whittling and whistling sibilantly through his teeth.

"Well," Rafe asked belligerently after a time, "aren't you going to say anything?"

"Nope."

"No lecture?"

"Nope." Pete sighted down the bole of the piece of wood he was carving, blew away a shaving, squinted at it again with one blue eye, then resumed his whittling.

"You're a hell of a lot of help," Rafe grumbled.

"Thought you didn't want any."

Rafe slammed his palm down on the table. "Damn right! I can take care of myself and my wife without any interference from you, old man."

"Doing a mighty fine job of it, too," Pete returned mildly.

Rafe made a sound like a growl, then threw the contents of his cup down his throat. The whiskey curled in his belly like warm smoke. He rubbed his mouth and glared at Pete. A hint of a rueful smile twisted his lips. "Yeah, a helluva fine job."

Pete's disinterested guise disappeared, and concern

etched his weathered visage. "You want to tell me what's troublin' you, son?"

Rafe laughed, a low harsh sound that grated on overstretched nerves. "Besides the fact that my wife is trying to leave me and someone wants to kill me, I'm in fine shape, old man."

"Kill you!"

Rafe told Pete about the bomb in Dallas and his theory about Larosse. "That's why I'm so anxious to get Brenna out of this part of the country. That killer made an extra effort to get to her before. What's to stop him from trying again? But how can I protect her if she won't trust me? Damn! She doesn't even want to live with me!"

"I think she wants to trust you," Pete said slowly. A murmur of voices caught his attention, and he glanced briefly at Johnston, who was engaged in conversation with two dusty cowboys. Their hats were pulled low over their faces. Pete returned his attention to Rafe. "The thing is, she hasn't had much opportunity to learn how to trust a man. She's been running away from trouble all her life."

"She's still at it," Rafe said bitterly. "Did you know she was trying to get a job as a damned governess?"

"Well, she ain't done it, has she?" Pete demanded with a truculent jut of his grizzled chin. "No, she's put up with your gallivantin' and learned to run your ranch, that's what! Maybe she's reached a point in her life where she wants to stop running, for the child's sake, maybe even for yours."

"I wish I could believe it. Dammit, Pete! If I thought she cared even a little . . ." Rafe trailed off, staring sightlessly into space. Why should it matter so much? She belonged to him, didn't she? The door slammed shut behind the two departing cowpokes, and the sound jarred him from his reverie. "All I want is to take care of her and the baby. Why won't she give me a chance to prove it? Is she never going to forgive me for the way we began?"

"She was upset when you left like that. I think she cares a lot, maybe more than she knows herself," Pete said. He clamped a companionable hand on Rafe's shoulder. "You done yourself proud when you married that little filly. She's a match for you in spirit and sass.

Don't throw something precious like that away out of pride and stubbornness.''

"I don't intend to. And I won't let Brenna, either.'' Rafe's jaw tightened with determination. "Maybe I jumped the gun back there, but she's my wife and she's carrying my child. I'm done with handling her with kid gloves. We're going to be together from now on, and she'll learn where she belongs!''

"Just remember she's a lady.''

Rafe slumped. "That's the hell of it. If she weren't, maybe I wouldn't want her so damn much.'' A tad embarrassed by this rare bit of honesty, Rafe met Pete's understanding gaze. "Thanks, partner.''

"Anytime, greenhorn.'' Pete folded the blade of his knife between his callused palm and his denim-clad thigh, then dropped it into his shirt pocket. He passed Rafe the small dumbbell-shaped object he'd finished. "Something for that baby to play with when he gets a little older. To remind him of old Pete Hooke.''

Rafe turned the rattle with its carved ball ends over and over in his palm, struck by Pete's unquestioning acceptance and affection. He knew the old Ranger would miss them, and Brenna perhaps most of all. He tucked the rattle into his vest pocket and cleared his throat self-consciously.

"You—you wouldn't want to come north with us, would you?'' he asked. "At least until the baby comes?''

"Naw, that ain't for me. I'd be like a catfish outta water and about as useful. I'll just stick around the spread for a while, maybe until you can find a couple to manage it.'' Rafe nodded agreement at this suggestion, and Pete continued. "I'm getting a mite fidgety anyway. Think I might go out to Waco and see if I can join up with a scouting party.''

"Got the wanderlust, have you?'' Rafe laughed. "You'll never change.''

"Rangering is all I know, son. You plan on bringing that little feller of yours to see his old Uncle Pete, you hear now? I'll teach him to sit a horse proper like I taught his daddy.''

"That's a deal.'' Rafe offered his hand, and they shook hands solemnly to seal the promise. Rafe felt an overwhelming love swell in his heart for Pete, but he knew he would only make the old Ranger uncomfortable if he voiced it. Instead, he said gruffly, "Let's go home."

Old Man Johnston carried a crock of pickled hog knuckles in from the storeroom after Pete and Rafe left. Puffing, he lugged the crock to the counter and set it beside the tins of sardines and jars of licorice whips. The clatter of horses' hooves faded in the distance, and he suddenly realized he hadn't asked them if they knew those two strangers. The cowpokes hadn't offered their names, but they sure wanted to know a lot about the folks around here, especially the Sinclair spread. And when he'd pointed out Rafe and Pete sitting over in the corner, they'd left in a big hurry.

Well, too late now, Johnston shrugged. Maybe he'd better send word over that way in the morning, though. Things were kinda suspicious, he reckoned, and it didn't pay to take chances, even in this modern day and age. And besides, that one feller with the single cold, black, beady eye was enough to give any Christian man a case of the willies. That decided, he went off toward the back of the house, hollering for his wife. It had been a long day and he was hungry.

Brenna heard the hoofbeats coming and hurried anxiously to the front porch. She had bathed her eyes and tidied her hair. She would make Rafe listen this time, she *would!* She chewed on her lip. She would, *if* Pete had been able to bring Rafe back.

Two riders came into view, and she breathed a sigh of relief, then straightened her shoulders and lifted her chin. It was time Rafe understood a thing or two about Brenna Kathleen Galloway Sinclair!

Rafe and Pete galloped toward the house, reining in with a dancing churn of sharp hooves. Rafe swung off the saddle and jerked his rifle free in one movement, then sent the bay off with a slap to his rump. Brenna looked on in surprise, open-mouthed.

"How many?" he shouted.

"Dunno," Pete returned, sawing at his reins as his own horse whirled in a circle. "Six, maybe eight. I'll get the boys."

"Right." Rafe bounded up on the porch. "Go inside Brenna."

"Rafe, what is it? I have to talk to you!"

"Get in the house, woman!" Rafe yelled, grabbing her arm and propelling her in through the door. "You and Juanita get to the back of the house and stay down!"

He gave her a shove, then turned and pumped a shell into the chamber of his Winchester. He used the barrel of the rifle to push aside the calico curtain that covered the open window beside the front door.

"Rafe, please!" Brenna gasped. "What's the matter? You're frightening me!"

He glanced back over his shoulder. "Just do as I say, Red. You'll be all right. Somebody was following us. Neither Pete nor I like the looks of it, but it's probably nothing. Stay back until we find out just who our visitors are."

Pete burst in through the back door, dragging Juanita after him.

"Madre de Dios!" Juanita exclaimed, jerking up her skirts and slamming down her garden basket of vegetables. She launched into a spate of Spanish and vigorous gesticulation that was totally ignored by the two men.

"Got Ned on the barn roof to cover the house," Pete said tersely, joining Rafe at the window, his Colt drawn and ready. "Other two are inside the barn. We'll catch 'em in a crossfire if Kelly and Matt don't fergit what they're doing. First time I noticed they ain't got much stomach for this kind of thing."

"It'll have to do." Rafe's words were clipped. "Here they come. Let's see what they want." He stepped out on the front porch, the rifle resting easily in both hands.

Brenna gasped and took a step forward, but Juanita grabbed her arm. "No, *señora!* Get back." Juanita tugged her into the kitchen, making Brenna crouch down between the stove and the table.

Brenna heard the thunder of hooves and sensed the horsemen circling the house, trampling the garden, trying to peer in through the calico-clad windows. Rafe's voice lifted in a terse greeting, but there was no answering shout, only the sudden explosion and whine of a rifle.

Brenna jerked and smothered her startled cry with her hand.

Rafe jumped back into the room, slamming the door and crouching beside the other window. His grin was a white slash under his mustache, and the fire of battle made his eyes burn with a white-hot light.

"Seems they want a fight," Pete said calmly.

Rafe nodded. "Let's give them one."

The room exploded with the smell of gunpowder and hot steel. Window glass shattered into deadly needles that tinkled musically to the floor. Rafe and Pete spaced their shots, making them count. Spent shells bounced and rolled like a bagfull of a kid's favorite cat's-eye marbles. Cartridges slammed into the thick wooden walls, scarring the old wood with bright pock marks. Horses shrieked, bullets whined, men screamed in agony. A long howl, cut off suddenly, made Brenna's skin crawl.

"They got Ned," Rafe muttered.

Brenna held her hands over her mouth to keep from screaming. Fear clogged her throat, and her ears rang with the shrill blast of gunfire. Beside her, Juanita huddled on the floor and sobbed and prayed in Spanish.

"Where the hell's Kelly?" Rafe demanded, pumping another shell into the rifle. He aimed it out the window, following an unknown horseman, fired and smiled grimly. "Another one—" He gave a sharp grunt of pain and spun away from the window, clutching his left side. A spot of crimson blossomed on his white shirt.

Brenna screamed. "Rafe!"

"Stay back! I—I'm all right." Left arm stiff, he picked up the rifle with his right and crawled back to the window.

"Pete!" Brenna cried. "Rafe's been shot! Do something—" Her eyes widened. Pete lay in a heap under his window. She crawled forward, reached for him, turning him over. Her hands came away red and sticky with blood. "Oh, no, Pete," she moaned. She looked at her hands for a helpless second, then jerked down the calico curtain, wadding it up and holding it to the growing blotch on Pete's chest. His eyelids flickered.

"Little gal . . ." The words were no more than a sigh.

Anger raged through Brenna. *Not Pete!* her brain

screamed. Why would anyone hurt good, kind Pete? Who were these men who could do such a thing? What did they want? Damn them, they had no right!

She picked up his pistol in a cold fury. Remembering Rafe's instructions, she sighted and gently squeezed the trigger. A rider tumbled off his saddle backward, but she felt no satisfaction. She aimed again, then gasped, biting her lip so hard she tasted the salty-sweet flavor her own blood. The barrel of the pistol wavered uncontrollably. The one-eyed man!

Hatred and fear blazed in Brenna. She pulled the trigger, but the hammer fell with an impotent click on an empty chamber. Rafe's rifle felled another horseman. With a shout, the remaining marauders wheeled about in retreat, leaving a litter of crumpled bodies behind to defile the yard. Brenna closed her eyes on a violent shudder of relief.

She opened them to find Rafe swaying over his friend, his face a twisted mask of rage and utter devastation. He reached out and blood dripped from his fingertips to mingle with his tears.

"The bastards," he choked. "They've killed Pete."

Chapter 16

There was no light in Pete's eyes. Only a sightless blue glazed over with death. The hollow shock of loss made Brenna numb. She tenderly closed his blind eyes with her open palm.

"Damn you, Pete!" Rafe mumbled, his voice broken. "Why'd you have to go and get yourself killed?" His face was ashen. The bright red of fresh blood painted a crimson river from his shoulder to his hip.

Brenna stirred herself. She could not afford the indulgence of grief, not when delay might mean another life to mourn.

"Rafe, sit down. Let me see," she said, urging him down, his back against the wall for support. *Oh, God!* she thought wildly. *What can I do?*

"Got to . . . be ready. In case those bastards come back," Rafe muttered, clenching his teeth. He tried to get to his feet, but fell back, grimacing in pain.

"You can't do anything until I stop the bleeding." She pulled open his shirt and vest, trying not to retch at the sight and smell of so much blood. "Now be still!"

It was hard to judge the extent of the wound for the ragged gouge across his rib cage. All she could think of was stopping the flow of blood. Her mind raced. She needed bandages, something clean and . . . diapers!

"Juanita, help me! Bring some water, quickly!" Brenna cried, struggling to her feet.

"Oh, *Dios!*" Juanita shrieked. She stood in the doorway to the kitchen, crossing herself, her face streaked with tears and panic. "Mother of God! Both dead!"

Turning, she dashed out of the kitchen, screeching and praying.

Brenna glanced back at Rafe. He was slumped over in a swoon beside Pete's body. No wonder Juanita assumed the worst. She hurried to her valise, pulling out several neatly hemmed diapers in frantic haste, then snatched up a bowl of water.

She worked to staunch the flow of blood, washing away the clotting mass, then pressing pads she folded out of the diapers along the path of the wound. Outside, a man moaned, Juanita screamed in Spanish, and harness jingled.

"*Señora,* come quickly!" Juanita reappeared in the doorway. "We will take the wagon. We must be gone from this place of death!"

Brenna did not glance up from her work. "Where are the men? I can't lift Rafe by myself."

"Ned is killed, and Matt shot, here, in the leg. Nowhere do I see Kelly. Please, *señora,* the others will return! We must go!" Juanita tugged at Brenna's arm.

"Stop it!" Brenna ordered, shrugging her off. "I have to see to Rafe."

"Leave him!" Juanita shrieked. "He is dead—or as good as dead!"

"No!" Brenna wrapped a diaper over the pads and knotted it tightly across Rafe's chest. "He's just lost so much blood, that's all. We'll wait until he comes around . . ."

"*Madre!* You are crazy! Stay if you want, then!" Juanita spat. "Me and my man, we choose to live." She spun around and ran from the house.

"Wait! Juanita, come back!" Brenna lurched to her feet and stumbled to the front porch. Juanita, perched in the high spring seat of the wagon, shouted and whipped the horses, heading them out of the yard. Brenna caught a glimpse of a white-faced Matt in the bed of the wagon, then they were gone.

Brenna swayed, caught herself on a post, and stared after the retreating wagon in undiluted horror. She couldn't force herself to look at the crumpled bodies lying still in the dusty yard. A riderless horse ambled around the corner of the house. It was unbearably silent.

"Brenna."

She whipped around at Rafe's hoarse call and hurried inside. He was using his good arm to push himself to a sitting position.

"I'm here," she said. "Please, Rafe, be still. We've got to get the bleeding stopped."

"Thought you'd gone," he mumbled.

"No. I won't leave you." The force in that promise surprised even herself. But they had no time. Larosse and his cutthroats might be back any moment to finish the job they'd started. "Can you walk?" she asked anxiously. "Everyone's gone. We've got to get out of here."

"Help me up." Using Brenna's shoulder for leverage, Rafe painfully pressed himself to his feet. Her arm went around his waist in support, but he swayed alarmingly. His voice was heavy. "We have to take care of Pete."

She glanced at the old Ranger and sent a silent prayer heavenward for his soul. She urged Rafe toward the kitchen door. "We can't now, Rafe. Pete would understand. You need help. We—we can go to the Henigan place. They'll send someone to take care of him. Please, Rafe!"

"Get—his knife," Rafe said, swallowing hard.

"But—" She looked at his stricken face, the strain of pain and grief, and understood his need. "Wait here."

Tears streaming down her face, she retrieved Pete's whittling knife and left Rafe turning it over and over in his palm while she scurried around the house, grabbing the valise, canteens, and Rafe's saddlebags and rifle. Luckily it was a small matter to catch the loose horse, but the effort it took for Rafe to mount made beads of sweat pop out on his forehead.

She awkwardly climbed up in front of him and sat sidesaddle, ignoring her own discomfort and worrying that all this movement would start Rafe's bleeding again.

"Hold on to me," she ordered. "We'll go across the ridge to Sarie's. It's closer and I think we'll be less likely to run into Larosse again."

"So you recognized him?"

"Yes."

"He'll kill us both if he finds us, you know that, don't you?" Rafe asked hoarsely. The swinging motion of the

horse aggravated the band of fire running across his side,
and he had to concentrate hard to remain upright.

"Yes, I know." She clicked at the horse, urging him
toward the ridge behind the house.

"If it comes to that, I want you to take the horse and
go."

"I won't leave you."

"You're a damned stubborn woman, Red," he said.
He almost smiled.

"We'll be all right. Just save your strength. Our baby
is going to need his father."

"Yes, ma'am."

Brenna knew that he mocked her, but she couldn't be
angry. He wasn't hurt so badly if he could still laugh at
her. The horse trudged steadily, and Brenna anxiously
checked Rafe over her shoulder every few steps. He
maintained a stoic silence, but she saw the tension in his
jaw and the way he gripped the saddle horn to keep from
falling, especially after the ground began to rise and the
trail got rougher, the forest thicker. More than once,
Brenna thanked her inclination for exploration. She'd
walked this way many times. It wouldn't be hard to find
their way to the Henigans', even though the light was
beginning to fail.

The sounds of shots brought her up short.

"Damnation," Rafe gritted. "They've come back to
finish us off."

They were high on the ridge now, nearly to the blasted
tree at the top. Peering through the lush summer growth,
they could see riders circling the compound, discharging
their guns aimlessly against unseen enemies. But there
was no one to defend the homestead except a dead man.
One rider was obviously interested in the tracks leading
from the rear of the house.

"Oh, God, Rafe! He's found our trail!" Brenna cried,
almost frantic. Rafe bent over, moaning softly, and slid
to the ground. Brenna gasped, "Rafe!" She scrambled
down to him as he struggled to his knees.

"Send the horse—back down," he said, his face white
and his hand clutched convulsively to his side in agony.
"Maybe they won't worry about another stray."

"Yes, all right." Brenna ripped the saddlebags, valise,

and canteens off the horse, handing Rafe the rifle, then turned the animal and gave it a sharp slap on the rump. The horse trotted obligingly down the hill. She prayed it wouldn't stop until it reached the bottom.

"We've got to find some cover," Rafe groaned, his face taut with pain.

"The shack! We're almost there." Brenna nearly sobbed with fright and fatigue. "Can you make it?"

"I can try."

Painfully, supporting each other, they climbed the rest of the way to the abandoned cabin. It looked like a mansion to Brenna. Once inside, she spread a blanket from the saddlebag and helped Rafe stretch out, then clung to the door facing, trying to catch her breath.

"Oh, no!" she whispered.

"What?" Rafe's voice was weak but adamant. "Brenna, what is it?"

"They're burning the ranch." Her voice was lifeless, defeated.

The sun was a hot orange ball on the western horizon, and below them, hot orange flames licked at the shingles, engulfed the barn, skittered along the porch railings. Helpless tears slipped down her cheeks as she watched the home she'd grown to think of as her own become an inferno.

"Why, Rafe? Why burn us out?"

"He's an animal, but he's getting his orders from someone. I hope he thinks we're inside there," Rafe muttered. He closed his eyes and stifled another moan.

She kneeled down awkwardly beside him, biting her lip at the red stain that bloodied her makeshift bandage. Her fingers worked at the knot. "But why, after all this time?"

"It's not only you he wants." He told her in a few brief, pithy sentences of the events in Dallas. "I nearly had him. He must be getting desperate to risk this."

"All this because I saw him kill Mr. Plummer?"

"It's got to be more than that." Rafe's hand caught her wrist in a surprisingly strong hold, and his voice was deadly. "This attempt cost him, but not enough. I swear on Pete's grave, I'll make Larosse and whoever is behind him pay!"

"Yes, I know," she soothed. "Lie back, Rafe. You're bleeding again. We're safe here, at least for the moment. Let me see what I can do."

"Go ahead. It hurts like a bitch."

She unwrapped the wound and probed gently with her fingertips while fresh blood oozed. He stiffened but did not cry out. "I—I think the bullet's still in there," she said, faltering.

"You'll have to dig it out." The words came out around clenched teeth.

"I can't!"

"Do it, Red. There's some whiskey in the saddle-bags."

"But Rafe . . ." Her lips trembled and she pressed a white-knuckled fist to her mouth.

"It won't stop bleeding until you do."

"All right," she whispered, terrified, yet even more scared that he would bleed to death if she did not try.

She gathered the small flask of whiskey from the bag and several more diapers, reflecting a bit hysterically that it was not the use she had envisioned for the small garments.

"Give me a swig of that first," Rafe said between gritted teeth. She helped him raise high enough to take a hearty swallow of the liquor. He fell back, exhaling harshly. "My knife's in my boot. Or use Pete's."

"Yes. You'll have to be very still," she warned, retrieving the knives and pausing uncertainly.

"Go ahead."

Brenna bit her lip, and splashed some whiskey on Pete's knife. Then she poured some of it directly on the wound. Rafe jerked and moaned and his face paled further.

"Oh, Rafe, I'm sorry," she whispered.

His jaw clenched. "Just do it."

She took one last glance at his taut features, drew a deep breath, then probed the wound as gently as she could with the knife blade. She sensed Rafe's flesh quivering, but he didn't move. She felt the blade touch something.

"There it is," she muttered.

But Rafe didn't hear her. It took her a second to realize he was limp. He was out cold. She breathed a silent prayer of thanks that he was to be spared this ordeal, at least, and concentrated her efforts.

Please, God, she prayed as she worked, *let him live*

No matter what their differences, she cared about this man, her husband, the father of her child. She prayed that she would have the chance to tell him. *I'll be a good wife,* she vowed. *I'll be everything he wants. Just give me another chance. Give me a chance to tell him—I love him.*

The realization checked her careful movements for a long moment. She looked at Rafe's face, the long lashes, the strong nose and cheekbones, and knew the truth. She was in love with him. How had it happened? After all they'd been through together, how was something so impossible now *possible* and right? It was no matter. She loved him with all her heart, and it would be too ironic if he never knew. He couldn't die! She wouldn't let him!

Several minutes later, her brow beaded with sweat, and every muscle in her body clenched with effort, she gingerly drew the bullet free. She slumped over her rounded belly, panting and trembling with relief. Choking back a ragged sob, she kissed Rafe's forehead, tasting the salty essence of him on her tongue and murmuring her love and need into his unconscious ears. She'd done her best. Now the rest was up to him.

After a moment, when her hands stopped shaking quite so violently, she poured more whiskey over the slash of torn flesh and replaced her makeshift bandages, using more diapers, then tearing another into strips to bind the dressing tightly into place around Rafe's chest. This done, she made him as comfortable as possible, sponging his forehead and face with water from a canteen and removing his boots. She threw the bloody bullet into the rough fireplace as if it were something obscene, then she cleansed Pete's knife and carefully put it away, convinced in her own mind that Pete had somehow guided her hand.

She moved quietly about the little shack, arranging things, moving things from here to there in an effort to keep terror at bay. At least no inquisitive marauder had climbed the ridge, and they all had vanished as they'd come. She watched the ranch house burn down to nothing more than glowing embers. She drank a little water, then

a burning sip of whiskey, surprised at the warmth
caused in her middle. The baby stirred, and she wa
suddenly overwhelmingly aware of her fatigue and th
dull ache in the small of her back. Anxiously, sh
hovered over Rafe, but he showed no signs of regainin
consciousness. She knew they couldn't hope to reach th
Henigans' tonight, not in Rafe's weakened state, even i
he should wake soon, and so she prepared to wait it out

At last, when the darkness became a tangible thing,
living, breathing entity both inside the cabin and out, sh
lay down beside Rafe to rest and wait. She listened to hi
breathing, shallow and quick in his unconscious condi
tion. From far away, the hollow hoot of a tree ow
echoed. Crickets chirruped and the wind carried the faint
acrid odor of smoke. Brenna's fingers lightly caresse
Rafe's chest, gently testing the spring of the dark whorl
of hair, feeling the reassuringly steady pump of his heart
She was careful not to jar him, but took comfort i
touching him, in being close. She dared not risk a fire
but the night was warm, and after a while her eyelid
grew heavy.

Rafe's groan of pain woke her.

"What is it? I'm here, Rafe." She could see his gray
outline against the darkness and reached for him. His skir
scorched her fingers. Fever! She scrambled up.

"Thirsty . . ." he rasped.

"Don't try to move. You'll open your wound again,"
she warned. She grabbed a canteen and held it to his lips.
"Here." He drank, then coughed.

"Musta been a helluva fight," he muttered. "We
Hell's Kitchen Boys can really scrap, can't we?"

"What?" She was confused, then realized the fever and
pain were making him delirious. "It's all right. Just go
back to sleep, darling."

"Edith, is that you? Light the lamp, will you? I can't
see your lovely face. Why'd you do it, Edie? Why marry
a weakling like George? Wasn't it good between us?
Edie . . ." His agonized mutterings slurred and ran
together into incoherence.

Brenna felt her world teeter and slip. For an agonizing
moment, her lungs refused to draw oxygen, her heart
refused to beat. When at last they did, she inhaled

sharply, her heart pierced by a pain that made her whimper.

Her dismay knew no bounds. Rafe was still in love with Edith, no matter what he'd told her before! Where were her feeble dreams now? How could she confess her love, when even in his unconscious state he yearned for someone else? How could she complicate an already grossly complicated relationship by sharing her feelings when her husband nursed a years-old passion for another man's wife!

Bitter tears burned behind her eyes, and she swallowed a thickness in her throat. No, she vowed to herself, she could never tell him how she felt. It would be an unnecessary humiliation, a needless embarrassment. Their marriage was an affair of convenience, a business arrangement meant to provide him heirs and a respectable wife, and to give her a means of support for herself and her sisters. It could be nothing more, no matter how foolishly her heart behaved. She would not be one of those pitiable women who hung on a man's every word, begging for the smallest notice. Not revealing the truth was the tiniest measure of independence, but it was her only defense against total surrender and the final submission of her soul. Rafe had everything except her admission of love, and that she must reserve if she were to survive. She could stand his scorn, and even his indifference, but she could not live with his pity.

Brenna bathed Rafe's face and arms, and forced sips of water down his throat, ignoring the scream of her own tired body and the occasional twinges in her lower back from bending over him. She wished for some of the willow bark tea Rafe had used on her fever, but did the best she could for him, alternately praying and cursing, urging him to fight and closing her ears to his muttered entreaties for a woman lost to him.

Pink streaks laced the horizon with filigreed fingers when he woke finally, lucid and sweaty with the moisture of a breaking fever.

"God, what a night!" He groaned, shifting stiffly. A haze of dark beard stubbled his cheeks, but his eyes were clear.

Brenna bent over him, her smile unconsciously soft

with love and relief, her fingers cool on his brow where
she pushed back the dark strands of damp hair. "You're
better, thank the Lord. You were dreaming."

"I feel like hell." He sat up painfully, cursing, and
eyed her blearily. "But you look like it."

Self-consciously, she touched her pale cheeks, her
snarled hair, her dirty, wrinkled wrapper. Her lips
trembled. "It—it's been a long night."

"What do you want, Red, gratitude?" he said harshly.
He was sick, and sick at heart. Pete was dead, the ranch
destroyed, his men scattered, and he and his woman
reduced to hiding in a hovel like sniveling cowards. He
picked up the canteen and took a swallow, his jaw set
against the pain the movement caused him. His shirt, stiff
with brownish-red bloodstains, hung open, revealing the
swarthiness of his skin against the stark white of Brenna's
makeshift bandages. He gave a chuckle that etched acid
chills along her nerves.

"You should have saved yourself the trouble. If you'd
played your cards right, you'd be a very rich widow now.
All your problems would be over."

A shaft of icy pain stabbed Brenna's heart, and she
gasped, helpless to avoid the blow his bitter words
inflicted.

"It—it's not the circumstances of your birth that make
you a bastard," she choked out, huge crystal tears spilling
over her dark lashes. "When did I ever covet anything of
yours? Not your wealth, nor your name—not even your
affection. I don't deserve this!" Her voice broke on a
pitiful sob, and she turned away, her slim shoulders
quaking as she hid her face in her hands.

"Brenna!" He struggled up, unmindful of his injury,
aghast at his unthinking words. "God, I'm sorry!" He
caught her, turned her, pulled her against his bare chest.
Cradling her with his good arm, he held her tenderly. His
voice was ragged with remorse. "I'm half crazy, Red. I
didn't mean it."

"Why do you want me to hate you?" she sobbed.

Stunned, he hesitated. Is that what she still thought?
"Don't, darling," he whispered. "Don't weep so."

"Do you hate me so much? I know I haven't been a
good wife—not any kind of wife—but I wasn't leaving

you, not after I knew for certain about the baby." Her words gushed out along with her tears, wetting his chest, draining her soul. "You've got to believe me."

"Brenna, stop. I know that now. Please, angel," he begged huskily. "I didn't mean to hurt you."

But she seemed beyond understanding, so deep was her fatigue and grief and pain. Rafe eased them both down next to the wall, holding her as she sobbed out her sorrow, knowing himself to be the lowest of all men for having attacked her with his cruel words when she had done everything in her power to care for him.

He rubbed her back, whispered soothing words into her ear, let his lips rest on the fragrant curls on the top of her head. After a long while, her weeping subsided into a series of soft, gasping hiccups. She quieted, relaxed, and eventually fell into an exhausted sleep cradled against him. Her distended belly pressed against his uninjured side, and he felt the baby move. His hand tightened on her shoulder, as if to forestall some unseen foe from ripping this precious possession from his grasp, and he swallowed harshly, his own throat thick with tears. Anger, fear, and grief mingled with self-loathing and an utter weariness of body and soul.

She was right. He was a bastard, in the harshest sense of the word, with no redeeming merits to lessen the condemnation of that verdict. Unforgivably, he had assigned to her his own faults, his own selfish, ruthless drive for money and success, and for taking action only if it afforded him personal gain. But her opinion of him had never been based on any worldly criteria, but on him as the man she knew firsthand—and in that he knew he had shown himself sadly lacking in character. No wonder she had contemplated escaping from him, from their farce of a marriage, and from the loneliness of life in exile at the ranch.

Brenna stirred, murmured, then lapsed back into slumber. Rafe reached for the blanket, tucking it over her. Outside, a raucous mockingbird trilled a greeting to the rising sun.

Yes, he'd made too many mistakes with Brenna. His lips twisted sardonically as he admitted to himself that he seemed particularly adept at that where she was concerned. Somehow, he had to make it up to her. When they got out of this mess, he'd see to it that they stayed together. She was the type of woman to whom a home and family would mean everything. Perhaps he could redeem himself in her eyes if he devoted himself to giving her that.

Brenna moved, then came awake with a startled gasp.

"Easy, Red. Are you all right?"

"I—yes. Let me up." Eyes wide, she picked herself up, drawing a deep breath as she straightened. One hand curved protectively around her tight, swollen middle. The other trailed outstretched along the rough log wall for balance.

"Are you rested enough to try to make it to the Henigans'?" Rafe began. "If we take it easy we can— Brenna! What's wrong?" She doubled over, her face contorted. Rafe held her arm awkwardly. "Are you hurt?" he demanded.

"No." She shook her head, her rosy-gold cascade of hair shimmering in the gradually lightening room. "It's nothing. . . ." Her sharp cry of surprise cut off her words, and she looked down at her feet in wonder at the rapidly growing pool of fluid that gushed from between her legs. She lifted the soaked skirt of her wrapper away from herself. "Oh, dear."

Rafe's reaction was more graphic. He cursed roundly. "Is that all you can say? Jesus Christ! This means the baby's coming, doesn't it?"

"I'm all wet," she complained softly.

"This child has the world's worst timing, and you're concerned that you've wet your drawers!" Rafe threw up his good hand in a gesture of mixed disgust and amazement.

"But, Rafe . . ."

"Oh, hell! Here, let me help you. And no false modesty, either." He helped her slip out of the sodden, pink-stained undergarment, ignoring the blush that colored her cheeks. "Come lie down."

She shook her head. "It's better if I walk as long as I can." She smiled, laughing slightly at her husband. "Relax, Rafe. It takes a long time for a baby to be born. We'll be at Sarie's well before then."

"Have you lost your mind? You stay right where you are! I'll go."

"You're weaker than I am. You lost a lot of blood," Brenna argued. She stiffened and began to pant, her attention turning inward.

"I'll be back with help before you know it." Rafe watched his wife with increasing nervousness. "Brenna?"

"No." Her hand waved blindly toward him, caught his. Her fingers dug into his palm with surprising strength. "I—I seemed to have miscalculated. This baby's coming now."

"It can't be!" A hint of panic tinged Rafe's voice, something so foreign to him that Brenna glanced up in surprise. He had faced danger and death coolly, but this was totally outside his experience. Brenna's lips quirked in a half smile of sympathy.

"Try telling that to the baby." Another contraction caught her. "Sometimes," she panted, "they're more in a hurry than others. I think I'd like to lie down now."

"Look, Red," Rafe said, spreading out the blanket and helping her down, "I'll go for Sarie and—"

"Rafe, you can't! I'm going to need you. Please don't leave me!" She lay back, groaning.

"But I don't know anything about . . . about . . ."

"But I do! It's your child, too, damn you!" The spasm wracked her and her hand twisted into the fabric of his shirt front. When she opened her eyes again, they were a tumultuous, frightened turquoise. "Please, Rafe! Don't leave me alone. I don't want to die like my mother!"

Something twisted in Rafe's gut. Somehow, he'd never considered that possibility. He reassured her hurriedly. "Hush, now, Red. Nothing like that's going to happen. We're in this together, just like always. I'll stay right here, just tell me what to do."

"Yes." The fear receded from Brenna's eyes, to be replaced by a look of acceptance and absolute trust. Rafe felt humbled by that trust and was determined never to betray it. He took her hand and pressed a kiss into her palm in silent token.

Rafe helped make her comfortable, peeling her voluminous wrapper off and leaving her in her thin chemise so the tepid air could cool her sweating, straining flesh.

Between contractions, she gave him rapid instructions. There was whiskey to disinfect Pete's knife again, and strips of cotton from yet another diaper to tie the cord. From the valise, he set out more diapers, a tiny gown, and several soft baby blankets ready for use. He listened seriously to her explanation of how he might need to make a tiny cut to make enough room for the baby's head, but found her assurance that she wouldn't feel it hardly credible. Only her absolute certainty in his ability to carry out her instructions kept his courage from flagging.

He let her suck on the corner of a moistened diaper, then wiped her face and neck, marveling at the silent strength of her striving. Brenna raised up on her elbows, knees spread wide, only the edge of her chemise veiling her modesty.

"I think it's coming," she gasped. "Can you see?"

Rafe swallowed, then took his place between her knees, gently pushing aside the chemise. "I can't . . . yes! Push, darling. You're almost there!"

Brenna strained mightily, Rafe giving encouragement. She fell back, panting harshly and shaking her head.

"I can't, Rafe, I can't."

"Push, Brenna! You're no quitter. Do it, Red! Now!"

She pushed, a low, long, guttural cry breaking from her throat and changing into a shrill scream.

"The baby's got black hair, Brenna," Rafe said excitedly. "Come on, love, push!"

One more gigantic effort, and she fell back, weak and exhausted. "I can't anymore, Rafe, please."

"We have a son, Brenna." Rafe's voice was awestruck and gravelly with emotion. A baby's thin wail of protest split the air.

"Oh! Oh, let me see!" she said, laughing and crying. Rafe quickly tied and cut the cord, then wrapped the red-faced, screaming infant in a blanket and laid him in Brenna's arms. "Oh, Rafe," she breathed, wondrous.

Her son waved his tiny fists in a fit of rage. His head was covered with fine black hair, slick and wet now, but otherwise a perfect match to his father's raven's-wing blue-black. He was the most beautiful thing she'd ever seen.

"He looks like you," she said and laughed, euphoric.

Rafe gingerly lifted the small, squirming bundle, and swallowed on a lump of love and reverence so powerful it changed him forever. A tiny life, sprung from his loins, a helpless bit of humanity, totally dependent on him. He gently kissed his bawling son's soft scalp, his heart swelling with a father's pride. He had missed that in his own life, but he vowed that his son would not. He raised his eyes to his wife, and his smile was a bit shaky.

"And he's got your temper. I—I've got a name for him."

"What?"

"Sean. Sean Sinclair."

Brenna's heart melted and her cup overflowed. In that gesture, Rafe absolved himself of any involvement in her brother's death, totally and forever. She gazed tearfully at her husband, his large hands gently supporting their son. Her eyes were luminous with pure adoration.

"Oh, Rafe!" A little gasp cut off her words.

"Do you mind?" he asked, almost diffidently.

"No, of course not, but Rafe?"

"What, darling?" He glanced up from the shining joy of his son's face and was instantly alerted by the sudden consternation in Brenna's.

"You'd better find a place to put Sean down. We— we're not finished!"

"My God, two!"

Rafe raked shaking hands through his hair and knelt beside Brenna. Several minutes of frantic activity were behind them—and with such results!

Brenna lay on the blanket, clean and as comfortable as he could make her, covered with her own wrapper, holding two tiny bundles. "Aren't they beautiful?"

He drew a deep breath, releasing it in a quavering rush. "Yes, but twins! Boys! I can't believe it!"

Brenna laughed softly, a weary but proud sound. "You never do anything by half measures, Rafe."

"Nor do you, darling." He leaned over and kissed her, a gentle, lingering salute that drew forth a sigh. Pulling back, he gazed at her, knowing he had never seen her look more beautiful. Even though her features were etched with the fine imprint of the trial through which she had passed, her face was serene with a calm womanliness that spoke of strength and inner peace. It humbled him and elated him, and he smiled tenderly. Brenna's smile in return was tremulous. A small cry warbled from one of the red, wrinkled bundles, and she shifted her attention, making low crooning noises.

"Sean appears to be the vocal one, doesn't he?" Rafe asked with a grin.

"That's not Sean," she corrected. She nodded to the other baby. "That's Sean."

"They look alike. How can you tell?"

She gave a little indignant sniff. "I just can."

Rafe's grin widened. "And who might this be, then?"

"Why, Peter, of course."

A sudden lump formed in Rafe's throat. "Yes," he said huskily, "of course."

She had named their second son with a natural assurance and subtle intuition that touched him deeply. Rafe knew his old friend would be honored. He brushed a springy red-gold curl at her brow, gently smoothed it back, then kissed her again.

"Thank you for my sons." The words were a pleasure to pronounce, and a fierce, warm glow of pride and protectiveness spread through him.

"I'm so glad you were here," she whispered.

"So am I. That feeling, in that first moment when I held Sean, and then Peter . . . what we shared . . ." He shook his head in wonder. "Such a gift! I'll never forget it, Brenna."

"They are lucky boys," she said in a drowsy voice. "They have the finest gentleman in the world for a father."

"You're too forgiving, love." He glanced around the squalid little shack. "How I let you come to this . . ." He swallowed convulsively, then pulled his silver chain over his head and placed it around her neck, settling the dime-sized medallion between her breasts.

"Oh, Rafe! Not your mother's medal. I couldn't!" Her fingers touched the cool silver coin, trembling in agitation.

Rafe's expression was solemn, and his hand closed over

hers, stilling her anxious fluttering. "I haven't anything to give you, Brenna, but this and my promise that you and the boys will never want for anything, not as long as I draw breath. So wear it for me and for our sons with that in mind."

Brenna bit her lip, then nodded slowly. "I—I'll treasure it. But . . . just love them, Rafe. That's all that really matters." She sighed and her lashes swept down, casting shadows on the fragile porcelain of her cheekbones.

I'm beginning to understand that, Rafe thought, moved to his core by an emotion so intense it made him shudder. And what of his wife? Would she ask him to love her, as well? Or was that too much to hope for? Was it still possible for her to come to care for him, not just for passion's sake, but with the communion and intimacy of a mature, lasting relationship? Perhaps their sons would be the common bond that drew them together. With all his heart, Rafe prayed it would be so.

"Rest now, sweetheart," he said. He pulled himself to his feet, grimacing at the soreness of his side. "I've got to get us all to some place safe. Will you be all right if I go for a while? I'll head for the Henigans'."

"Yes, I think all three of us could rest now," she murmured.

"I'll hurry." He set the canteen nearby and tucked the edges of the wrapper around them.

"Be careful of your side," she warned sleepily.

He touched her hair lightly. "Don't worry, Red. After today, I feel I could easily carry the world on my shoulders."

In the end, Rafe only had to climb down the ridge. Old Man Johnston's oldest boy had been sent early with a message to the Sinclair place and, finding only carnage and death, had hightailed it back for help. When Rafe left Brenna and the babies, he saw a group of horsemen poking around the ruins of his ranch. He recognized Johnston's portly figure and Paul Henigan among the group. His hallooes brought help and plenty of questions, but his main concern was for Brenna.

By the time she and the twins were carried down from the shack, loaded carefully into a waiting wagon, and whisked swiftly into Sarie Henigan's safekeeping, Rafe had seen enough to know that no answers would be gleaned from the dead members of Larosse's gang. Kelly was still nowhere to be found, and Rafe assumed he had escaped unharmed before the shoot-out had even begun. Juanita and Matt seemed to have left the country, too, and Rafe reflected that it was just as well when he heard the story of their panicky defection. He couldn't have held himself accountable had he come face to face with any of them.

The men gave the three dead marauders a perfunctory burial, but interred Ned's and Pete's remains with proper solemn services near the ranch. Soon only the charred timbers of barn and house stood in mute evidence of the violence that had taken place.

As before, Larosse himself disappeared, vanished like mist rising over the Sabine River basin, and completely eluded all attempts to follow his trail. Frustrated almost past endurance, Rafe knew that he was no closer to the killer than he'd been at the beginning of this deadly game. But with two new lives to protect, the stakes had become even higher.

Chapter 17

Sean Sinclair nuzzled hungrily at his mother's breast, making small, greedy noises. Brenna smiled and cuddled him closer, stroking his fine black hair with a loving touch. It was hard to believe how much he and Peter had grown in scarcely a month. They seemed to thrive on change, and God knew, they'd had enough of it.

From the deserted shack where they'd been born, to Sarie Henigan's ranch house where they'd all rested and gained strength, Rafe included, then back to Marshall and those days traveling north in the swaying, clicking private railcar, and finally to this luxurious brownstone in the heart of New York City. It was enough to boggle the most sophisticated traveler, yet the boys took every upheaval in stride, growing plump and contented.

"My land! I swear these boys're part catfish, they love to wet so much," Annie Barlow mumbled around a steel diaper pin. She bent over one of the two lace-draped cradles, working quickly, then lifted the fretting infant and gently bounced him in her arms. "There, now, Peter, hold your horses! It'll be your turn for dinner soon."

Brenna gazed at her friend with warm gratitude. "Annie, I don't know how I'd manage without you. Have I thanked you properly?"

"Not in the last half hour." Annie giggled, her warm brown eyes dancing. She absently swiped at the frizz of mousy hair falling over her forehead. Her starched shirtwaist and skirt were neat, but her apron sported the most disreputable bow imaginable, and Brenna hid a smile. As a nursemaid, Annie couldn't be faulted, but an elegant bowknot was still beyond her!

"I'm still amazed Rafe was able to convince you so quickly to come with us." Brenna's satin house slippers patted the Turkey carpet that covered the floor of her spacious bedroom, and the painted wicker rocker in which she sat rolled and creaked reassuringly.

"Your Mr. Sinclair just bowled me over with charm, that's all," Annie said, laughing. "And why not? I get to travel and see the most glamorous city in the world and earn a nice fat pay packet to boot. *And* get to take care of these precious, precious boys. You haven't been out much yet, Brenna," she chattered on, "but it's all so fascinating! Mr. Edison's electrical lights just everywhere, and the Liberty Enlightening the World Statue out in the harbor, and the horsecars and people bustling all over. Louise the kitchenmaid took me for a walk across that Brooklyn Bridge. Why, it fair took my breath away!"

"I'm glad you're enjoying it all so much." Brenna laughed, gently disengaging a milky, sleepy Sean from her breast. She traded infants with Annie, adjusting her lace-trimmed sacque and settling Peter into place at her other side.

"You know the best part?" Annie asked in a conspiratorial whisper as she gently thumped Sean's back. Her coffee-colored eyes snapped with good humor. "It's these newfangled indoor bathrooms. Imagine, no more walking to the privy in the rain!"

"Leave it to you to stick to practical matters." Brenna giggled. Then her face sobered. "Seriously, Annie. You're not missing home too much?"

Annie frowned slightly, and her hand slowed on Sean's back. Her voice was tart as she said, "If by home you mean Jimmy Teague, then no, I don't miss it. In fact, I quite relish playing lady's maid to your lady of the house. Remember how we used to pretend?" Sean gave a resounding burp, and Annie's good-humored smile returned. "What a good lad! Come now, time for bed."

Annie fussed over the infant, tucking him into the cradle and giving it a gentle push. Brenna watched her friend closely, trying to see beyond Annie's chatter. How badly had Jimmy Teague's cooling ardor hurt her?

"Annie, I'm sure Jimmy is still very fond of you in

his own way," she began. "After all, he did come to see us off at the station."

"Just in the hope of getting me to pass on information about Mr. Gould," Annie returned sharply. Her lips firmed to an unconsciously proud and stubborn line. "It don't matter, really. I know I'm no beauty, but it weren't that. Jimmy had changed over the last months. He weren't the boy I used to know, at all. It all comes from hanging around the wrong kind, I guess."

"He did seem different," Brenna acknowledged thoughtfully, remembering how the pale light in the young man's eyes had gleamed with fanaticism. He'd seen Rafe's offer to Annie as an opportunity to aid the Knights and willingly sacrificed Annie's affection for the cause, much to her dismay and ultimate disillusionment. But in the end, it hadn't been loyalty to the Knights of Labor but Annie's friendship with Brenna that was the deciding factor in her decision to come to New York.

"I guess what hurt was knowing that Jimmy's feelings weren't as deep as I hoped," Annie murmured, her chin trembling. "Not if he could ask me to spy on Mr. Rafe for the Knights. I wish the Brotherhood well, but I don't give two cents for their methods."

"I'm glad we're in agreement on that. We can't be forced into something so underhanded." Brenna's lips quirked. "Besides, what could the two of us learn of any importance? How to fold a diaper properly?"

Annie giggled behind her hand. "Maybe. Or how often I change my apron 'cause a little feller dribbles on me."

Brenna chuckled softly, trying not to disturb a placid Peter. "Don't pine over Jimmy. I think you can do a lot better. There's someone out there waiting for you who'll treat you like a queen. It might even be a Yankee."

"Hmph. We'll see about that!"

"One found me," Brenna pointed out quietly. Her lips curved softly as she gazed down at her son. There was a quiet rap at the dressing room door, and Annie scurried to answer it.

"Oh, sir! She ain't finished with the babies yet," Annie said, blocking the half-open door with her plump bulk.

"I'll come back later."

Rafe's deep voice flowed like thick syrup on Brenna's

suddenly quivering nerves. Since their arrival, he rarely sought her out. True, the babies took up nearly all of her time, but Brenna had been a little hurt by Rafe's seeming avoidance of her. She supposed that since his return to New York the pressures of work kept him away, and he had been all solicitousness regarding her comfort. Yet it was Rafe himself that she longed for, and since his visits were so rare she wasn't about to let Annie send him away now.

"It's all right, Annie," Brenna called. "Come in, Rafe."

Rafe, resplendent in full evening dress, stepped around Annie, his pale eyes twinkling at her expression of indignation.

"Well, sir, at least put out that cheroot," Annie demanded. "It ain't good for the boys."

"Yes, ma'am." Rafe's mustache twitched. "Perhaps you'd dispose of it for me on your way out?"

Annie accepted the still smoking cigar reluctantly, gingerly holding it between two fingertips, her plain face compressed in repugnance. "You need anything else, Miz Sinclair?" she asked.

"No, thank you, Annie." Brenna kept her lips still with an effort, but when Annie pulled the door closed with a resounding thump, she couldn't hold back her smile any longer. "Rafe, you scoundrel!" She laughed. "Why do you delight in teasing Annie?"

"She's a challenge," Rafe said with a grin, shrugging. "She's more protective of you than a mother hen. I get the definite feeling that I'm here only on her sufferance. Besides, I'll wager she tried a puff of that cheroot before she tossed it away."

Brenna laughed at that, then cuddled Peter closer when he protested her sudden movement. Rafe's eyes narrowed on the smooth white skin exposed by the lacy edge of her white peignoir, then he hurriedly bent over the other cradle to admire his eldest son.

"You're going out tonight?" Brenna asked hesitantly.

He nodded. "Yes. George and I have to meet Dillon to discuss the latest round of calls for demand notes at the Union Pacific."

"Is it serious?"

"Mr. Gould is still in Idaho, and poor Dillon is desperate. Giovanni believes this latest siege indicates someone is trying to make a drive for the Union Pacific itself."

"Is Mr. Rossini right?"

"Who knows for certain? The market is narrow, the Street edgy and waiting for disaster to strike. But if the U.P. goes into receivership, all hell could break loose."

"Would it hurt you?"

Rafe's expression was grim. "It wouldn't help. And I haven't been able to secure control of the Sante Fe line as yet. If Gould needs my assets to help shore up the Union Pacific, I may lose all the ground I've gained in that area."

"Why? Isn't the Sante Fe more important to you than Mr. Gould's Union Pacific?"

"I owe him, Brenna. If he needs me, I'll be there." Rafe's voice held an implacable element, and Brenna dared not push this particular question further.

"Perhaps it won't come to that," she murmured.

"Not if I can help it." Sean's small fist curled around his father's dark forefinger, and Rafe couldn't prevent the smile that curved his hard lips.

"It's all so confusing." Brenna shook her head. She saw Rafe's hesitancy with Sean and prodded him gently. "You can pick him up. He won't break. You of all people should know that."

Gingerly, Rafe lifted Sean from the cradle and sat down on the edge of the brocade-covered brass bed. Father and son gazed solemnly at each other for a long moment, then Sean gave a gigantic yawn that made his parents laugh, sharing the intimacy of the moment.

"He's grown," Rafe murmured. Involuntarily, his eyes strayed again to the swell of her breast where Peter suckled sleepily. His loins tightened with desire. His lips compressed in a self-derisive smile. He was jealous of his own son!

"They both have." Brenna looked up to find her husband's avid gaze upon her and she blushed. There was something so intimate, so disturbing, in feeding the babe with Rafe watching. Was she too immodest? Was it sinful to like the way your husband's eyes traveled over you?

Awareness flashed through her like summer lightning, distant but electrifying.

Rafe tore his eyes away and cleared his throat. "I meant to take you out of the August city heat, perhaps to the Catskills, but now with this latest crisis—"

"We're quite comfortable here," Brenna interjected. Surely he didn't mean to send her away again? Is that why he had all but ignored her since their arrival in New York? She had so hoped the tenuous thread of intimacy and communion they'd shared during the birth of their sons might be woven into the fabric of a real marriage. She tried to keep the quiver out of her voice. "It's no hotter than I'm accustomed to, anyway. And we're close to Central Park here."

Rafe rose and replaced the sleeping infant in his bed. He turned back to Brenna, watching her for a long, intense moment until the rosy color washed her cheeks again. Reaching out, he touched a soft tendril of fiery gold hair that fell over her shoulder. Following it down to where it curled softly against her breast, he played with the springy end.

"Are you happy with the room?" he asked.

"Of course." Her answer was rather breathless. "It's beautiful."

"I know you women like your own things. Feel free to add those scarves or drapes or whatever you all seem to like so well."

Her eyes flicked rapidly to the lace-hung windows with their tasteful overdrapes, the needlepointed firescreen and striped satin fainting couch, the new Tiffany lighting fixture. Soft blue walls contrasted with the dark wood occasional tables and creamy brocaded spread. The room was well-appointed but not ridiculously ostentatious, in keeping with the other portions of Rafe's house. To Brenna, it was the height of luxury and good taste.

"Thank you, but it's lovely the way it is."

"Yes." Rafe's voice was husky, and his eyes never left her upturned face. Their gazes tangled, meshed, and heat rose in his blood like deep, rich wine. Slowly he leaned toward her until his lips met hers, and he caught her soft sigh with his mouth. She was lovely and utterly desirable and smelled of lavender and faintly of milk. Rafe groaned and deepened the kiss, his tongue probing forcefully, his fingers moving restlessly through her captured curl to explore the roundness of her swollen breast beneath the lace-trimmed sacque.

Trapped by his hand, his lips, and the babe at her breast, Brenna's head whirled with the clusters of sensation that stormed through her veins, tugging at her nipple, teasing her lips, and contracting to a throbbing core deep within her. Desire thundered, and he swallowed her small, hungry whimper with a consuming voraciousness that made her weak.

Peter's startled wail broke them apart. Rafe stepped away, and Brenna immediately moved the squalling infant to her shoulder, patting him and whispering love words against his fringe of fine black hair. Her face flamed and her breathing was ragged.

"It seems the boy objects to being ignored," Rafe said, trying for lightness. He could have kicked himself, allowing his own base desires to surface at such a delicate moment. What must Brenna think of him? Still, a man had a right to know about certain things, and he could not stop himself from asking, however obliquely, about the concern that was foremost in his mind. "Ah—I haven't inquired about your health. Are you regaining your strength?"

Brenna shot Rafe a startled glance, then hurriedly rose from the rocker and set Peter in his cradle. "Well enough, thank you."

Was he asking her what she thought he was asking? He'd left no doubt about his desire for her before the babies came. Was he asking her to take her rightful place in his bed as his wife now? Brenna's heart thumped, excitement and apprehension dueling for superiority within her. He never spoke of love, yet would knowing that he wanted her be enough?

The throbbing deep in her middle resumed its beat, and her blood thundered in her veins. Her body said it was enough. Her head whispered he belonged to another. And her heart? Her heart shouted that if passion was the only way she could tell Rafe she loved him, then so be it. She owed him—and herself—that much, at least. She tucked the blanket around the baby and straightened, giving Rafe a direct look with her green gaze. "I should be fully recovered in another week or two."

He was taken aback by her candor, then his eyes blazed, hot and silver with promise. His voice was gruff. "Good. You'll be able to get out more by then. I'll get theater or opera tickets, shall I? And we can dine afterward at Delmonico's."

Pleasure glowed in her eyes, and she bit her lip to control her delight. Was he actually going to court her? "I—I'd enjoy that," Brenna murmured. "Although I don't know anything about opera."

"That's all right, neither do most of the patrons who attend," Rafe said with a sardonic twist of his lips. "Most are more interested in the social parade than in the singing. But it will give me the opportunity to show off my beautiful wife to the world."

"Oh." She'd forgotten that part of their marriage agreement included making a respectable appearance in that role. Was that part of Gould's plan, too? Her hopes dipped and soared like the Coney Island "Shoot the Chutes" ride Annie raved about. Bruised feelings made her teeth snap together and her voice acid. "I hope I don't disappoint you."

"Of course you won't!" Rafe grinned, oblivious. "Why, Red, you'll be the talk of the town! Have the seamstress, Mrs. What's-her-name, make you something special."

"Mrs. Oliver. I have several very nice things already," she replied, thinking of her bulging closets and dressers, filled at Rafe's orders with the most exquisite garments the talented modiste could provide. But, of course, Mrs. Sinclair must look the part at all times, and clothing was a part of it. She tried to keep her tone even. "You've been most generous."

"It's no more than the mother of my children deserves," he said carelessly, and Brenna barely checked a wince of pain. He patted his waistcoat. "Here. I've something I want you to keep for the boys." He removed a small carved rattle from a pocket and handed it to her. "Pete gave it to me the day he died. I had it in my vest pocket."

"Dear Pete." Brenna turned the small carved object

over and over in her hand, thinking of the kindly old man who had loved her. She moved to the mantel and laid the rattle beside a small carved cradle. "He made this, too, I'd dropped it in the valise."

"He was quite a whittler, all right. Always had to keep busy," Rafe said gruffly. He turned away abruptly, shoving his hands deep in the pockets of his trousers. Brenna looked at his bent head with pity, and her annoyance vanished. She walked up behind him, her long robe sweeping around her ankles, her satin-shod feet whispering across the carpet. She rubbed her hand up the tense wall of his spine.

"You miss him." It was not a question.

"Yeah."

She stroked the fine fabric of his evening jacket and laid her cheek against his back in a spontaneous gesture of comfort. "I do, too."

"His death won't go unavenged, I swear," Rafe muttered darkly. "That's another reason why . . ."

"Why what?"

"Why we need to be seen in public. It's important that some information gets to the right ears."

"I don't understand." Brenna wore a perplexed expression. Rafe swung around, grasping her upper arms. "It isn't just Larosse, Brenna. From the very start, he's worked for someone. A mastermind who's trying to destroy all I've built. Giovanni and I have decided that we'll never get to him through Larosse. Our only hope is to lay down a network of lies, a smokescreen of sorts, and try to make whoever it is overconfident. Maybe then he'll overplay his hand. Once we know who we're up against, then we can deal with him and Larosse, too— permanently." His face took on a tremendous ferocity, and Brenna shuddered with sudden fear.

"Who would do such a thing?" she asked.

"I've made enemies along the way, and I've inherited some of Mr. Gould's. It's hard to say."

"But they've tried to kill you twice! Are you going to use yourself as bait for some sort of trap?" Her voice was shrill.

"No, nothing like that. Relax, Red. I'm taking every

precaution. And you must promise to, as well. Never leave the house without an escort.''

She chewed her bottom lip worriedly. ''Is it really necessary?''

''No chances, Red,'' he said sternly. ''We'll snare our culprit by outwitting him at his own game. It all started with the Southern Pacific deal. A few false rumors of my impending bankruptcy, a carefully planned foray into the market to expose a 'weakness' in my finances, and perhaps we can force whoever it is out in the open.''

''You're frightening me.'' She shivered and Rafe pulled her against his chest.

''Don't worry, Red. I told you before, I'm not going to let anything happen to you or the boys.''

''It's you I'm worried about!''

''I can take care of myself.''

Brenna groaned inwardly. Overconfidence could prove to be Rafe's undoing just as well as his enemy's. She pressed against him, inhaling the intoxicating scent of clean male and starch and bay rum. She didn't care about revenge or success or even independence at this moment. Somehow falling in love made all that seem unimportant. But she was afraid her love was a pitifully frail restraint on Rafe's dangerous pursuit of his goals, and her helplessness scared her.

Rafe ran his hands down her back, touching the soft swell of her hip, then pulling her close to the hardening proof of his desire with a sudden movement that left no doubt about the depths of his need.

''God, Brenna! You feel so good,'' he said thickly. Lifting her chin with a knuckle, he gazed down into her rosy, soft-eyed countenance for a long moment and finally dropped a swift kiss on her parted lips. He swallowed with difficulty, then reluctantly set her away, a rueful smile twisting his mouth.

''We'll postpone this conversation for two weeks, sweetheart. I'll bid you good night for now.'' He paused at her door and his grin widened, his eyes sparkling with a slightly wicked, teasing light. ''Perhaps in the meantime the twins should move into the nursery? I'd hate for anything to, ah, disturb their sleep.''

He pulled the door shut quietly after him, and Brenna

pressed her hands to her flaming cheeks. Two weeks! Her heart pounded with anticipation. Two weeks, and she would be Rafe's wife again in more than name alone.

"Be still, can't you?" Annie asked in exasperation. "How am I ever going to get your hair up?"

"I'm sorry." Brenna clasped her hands nervously and studied her reflection in the vanity mirror, watching Annie struggle with the curling tongs and hairpins over the elaborate hairdo Mrs. Oliver insisted would be perfect with her modern classical evening dress. "No, it just won't do," Brenna said suddenly and began tugging at the carefully placed pins.

"Oh, now what?" Annie wailed. "You're going to be late for the opera, and Mr. Sinclair will blame me!"

"No, of course he won't," Brenna assured her, vigorously brushing out Annie's handiwork. "But I don't look like myself. It's got to be simple. Where's that gold ribbon?"

After another minute, Annie found herself nodding. Brenna's mass of strawberry hair was secured high on the back of her head in a loose pile with the ribbon woven through its shiny mass. Artful tendrils softened her temples and nape in a Grecian manner. "That is better. Very elegant. Now, hurry into your dress!"

Soon Mrs. Oliver's creation was settled and secured, and Brenna smoothed her elbow-length kid gloves, anxiously chewing her lips. Butter leather evening slippers peeped from beneath the hem of her gown with its elaborate Grecian key embroidery. She couldn't have felt more like Cinderella than if her shoes were indeed made of glass. For a moment, trepidation ruled and she thought wildly of that day in the depot's attic when she'd danced in new shoes with Annie. How far she'd come since that carefree moment! She touched the silver medallion she wore at her throat for courage and turned to her friend.

"Well, Annie? Will it do?"

"You look beautiful!" Annie stood awestruck. The gold crepe gown with its simple drapery across the bodice and skirt and delicate golden fringe showed off Brenna's unusual coloring and splendid slimness with understated elegance. Annie gave herself a shake.

"Hurry down now, and have a good time. I'd never thought you'd be this jittery over a visit to the opera!"

Brenna grabbed up her *sortie de bal*, the hooded evening cloak that matched her gown, and her small beaded evening bag, hoping that Annie thought her high color was due to the excitement of the evening before her. Annie didn't realize it, but Brenna's nervousness didn't concern her debut into New York society, at all. No, it was her darkly attractive and exceedingly virile husband that had her all a-flutter! Brenna forced herself to take a calming breath. How would a real lady, someone like Shakespeare's Desdemona, conduct herself on this all-important occasion? Brenna mentally shook her head. This was no part she play acted; it was her own life, and she would take hold of her destiny! She squared her shoulders and lifted her chin.

"Thank you, Annie." Brenna gave her friend a peck on the cheek. Her eyes glowed with determination. "I intend to have a wonderful evening."

Brenna descended the staircase into the marble-floored foyer. Her slippers made little noise on the multicolored Oriental runner, but Rafe appeared suddenly in the opening to the drawing room and watched her silently. He met her at the bottom step and took her hand, his pale gray eyes sweeping her from head to toe. The husky word he murmured made Brenna's heart race.

"Magnificent."

"Thank you," she whispered.

He helped her into her wrap, his smile slow and dazzling. "I'm afraid you'll make it hard for me to concentrate on Verdi's *Otello* tonight, my dear. I've eyes only for you, and the rest of New York will, too. Shall we?"

Overcome with a tremulous pleasure at his praise and compliments, Brenna returned his smile and nodded her agreement. He was dark and elegant in evening attire, and his magnetism and masculinity reached out to her in waves that made her quiver with anticipation and the first curling tongues of arousal. It was little wonder that she also found it hard to think of anything but the handsome man beside her. The ride in the hansom cab to the Metropolitan Opera House passed in a blur, as did, regrettably, the soaring score and virtuoso performances of the opera stars in the parts of Otello the Moor, his faithful Desdemona, and the evil Iago.

Once they were settled in their box, it seemed that all of Rafe's friends and associates visited to make her acquaintance, ignoring the impassioned tale of jealousy and deceit on the stage below. Brenna nodded and smiled politely and answered questions in her soft, lyrical voice, her innocent air and charming laugh garnering approval of the self-made elements of New York society. She did not know, nor would she have cared, that the old scions, the Astors and Vanderbilts and their friends, watched with equal interest, though their condemnation of anyone associated with Jay Gould was a foregone conclusion.

Whispers of gossip hopscotched back and forth between the boxes, and it was with some chagrin that nothing crass could be found about the charming new wife of that sinfully handsome and ruthlessly ambitious Raphael Sinclair. Eventually the consensus reported she was a daughter of some New Orleans or Atlanta magnate, a cultured, blue-blooded daughter of the Confederacy. A few disappointed mommas sniffed that it was too bad some men felt they had to look outside of New York to find wives. And when Rafe heard this, he grinned, well pleased with Brenna's success, just as he'd envisioned.

The interest continued unabated after the performance. Brenna held Rafe's arm as they promenaded down the grand staircase of the Opera House, mingling with and greeting other patrons. Brenna felt a giddy excitement at the apparent warmth of her welcome into Rafe's circle and real pride that she was the woman on the arm of such a devastating gentleman. There were many who saw her delightful smile and glittering vivacity and envied Rafe Sinclair that night. Although their conversation was light, tension crackled between them, and Brenna wondered if Rafe might suggest they forego their supper.

"Rafe! I say, wait up!" a voice called over the crush.

Rafe frowned slightly, his mouth compressing in irritation. He pulled Brenna against the banister to wait for the fresh-faced young man with the handlebar mustache who approached with a beautiful, dark-haired companion on his arm.

"What luck!" the man said, grinning ingeniously as he joined Rafe and Brenna. "I've been trying to speak to you all week, Rafe. Papa especially wanted me to discuss my ideas for that new spur line with you, but you've been a hard man to see."

"I've been rather tied up," Rafe evaded. Damn! he thought, fuming. Not another half-baked scheme. Why was Rafe always the one obliged to tactfully point out the flaws in the heir apparent's thinking? And this meeting couldn't have occurred at a more inopportune moment. His eyes darted to the woman standing quietly beside her husband, then quickly to Brenna's politely interested face. "Could it wait? We have dinner reservations."

But the young man was oblivious to Rafe's subtle hint.

"Splendid! Delmonico's, of course. Why don't we join you? Combine business with pleasure, so to speak. I'll be able to report our talk to Papa first thing in the morning. Besides, we've been wanting to make the acquaintance of your wife." He turned to his companion. "Isn't that right, m'love?"

"Of course, George. How are you, Rafe? You wouldn't mind a couple of extra dinner companions, would you?"

Rafe groaned inwardly and gritted his teeth, seeing no graceful way to refuse without appearing rude and insulting before the cream of New York society. His well-laid plans for an intimate dinner in the company of his wife went quietly up in smoke at his stiff reply. "No, of course not."

Brenna had felt her husband's instant tension through the gloved hand she rested on his arm and was puzzled. Her glance flicked to the burgundy-gowned woman whose sultry gaze sought Rafe's in a knowing look before turning to Brenna. Dark, almond eyes examined her carefully, then paused and narrowed in recognition on the medallion in the hollow of Brenna's throat. Brenna touched the silver coin with fearful, possessive fingers, knowing all at once whom she faced.

"Brenna," Rafe said, "I'd like you to meet George Gould and his wife, Edith."

Cold tremors chilled Brenna's bones. She felt pale and insignificant next to Edith Kingdon Gould's rather barbaric and sensual beauty. So this was the woman Rafe still loved, in spite of the fact that she belonged to his benefactor's son. Jealousy and resentment flared within Brenna. How could she hope to compete with someone so earthy and beautiful, yet so unattainable? Had Rafe chosen Brenna as his wife of convenience because she could never displace Edith's claim on his heart? Or for something as nebulous and fanciful as their faint resemblance? Rafe's tension gave him away. He was not indifferent. The knowledge that she was a poor second choice shattered Brenna's hopes, but she would not show her pain. Reaching deep for courage she did not expect to find, she stiffened her spine and extended her hand.

"How do you do," she murmured. "Rafe has told me so much about you both."

Chapter 18

The dinner party at Delmonico's elaborate establishment was no less than sheer torture to Brenna. Rafe and George discussed the new spur line, and Brenna forced herself to smile and nod at Edith's uninterrupted stream of chatter. While Brenna simmered with growing resentment, George called for champagne, his convivial mood setting her teeth on edge. Her nerves were shattered by Edith's penetrating inspection and the smoldering looks she cast Rafe from under her dark lashes. That Rafe seemed not to notice made little difference. Brenna did not taste a single dish that was set before her.

She could make no guesses about the motives behind Rafe's gracious manner. He smiled at Edith's malicious little *on dits* and chuckled at George's jolly Wall Street tales, his earlier tension vanished. Did he care so little for her that he could not sense how awkward and difficult this dinner had become? Why did he not rescue her from the interminable situation? Her face was a cool, polite mask that hid her growing fear that it was Edith's fascination that held Rafe in thrall. She longed for some sign that his earlier warm regard had not fled, but as the miserable meal wore on, her hopes died.

Betrayal was as bitter as the coffee that ended the meal, her budding trust in Rafe and hope for their relationship crushed like the linen napkin left in her chair. It had been easy to ignore the knowledge that Rafe's heart was engaged when there had been no face or form to make that threat real. Now she knew how foolish she'd been. A cold ball of hurt filled Brenna's chest, and her warm feelings for Rafe retreated until all that was left was an icy knot of pain and humiliation.

She had a piercing headache and her breasts were uncomfortably heavy by the time they made their adieus. Brenna climbed into another hansom cab, grateful there was no need to keep up the pretense of a smile any longer. She lay her aching head back against the padded leather interior and tried to make her mind mercifully blank.

Rafe gave the address to the hack driver and settled his long length beside her. He took her hand with great solicitousness and squeezed it gently. "I hope the evening hasn't been too much for you, my dear."

Brenna jerked away and her breath hissed past her teeth in indignation. Hostility and resentment radiated from her. "It certainly was. *Much* too much!"

Rafe frowned. Vexation curdled his stomach. Why tonight of all nights did Edith have to appear? Brenna was stiff and as prickly as a cactus with offended pride. Where was the soft and willing woman who'd smiled with shy invitation earlier in the evening? Heat stirred his loins, and he stifled a groan of irritation. She was all too easy to read, but how could he wait to woo her back to pliancy? He fought the temptation to flip her skirts then and there, to bury himself in her velvet softness, and propriety be damned! He drew a tight rein on his rampaging desire and tried to tread lightly. "Didn't you enjoy yourself?"

"You can ask me that? After watching *her* all night? How could you!"

"Don't be a child!" he snapped, losing his patience. "You'll have to learn to curb your squeamishness because we'll be seeing George and Edith often. After all, we're quite a bit more than mere business associates."

"I'll just bet you are!" she spat, trembling with suppressed rage. Her only defense against hurt and jealousy was anger, and she allowed it full reign. She now knew firsthand the murderous fury that had been Othello's tragedy, yet she took no measure to curb it. "I won't be placed in that position ever again, do you hear? I refuse to be humiliated by your—your mistress!"

His jaw tightened and his face was a dark shadow in

the dimness inside the carriage. The steady *clop-clop* of the horse's hooves on the cobbled pavement was a rhythmic counterpoint to his cold, measured phrases. "You assume too much. I told you, whatever was between Edith and me was over long ago. Why, look at her! She's a respectable married woman with a family."

"Who thinks her husband's a fool and looks at you with hungry eyes! I'm not blind and I won't be used. Not again!"

The cab drew to a halt with a jerk and a jingle of harnesses, cutting off Rafe's furious reply. They entered the townhouse, and Brenna marched directly to the staircase, intent only on escaping the searing disappointment that scalded her veins. She had been wrong. Mere desire was not enough, not for her. She couldn't come to Rafe's bed each night, knowing that she was a substitute for another woman. She had more pride than that! Rafe's rough words halted her on the first tread.

"Where do you think you're going?"

She swung around, fixing him with a haughty stare. "I'm tired. I'm going to bed—alone."

Rafe's face hardened. His long stride brought him to her side, and he leaned over her threateningly, his eyes angry slits of silver. His breath was hot on her cheek. "So that's the way it's going to be, is it? Dammit, Red, I'm a man! I'm not made of stone."

The heat and solidity of him made her tremble, but she glared her defiance with eyes that blazed emerald fire. "And I'm a woman! With all the tender qualities that the name implies. Will I never be allowed to decide my own fate?"

Frustration and thwarted passion filled Rafe with a savagery he could barely constrain. "God damn you!" he thundered. "What do you want from me?"

The one thing you no longer have to give, she thought wretchedly. *Your heart*.

But she could not put her hopes, her longing, her dreams into words, only to have him crush them beneath his heel with his laughter, his contempt, or worse, his pity. Her shoulders slumped and her throat felt thick with tears.

"Nothing," she whispered. She shook her head, half

blinded by the gleaming crystal moisture that sparkled on her sooty lashes. "I gave you sons. Now all I ask is that I be left in peace."

Rafe gazed at the soft red-gold curls crowning her bent head and inwardly cursed God and heaven and hell. Was he forever to yearn for that which would always be out of his reach? Like Sisyphus, condemned to labor endlessly because he dared covet those things other men found so easily?

He'd always thought success at any price was worth it, but with Brenna his certainty faltered. He could take her, he knew, by force or seduction, but what purpose would it serve? Would he kill what little respect she might have for him? What satisfaction could he find if he broke her spirit? No, he cared too much for this elusive, plucky woman. She'd carved her place indelibly in his soul, and now this was the price he must pay.

Why was he surprised? A woman's faithlessness and inconstancy were nothing new to him. His lips thinned in self-derision. But this woman had already suffered much at his hands. If he couldn't make her happy, at least he wouldn't hurt her further.

"So be it then, madam," he said, his voice stiff in his own ears. He took a step back. "Within these walls you'll have your wish. But know that I expect you to fulfill your role as my wife in every other aspect. You'll make your public bows prettily, and raise our sons, and run our home." His face darkened ominously and his voice was low and dangerous. "And never, *never* will you again take me to task about where I find what you deny me."

Brenna's head jerked up, a sudden horror overwhelming her. Aghast, she realized what she had done in her jealousy—driven him away forever with her hasty, foolish words, straight into another's arms! A sob tore through her. Her fingers pressed against her lips but could not contain the ragged, wrenching gasps of pain. Blinded by tears, she clutched her skirts and fled up the stairs in an agony of remorse.

Watching the flounce of her hem disappear, Rafe was nearly overcome by a sorrow that cut deep and a piercing self-mockery that the reprieve he'd given her had brought her such tears of relief.

* * *

Brenna never guessed that her acting ability would be put to such a test. Da would have been proud of the way she played her part. True to his word, Rafe saw that she was at his side in public, although each new round of parties or concerts tried her sorely. She longed to retreat to the sanctuary of the nursery, but nearly every evening during the following weeks found her bedecked in her new finery and attending the most glittering functions.

She knew that on these occasions Rafe found the opportunities he wanted to drop careless secrets into avid ears. The knowledge that he was setting his trap for Larosse and his unseen nemesis chilled her bones. But for all the courtesy and doting affection Rafe showed toward his wife in public, Brenna paid a high price in private pain, for she knew his attentions were no more than the polite constraint of a total stranger. Hiding her unhappiness became a bigger task than playing the great lady, and the effort left her limp and miserable, though only Annie saw it.

Only with the babies or during her visits to the cool, cloistered vaults of St. Patrick's Cathedral a few blocks away did Brenna find serenity and peace. Amid the round of shopping and receiving and returning calls, she had discovered the Gothic edifice to be an oasis of calm in the noisy Manhattan bustle. The familiarity of the Mass, the intoned Latin liturgy, the scent of incense, all offered comfort, yet she could not pray, could not find the solutions that would change her unhappiness into acceptance. She wanted to ask God to release her from the burden of her love for Rafe but could not voice the words, as if it were a blasphemy too horrible to be uttered.

As September drew to a close, Gould returned from the west, and Rafe was absent a great deal attending his mentor. The newspapers howled about Gould's latest perfidy, an apparent attempt to hold up J. P. Morgan's bail-out of the Union Pacific's troubled finances. Brenna paid scant attention to the Wall Street news, for Rafe was confident plans were going forward to secure the needed mortgages from Morgan's bank. He laughed at the screaming sensationalism, noting that the idea had originated with Gould himself at Dillon's request, so he would scarcely be working to prevent it. Of more import was the rumor that Gould's Missouri-Pacific line would pass on its quarterly dividend.

Brenna was aware of these things, but only with passing interest, for her energy was consumed in keeping up her shaky façade of calm and dignity. Only her pillow knew the tears she'd wept over her miserable condition of loving a man who saw her only as an asset to be added to his financial statement and, if he had his way, a convenient receptacle for his lust. She wondered if she could stand a lifetime of longing for his affection, yet denying them both the release of passion. She knew that she must for her sons' sakes, even though being near Rafe was an absolute agony.

She was rigid with relief that another evening was over the night they saw Barrymore play Hamlet. Shakespeare's familiar words had come to life on the stage, the tragedy of ambition and death and revenge touching Brenna with its dark overtones of choices made and immutable. Memories of Da haunted her, and the worn visage of her mother mocked her. Was there nothing more to life than endurance and survival? Ophelia's passion for Hamlet had driven her mad. Brenna knew that she was made of sterner stuff, yet Ophelia at least had seen an end to her suffering. What relief did Brenna have to look forward to?

Brenna stepped into the foyer while Rafe paid off the hack driver. Her brain swirled with confusion and disillusionment, and she tugged off her gloves in weary misery. They'd spent another strained evening making polite conversation for the benefit of others. How much more of this torture could she endure? So attuned to her inner turmoil was she that she failed to notice the elegant figure with cane and bowler waiting quietly on the Empire settee until Giovanni Rossini rose to greet her.

"Good evening, Mrs. Sinclair."

Brenna started, then a warm smile curved her lips. The Italian had been very cordial to her in their brief meetings, and she liked him for his quiet manners and meticulous courtesy. She extended her hand in greeting. "Mr. Rossini, what a pleasant surprise! Have you been waiting long?"

He took her hand and bowed over it. "Your excellent butler, Mr. Carlisle, assured me you would not be long in coming. I trust that your evening at the theater was a success? I hate to curtail it in this fashion, but it is rather urgent that I speak with your husband."

"He'll be here in a moment. Please, may I offer you something? Coffee, perhaps?"

"With thanks, no. And how are those fine sons?"

"Growing and healthy. Would you care to see them?"

Giovanni shook his head, but his expression was regretful and a bit wistful. "It is late. I would not disturb the young ones. Perhaps if I might another time?"

"Of course. I would be delighted to show them off."

"It is a regret of my life that I have no sons," Giovanni admitted softly.

Brenna's heart went out to the older gentleman. She wondered if his bachelorhood was a result of a lifetime of devotion to Gould's interests at the expense of his own. For all his continental urbanity, she sensed the same loneliness she had seen sometimes in Pete Hooke's eyes. It was a terrible burden to be alone, as well she knew. "You must feel free to visit us as often as you can," she hastened to assure him with genuine warmth.

"You're most gracious to indulge an old man's fancy. Rafe was fortunate indeed that circumstances brought him so lovely a wife. Ah, here he is now."

Rafe paused in the doorway. "Giovanni? What is it?"

"A moment of your time," Giovanni replied, his dark eyes flashing an enigmatic message. "Will you excuse us, my dear?"

Brenna quietly bid them good night and mounted the stairway, her glance thoughtful on the two dark heads moving into the drawing room, one raven's-wing dark, the other equally black where not threaded with silver. She listened to the deep, concerned timbre of Rafe's words, storing up the sound in her heart. Then with a sigh of regret as deep as Giovanni's, she sought her own chamber for another empty night.

Annie awaited her there, dozing in the wicker rocking chair. Yawning and rubbing her plump, sleep-flushed cheeks, she rose to help Brenna undress.

"You shouldn't have waited up," Brenna chided gently.

Annie shrugged, loosening the laces and tapes and buttons on Brenna's moss velvet and black lace gown. "Ain't no trouble. I checked on those boys and they're sleeping like two angels, though I know they'll be howling at first light for their mama."

Brenna smiled and slipped into a paisley silk dressing gown. "And your evening? How was it?" She sat at the mirrored vanity and slowly pulled the pins from her hair, spilling it to her waist.

"Right nice. That feller Jimmy wrote me about came 'round, you know, and took me and Louise down to Child's Lunchroom for ice cream. Vanilla, with fudge sauce." Annie smacked her lips and hung up Brenna's dress. "Tommy Black's his name, though he likes to be called Thomas. He's got a nice set of whiskers, but he asked the most questions of anybody I ever seen."

Brenna ran her silver-backed brush through her hair. "I'm glad you had a nice time," she murmured.

"What about that there play? Did you and the mister enjoy it?"

Brenna stared distractedly at her pale reflection in the mirror. "What? Oh, yes, fine."

"Well, you don't much act like it," Annie grumbled.

"I—" Suddenly, Brenna's lip trembled.

Annie's plain face softened and she gently touched her friend's shoulder. "What's the matter, honey?"

Brenna's eyes swam with unshed tears. "Oh, Annie, what am I going to do?" she whispered miserably. "I can't stand it, he treats me so coldly."

Annie cleared her throat uncomfortably. She didn't have to guess who "he" was. "Well, it ain't my business to mention such, but I was wondering . . . well, you know . . . since the babies moved into the nursery . . . why the mister ain't been to visit. You know, at night . . ." Annie's face was scarlet. "It ain't none of my business," she repeated staunchly.

Brenna gave a strangled laugh and wiped the moisture from the corners of her eyes with her fingertips. "If our problems were that easy to solve, I'd do the visiting myself."

"Well, why don't you?" Annie demanded.

Brenna gave her an astounded look, then shook her head, unable to contain her bitter anguish any longer. "You—you don't understand. He loves someone else."

Annie gave an unladylike snort. "I don't believe it, not the way I've seen him look at you! Hungry-like."

"It's true, though. I thought it wouldn't matter, but it does. Oh, Annie," Brenna cried, "I love him so much!"

"Well, then, you'd better fight for him! And the best way to do that is to make him happy in your bed."

"You mean—seduce my own husband?" Brenna's cheeks flushed a delicate peach.

"You're his wife, ain't you? Who has a better right?" Annie demanded, her brown eyes snapping. "Listen here, Brenna. My ma was just a country girl, but she always said if you keep your man busy and satisfied, he won't have time to think about another woman."

Brenna bit her lip. "But what if he doesn't want me?"

Annie gave her a look of disgust and pushed her around so that they both stared into the mirror. "Look at yourself. You can *make* him want you. And he can learn to love you. But you got to take the chance."

Annie gave Brenna one last encouraging pat on the shoulder and quietly left the room. Brenna stared into the troubled, turbulent eyes of the woman in the mirror. Could she make Rafe desire her again? Could the reality of a flesh and blood woman in his bed replace his longing for Edith? And what of her pride? Brenna trembled. Pride was a lonely companion. Annie was right. It was a chance worth taking if she wanted to win Rafe's love. But did she have the courage to do it?

Rafe strode into his darkened bedroom, tugging at his tie and unfastening the studs on his shirt. His mind whirled with the disturbing news Giovanni had brought. Gould had all but collapsed at the Missouri-Pacific's quarterly meeting and was now under Dr. Munn's care. Rafe knew Gould's oldest daughter, Helen, would see that her father followed the doctor's instructions to the letter, but he doubted if there was anything, including ill health, that would keep the little man locked within the confines of his Fifth Avenue mansion for long. Perhaps the doctor would suggest he recuperate at Lyndhurst, Gould's country estate on the Hudson.

At any event, the press was sure to have a field day, and the market itself was liable to fluctuate wildly at the mere rumor of serious illness. It couldn't have come at a more inopportune time for Rafe, right in the middle of delicate negotiations that would give him controlling interest in the Santa Fe line. If the market climbed, he might have to pay double for what he wanted. Rafe's lips thinned. No matter. He'd have that stock, whatever the cost, and then Smitherman would have to deal. No doubt Gould would be very grateful when Rafe dropped both the Santa Fe and Southern Pacific in his lap. Denied by the one woman he wanted to the point of obsession, and unmanned in his own home, at least his climb to the top of the business world's ladder would be some solace. It was all he had.

Rafe tossed the studs on top of his mahogany chest-on-chest and turned, reaching for the lamp on the table beside the bed. He froze. The pale oval of face was too dimly lit to reveal her features, but he knew that fall of strawberry hair that shimmered with a light of its own.

"Brenna? Is something wrong? The boys . . . ?"

The chair in which she sat creaked slightly as she rose slowly to her feet. She took a tentative step toward him, and her voice was low and strangely husky. "No, nothing's wrong."

He pulled the chain on the leaded glass Tiffany lamp with a flick of irritation, flooding the room with a soft, multicolored glow. She stood blinking, her hair falling across her shoulders in soft waves and the medallion he'd given her nestled between the swell of her breasts. Rafe sucked in a breath between his teeth at the sight she made, wrapped in the swirling paisley dressing gown that clung to her slim curves, revealing and tantalizing so that he ground his teeth to keep from reaching for her.

"What do you want? What were you doing sitting in here in the dark?" he asked. He pulled his tie free from his stiff collar and threw it on top of the studs, then shrugged out of his dinner jacket.

"Just sitting. And thinking." She hugged herself as

though she were cold. "I've been doing a lot of that lately."

"Have you?" He made his tone purposefully disinterested. He tugged his shirttails from the waistband of his trousers and removed his cuff links, then paused, his shirt hanging open. His eyebrow lifted and his lips curved in a mocking line. "I don't wish to offend your modesty, madam, so perhaps you'd better leave. It's been a hellish day and I don't sleep in a nightshirt."

Her eyes were wide and her voice was a bare whisper of sound. "Rafe?"

Suddenly wary, he eyed her uncertainly and with a modicum of belligerence. "What?"

If possible her eyes became even wider, each dilating until there was only a thin ring of green around the circle of black pupil. She swallowed and visibly gathered her courage.

"May I stay?"

Thunderstruck, Rafe could only stare for a long moment. Then an angry flush surged up his neck, darkening his swarthy face under his tan. "What sport is this? Don't play your games with me, Red." He was afraid to touch her, afraid of the violence that threatened if he should lose his hard-won control.

She chewed on the swell of her lower lip in an unconsciously provocative fashion and shook her head. "It's not a game. I want . . ." She faltered to a stop at his ominous expression.

"What? What do you want?" he demanded thickly.

Brenna took a step closer, then another and another, until he could smell the scent of lavender and feel the womanly warmth of her skin radiating through the thin silk. Hesitantly, she reached out, laying her small palm over the place in his chest where his rampaging heart threatened to tear loose from its moorings. "I want . . . you. I want to be your wife in truth." Her small, rounded chin quivered with vulnerability, and her voice dwindled to a gossamer wisp of sound. "I want it to be like it was between us—that first time."

Rafe's hand covered hers, squeezing the delicate bones in a crushing grip. "Why?" he rasped hoarsely.

"Is it important?"

He nodded, his eyes narrowed, his brows a straight glowering line. She gave a shuddering sigh, and rosy color stained her cheeks.

"When you were shot, I promised God that if He let you live, I'd be a good wife to you. But I let pride and fear and jealousy get in the way of that promise and . . . and both of us are suffering for it." She swallowed and stumbled on. "I've been sitting in St. Patrick's, day in and day out, trying to find a way to tell you I was wrong—about so many things."

"Did you confess to a priest? Did he tell you to do your duty to your husband?" Rafe demanded. God had played too many tricks on him in his life for him to be easily swayed by such an argument. "I want no cold female in my bed doing her duty!"

"I spoke to no one. Please, Rafe. Nothing has ever been easy between us, but this marriage is all we have, for better or worse. Let's try to make it better." She rose on her toes, one hand caught in his, the other resting lightly on his shoulder, and pressed a gentle kiss against the unyielding line of his mouth. "For me it's much more than duty. Though I've tried hard to deny it, I've never stopped wanting you. Please let me stay."

Her whisper was raw with an honesty that pierced the hard, defensive shell around his heart. A giant shudder racked him. Suddenly, he didn't give a damn if it was her sense of duty or God's will or sheer madness that brought her willingly to him. He had to have her—now. He wrapped his arms around her, pulling her into the cradle of his thighs, letting her feel the hard power of his desire. His mouth sought hers blindly, with a ravenous hunger that plundered her lips and the sweetness within like that of a starving man. She whimpered deep in her throat, and he pulled away, burying his face in the delicate curve of her neck.

"Be sure," he gasped, knowing he'd surely die if she stopped him now.

"I am. Oh, Rafe, kiss me again."

That was all the encouragement he needed.

He plunged his fingers into the silky skein of her hair, holding her head so that his lips could drink their fill, tasting her nectar, nibbling and sipping, her tongue meeting his in an electric surge of passion long denied. Her hands slipped under his shirt, exploring the muscles in his chest, the new lacing of still-tender scar tissue on his side, the valley of his spine, the hard ridges of his belly. Her fingers played through the soft whorls of chest hair, found and teased the flat male nipples, eliciting a groan from him.

Sliding his hard palms down her back, Rafe smoothed the flare of her hip and stopped, startled to discover that she wore nothing underneath her dressing gown. Flames heated his blood and throbbed in his loins. Cupping her buttocks, he lifted her against him, moving and circling their lower bodies while their mouths clung. Eagerly, she responded, pressing forward, darting her tongue to twine with his, using her hands to incite him, nearly pushing him over the brink.

He fell with her onto the bed, pinning her with his thigh and holding her wrists at the side of her head. He kissed her mouth, her chin, the slim column of her throat, then pushed aside the edges of the dressing gown with his nose. She writhed beneath him, her breath shredding, her hunger growing in league with his to scatter all hesitancy and destroy all restraint.

Drawing back, he drank in the beauty of her perfect breasts, fuller now, with their coral tips and the creamy whiteness of her blue-veined skin, marred only by that sprinkling of freckles. He pressed his mouth against the star-shaped freckle on the upper curve of her breast and felt her sigh. His lips continued across her skin, barely touching her, brushing the sensitized flesh with just a hint of his mustache, his breath blowing hotly across the budding nipples. He smiled as they puckered, responding involuntarily to his teasing, and Brenna moaned, tugging at her wrists.

"Let me touch you," she pleaded.

"Not yet. Not until you know the madness of wanting that I've felt all this time." His tongue flicked out, scalding the hard budding flesh. She tasted of woman and the faint residue of milk. He laved the tip with the tender-rough surface of his tongue, then watched, fascinated by the tiny blue-white liquid pearl that formed.

"I should not drink where our sons so often sup, yet

I'll wager they'll not begrudge me this small taste of paradise," he murmured. Slowly, he bent his head and nipped the droplet onto his tongue, savoring her essence. Brenna gasped and arched against him, her eyes wild with the sheer eroticism of his gesture.

"Rafe, please!"

"Be patient, Red. I've had to learn much of that virtue, and now so must you." So saying, he pulled her hands down beside her hips, still holding them fast, and blazed a path across the downy planes of her belly, dipping into her navel and lower. The belt of her gown fell away, and he nuzzled within the musky triangle at the top of her thighs, letting his sweet torture wring gasping cries of delight from her parted lips. He released her hands, and her fingers dug into the thick silkiness of his hair. She moaned his name, her voice frantic with desire.

And that's how Rafe felt—frantic, and consumed by the ache that severed his control. He tore off his clothes, unable to spare another minute, and found that she met him with a fiery hunger of her own. Their joining was fast and furious, demanding and insatiable, out-of-control and joyously abandoned, with no more time or need for tenderness. Only the powerful surge and thrust, parry and plunge of absolute need, with a burning, all-consuming passion that took them higher and higher until the white-hot conflagration exploded, shattering them with pleasure given and received.

Brenna sobbed her happiness against his sweat-drenched neck, and this time Rafe did not question her, but held her close and felt his own eyes prickle with moisture.

Brenna eased out of Rafe's loose embrace in the gray pre-dawn light, careful not to disturb him. A deep contentment and joy filled her, and she blushed with the night's remembered passion and pleasure, but duty called. She swung her feet to the floor, then felt Rafe reach for her, his voice muffled by sleep.

"Don't."

She smiled, warmed by his possessive hand on her waist. She turned back to him, drinking in the hard planes of his face, softened in passion's aftermath, the dark tousled hair, combed into disarray by her eager fingers.

Greatly daring, with the euphoria of newfound confidence, she brushed a strand of hair back from Rafe's forehead and bent to kiss the corner of his mouth.

"Good morning," she whispered.

He grunted and tugged her over to lie on top of him, peeking at her lazily through his thick lashes. His hand roamed over her silky thigh and across the mound of her bare buttock. "Who gave you permission to leave my bed, wench?"

"Much as I've reason to stay, I must go," she murmured. "Your sons call."

He opened one eye and listened, hearing indeed the faint wails from the nursery. "Good God! Do they always arise at this ungodly hour?"

She laughed. "Of course. They're too young to know their manners yet." Dropping a swift kiss on his lips, she tried to slide away. "I must go."

"Not so fast, Red." He rolled her over and ravished her mouth with a kiss that took her breath away, then bounded out of the bed. He grinned and stretched, a magnificent male animal resplendent in his unselfconscious nudity. "Stay there. I'll fetch them for you."

"But, Rafe . . ."

Too late, he disappeared down the corridor. A moment later a shrill shriek split the air, then Annie rushed past the open door, her apron thrown over her head, giggling to split her sides. Rafe reappeared in the doorway, a bright-eyed, black-haired infant balanced on each thick forearm. He kicked the bedroom door closed, and a ruddy color suffused his dark face.

Brenna took one look at his chagrined expression and doubled over in peals of helpless laughter.

"Jesus Christ!" Rafe grumbled, perching on the side of the bed. "What does a man have to put up with in his own house?"

Brenna reached for Peter, who was now chortling noisily in time with her own giggles, and settled him to her breast. "I'm sorry, Rafe," she said, "but I tried to warn you."

Rafe bounced Sean on his knee, his smile sheepish. "Hell of a note, ain't it, boy?" He cocked an eyebrow at Brenna. "Just what did Annie mean by 'Thank the Lord!'?"

Chapter 19

Along the "Queen of Avenues" foot traffic was brisk. Ladies in tall hats and short, fitted jackets strolled with a fistful of skirt in one hand, the "skirt clutch" technique that saved their sweeping hems from the worst dirt. In dark frock coats, bowler hats, and an occasional fedora, gentlemen nodded politely but continued their earnest conversations. Couples visited on the wide front stoops of some of the city's most handsome residential dwellings, including the Gould mansion at the corner of 47th Street and Fifth Avenue. Here and there a street vendor sold gumdrops or roasted peanuts under a makeshift canvas awning.

The street was filled with broughams and hansom cabs and the tinkling ring of bicycle bells. An open horsecar, its striped awnings raised to admit air and light, moved across an intersection, heading for the river and the ferry landing. Farther down the street, visitors to the city lounged in the lobby of the elegant Hotel Windsor, and St. Patrick's twin spires poked dual holes in the blue sky.

"Good day, Mrs. Sinclair, Miss Annie."

"Hello, sir." Brenna smiled her greeting.

Giovanni Rossini fell into step beside her on the wide, paved Fifth Avenue sidewalk. She and Annie pushed identical high-wheeled wicker baby carriages through the sun-splashed October afternoon.

"I see you've been taking advantage of the marvelous weather," Giovanni murmured, peering eagerly into the carriages. Sean and Peter made baby noises and blew spittle bubbles at him, their blue gazes locked with interest on this new face.

"We've been to the park," Brenna replied, turning the corner of 57th Street. Her Neapolitan braid hat with its mint ribbons perched jauntily on her strawberry tresses, drawing many an admiring glance. "The day was too beautiful to ignore, though I've been warned that it can't last."

"Indeed, Old Man Winter will be bringing his ice and snow sooner than we know. Central Park can be very pretty then, as well."

"Will you come in and visit awhile?" Brenna asked as they approached the middle of the quiet block. The tall, narrow windows of the Sinclair brownstone gleamed brightly in the sunlight.

"Gladly. As it happens, I'm on my way to have a word with Rafe," he added.

She smiled at him with an impish lift to her lips. "Wouldn't it have been simpler to telephone?"

"Ah, a diabolical instrument." Giovanni laughed. "But in that case, I would have missed the pleasure of your company, Mrs. Sinclair."

"Please, call me Brenna." She tucked her arm into his and smiled charmingly, her happiness sparkling in her eyes. "We must become close friends. My sons have no grandfather to spoil them, and I know you have always been an important part of my husband's life."

"Thank you, my dear. And I am Giovanni. It's true I've been involved in Rafe's education, sometimes to his great annoyance, but it's Mr. Gould who has been his benefactor all these years."

"Why would Rafe be annoyed?" she asked, curious to know all there was about her love, her husband, the man who made her days smile and her nights weep with joy.

Giovanni laughed softly. "We have always butted heads, about nearly every subject, since Rafe came under my care. As a boy, he was a fighter. It serves him ably now, although I think you have mellowed him, my dear."

"Perhaps having a family of his own around him is the reason for that," Brenna murmured. "He told me he was on his own, a mere child, surviving as he might when he first came to Mr. Gould's notice during the Fiske days."

"Yes, Diamond Jim and the Grand Opera House." Giovanni shook his head, remembering. "Those were wild times, best not repeated. Rafe showed promise, even then. He was a shrewd street urchin determined to succeed. It was those qualities that encouraged Mr. Gould to subsidize his education, and an able student he was, although a bit of a scrapper. I had more than one conversation with the headmaster of the boy's school Rafe attended.'' He shook his head, chuckling. ''Although the sisters at the Ward of Mercy had fostered him with Mr. Gould's help ever since he was a baby, I think they drew a sigh of relief the day Rafe left Mulberry Street behind.''

''I don't think I understand. I thought their association began during the Fiske days,'' Brenna said, puzzled.

''No, long before that. It was not uncommon, even then, for the Goulds to quietly choose some philanthropic cause and carry it out anonymously. Of course, as Mr. Gould's private secretary, I was privy to that information. We kept a quiet eye on several such children. Mr. Gould's family was always his primary concern, and he felt keenly for the orphans. When Rafe ran away from the home that last time, the old nun and Mr. Gould decided between them that ours was the best way. Mr. Gould's investment in Rafe has been paid off a hundredfold in loyalty and monetary success.''

''It's hard to think of a child as an investment,'' Brenna returned distastefully, her eyes on her two small sons.

''An investment in the future, my dear. What would Rafe be today but for Mr. Gould's interest?''

What indeed? Brenna asked herself. What would Rafe be without his unquestioning loyalty to so powerful a man? Would he be driven to such lengths to succeed, to fashion his destiny in the business world at any cost? She had no doubt that Rafe's character would have overcome any hardship to become whatever he wanted. But would he have been happier as a simple farmer or a small shop owner? She shrugged to herself. Those questions were merely flights of fancy. Rafe was Rafe, and the man she knew now was the one who was precious to her.

She took secret pride in the knowledge that she made him happy, that for some brief moments, she alone could make him forget the demons that drove him. Though the word *love* never appeared in their conversations, she had hopes that in time that would come. For now, the growing contentment in their household and the private ecstasy of their bedroom were sufficient.

"I like to think that I was in some small part responsible for Rafe's growing into such a successful young man," Giovanni continued quietly. His dark, liquid eyes were suddenly melancholy. "If things had been different, my beloved Ingrid and I might have . . ." He broke off as they reached the brownstone's stoop, and he cleared his throat gruffly, as though a bit embarrassed at his momentary lapse into his private memories. "Well, no matter. Ah, here we are! Let me assist you with the carriage, and you, too, Miss Annie."

The general uproar involved in getting the twins inside and the carriages put away gave Brenna time to reflect on that last revealing statement. So Giovanni had indeed loved someone in his youth, she thought. Whatever had happened to keep them apart, Brenna was sympathetic, and promised herself to be exceptionally kind to the older gentleman because of it.

Annie disappeared upstairs with two sleepy babies. In his shirt sleeves, Rafe appeared from his study, where he'd been working, to greet Giovanni. Rafe's eyes glittered at the sight of Brenna in her flirtatious hat, and his lips bore an indulgent smile that made his handsome face devastating. Brenna took off her hat and repp silk jacket and asked Carlisle to send coffee to the study.

She served the coffee from a chased silver service, chatting lightly and teasing Rafe about the condition of his desk, which was piled high with documents and bound volumes of minutes from his various railroad holdings.

Rafe accepted the cup she brought to him, balancing it on his knee and squeezing her hand. "Complain all you want, Red," he said with a lazy smile, "but if you extend your cleaning campaign to my study, you'll risk my wrath. So proceed at your own peril!"

Brenna's laugh tinkled like a silver bell in the heavily appointed room. "Since when have I been able to resist a challenge like that, sir?" she teased. "I'll excuse myself now, for I know you gentlemen are dying to discuss business." Her hand lingered for a sweet moment in his, and then she departed with a swish of skirts and a hint of lavender.

"She adds much to this house," Giovanni remarked as the door closed quietly behind her.

"She adds much to my life." Rafe reached for a thin cigar and lit it, puffing silently for a moment.

He was loath to examine too closely his contentment these days, fearing like a child that it would prove insubstantial and ephemeral. Yet each morning he awoke with new purpose, finding the woman in his bed no dream, but real warm flesh and ever-surprising passion. Yes, she added new meaning to his life, and for the first time he was beginning to believe that the subtle changes she wrought in him with her tender ways were strengths and not weaknesses. It made every success that much sweeter.

He leaned back in his leather armchair, and his lips curled upward with a satisfied smile. "Well, Giovanni, I've done it."

"What? Married well, in spite of yourself?" the older man asked. "So I've noticed."

Rafe chuckled. "Yes, that, too. But I was referring to the Santa Fe line. By the close of the Exchange today, I'll be majority stockholder."

Giovanni's silvery brows lifted in acknowledgment. "Congratulations. That is no small accomplishment, considering the circumstances."

"Yes, having to use dummy companies and proxies complicated the matter immensely, yet I cannot complain. The hounds of Wall Street are baying at my heels at this very moment, ready to tear me to shreds when I trip and fall." He grinned. "Too bad I'll have to disappoint them."

"And have you discovered the leader of this pack?"

Rafe frowned and ground out his cigar in a porcelain dish. "Unfortunately, no. One seems as eager to see me ruined as the next, but they are all petty thieves. I know names, yet no one to whom I can connect that villain, Larosse. But I haven't given up. Our attempt to thimblerig this game may yet prove fruitful."

"I find it extremely odd that the missing securities have never surfaced. After all, it's been a year now since Plummer's murder."

"Whoever has them is too wily to let that happen."

"But what good are they in that case?" Giovanni

asked, setting his empty cup aside and straightening the precise crease in his trousers.

Rafe rose, shrugging. "I don't know. Collateral for a private loan, maybe. Or for use against Gould's acquisition of the Southern Pacific."

"I'm afraid Mr. Gould's heart is no longer in that project. His precarious health and the damned persistent rumor that he is short on the market with the U.P. takes all his energy."

"Perhaps with the Santa Fe on the bargaining table, he will change his mind."

"Yes, I'm sure he'll be quite proud of your accomplishment," Giovanni agreed, folding his long-fingered hands beneath his chin thoughtfully. "Although it chagrins him when you succeed with an initiative of your own where George cannot."

"George is able, but more interested in the things money can buy than the making of it," Rafe said, dismissing George with a wave of his hand.

"Take care you never come between them," Giovanni warned. "Make no mistake, Gould would have no qualms about squashing any threat to his son, no matter who's involved."

Rafe stiffened. "No need to recite me that lesson. I know what I owe and to whom I owe it."

Giovanni stifled a sigh. Sometimes the young man could be unbearably tiresome. "It is just as well we never told him of our fears of a conspiracy. Perhaps this Larosse was working alone, after all."

"No! I don't believe that." Rafe paced up and down on the Oriental rug before his desk. "There are too many coincidences. And as long as Larosse is on the loose, he's a threat. Don't forget that Brenna was a witness to Plummer's killing. I won't rest until he's brought to justice."

"Our agents believe he may have headed north again, but he covers his trail well. They're still working on it."

"Then tell them to work harder! Dammit, Giovanni, a man like that just doesn't drop off the face of the earth! Where can he be hiding?"

"You know yourself that Hell's Kitchen and Five Points can swallow a man alive. A villain may hide himself in those cankerous nether regions and never see the light of day.''

''Until his master calls him and he crawls into the sunlight again,'' Rafe replied. His eyes were hard. ''And that, Giovanni, is what scares me.''

''You there! Watch what you're doing. You ruin me mums and I'll have yer ass!''

''Aye, sir.''

The answer was more a sneer than a respectful reply, but Edgar Larosse wasn't concerned. He insolently dropped the pots sporting yellow blooms beside the gardener digging in the flower bed. The other hired men were afraid of him, and for all his big talk, so was this one. It suited him to have it so.

The thin silver ribbon of the Hudson glinted through the trees. But the beauty of the extensive grounds made no impression on Larosse, who turned a surly face to gaze with one black eye at the tall, mullioned windows of the manor house. He spat in the dirt, grumbling inwardly.

Damn him, anyway! Sitting up there like a damned fat spider in a web while a man's talents went to waste.

What was a man supposed to do out here in the boondocks with no proper whorin' or drinkin'? Hiding out wasn't his style, anyway. Better to go after that cursedly lucky Sinclair and his red-haired bitch straight out. But no, the old fox wants it done his way, pitched a flat-out fit when he learned Edgar had taken matters into his own hands down in Texas.

''You there! Get back to the greenhouse. I need more mums.''

With a curse, Larosse stomped through the bed, crushing yellow petals beneath his heavy heel. Stalking away, he snarled to the startled gardener, ''Get 'em yourself!''

If he didn't get out of this blasted flower garden soon, the old fox was gonna lose one of his pansy-pickers for sure!

Larosse's lip curled. In the meantime, what was to keep him from making a little visit back to his old stamping grounds? After all, a man was entitled to a little fun, even if he was waiting things out. Never knew what a body might pick up down there, either. No sir, you never knew.

"Annie! Where are you? Oh, wait until you hear!" Brenna burst into Annie's modest but comfortable third-floor bedroom, her face alight, waving a letter. "They're coming!"

Annie whipped around, pushing her disheveled, mousy locks back over her forehead. She sniffed and forced a smile as Brenna rattled on, her slim fingertip following the line of childish scrawl.

"Mother Superior has given them permission . . . for three weeks! They love their new dresses . . . can't wait to see their nephews! Oh, Annie, isn't it wonderful? Maggie and Shannon will be here for Christmas! We must plan something fabulous and . . . Annie? Is anything the matter?"

Annie's plain face glowed with a painful redness, but she shook her head, bustling past Brenna. "No, it's just such powerful good news, that's all. Lord, look at the time!" She was halfway through the door, but Brenna's feet didn't budge.

"What were you doing?" she asked, her eyes skimming the piles of clothing resting on the foot of the iron bedstead and in the seat of the spindle-backed rocker.

"Just going through some old things. I'd better hurry. It's time for the boys to get up."

"If I didn't know better, I'd say you were . . ." Brenna swallowed on a suddenly dry throat, and her eyes pleaded for a denial of her suspicion. ". . . packing?"

Annie's brown eyes dropped, and her stubby fingers twisted the corner of her apron into a wad. Brenna hesitated, her brain whirling. She touched Annie's arm.

"I feel so foolish and selfish. All I've been thinking of lately is my own happiness. I'm sorry, I didn't realize you weren't happy here, too."

"It ain't that, exactly," Annie muttered, her tone wretched.

"Would—would you have left without telling me?" Brenna couldn't keep the hurt out of her voice.

"I wouldn't have wanted to, honest! It's just that I can't think of anything else to do." Annie's lower lip quivered and her face crumpled, tears spilling down her plump cheeks.

Brenna put her arm around Annie's quaking shoulders and guided her to the edge of the bed. "What is it? Please tell me. Is it something I said, something I did?"

"No, no, you mustn't think that! You're the dearest friend I'll ever have. That's why I had to go. I'd never do anything to hurt you and the mister, but . . ." She took a ragged breath, scrubbing at her cheeks with the ball of her fist.

"But what, Annie?" Brenna urged. "Tell me what's troubling you so."

Annie's face worked for a long moment, and then it all came out in a rush, as if she couldn't bear to keep her misery packed inside another moment. "It's that Thomas Black! You know, the one who knows Jimmy. Black's the name for him, all right—black-hearted devil that he is!"

"But what's he done? He didn't foist himself on you?" All sorts of horrible visions clouded Brenna's imagination.

"That I could deal with! But he talked so sweet and got me to likin' him. Oh, Brenna, he's in with the Knights of Labor, too! Jimmy must have told him all about us, because Black is trying to make me pass on anything that could hurt Mr. Rafe and that there Gould. He—he said I should go through Mr. Rafe's desk and such, but I wouldn't do such a thing and I told him so. You gotta believe me, Brenna, I wouldn't!"

"I know that," Brenna soothed, patting Annie's shoulder. "So you told him no. That should have been the end of it."

"You don't understand. He won't leave me alone. He's there every time I leave the house, constantly warting me, sending me notes, talking about my duty to the Knights."

"Well, we can do something about that! I'll have Rafe call the police." Brenna's tone was high with indignation.

"No! Thomas Black said something awful would happen to me if I told. He's sent word that if I don't bring him the information he wants tomorrow, he's gonna go to Mr. Rafe himself and tell him I've been spying on him all this time. He says he's got something as proof that'll make it seem as if I had!''

"Rafe wouldn't take his word against yours, Annie," Brenna protested.

"He don't know me. What's he to think? Anyway, it's just better that I leave. That way, Black can't use me anymore.''

"There's got to be another way. I don't want you to leave. I need you!''

"You can get another nursemaid.''

"Oh, Annie, sometimes you're so addlepated I could just shake you!'' Brenna said in frustration. "We're friends first! You should have come to me at once with this. We won't let some no-account scare you away. Unless you really do want to go back to Texas.''

"I like it here,'' Annie replied simply. She shrugged her shoulders helplessly. "But there's nothing I can do.''

"Poppycock! We'll just see about that.'' Brenna's chin firmed with determination. "Mr. Black may not know it, but he's just bought himself a pack of trouble!''

"You sure this is where you want to go, missus?'' The cab driver leaned over his perch and cast a dubious glance at his female passengers. "Five Points is kind of rough. Ain't no place for ladies.''

"Are you certain this is the place, Annie?'' Brenna asked anxiously. Now, a day later, her idea to confront Black in his own den seemed suddenly the height of foolishness. They'd driven through sections of the city that appalled her. Life teemed in abject misery where the very poorest inhabitants of the city dwelled. The Bowery was one saloon and flophouse after another, with an occasional mission dotting the sordid landscape. No wonder it was known as Skid Row.

"Third Avenue el station in Chatham Square is what he said,'' Annie replied, coughing. Smoke and cinders blew in the window from the noisy, steaming locomotive racing over their heads. Elevated railway trestles undulated like giant snakes over the muddy boulevard, cutting off light and air from the unfortunate pedestrians beneath it. It was a region of shadows peopled by the most shadowy and squalid of creatures. It was a far cry from the genteel environment of "uptown."

"Maybe we ought to fergit the whole thing," Annie said, looking increasingly uneasy. She shivered and pulled her black wool jacket closer to ward off the frigid air. An overnight dip in the temperature had plunged the city into winter.

Brenna took a deep breath. The cold air steadied her. "No. We've come this far. I'm not leaving until I've had my say with Mr. Black. Do you see him?"

"No . . . wait! There he is."

Annie pointed to a nattily dressed man with heavy side whiskers, who was loitering near the entrance to the station. The driver went to fetch him at Brenna's request, happy to be of service when she pressed a bill into his palm. Brenna sat back in the shadows of the cab and pulled her black net veiling over her face, hoping it made her look more severe. She straightened her spine and steeled herself. She could be as vicious as Lady Macbeth, if needed, to protect her own.

"Get ready," she hissed at Annie.

Thomas Black was a short, stocky individual whose beefy features were pleasant enough when taken singly. As a whole, however, they formed a permanent glower that he was doing his best to live up to. He approached the carriage with a swagger, his nose twitching in satisfaction at Annie's rigid profile in the cab window.

"Well, now, Annie, you're traveling in style," Black said affably. "And did you bring me what I wanted?"

"I brought something." Annie pushed open the cab door. "Get in."

"Now that's more like it." Black levered himself halfway through the door, then jerked. His gaze ran from the tip of a black leather shoe, up the graceful folds of dark skirt and fur-trimmed jacket, to the elegant but blurred face that regarded him from the corner of the coach. "What the—?"

"Please, Mr. Black," Brenna said, her voice a silky purr with a hint of steel beneath it. "Make yourself comfortable." Her rap on the coach door set the cab in motion. Black staggered and fell into the seat opposite.

"Hey! What is this?"

"Just so that we will be undisturbed while we have our—discussion," Brenna answered.

"Mrs. Sinclair, ain't it? This ain't got nothing to do with you!" Black blustered.

"When you insist my friend spy on my husband, I can assure you that it is most certainly my business." Brenna made her voice icy.

"I knew I shouldn't of trusted her to keep her mouth shut," Black mumbled, scowling at a stone-faced Annie. "I oughta—"

"We've had enough of your threats, Mr. Black," Brenna snapped. "Your inept and cowardly methods will certainly do the Knights of Labor more harm than good."

"I thought you was supposed to be with us," Black muttered resentfully. "The both of you are turncoats!"

"It is only my sympathy with the Knights that has kept me from mentioning you to my husband thus far," Brenna returned. "But you will cease badgering Annie or any of my employees from this moment on."

"If you cared about the Brotherhood, you'd help us," Black whined. "The next strike must come at the right time to be effective. You've got to give the working man a fighting chance!"

For an instant, Brenna hesitated, her old loyalties warring with the new. Then she shook her head. "I can't help you. Not this way. But my husband is not unaware of the plight of the laborer, and he is working toward solutions."

"In a pig's eye!"

"Believe what you like, but if you bother us again, I will not hesitate to enlist his aid. His methods of dealing with scum are not as gentle as mine. You will not get off this lightly again, sir." She knocked on the door, and the cab swayed to a stop. "Now get out!"

Black scrambled out. "You ain't heard the last of this!" he snarled, his bulldog face mean with hate at this humiliation. He plunged into the noisy mass of people and pushcarts and wagons that crowded the narrow street, disappearing within seconds.

"Oh, he's an awful one." Annie shuddered. "How did I ever think he was nice?"

"We've seen the last of him, I'm positive," Brenna

assured her with more certainty than she felt. She glanced away, her gaze scanning the teeming street. People milled everywhere, and pushcarts loaded with produce and merchandise lined both sides of the broken sidewalks. Women in tattered shawls bartered loudly for potatoes and cabbages and sausages. The shrill cries of vendors cut across the *clop* of horses and the unfamiliar melody of another language.

"Fresh fish today!"

"Cash for old clothes!"

"Saws sharpened!"

Bits of laundry dried on the cast iron fire escapes of tenement buildings that made the street a gloomy canyon. The tinkle of a piano came from the corner saloon, and on another corner children droned the alphabet at a public school. The cold air was fetid with the smell of rotting garbage, unwashed bodies, and cheap beer.

A part of her recoiled, but another part of her was fascinated by the panoply of life so different from anything she'd ever known. Brenna called out to the driver. "What is this place?"

"Part of Little Italy, ma'am. We're coming up on Mulberry Street. Where you want to go now?"

"Mulberry Street?" Brenna's brow creased, then she remembered. Rafe had grown up on Mulberry Street. Something stirred within her, part curiosity, part hope. Perhaps this was an opportunity to learn more about her husband, to understand why he built walls around his innermost self. His earliest memories had been forged here, and although he wouldn't share them, perhaps she could gain a deeper understanding of his needs if she knew something about them. She made a sudden decision.

"Driver, do you know a place called the Ward of Mercy?"

A coal fire glowed in the grate, making the nursery warm and cozy, but outside rain mixed with sleet, turning the city gray and slick. The strollers and vendors had vanished, and only an occasional disembodied umbrella scurried down the deserted street. Brenna shivered and dropped the curtain back in place. Turning, a loving smile lifted her lips.

Sean and Peter lay on their stomachs on the rag rug carrying on an unintelligible conversation of shrieks and chortles. They challenged each other nose to nose, two strong personalities testing the mettle of the nearest adversary. Suddenly, Peter arched, chubby fists flailing the air. One connected solidly with the side of Sean's head. A wail split the air. Sean buried his nose in the rug and shrieked while his brother froze in an attitude of pure amazement. Brenna laughed and joined the duo on the floor, lifting Sean to comfort him.

"Don't cry, sweetheart," she crooned, bouncing him gently. "Look, Mama's got something pretty."

She tugged her medallion out of the neckline of her patterned blue silk shirtwaist and tried to distract him with the shiny object. Tears forgotten, Sean reached for the necklace. Brenna cast a glance at her other son. "You needn't smile at me, young man," she chided with laugh. "I saw you do it!"

Peter flashed a toothless grin and proceeded to maul his fist with his gums. Sean, by this time thoroughly entangled with chain and medallion, gave a squawk and threatened tears again. Brenna sighed in mild exasperation, gently untangled fingers and chain, then propped the child against her knee. She pulled the chain over her head and dangled it just out of Sean's reach, smiling at his determined attempts to claim the prize once again.

They were both like their father, she thought, her eyes lingering on the flashing silver circle. Strong-willed and determined. Her gaze became unfocused and her expression sobered. Rafe had needed those qualities to survive on Mulberry Street.

The Ward of Mercy wasn't what she'd expected. The nuns were harried and overworked, the number of homeless, unwanted children staggering. It was clean, desperately poor, and God-fearing, and Brenna knew that the well-meaning sisters tried very hard. But her visit had left her depressed at the grayness, the lack of hope, the sterility. How had Rafe managed to become what he was today when he had started with so little hope, so little love? It was a miracle he could give anything at all to another person.

Only the oldest nun, half-blind Sister Magdalene, had

remembered him after all this time. Frail and soft spoken, she had sat in a creaking rocking chair, cuddling the tinicst infant against the front of her starched habit. Yes, she remembered black-haired Raphael, the boy with eyes like steel, who never cried. He had the face of an archangel, or of a devil. He fought the battles for the little ones who could not defend themselves from the inevitable bullies, then took the whippings for fighting without a whimper. Yes, she remembered her favorite and smiled.

Brenna had left them dozing, the infant and the elderly nun. God had a way of putting people together who needed each other, she supposed, and gave every cent she had with her to the harassed but cheerful nun who showed her out. Rafe's generous allowance would go far here.

Rafe had studied her curiously over the dinner table that evening, and she was afraid that her thoughts were revealed too plainly to him. It wasn't necessary to burden him with the problem of Thomas Black, not now that he had been dealt with, and as for her visit to the Ward of Mercy . . . well, that, too was perhaps best not spoken of. Doubtless, he would question her motives. So when he accepted her explanation that her afternoon shopping for Shannon and Maggie's visit had been tiring, she breathed a quiet sigh of relief.

She stared at the twirling circle of silver with its little filigreed cross. No, by now she knew Rafe well enough to guess he would not welcome any curiosity on her part about the mother who bore him, then abandoned him to the nuns' care. That particular vulnerability could not bear probing, not yet. A quiet knock on the nursery door disturbed Brenna's pensive reverie. Giovanni Rossini stood hesitating on the doorsill.

"Am I disturbing you, my dear?"

Brenna smiled. "Of course not, Giovanni. It's playtime. Come, sit down and join us."

Giovanni drew up a straight chair and perched on its edge, his expression a bit diffident.

"I brought something for the twins." He reached into his side coat pockets and withdrew two soft, multicolored striped cloth balls.

"Oh, Giovanni, thank you. That's very kind." His hesitancy and the loneliness in his dark, sad eyes touched her. Getting to her knees, she lifted Sean so that he could see, but he grabbed at the medallion that had eluded him until that moment. "Look, darling, a new toy! No, don't chew the chain, Sean. He's been fascinated by it all—" She broke off, startled by Giovanni's shocked gasp and sudden pallor.

"Giovanni! What is it? Are you ill?" She scrambled up, setting Sean down beside Peter. "I'll get you some water."

"The charm," he croaked, coming to his feet.

"What?" She gaped at him.

A spate of vicious Italian hissed from between his teeth. Despite his ashen face, his fingers were hurtfully strong, tearing the necklace free from her stunned grasp. She had never heard him speak anything other than flawless English, never seen him be anything but polite. Now, studying the medallion, his eyes burned black with an unholy light, and his expression made her take an involuntary step back.

"Where! Where did you get it? Tell me!" he demanded.

"I—I—" She shook her head in confusion. "Why? What's the matter?"

Giovanni's dark fingers curled like talons around the silver chain, and his face worked with a terrible emotion.

"It is *hers*. My Ingrid's. How came you by it? Did she give it to you? Before God, I must know! Are . . . are you my daughter?"

Chapter 20

"Your daughter?" Brenna's mouth dropped open in astonishment. She shook her head and felt pity stir as the hope died in Giovanni's eyes. Her voice was gentle. "No, I'm sorry, but that's impossible. Rafe gave the medallion to me. It was his—" She broke off. A sudden, terrible premonition squeezed her heart and stopped her breath.

"Rafe?" Giovanni repeated, a dazed look in his eyes.

"Oh, God," Brenna breathed. She reached out, her trembling fingers covering his. "Giovanni, it belonged to Rafe's mother."

He stared at her uncomprehendingly, his expression blank and haggard, then he swayed, reaching blindly for the chair. His legs collapsed under him, and he sat heavily.

"How could it be?" Brenna asked anxiously. "Unless . . . unless . . ."

"All these years! All these years . . ." Giovanni shook his head in wonder and chuckled, a particularly mirthless sound that chilled Brenna's soul. He buried his face in his hands and a hard, dry sob tore through him.

Alarmed, Brenna ran to the door. "Annie!" she shouted. Both babies started at her sudden eruption and began to scream. "Annie!"

Annie appeared in the doorway. "My lands! What is it?"

Brenna scooped up the infants and thrust them into Annie's arms. "Here, take the boys. Get Rafe, quickly! And send for a doctor!"

One look was enough to convince Annie to hurry.

Brenna returned to Giovanni's side and put her arm around his shaking shoulders.

"My poor Ingrid." Giovanni gasped, struggling for breath. "What did I do to you?"

"Calm yourself, Giovanni," she pleaded, her own throat tight with unshed tears. "We know nothing for certain."

"Brenna, what is it?" Rafe strode through the nursery door, his dark face etched with concern.

"Help me, Rafe. He's had a—a shock."

"I'll get some brandy." Rafe, frankly puzzled, was no less alarmed by Giovanni's frightful pallor and shallow breathing. Giovanni stopped him with a sharp gesture.

"No, stay." He paused and rose unsteadily to his feet. He searched Rafe's face with a fearful intensity that unnerved the younger man. At last he drew a deep, steadying breath. He opened his palm, revealing the chain and medallion he still clutched. "I must know—where you acquired this."

Rafe frowned and glanced at Brenna. Giovanni's sudden attack frightened her, he could tell, but there was something more . . . something that made it impossible for her to meet his gaze, something that made her mouth soft with pity and her eyes wide with compassion.

"All right, Giovanni," he placated, "but after you see Dr. Munn."

Giovanni made a dismissive wave. "Forget the doctor! I'm not ill. But I must know . . . it's important."

"It was my mother's," Rafe said stiffly. "I never knew her, but Sister Magdalene said she left it with me. They said she died shortly after. That's all I know."

"Then it's true. How desperate she must have been," Giovanni murmured sorrowfully, rubbing the medallion between his fingers. "Poor Ingrid."

"You knew her?" It was Rafe's turn to feel shocked.

Giovanni's gaze turned inward on some locked-away memory. "Knew her? Yes, more than that, I loved her."

"What!" Stunned, Rafe stared at Giovanni, then his mouth twisted as anger replaced surprise. His fists bunched in white-knuckled balls. "I don't know what the hell you're talking about. My mother was a whore."

"Never! She was a lovely immigrant girl who worked

in a fine household." Giovanni's voice took on a new burden of anguish. "I left her pregnant and alone. What must she have gone through? I loved her! Why didn't she wait for me?"

"Don't do this to yourself," Brenna urged. "Something terrible must have happened."

"Or she was as faithless as all women," Rafe said, his face hard with tension. "She may have betrayed you with another and run away in shame."

"You are no bastard! I'll not have you think such calumny of Ingrid," the older man returned harshly. Then his voice softened. "She had no reason to flee. You see, she was my wife."

"Your what?" Rafe's disbelief was reflected on his face.

"We were so young, so very much in love. We were married only a week before I sailed for Europe. It was only for a time, we thought, and knowing we were one made the thought of separation bearable. No one knew our secret."

"Why did you leave?" Brenna asked softly.

"It was in the early years with Gould. He hadn't gotten his start on Wall Street then, but I knew he was going places. I was working in his leather merchant's office when I met Ingrid. The crisis at the Gouldsboro tannery and Leupp's suicide made my future uncertain. Gould sent me to Europe to scout markets for his hides."

Giovanni shook his head. "I was to return in two months, but the time stretched out, one delay after another, then her letters stopped. I was frantic with worry. It was then that I told Gould of our marriage. He was a great help, but she had left her job and disappeared. I searched a long time. And then the war came. All these years, never knowing, constantly wondering . . . until now."

Rafe felt Giovanni's gaze on him, but something stubborn and hard inside refused to believe. "Impossible! You base this incredible postulation on flimsy evidence. How many of these simple religious medals exist? Thousands, I'm sure, and they're all practically worthless. It was a small token from a whore to the child she abandoned, a salve to her meager conscience."

"I said she was no whore!" Giovanni declared angrily. "Believe me, Rafe! Your mother was an honest woman and true. This I know. If you are Ingrid's son, then you are mine! Whatever happened, it must have been dire indeed for her to hand over that medal. She was keeping it for me and she knew what it meant. Garibaldi himself gave it to me before I left Italy. It was the one thing I prized above all else when I came to this country. Would I forget such a thing?"

"Then prove it!" Rafe covered Giovanni's hand. "There was once an engraving on the back. What was it?"

Giovanni relaxed, and a little smile curved his lips. "A single date—1859. The year of our marriage."

Rafe jerked back as though stung. Confusion reigned within him, stirring his emotions into black turmoil. His world tilted, skewed at an angle, sending all his long-held beliefs skittering across his consciousness like stones skipped across still waters. He looked into those waters for a reflection of himself, but saw only a murky darkness, terrifyingly empty. He didn't know who he was anymore, nor who he could become.

"What do you find so hard to believe?" Giovanni asked quietly. "That she was no whore, or that I am your father?"

"I don't need a father. I don't need anyone," Rafe muttered, running his hands through his dark hair. His movements were jerky, restless. In his agitation, he failed to see the color drain out of Brenna's face.

"That comes as no surprise," Giovanni said, his tone stony. "But I need you. I need to see Ingrid living in you and those boys of yours. I know now why I felt so drawn to them. Their eyes are the same blue as hers were. God in His mercy has—"

"Mercy!" Rafe roared, his face livid. He slammed his fist into the wall, seeking release from spiritual pain in a violent physical act. "Dammit to hell! What's merciful about this? Can't you see? It's some kind of cosmic joke. All this time we've been together, yet not together, and felt nothing. We don't even like each other! My life's been one cruel joke after another, and this is no different."

"Stop, Rafe," Brenna pleaded. "Don't say these hurtful things."

"What the hell do you know about it?" he said, lashing out. He hated himself for hurting her, but he couldn't help it. "God damn it, just leave me alone!"

"Can you not look into your heart and accept the truth?" Giovanni demanded. "What will it take to prove it to you?"

"More than merely your word!" Rafe hurled.

Giovanni's expression altered, took on the implacable blandness that Rafe had come to know as his hallmark. "Then I suggest we go back thirty years to the place where this tragedy—or is it comedy?—began. The answers we seek must lie within the Ward of Mercy."

Rafe scowled. "Now? Tonight?"

"If you have the stomach for it—son."

Black eyes clashed with silver for an interminable moment. Mockingly, Rafe bowed, extending his hand toward the door. They left the nursery, sparing Brenna neither word nor glance.

Brenna shivered and pulled her velvet dressing gown closer. Outside, the wind howled and the sleet continued to coat the streets. Rafe and Giovanni had not returned. She tiptoed down the hall and let herself into the quiet nursery, too keyed up to sleep.

She stood over the cradles for a long time, watching her sons sleep. She smoothed the soft black down on their heads and set a soft kiss on each sleeping face, careful not to disturb them. Her heart was full, and she felt a tear trickle down her cheek. So must the ill-fated Ingrid have lovingly touched her own baby. How desperate, how hopeless to know that it was farewell. What circumstances had forced her to abandon her child to another's care? Surely her mother's heart had broken in that instant.

What cruel fate had carved Ingrid's destiny into tragedy? Brenna bit her trembling lip, knowing that only luck had prevented her own life from following similar parallels. Across the distance of time, Brenna felt deeply for the unknown Ingrid and prayed that she find peace and rest. And she promised Ingrid that she would always care tenderly for her son and her son's sons.

Downstairs, the front door opened and closed, and there was the low murmur of men's voices. Brenna hastily wiped her damp cheeks and crept out of the nursery. She hovered like a wraith at the top of the staircase, uncertain, yet consumed by a burning need to learn the outcome of the night's investigation. Had the truth been brought to light at long last?

No conversation drifted to her ears. On silent, slippered feet, she stole down the stairs. A shaft of pale light poured from the open door of Rafe's study. She walked hesitantly forward, then paused in the doorway, mesmerized by the companionable tableau. Rafe slouched low in one deep leather chair, his long legs outstretched before him, a snifter of brandy loosely cradled in one hand. Giovanni sat opposite in a similar position. Both stared moodily off into space.

"Rafe?" Her tone was tentative, her expression questioning.

Rafe flicked a glance at her. His gray eyes were smoky with a mixture of emotions she could not identify.

"My dear Brenna. Come in." He straightened, gestured lazily with his glass, and took a deep swallow of the fiery liquor. "I want you to meet—my father."

Brenna's head jerked toward Giovanni, and she saw the same emotional turmoil in his dark eyes. Without conscious thought, she moved to his side and took his hand. Her soft smile was a mixture of relief and affection and welcome. "I'm so glad. For both of you."

Giovanni lifted her hand to his lips. "Thank you, my dear."

Brenna sat down on a leather ottoman. "Will you tell me?"

"Perhaps you can tell us," Rafe said sardonically. "I was amazed to learn we weren't the only visitors Sister Magdalene has entertained recently."

Brenna's smile faltered and she blushed guiltily. "I— I'm sorry I didn't tell you. It was an impulse visit. I—I wanted to know what it was like for you, that's all."

"Perhaps it was just as well," Giovanni said. "Sister Magdalene's memory was jogged by your interest. Poor old soul, she remembered it all."

"What? What did she tell you?" Brenna asked.

"Rafe is Ingrid's child," Giovanni said heavily. "She came to the sisters, half-starved, destitute, and heavy with my child. They took her in, but she had no hope. After the baby came, Sister Magdalene said they weren't surprised when she simply . . . let go of life."

"Oh, no. How terrible and sad," she whispered.

"It was murder, pure and simple," Rafe snapped. "She'd gone to Gould for help when she realized her condition, and he turned her away."

"What?"

"Worse than that"—Giovanni groaned into his hands— "somehow he made her believe I regretted our relationship and wanted to be rid of her. The sister told us Ingrid believed I would stay in Italy for good."

"But why?" Brenna cried, horrified.

"I'm not sure. I remember he advised against romantic entanglements. Said my career should come first. I don't know. Maybe he was afraid he'd lose my services at a crucial time." Giovanni shrugged. "My letters passed through the business office. It was an easy matter to stop forwarding them, easier still to withhold my whereabouts."

"But surely not," she said, although reluctant to defend Gould. "Why has he been so kind to Rafe all this time?"

Rafe laughed, a harsh, ugly sound. "Can you believe a guilty conscience?"

"He didn't know we were legally married until I told him," Giovanni said slowly. "By then it was too late."

"I just can't believe it, even of him," Brenna said. "It's too horrible."

"I can," Giovanni said bitterly. "I've seen it before. Gould has never given a second thought to double-crossing a compatriot to get what he wants. Look at what he did to Jim Fiske. Left him high and dry when they tried to corner the gold market. And he even liked Fiske!"

"He's been playing us off each other for years," Rafe said, his voice echoing Giovanni's bitterness and disillusionment. "The irony of it must have made him laugh. Sitting there, playing God with my life!"

"What will you do?"

A lengthy silence answered her question. Finally

Giovanni passed his hand over his eyes and sighed. He looked old, beaten.

"I can't think. I'm too tired. I—I think I'll go home," he said. He rose stiffly to his feet.

Rafe followed him to the front door. "We need to talk."

"Yes. Remember, he did this wrong to me first of all. You won't do anything rash?"

Rafe showed his teeth, but it wasn't a smile, and Brenna shivered with the knowledge that below the surface lay a towering rage.

"As I said," Rafe replied. "We need to talk."

"Have you a carriage?" Brenna asked behind them.

"The cab is waiting," Giovanni answered.

He seemed so alone that she impulsively brushed his haggard cheek with a brief kiss. "Take care. The streets are treacherous."

Giovanni's smile was wan. "It is a night for treachery. Good evening."

The door closed behind him with a whoosh of icy air. Brenna looked at her husband and chewed her lip worriedly.

"Will he be all right? Maybe we should have insisted he stay the night."

"Leave him. He needs to be alone, as do I," Rafe said, turning away. His voice was tight and closed, and he walked toward the study.

Brenna tried to conceal her hurt. She realized he had a lot to think about, but she thought husbands and wives should share each other's joy—and pain. Still, if his solitude was what he needed, then he would have it. She began to climb the stairs. "I understand. Don't stay up too long."

"Yeah, Red. Good night."

Halfway up the flight, she paused. "Rafe? You don't mind too much, do you?"

He returned to the bottom of the stairs and stood looking up at her. "Mind what?"

"About Giovanni. Knowing at last your heritage. You should see it as a gift."

"I've always respected him. I think I can become accustomed to the idea."

"Yes, but how do you feel, knowing he's your father?"

"It's a little late to develop the emotional ties of a filial relationship. And neither of us wants it, anyway."

Brenna tried to read the true meaning behind his harsh words. "It's the truth about Gould's part in all this that's upset you, hasn't it?" she asked in a flash of perception. "You've always given him all your loyalty, and now to discover he didn't deserve it—"

"Shut up!" His hand knotted about the newel post.

She gulped, stricken. "I'm sorry." Picking up the hem of her robe, she turned to flee.

"Red, wait."

She hesitated, then slowly swung back to face him. He ran his palm down his face, rubbed his mustache, and sighed. "Sorry. I don't mean to take it out on you," he said gruffly. "You'd better go on to bed."

She came down a step. "I know it hurts," she whispered.

Rafe's jaw worked and when he spoke, his words were rife with emotion he could no longer conceal. "I feel as though I've been raped. My insides are torn up. Everything I believed in is gone. Gould took it all, everything I could give and then some." His voice was tortured. "I've been his whore! And I never questioned a thing! I took it all on blind faith, as obedient as that lap dog you once likened me to. What kind of man does that make me?"

"Your own man." She came down another step. Her eyes were luminous, green pools that a man could drown in. "A man who's able to make mistakes. A man who stands by what he believes in, however misguided. A good man. And the man I love."

Her last whispered declaration soaked into him by degrees. She saw him swallow, as though his throat were suddenly thick. He climbed another step, and his voice was a gravelly murmur. "Whether that's true or not," he said with raw honesty, "it's what I need to hear. Come here."

Brenna saw his hunger and exulted in it. She glided down the remaining steps between them, coming level with him and sliding her arms over his shoulders. "It's true," she murmured, melting against him and raising her mouth for his kiss.

Rafe groaned and took her lips, instantly deepening the kiss to taste her sweetness. He pulled her close, letting her curves fit into the hard planes of his body.

"Oh, God, Red! I need you. I need you so bad!" he said on a ragged cry.

"Yes, I know," she breathed.

He lifted her in his strong arms and carried her up to their bedroom, where Brenna learned the depth of his need again . . . and again . . . and again.

And if, in his turmoil, he found solace in their passion, that was as it should be. For love and need were often found one in the same, and with that thought, Brenna was content.

She woke suddenly, naked and alone. The pillow next to hers still held the indentation of Rafe's head, as the sheets still held the warmth of his body. She sat up, her hair spilling down her shoulders, strangely chilled by his absence after the closeness they had shared. It was not yet dawn, but the gray sky reflected the gray, ice-crusted city outside her window, and she shivered. Pulling on her velvet robe, she left the room, compelled to discover what had drawn him away from her at so early an hour.

Brenna found Rafe at his desk, pouring over piles of reports. He'd pulled on trousers, but his shirt lay unbuttoned against his bronzed chest. His face held a hardness that matched the diamond-bright glitter in his eyes. As she moved hesitantly toward him, he looked up, tossing a sheaf of papers down on his desktop.

"I've been looking in the wrong place," he announced. His mouth twisted. "It's been right here under my nose all the time. I just didn't want to see it."

Brenna blinked in confusion. "What has?"

"It's Gould himself who's trying to ruin me. Everything falls into place. And it makes sense in a perverted way. He warned me repeatedly about tracking down Larosse. And then he needed my assets, just when it hurt me the most, but he knew I'd come through, even at my own expense. And the market forays against my holdings. Only someone as powerful as Gould could have manipulated the market like that. It's all right here, Brenna,'' he said, slapping the stacks of reports. ''I was just too stupid to figure it out.''

''But why would he, Rafe?'' Shaking her head, she went to his side and rubbed the tense muscles in his shoulders. ''I don't understand why he'd want to do such a thing. You're not rivals; you're partners. Your success is tied with his own.''

''Who knows? Conventional morality has never bound him in anything, as proven by his treatment of Giovanni and myself. Maybe I'm growing too strong, too independent. Maybe it's jealousy. George is a weakling, but he's the favored son. Maybe it's his way of slapping my hand, showing that the protégé can never outstrip his master.''

''But now that you know, you'll be able to protect yourself?''

''Oh, yes.'' Rafe's smile was the feral snarl of a cornered cougar. ''Two can play at this game.''

A trill of alarm raced over her nerve endings. ''What do you mean?''

''He's used me and manipulated me all my life. It's time he paid. When I get through with Jay Gould, he'll rue the day he was born.''

''Rafe, you can't mean that,'' she said, gasping. ''He's too powerful.''

''Ah, but you see, Red, I have the advantage. He doesn't know that I'm on to him. And I know all his weaknesses. He'll find that he's not the only one who can use subterfuge and deceit. He still wants the Southern Pacific, and his greed will be his undoing. Only, instead of a southern rail route, I'll bring him his own head on a platter. And if I accumulate his fortune along the way, so much the better. The world will know then what kind of man Raphael Sinclair is.''

Brenna listened in growing horror at Rafe's grim words. Her hands fell still on his shoulders. ''Rafe, you can't do it.''

He shot her a sharp, sardonic glance over his shoulder. ''Don't worry, Brenna. I've got it planned precisely. Your quality of life won't suffer, I guarantee.''

''That's not what I mean!'' Brenna snapped, hurt at his assumption that her concern was for herself. ''I was as content on the ranch as I am in this fancy townhouse. I know you're angry, but taking revenge on Gould isn't the way.''

"You plead for Gould? I find this most ironic, considering your history of hate for him. What's caused this change of heart?'' He pushed away from the desk and stalked to the marble fireplace. He poured coal into the grate and stirred the ashes to life.

Brenna twisted her cold fingers in agitation. "I plead not for Gould, but for *you*. Oh, Rafe, don't you see?''

"I only see that when I need your steadfast devotion, you fail me,'' he said, his voice hard. He stared into the glowing fire.

"Darling, please! Think this through,'' she begged. "You can't betray Gould in this cold-blooded fashion. If you do, you'll be turning away from the thing that is strongest and noblest within you—your sense of duty and loyalty.''

"You want me to show my belly and grovel like a hound? Is that it, Brenna? Just let Gould finish the task he's begun? Lick his hand like a dog as he plunges the knife into my heart?''

She shook her head. "No, no. Break with him, dissolve your business relations, whatever is necessary. But do it in the broad light of day, not like a thief in the night. His methods are not yours.''

"You know so much about my ways?'' he mocked. "I assure you, madam, that I've done the same and worse many times over!''

Brenna's lip trembled and her voice fell. "Perhaps you have. But I'd stake my life that you never betrayed anyone to whom you'd sworn your loyalty.''

Rafe scowled and kicked the brass fire guard violently. "Dammit, Brenna, he betrayed me! From the minute I was born—even before! He doesn't deserve anything better.''

"No, you're right, he doesn't. But the loyalty you gave him is no less precious because he was undeserving.'' She approached him, her hand lifted in supplication. "Don't do this, Rafe. If you deny the one thing that's given you purpose all your life, you'll destroy the best part of yourself along with Gould.''

He stared down at her, his silver eyes narrowed, as if he was seeing her for the first time. One dark hand reached out and gently fondled a curling strawberry lock. "You're quite the philosopher tonight, Red."

Brenna's breath caught in her throat. Had her words struck home?

"Please, Rafe," she murmured huskily. "We've been so long finding happiness together. Please don't risk it on this madness."

Rafe's long fingers trailed down her slim throat, dipped into the V at the base of her neck, then traveled down her breastbone. His hand splayed out underneath the edges of her dressing gown, lying possessively on the swell of her breasts.

"Lovely, lovely Brenna." He bent, and his lips grazed her earlobe. "You are all a man could ever want. But your sweet words cannot sway me. A man must do what he must."

"But at what cost?" She moaned, leaning against him. Her core heated with the embers of smoldering passion. She could feel the answering tension in him. Abruptly, Rafe set her aside. She jerked in surprise.

"A man does not count the cost of success," he said harshly.

Reeling, Brenna bit her lip to forestall the hot tears that burned behind her eyelids. "Even if that price is his wife?"

"Even so. If you cannot stand beside me, then seek for yourself whatever it is you want—including a divorce!"

"No!" She pressed white knuckles to her trembling lips.

"That is the price of your betrayal, for that's what this is, is it not? You once vowed to make me pay for the wrongs I did you. Must I lock you in that room now to keep you from shouting my secrets to the world?"

"You throw at me words spoken in the heat of anger," Brenna said bitterly. She stirred uneasily at the thought of Rafe's rage should he learn of Thomas Black's spying. Would Rafe assume that Brenna had a part in that? She sighed deeply and raised her eyes to her husband.

"Revenge is a two-edged sword, if only you would

take note of the lesson. The Prince of Denmark avenged his father, but at what price? Will you throw away everything we have together just to seek your vengeance? It will be small comfort to me to carve Hamlet on your headstone and wear widow's weeds.''

"You have a pretty tongue in your head, madam," Rafe said wryly, "but either you stand with me or against me. Which shall it be?"

She swallowed her despair, knowing herself beaten. They had shared much in hardship and joy, and she had learned him slowly and carefully. He was no weakling as her father was, nor a bully like Malvin O'Donnell, nor even quite the gentleman like Giovanni. He was a man like no other in her life. With care and strength and tenderness he'd taken from her not only her heart, but also the commitment that for so long she had been afraid to give. Right or wrong, her life was with him. She gave him the only answer possible.

"I was long in learning to trust a man," she answered slowly. "Longer still in learning to love one. Though I fear the mistake you make, I can never stand anywhere but beside you, Rafe."

He grunted. "So be it, then. We'll tighten the noose around Gould's neck together. We'll set the first knot in place at Helen Gould's coming-out reception."

"Oh, no! I couldn't!" Brenna gasped. "How can I bear to face any of them, knowing what you plan?"

"You will because you must. You must give a performance the finest actress would envy. No one must suspect until the trap is sprung."

Brenna shuddered at the violence in his tone. "I'm frightened, Rafe."

He shot her a piercing look. "Have no fear that I'll end Gould's puny life with my own hands, or even resort to hiring a cutthroat, like he has with Larosse." He nodded as he saw her start of surprise. "Oh, yes, you can be assured Larosse is his man. But my methods will prove more painful. Once Jay Gould is reduced to ruin, the world will not only despise him, it will laugh at him, as well."

Sweat trickled under Edgar Larosse's wool underwear. He swore and scratched. It might be freezing outside, but the hot house was ninety degrees and as humid as the Amazon jungle. The metal superstructure of the massive four-acre greenhouse allowed the weak December light to stream in through the steamy glass panes. Larosse ducked under a palm frond. The lush potted foliage of the palm court made him uneasy with its exotic collection of elephant ears, zebra plants, coconut palms, and trailing vines. But the section of the greenhouse that really gave him the willies was the master's favorite. He followed the narrow walk between sections of carnations, crotons, and ferns, and paused at the eerie and obscenely colorful display of hanging plants. Jay Gould's pride and joy—the orchid house.

A small figure moved along under the greenery, touching and admiring the blossoms with the delicacy of a woman. But his body rattled around inside his clothes, and his features, chiseled by age and illness, seemed oversized for his frame. He spoke, and Larosse jumped.

"Come closer, Mr. Larosse."

Larosse edged forward, wondering if the man had eyes in the back of his head. "Yes, sir?"

"This is a particularly fine specimen, don't you agree?" Gould took a small pair of clippers and snipped a ruffled, crimson orchid. "Very festive, in keeping with the Christmas season. You have news?"

Gould's abrupt question made Larosse feel off balance. "Uh, yeah."

The little man turned and fixed beady black eyes on Larosse. "Well?"

"They was poking around Mulberry Street, sir. Saw someone in the Ward of Mercy. Couldn't find out who, but it was Sinclair and Rossini, no doubt about it."

Gould gave a noncommittal grunt and snipped another bloom. "No matter."

"In fact, they been together a lot. Lot of coming and going at the Sinclair house, business types. I got, er, acquaintances in the Knights of Labor who're mighty interested in Sinclair right now."

Gould laid the orchids in a flat basket. "Is that so? It might be well to take advantage of that fact."

Larosse grinned. "Yes, sir, I can sure do that. You want me to do anything else?"

"In the fullness of time, Mr. Larosse. Good day."

Larosse watched the most hated man in American walk away. Gould hadn't let on if this news bothered him. If he was making adjustments because of it, nobody knew but him. Larosse scratched his crotch and wondered if anyone really knew what went on behind that bushy beard and inscrutable expression. He knew one thing: you might underestimate Jay Gould once, but you wouldn't make that mistake ever again—if you survived.

Chapter 21

"I can't do it."

"Yes, you can."

Rafe placed Brenna's gloved hand in the crook of his arm and squeezed it in warning. A chill Christmas wind swept down the length of Fifth Avenue, tugging at the coats of the milling reporters and gawkers outside the Gould mansion at Number 579. In swallowtail coat and top hat, Rafe urged Brenna forward to join the guests arriving at Helen Gould's afternoon reception.

"Come on, Red. Show me some pluck," Rafe whispered in her ear. "Smile. We won't stay longer than necessary."

Brenna swallowed nervously and nodded. They filed into the foyer, where a liveried servant took their wraps. She settled the folds of the reception gown Mrs. Oliver's skilled needle had fashioned after Worth's model; the dress was a maroon and beige stamped velvet, fitted, with floor-length shoulder drapes and heavy lace at throat and cuffs. She also wore Rafe's Christmas gift, a sumptuous strand of pearls and matching earrings, presented just the day before at the family Christmas Day celebration.

The holidays should have been a time of joy, but for Brenna the past weeks had been a season of strain. The arrival of her sisters and their happy reunion helped take her mind off Rafe's impending vendetta. It was hard not to get caught up in the girls' rapturous excitement over their visit to New York. For Maggie and Shannon's sake, she tried to conceal her growing worry, throwing herself into making their visit a memorable one.

Brenna filled their days with shopping and sightseeing,

their evenings with visits to the opera and theater. At home, they talked and shared secrets. Shannon with her impish smile and bright red hair would play with the twins while brunette, blue-eyed Maggie would report on their progress in school. They even begged their older sister to consider letting them come to New York next term to attend a young ladies' academy. Fearful and unsure of the future, Brenna weakly put them off for the time being with promises to ask Rafe about it.

As their new brother-in-law, Rafe charmed the girls—that is, whenever he emerged from his study or returned from his downtown office long enough to spare them a word. He and Giovanni closeted themselves for hours on end, and there was a never-ending series of visitors whose solemn expressions indicated the seriousness of their business. Brenna knew that the assault on Jay Gould's empire was imminent, and it made her edgy and anxious.

Her relationship with Rafe was tense, but there was nothing either of them could do to remedy it. Rafe sensed her unease and disapproval and withdrew into a dark, brooding shell that admitted no need for her. Although he still reached for her in the night, their lovemaking possessed an edge of desperation. Even the pleasure of having Father Christmas visit the twins for the first time, and their wide-eyed enchantment with the decorated, candle-lit fir tree in the parlor, had been overshadowed by Rafe's preoccupation and Brenna's battle for a composure that was brittle at best. Guiltily, she looked forward to the girls' departure in two days' time. At least then she would be relieved of the stress of putting on a cheerful, false front, a mask over her overstretched emotions like the one she wore now for Helen's debut.

Brenna touched the pearls at her throat. *Pearls for tears*, she thought, with an ominous shiver, and prayed she would hold up through this ordeal.

The lilting strains of the Hungarian Orchestra of Munczi Lajos filled the Gould house, which had been transformed into a bower of green with a profusion of ferns, palms, holly, mistletoe, and laurel. Potted plants and cut flowers were everywhere, and an occasional tantalizing whiff from the lavish buffet laid out by Delmonico's mixed with the floral perfume.

Brenna held Rafe's arm and moved forward with the crush toward the reception line. Her first sight of Jay Gould shocked her. In the months since her wedding, he seemed to have shrunk. Pale and nervous, he greeted each guest in turn in his soft voice, sometimes clearing his throat once or twice as if to restrain a cough. Beside him stood his daughter Helen, shyly smiling at each introduction, her demure form and features shown off to best advantage in a gown of blue satin and silver brocade.

Feeling very much a hypocrite, Brenna acknowledged Gould's pleasantries and congratulated Helen, drawing a grateful breath as they finished and could move down the line. She was amazed at Rafe's coolness as he exchanged quiet words with his mentor and nemesis. Her relief was momentary, however. Overshadowing Helen's quiet person in a gown of canary-yellow silk, Edith Gould held sway over the end of the line. She greeted the Sinclairs with a smile as dazzling as the diamond ornaments that adorned her splendid bosom and the bouquet of orchids she held.

"My dear Brenna," Edith said, pressing her cheek to Brenna's, "how lovely you look!"

Brenna swallowed and cast a glance at Rafe, who was now busy complimenting a blushing Helen. "Thank you, Edith. This is a wonderful success for Helen."

Edith followed Brenna's glance, and her dark eyes took on a knowing but somehow kind expression. "You mustn't concern yourself about Rafe," she murmured in a low voice.

Brenna jumped guiltily. "What—whatever can you mean?" she asked, faltering.

Edith gave a throaty chuckle. "I see you've brought him to heel. Who'd ever have guessed he'd make such a good husband? You have my congratulations. I could never have been happy with him, you know."

Brenna's lips parted in amazement and her cheeks blazed. "I—I—"

"Now I've embarrassed you." Edith laughed. "I merely meant to reassure you. As fascinating as I found Rafe when I first knew him, it was clear that George was the man for me. I think I hurt Rafe's pride more than his heart," she confided. "But you see, he didn't need me, and George did."

"Sharing secrets, Edie?" Rafe asked dryly.

"We have none, do we, Rafe?" she answered gaily. "Your pretty wife might be jealous of your old friends unless she knew better."

"Why should she? You and George are the picture of domestic bliss."

"Oh, yes, indeed." Edith dimpled and lowered her voice in a conspiratorial whisper. "Speaking of secrets, George and I will be welcoming another addition to our family in a few months' time."

"Congratulations to you both," Rafe said. "That makes—?"

"Our fourth. You and Brenna will have to do something about catching up."

"Perhaps another set of twins?" Rafe chuckled. "What do you say, Brenna? Daughters this time?"

"Not just yet," Brenna replied, blushing.

"Give her some time!" Edith laughed. Others waited, so she gave Rafe's arm a final pat. "Do visit the buffet. Although I'm watching my weight, I can recommend the marmalade cake."

Rafe steered Brenna away. "She'd better curb that sweet tooth or she'll run to fat," he remarked in a low, amiable voice. They circulated through the murmuring, fashionable crowd, nodding to acquaintances and neighbors.

"She's still very beautiful and glamorous." Was it a hint of lingering jealousy that made Brenna probe Rafe's apparent indifference to Edith? Although their physical relationship was all she could want, Brenna still hoped to someday hear Rafe's pledge of love.

Rafe shot her a silvery look, and his lips tilted upward. "Don't worry, Red. You'll never be fat. You have good bones."

"Bones have nothing to do with it," she said tartly.

"Are you trying to tell me you're expecting again?" he teased. "So soon?"

"No, so don't puff up with pride like a bullfrog." Her cheeks were rosy again. In the drawing room, the press

was not as thick. Rafe snatched two cups of punch from
a waiter and passed her one.

"It's not from lack of opportunity. We must not be
concentrating hard enough," he said next to her ear.

Brenna sipped thirstily, her eyes anywhere but on Rafe,
mortified by the conversation yet excited, as well. He
laughed gently at her discomfiture.

"When this is all over, we'll go somewhere, just the
two of us. There are still things we need to work out,
aren't there?"

She met his gaze and saw the softness behind the steel,
a softness she knew was only for her. He loved her. She
knew it with a woman's instinct. Would he ever trust her
enough to tell her? Would he have the chance, or would
his quest for vengeance and thirst for monetary success
overshadow and eventually kill those tender feelings?
Chill fingers of dread caressed her heart.

"Promise me," she said, slipping her hand into his and
clutching his words as her lifeline of hope.

"I promise, Red."

A voice intruded on their moment. Rafe looked away,
frowning. Giovanni approached, superbly tailored as
usual, but his normally placid countenance rippled with
an inner disturbance. He drew them to the side of the
large drawing room table and pretended to admire the
expansive display of crimson orchids in its center.

"Mr. Gould has outdone himself this season with his
collection of orchids. I understand the greenhouse at
Lyndhurst is a fabulous sight," Giovanni commented
loudly enough for others to hear. Then he murmured to
Rafe. "I must speak with you."

"What is it?"

"We must move—and quickly," Giovanni said. He
cast a furtive glance over the crowded room. "Gould told
Ames to defer all railroad construction a fortnight ago."

Rafe cursed under his breath.

"What does it mean?" Brenna asked, feeling the
charge of tension between them but not understanding.

"The last time it happened, he launched the attack that
won him back the Union Pacific." Giovanni toyed
absently with a blood-red blossom. "He knows, or else
is planning something we have no knowledge of."

"It's too soon," Rafe ground out. His fists clenched at his side. "We're not ready. Smitherson can't be counted on, yet."

"If we wait, we'll lose the element of surprise, and that's our only chance. We do it now, or not at all." Giovanni's hand closed around the delicate scarlet bloom and crushed it unknowingly.

"Then there is no choice," Rafe said, his voice hard. "It begins."

Numb with rising fear, Brenna followed Rafe out of the room, but in her mind's eye all she could see was the bloody pool of the broken orchid against the polished table top.

Two days later the Sinclair household was in an uproar, but it had nothing to do with Rafe and Giovanni's campaign in the stock market. Indeed, Rafe marshaled his forces with the skill of a general, disappearing into his study or remaining downtown at his offices while he directed his brokers into the foray as if they were seasoned troops.

He had reached an agreement with Smitherson, and in a choice bit of negotiation had the Southern Pacific's assurances behind his drive to force Gould out of the market entirely. He bought up immense blocks of stock, using his resources in the Santa Fe line as collateral, and soon he had amassed, through various sources, blocks in Gould's own Missouri-Pacific, Richmond Terminal, Pacific Mail, Katy, and Texas & Pacific lines. When Brenna asked how much it cost him, Rafe grimly answered, "Every penny," and went quietly back to work.

No, the uproar was due to Maggie and Shannon's imminent departure, the classic problem of being unable to get their trunks closed, the lost gloves, the tearful excitement of another separation. Assuring her sisters that they would indeed be expected to come for the summer, Brenna sent them off to locate their hats and coats. The weather was overcast and there might be snow before nightfall, but the girls insisted Sean and Peter be brought out to see them off, and Brenna couldn't deny their request. Feeling as tense as an overwound watch spring, she hoped the trip to Grand Central Depot would clear her head. At the very least, the ride would tire the boys out and they could all get a good night's rest later.

Brenna set her ruffed velvet hat on her head and pinned it carefully. The door opened behind her.

"Are the boys bundled up well, Annie?" she asked, then turned and gasped. "Annie! You're white as a sheet. What's wrong? Is Rafe—?"

"It's him, that Tommy Black again," Annie interrupted. "At the back stairs. He wants to see you. Said to give you this."

"Downstairs now?" Brenna repeated. She rapidly unfolded the note and scanned its contents, her color receding with each scrawled line she read. She balled the paper up and threw it across the room. "Damn his eyes! Why did he have to come now?"

"He said he means it this time. You'd better come."

"I've got to think," Brenna said, pacing and muttering. "How did the Knights know about Rafe's stock market negotiations, anyway? I can't just hand over everything I know to help them call a strike, even if Black *is* threatening to go to Rafe with lies that I've been spying for Gould."

"Mr. Rafe knows better than that!" Annie argued.

"Does he?" Brenna walked to the window and chewed her lip worriedly. Did Rafe trust her enough to take her word in this matter? Or would he only remember her opposition to his plan for vengeance and wonder how Gould knew something was afoot? Could she take the chance when Rafe's plans were even now at the detonation point? She squared her shoulders. Thomas Black was a bully, and she knew how to deal with his kind. Hadn't she sent him packing once before? She'd do it again, too, she vowed.

"What should I tell Black?" Annie asked.

"Tell him I won't see him here. I've got to get Maggie and Shannon to their train. Tell him to meet me outside Grand Central Depot after the eleven-thirty departures. Run! I'll get the boys. Meet me in the hall."

Minutes later, Annie joined her downstairs, and there was great confusion until the trunks were loaded into the enclosed hansom cab, Maggie and Shannon each settled with a twin on her lap, and Brenna and Annie handed in. There wasn't room for another passenger, and Carlisle drew a dignified sigh of relief when Brenna told him to stay behind.

The girls chattered and played with the excited babies on the trip to Park Avenue and 42nd Street, where the Grand Central Depot stood in high-domed splendor. Horse-drawn cabs and Express wagons and jitneys vied for position on the busy street. The familiar howl of train whistles split the air. Brenna caught Annie's eye, and they shared a smile at the memory of their lives at the Marshall Depot.

They exited the cab, and Brenna hailed a porter to see to the girl's baggage. With Sean on her hip, she directed the man to the correct train. As the others followed him out of the wind, Thomas Black appeared at her side.

"I don't like to be led on no wild-goose chase, Mrs. Sinclair," he said belligerently, his thick side whiskers bristling with anger.

"I'm not concerned with what you like, Mr. Black!" Brenna snapped. "I have to see my sisters off, then I'll talk to you. Wait in the cab until then." She turned and left him without waiting to see if he would do her bidding. Sean sensed his mother's agitation and stuck his thumb in his mouth for comfort. He soon cheered up, however, waving and gurgling at the sight of the steaming monster locomotives inside the terminal.

Soon the girls were settled into their private compartment, innumerable kisses and hugs had been exchanged, and Brenna and Annie stood on the platform, holding the twins and waving good-bye. The unexpected toot of the train whistle made the babies cry as the locomotive pulled away. Brenna had her hands full calming them down and didn't have time to feel too sad.

Walking toward the entrance and the waiting cab, Annie asked, "What are you going to tell Mr. Black?"

"I'll have to play the businessman and bluff him," Brenna replied with a grim smile. "Rafe doesn't need any more trouble at present. Now, where is that cab?"

She spotted it parked out of the mainstream of traffic near an alley between the Grand Union Hotel and the elevated station of the Third Avenue spur line. She hurried toward it, anxious to get the babies out of the cold wind, and even more anxious to deal with Mr. Black once and for all.

"All right, Mr. Black," she said, climbing into the enclosed cab. Annie settled beside her on the seat, and Peter and Sean crowed at each other noisily. Black sat against the corner of the opposite seat, his bowler tipped over his face, as if, Brenna thought, he had all the time in the world for a little snooze!

"You, sir! Wake up!" she snapped, irritated, and nudged his ankle with her toe. To her horror, he fell over sideways, staring up at her with sightless eyes.

A black shadow loomed at the door, climbing inside as the cab took motion. Before they could even gasp, a massive fist slammed into the side of Annie's head, and she slumped soundlessly against the corner.

Brenna clapped a hand over her mouth to stifle her scream and caught the toppling Peter with the other. She clutched her sons to her and shrank back against the seat, her brain shrieking silently in terror while the babies protested their rough treatment.

"That's right, missy," Edgar Larosse said with a sneer, his single black orb piercing her. He showed her a silver-bright blade streaked with crimson. "Keep quiet, else your whelps will feel my steel like our friend Black, here. And that would be a pity, now wouldn't it?"

He showed his yellow teeth and began to laugh. Brenna knew it was the sound of hell itself.

Terror stretched time into an eternity. Brenna couldn't guess how long they'd been traveling. The moist gray daylight formed a cocoon around the swaying carriage, which muffled the sounds of the receding city and warped her perception. She cowered behind the wall of her mind, too shocked to do more than cradle her drowsing sons in her tired arms. It barely registered when the cab slowed in a wooded area and Larosse dumped Black's limp body out the door, then unceremoniously threw a still-unconscious Annie out after him.

Fear and the ghoulish, perverted pleasure that curled Larosse's lips as he fed on her horror kept her silent, stilling her questions before they were formed. She could guess his mission, and if she were right, then she'd know soon enough. If she were wrong—well, soon it wouldn't matter.

Larosse slammed the cab door and sat back again, but Brenna merely stared woodenly. She dared not show the flare of hope that surged at the faint sound of Annie's groan. At least Annie was still alive and now free. She'd find Rafe and tell him, Brenna assured herself. *If* she wasn't too badly hurt. *If* someone found her. *If* she didn't die of cold and exposure first.

After a long time, the carriage slowed again. Larosse grunted in satisfaction, and Brenna shot him an uneasy glance. She peered surreptitiously out the small window, seeing only the vague outline of a tree-lined drive through a misting rain that was slowly turning to snow. Suddenly, a hugh white castellated shape materialized, and Brenna gasped, struck with foreboding at the brooding, fortress-like mansion.

The cab halted under the elaborate porte-cochere, but no servants met them. Indeed, the entire place had an abandoned air about it, as if it had been closed up for the onset of winter. Larosse climbed out and made a sharp gesture.

"Get out."

Brenna licked her dry lips, tugged the blankets securely around the babies, and slowly descended. Larosse reached for one of the bundles she so precariously held, but she jerked away.

"No!"

Her face held the fierce expression of an aroused she-lion, and she defiantly balanced her children and stepped out unassisted. Larosse merely shrugged, then pushed her through the ornate portals and an entrance hall decorated with marble floors and vaulted *trompe d'oeil* ceilings. It was warmer inside, but dim and deserted. Brenna shivered, gripped by the fanciful notion that the only thing lacking from this modern castle was a moat, and that soon she'd find herself locked within its dank dungeons.

Larosse shoved her forward, then left through an arched doorway. Brenna stumbled to a halt, overwhelmed by the vast drawing room with its groined ceiling and intricate fan tracery along the columned vaults. Long, mullioned windows with stained-glass diamonds above lined the walls and the oriel that jutted out into the arcaded piazza outside. In the bay of the oriel, there was a nearly life-sized alabaster sculpture of a winged Cupid and Psyche cavorting.

"Come in, my dear."

Brenna looked for the author of that softly spoken command, her eyes scanning the confusing array of tasteful velvet-covered chairs and marble-topped tables. Bowls of exotic blossoms dotted the room. The crystal chandeliers hung unlit, and her eyes strained in the rapidly diminishing afternoon light. A flicker of movement brought her attention to the small bearded figure sunk in the depths of a heavily carved armchair. She suddenly knew where she was. This had to be Lyndhurst, near Irvington on the banks of the Hudson River, and none to her surprise, her host was Jay Gould himself.

"Why—" Her voice quavered and she stopped, forcing strength into her tone. "Why have you brought me here, Mr. Gould?"

"You disappoint me, my dear. I should have thought that was obvious. But I forget my manners." He gestured her toward a chair, his white hands spidery with menace. "Sit, please. And what have you there? Not both children? How delightful. Mr. Larosse, see that a tea tray is sent immediately."

Larosse disappeared, but Brenna did not relax. The babies fretted and began to squirm as she dropped into the offered chair. She loosened the twins' and her own outer clothing, then defiantly removed her hat, sending a furious glance at Gould.

"Perhaps obvious to you, sir, but not to me. This is outrageous! That—that vile creature killed a man and attacked my maid! For what purpose do you employ a villain like Larosse? Rafe won't stand for this, I promise you!"

Gould's face tightened, and he stroked his silver-threaded beard. "Um. Unfortunate. Mr. Larosse is sometimes, er, precipitous in his actions on my behalf. But these are desperate times. Ah, here we are."

A blank-faced manservant carried in a loaded tea tray and set it on the table between them, then disappeared as unobtrusively as he had come. Larosse returned to loiter beside the door. He frowned at the howl the twins made at the sight of the crackers and shortbread on the tray.

"What's the matter with them brats, anyway?" he demanded.

"They're tired and hungry and wet," Brenna snapped, more angry now than fearful. Without waiting to be invited, she shoved a cracker into each baby's mouth and reached for the milk pitcher, glad they had been weaned. She couldn't have beared to nurse them under these men's eyes. Pouring a portion into a china cup, she let the boys sip the frothy liquid. She glared at Gould. "I think this has gone quite far enough. I demand that you let us go!"

"All in good time," Gould said mildly, daintily sipping his tea. "But first you must do me a favor."

"What kind of favor?" she asked suspiciously.

"A small one. You will write your husband a note with the details of your circumstances. You must make it clear that unless he drops his assault on the market, he will not see you again."

Brenna set the cup on its saucer with a harsh clash, ignoring Sean's protest. She settled a boy on each knee, and handed them another cookie with a shaking hand. Her voice was icy. "You plan to do murder, too, Mr. Gould?"

"Nothing so harsh, perhaps. But there are ways to make people disappear."

"Like the way you made Ingrid Rossini disappear?" she asked bitterly.

Gould hesitated, coughing. "So they know. I'm not surprised. It had to come."

"Why? Why are you doing this?" Brenna cried.

Gould waved a hand negligently and reached for his handkerchief. He coughed again, violently, then leaned back wearily. "The mistake of a lifetime. I sought to save Giovanni from that woman's grasping claws. But afterward . . ." He shrugged. "How could I tell my old friend the truth without losing him for good? It pleased me to succor his offspring, albeit with him unknowing. Little did I realize that I took an asp to my bosom! Rafe's ambition outstrips him. I know my Shakespeare, too, my dear. As Brutus said, 'Death for his ambition.' "

"You betrayed his trust! From the moment of his birth, you used him!" Brenna accused. "Can you blame him for wanting to avenge that wrong?"

Gould's pale brow flushed purple. "I nurtured him and provided for him. I prided myself in him, to my shame, sometimes more than my own son. All that he is, I made! And now he seeks to destroy me, the ungrateful wretch! That I cannot allow. I haven't the stomach or the time for a drawn-out fight. His machinations have run the market up beyond his limit. I must stop his drive temporarily, long enough to dump a quantity of stock so that he'll be caught short. That will finish his career on the Street. It would be the end result anyway, so why make the process any more painful than necessary? Your presence here will be a pressure he will not be able to resist."

"I won't do it," she said quietly. "Rafe has everything he owns tied up. I won't make him choose between his fortune and me. Besides, I don't think you can actually bring yourself to harm us." Her smile was the tiniest bit triumphant. She'd called his bluff.

Gould blinked at her, his black eyes as cold and lifeless as the marble statuary. He raised a finger. "Larosse. Take the children."

"No!" Brenna sprang to her feet, an arm around each boy. She looked frantically for escape, but there was none.

"Give 'em here, missy," Larosse growled, advancing on her. His knife appeared in his hand. "You know what I can do with this."

"Put that away, you fool," Gould hissed. He motioned to Brenna. "No harm will come to them if you cooperate."

"No," she whispered, tears of helplessness spilling from the corners of her eyes. Larosse continued to advance, but she was cornered. He slipped the knife back into his pocket and reached for the babies. Terrified, Brenna froze. Larosse jerked the babies out of her grasp, grinning at their screams of fear. Their frightened wails followed him out of the room, each shriek ripping into Brenna's lacerated heart.

"Now, my dear, perhaps you'd be kind enough to pen a draft to your husband?" Gould said at her elbow.

Dazed, Brenna allowed herself to be led to the small secretary with a bowl of crimson orchids gracing its polished surface. Gould lit a small coal oil lamp with a blown-glass shade and offered her the pen. Reluctantly, but with no hope of resistance, Brenna took it from his white hand. She wiped her streaming cheeks and took a deep breath.

"What do you want me to write?"

Excitement flowed around Rafe's office in tangible waves. Clerks and male secretaries moved briskly. The stock ticker kept up a rhythmic chatter. Occasionally the shrill peal of a telephone cut through the noise. The volume of information that had moved between the office and Rafe's brokers on Wall Street on this one day was a perpetual subject of amazed discussion. Rafe and Giovanni stood in the command center, Rafe's private office, looking out the door at the flurry of activity.

"He's on the run."

Rafe studied the reel of stock ticker tape in his hand, and allowed himself a little smile. "By God, I think you're right, Giovanni. We'll shore up our defenses before the closing bell, and Gould will be ours!"

"Huntington will be the first to achieve a transcontinental rail empire, from west to east. Your alliance with him should serve you well."

"With you to advise me, how can we fail?" Rafe laughed, clapping his father on the back in a rare show of the affection growing between them. Giovanni responded with an even rarer smile. United against a common enemy, they had at last found the rapport of father and son both yearned for.

"We'll tell Merritt to buy six thousand more shares of Pacific Mail before the end of the day," Rafe said. "With that and the bits of Union Pacific we're able to pick up, we should just about put the final nail in Gould's coffin."

He ran a finger under his collar. Despite the freezing temperatures outside, he'd worked up quite a sweat today. But the gamble was paying off. By the end of business this day, he'd be in the most envied position of all the New York financiers. Besting Gould at his own game was almost better than the fortune that came with it. Rafe grinned to himself. Almost, but not quite.

"Mr. Sinclair, there's a call for you," a clerk yelled across the expanse of desks.

"Not now," Rafe said with a dismissive wave.

"It's your home, sir. They say it's urgent."

Rafe shrugged and gave Giovanni a wry smile. "Probably Brenna wants to know if I'll be home for our dinner engagement."

"This day will be known on Wall Street as the day David slew Goliath. You should take that lady out to celebrate," Giovanni advised.

"You're right. It hasn't been easy for her lately." Rafe picked up telephone on his desk and spoke into the mouthpiece. "Hello?"

Giovanni watched curiously, then with growing alarm as Rafe's face darkened into a scowl.

"Well, look again!" Rafe barked. "Send someone back to the depot to ask. I'll get you some help." He slammed the receiver down, frowning.

"What is it?" Giovanni asked.

"Carlisle. Brenna and Annie haven't come back from seeing the girls off. It's been hours."

"Maybe they went shopping?"

"They had the boys with them." Rafe swallowed. "I don't like this. It isn't like Brenna. We've got too many crackpots walking around loose. Remember the bombing of Russell Sage's office, and those two maniacs who tried to kidnap Helen Gould?"

"I'm sure they've just lost track of time. They're probably visiting some neighbors," Giovanni soothed, but with no real conviction.

"Sure. Yeah, I'm sure you're right." Rafe shook his head as if to clear it. "There's no need to get worked up over nothing. . . ."

"Sir, this just came for you," a helpful clerk said, rushing to Rafe's side with an envelope in his hand.

The familiar feminine script leaped out at him, and alarm marched across his mind with banners flying. He ripped open the envelope and something red fell unnoticed at his feet. Scanning the single page, Rafe felt his stomach lurch as his world shattered. He fought down a

sick feeling of vertigo, and his face took on an implacable hardness. "That unspeakable bastard. Gould has
them."

"What? How?" Giovanni grabbed the letter, read it,
and his face blanched. "He can't do this!"

"He *is* doing it." Rafe reached for Brenna's note,
reading again Gould's succinct, devastating instructions:

> Stop all purchase of U.P. and other Gould stock.
> Make no move to cover calls on Santa Fe demand
> notes. Do not attempt to support price of Santa Fe
> stock. Consider all signature mortgages due and payable
> at Gould offices in twenty-four hours.

"I underestimated him," Rafe said bitterly. "How did
he know where I'd be most vulnerable? He's bought up
all my notes. While I stand helpless on the Street, he'll
dump thousands of shares of stock on the market, driving
down the value of what I own, then call in my mortgages.
I'm caught short on the right and pinched tight on the
left."

"We can fight him! We'll borrow more, then buy up
those shares to keep the price up."

Rafe shook his head. "I've already used every piece of
credit I could scrounge. And he'll know as soon as we
make a move. Then what will happen to Brenna?"

"He's bluffing."

"You know him. Do you really think so?" Rafe's
expression was bleak, his laugh mirthless. "Brenna faces
the same fate as my mother. He must be gloating to see
history repeating itself. Damn his rotten soul to hell!"

"There's got to be some way to prevent this,"
Giovanni said desperately. "You can't let Huntington
down now. If Gould doesn't ruin you, he will. *If* you've
got anything left."

"Don't you think I realize that?" Rafe shouted. His
fist crashed down on the corner of the desk. "Dammit!
Gould's got me by the jugular and he knows it. My
fortune or my family. Some choice. Even if I satisfy
Gould, Huntington won't stand for a double-cross like
this. Either way, I lose."

"No matter what," Giovanni said heavily, "I'm with you, son."

A bitter anguish etched lines on Rafe's features. "So I drag you down, too, eh, Papa? Yet how can I defy him, no matter what it costs me?" He leaned forward over the desk with arms braced, the note crushed in his hand, his head hanging in utter defeat.

Everything, he thought dizzily. *Gould will have everything of mine—fortune, reputation, and pride.*

He knew what was at stake. If he followed Gould's instructions, he'd be bankrupt, for there'd been no margin for error. By day's end, every share of stock he still owned would be next to worthless, and his creditors would be in a panic, pounding on his door, clamoring for either repayment of their loans or his head—or both.

He'd staked it all on this one great bid for fame, fortune, and revenge. And he'd lose it all because he'd allowed a woman to claim a place in his heart, and he knew he couldn't turn his back on that.

Brenna had taken his passion and shattered his defenses, replacing ruthlessness with tenderness, and stripping him of the hard ambition that had always driven him. What were fame and fortune without her by his side to share in his triumph? What value all the money in the world if it only bought an empty hearth and an emptier heart? No, money didn't make a man, and success was a seductive mistress that took and took until there was nothing left to give. With her unselfishness and her love, Brenna had taught him the magic of giving oneself wholly.

She'd tried to warn him, but like a fool, he'd been too sure of his own power, too positive of his ability to execute justice to listen, or even realize what he risked. She'd rewarded his cynicism with loyalty, his relentlessness with a softness that was the most powerful force in the universe. He'd promised her that he would take care of her, and now what had he brought her to in his stubborn quest for vengeance? With one brutal master stroke, Gould proved himself utterly ruthless and Rafe a mere amateur at the deadly game. He shuddered to think of the danger she faced in Gould's clutches, with certain knowledge that his threats were not idle ones. Yet in agreeing to Gould's terms, he'd have nothing left to offer her—except her freedom.

The taste of failure was bitter in his mouth, but financial ruin was nothing to the gut-wrenching agony he knew would be his if he lost Brenna.

"I love her," he murmured, at last admitting the truth to himself. He looked up at his father. "God, I love her! No harm must come to her, no matter what the cost. I can't risk the boys' or Brenna's safety now, even if I lose her later. I feel so helpless. We don't even know where she is."

"Maybe we do," Giovanni said quietly. He bent and picked up the crushed and bruised blossom that had fallen from the letter. Rafe stared at the crimson petal of an exotic flower, a hothouse bloom produced in only one place.

"Lyndhurst," Rafe bit out.

"It has to be. This was Brenna's way of giving us a clue, I'm sure of it."

A smile surprised Rafe's mouth. He shook his head in admiration for his strawberry-haired wife. Maybe there was still a way to salvage something.

"Damn, that woman's got pluck. If she hasn't given up, then neither can I."

Chapter 22

The drawing room door opened on silent, well-oiled hinges. Brenna rose stiffly from the velvet armchair, her movements jerky with tension, her heart thumping painfully, her words spilling from dry lips.

"I want my babies."

"When Rafe has seen reason, my dear," Gould replied.

Brenna's heart fell, watching Gould and his faithful shadow, Larosse, cross the cavernous room toward her. The door shut quietly behind them, secured by the several burly guards who watched and waited like mindless automatons. She'd been left alone for hours, it seemed, with only her scudding thoughts for company. Outside, the watery daylight had disappeared, replaced by a pitching, whirling darkness as the snowstorm became a howling, full-fledged blizzard. She wanted Rafe desperately, but her feeble attempt with the orchid petal did not offer much hope for help from that quarter. Fear choked her, fear for herself and for Annie, but most of all for her children.

"I did what you asked," she said, hating herself for pleading, but unable to curb the desperate petition. "Please, let me have my sons."

"They're quite safe. Mr. Larosse has seen to that," Gould said with an offhanded shrug.

Brenna's frightened glance flicked to the one-eyed assassin, and she couldn't repress a shudder. Peter and Sean dependent on a vicious killer who had plenty of reason to hate their mother? What guarantee did she have that her sons weren't already dead?

"I must apologize for leaving you to your own devices," Gould continued. "Why, it's grown quite chill in here. Mr. Larosse, punch up the fire, if you please. You understand it was necessary to keep you away from the few house servants still in residence, don't you, my dear? At least until this, er, unpleasantness is finished."

"I want to see my sons," Brenna repeated stubbornly. "Rafe will kill you if anything happens to them."

"Rafe has other things to concern him at present."

"He knows you're keeping me here. He'll come for us," she warned recklessly.

Gould chose a chair at the tea table, laughing softly. "I think not. Even if he guesses your location, we are quite fortified. He'll not get past the perimeter guards, nor risk the river on a night like this. You forget, of recent years I've had to protect myself from maniacs and anarchists. No, you must not count on rescue, but as soon as I have the word I want, you will leave."

"How do I know you'll keep your promise?" Brenna demanded.

Gould's smile was a slight, reptilian grimace. "You don't."

Brenna paled. Doubts assailed her. Did Rafe love her enough to give up everything? Or did he believe Gould was only bluffing with his threats and would not harm them as he promised? Was his revenge and the preservation of his fortune more important than anything else—including their lives? And if he gave it all up for her, could he ever forgive her for her part in his humiliation at Gould's hands? The thoughts that had plagued her as she sat alone forced a final question through her cold lips.

"What—what if Rafe doesn't agree to your demands?"

"That would be too sad to contemplate," Gould said sorrowfully. "You'd best pray that he comes to his senses—and quickly."

Brenna swung away, unnerved. Ignoring a grinning Larosse, she walked to the carved white marble fireplace and warmed her cold hands before the glowing coals. She stared into the flames, willing her features to expressionlessness, while her mind whirled in frantic activity, searching for a way out. Escape she must, but not without

her sons. She discarded one desperate gambit after another
until a soft tap at the door made her jump.

Larosse went to the door, exchanged a guttural utter-
ance with another guard, then crossed the room to
Gould's side, two white envelopes extended.

"Telegrams, sir," Larosse muttered.

Gould took a butter knife from the abandoned tea tray
and delicately slit the envelopes. He removed the slip of
paper inside one and glanced at it briefly, then studied the
second more carefully. "Very good. Take this to Mrs.
Sinclair, Edgar. I believe it holds some interest for her."

Larosse grinned. "Yes, sir."

Brenna accepted the telegram with the same repugnance and loathing she would have exhibited if asked to
caress a rattlesnake. She forced her eyes to focus on the
brief printed message:

IT IS DONE AS YOU WISHED. STOP. SINCLAIR.

"Oh, no," she whispered. The paper slipped from
nerveless fingers and drifted to her feet. The wind
whistled around the corners of the mansion and snow
pelted the mullioned windowpanes, forming sinister
shadows. She knew she should feel relieved, knowing
Rafe had sacrificed his entire fortune for her and their
sons, yet she felt his pain and frustration as keenly as if
a knife pierced her own heart.

"Why so sad, my dear? You should be happy that your
husband holds you in such high esteem. After all, it's not
every day a man gives millions for the woman he loves.
The bears and bulls dueled well today, but I'm afraid the
market has claimed another victim. George reports that
Rafe will not recover." Gould fondled his beard, and his
eyes gleamed with the first emotion Brenna had ever seen
from him. The fiendish delight and triumph repelled her.

"You've got what you wanted," Brenna said, her
bright head high with unconscious dignity. Her voice
quivered. "I'll take my sons and go now. My husband
will need me."

"I'm afraid that won't be possible."

Brenna stared. "What!"

"You didn't think I'd let Rafe off this easily, did

you?'' Gould's black eyes flashed. His white hands twisted in a rapacious gesture. ''Mere money is not enough. No, my dear, for his transgression, Rafe will pay with everything he owns. His sons are lost to him, and you, as well. Take her away, Larosse.''

''No!'' Brenna's horrified cry echoed off the ceiling vaults. ''What have you done with my babies? Where are they?''

''Where you'll never find them.'' Larosse chuckled as he stalked her, his yellow teeth bared, a lustful, covetous gleam in his single black orb.

Brenna backed away, bumping the secretary and causing the flame in the coal oil lamp to flicker and sway. Whatever fate Gould planned for her, it could be nothing worse than life without Rafe or their sons.

In an act of utter desperation, she seized the lamp from the desk and hurled it into the fireplace. Explosion and flames enshrouded the room.

Rafe crouched in the lee of the Lyndhurst piazza and squinted against the swirling snow, trying to make out the shadowy figures on the other side of the diamond-shaped drawing room windows. His booted feet were numb and his mustache was crusted with ice, but they'd made it, by God!

He shot a quick glance over his shoulder. He'd been afraid Giovanni couldn't keep up the pace, but the older man had surprised him, first by insisting he be included in the rescue, then by his stamina and stealth. Rafe only wished his hastily assembled posse were half as skillful. Rangers they weren't, but they were loyal men and brave, nevertheless. *Pete, where are you when I need you?* he thought with a grimace and pulled his hat lower over his forehead.

Not that Pete would have approved of the perilous boat ride through the icy Hudson in the middle of a damned blizzard. But the river was the only side of the estate not heavily patrolled. What fool would risk such an attempt, anyway? Only a desperate one, and Rafe was desperate. Now the trick was to locate Brenna and the twins before Gould learned his plan hadn't been a complete success. Rafe was afraid they were locked in some part of that damned tower, but it was dark and cold, and the only lights were from the kitchens on the north side of the mansion and the drawing room on the south.

Rafe gestured to his men. They peeled off by twos and melted back into the night. They had their orders. He drew his Colt and edged forward again, peering intently through the window.

A reddish gleam startled him, and his breath caught. Brenna. She was there, and unless he missed his guess, she was talking to Gould. He strained to hear what she said, but the wind whistled in his ears. Studying the long French-styled windows of the oriel, Rafe tried to decide whether to use them for access or if a frontal attack was too risky. Maybe they should concentrate on removing the foyer guards first. And where were the twins? He chanced another look.

That's right, Red. Keep him talking, darling.

A crimson flash blinded him. Shards of glass whizzed past his ear.

"Jesus Christ!"

Covering his head with his arms, Rafe kicked the window open, rolling forward into the room with the shriek of wood and crash of shattering glass. Cupid and Psyche looked on in silent wonder. Rafe landed on his feet, gun leveled, his eyes narrowed against the smoke billowing from the blackened fireplace. Small tongues of yellow flame licked at the edges of the carpet and smoldered out.

"What the—?" Larosse whirled around, reaching for his pistol.

"Don't try it!" Rafe barked, all predatory reflexes dangerously unleashed. "Drop it!"

Larosse's gun clattered at his feet, accompanied by a snarl of rage. Rafe swung his gun to where Gould sat shrinking lower into the depths of the heavy chair. Giovanni, gun in hand, climbed through the ruined window after Rafe.

"Rafe!" Brenna's glad cry sounded from the corner of the room where she'd been thrown by the power of the exploding lamp. She struggled shakily to her feet, unhurt except for a tiny cut on her cheek.

Rafe's steely gaze wavered. "Red! Are you all right?"

"Yes, I—" Her scream of warning came too late.

Larosse's wrist flicked like a snake. The knife thudded with sickening accuracy into Rafe's arm, spinning him around. His gun skidded across the floor. Rafe grunted in pain, clawing at the knife, as Larosse scrabbled frantically for the gun he'd dropped. Pulling the knife free, Rafe dove headfirst at the killer.

They grappled for possession of the gun and knife, rolling over and over, hand to wrist, wrist to hand, toppling chairs and tables. Giovanni couldn't fire for fear of hitting Rafe.

"Give it up, Larosse," Rafe snarled, his knife hand inching toward the killer's throat, the other wrestling for the gun.

Larosse swung his elbow, popping Rafe's head back. They rolled again. "I'll get you and that damned bitch, too," Larosse panted.

"You can't kill me. You've tried, but I just won't die, will I? You can't get to me like you did your friend Sully," Rafe taunted, his lips drawn back over his teeth. "You're nothing but an animal. You don't deserve to die like a man!"

Larosse gave an inarticulate howl of rage, rolling on top and forcing the gun down between their straining, writhing bodies. Rafe fought with ferocious determination, losing strength in his injured arm, yet grimly locked in mortal combat. The gun's deafening roar brought instant silence and utter stillness.

Larosse lifted his head, his one black eye bright with hatred. Brenna cried out in horror. He fell onto his back, the pistol clattering uselessly, and a red stain blossomed around the knife in the center of his chest. The cyclopean features clenched defiantly, even in death. Rafe rolled to his knees, clutching his arm, gasping but whole.

"Rafe!" Brenna's relief was so great she felt faint. With determination, she pushed the onrushing blackness aside and ran to fill her husband's arms. "Are you hurt?"

"I'm all right." Rafe's hands tightened on her. Nothing had ever felt this good, this right.

"Your arm?"

"A flesh wound."

"Rafe, the boys—"

The drawing room door opened behind them, interrupting her. Rafe turned to meet a new challenge, then relaxed. His own man stood before him, the others guarding a subdued group of Gould's bodyguards in the hall. It appeared they had won the day, as well.

"My compliments, Rafe."

Rafe jerked around, astounded at Jay Gould's softly spoken praise. The shrunken man folded his hands calmly and eyed the devastation around him—Larosse's cooling body, the sooty remains of the fire, the scattered furniture, the ruined glass windows where even now a small drift of melting snow accumulated.

"It was a game well fought," Gould said. "Pity the outcome wasn't altered. As it is, I must thank you for ridding me of a, er, considerable inconvenience." His eyes briefly, distastefully, lingered on Larosse, then edged away.

"You bastard. That's all it ever was to you, wasn't it? A damned game." Rafe's voice was scathing with bitterness.

"It was much more than that to me. Just as it was much more to you and Giovanni than a bid for revenge for a mistake I made thirty years ago."

"A mistake!" Giovanni raged. The barrel of his gun wavered. With a sound of disgust, he stuck it in his waistband. "My wife died thinking I had betrayed her!"

"Ah, old friend! It was an unfortunate series of events I did my best to rectify. Did I not succor your offspring?"

"It should never have come to that, *old friend*," Giovanni ground out.

"And hardly explains why you've tried to destroy me now," Rafe said in a tight voice.

Gould coughed, looking twice his age and utterly weary. "It was unavoidable, I'm afraid. You were expendable. You see, I had to take care of George."

"George? What's George got to do with it?" Rafe demanded. He allowed Brenna to examine his arm and bind it with her handkerchief, but his mind was spinning.

"Don't you realize yet who sent Larosse after Plummer?"

Rafe's jaw went slack. "George? But why?"

"Jealousy. Envy. A son's desperate bid to give his

father the one thing in the world I most desired, and an even keener desire to beat his rival for my affection and respect.''

Rafe's jaw hardened. "George ordered Andrew Plummer murdered to give you the Southern Pacific securities before I could?''

"Well, not specifically. Larosse had an unfortunate tendency to overstep his instructions. I believe the bombing in Dallas and the attack on your ranch were also the results of his impetuosity. He was reprimanded quite severely for both incidents.''

"How comforting!''

"You mean you've had the S.P. securities all this time?'' Giovanni demanded.

"Since January, actually. George was so proud to be able to supply them at such a critical moment. You remember how desperately we needed collateral to shore up the Union Pacific holdings. If you had just taken my hints to forget about them, Rafe, then none of this would have happened.'' Gould's tone was faintly plaintive, and he shrugged. "As it was, I had to do everything in my power to protect my son. He's a good lad, just overeager to please. I couldn't let one mistake ruin his career.''

"Mine, on the other hand, was forfeit, then?'' Rafe snapped.

"You shouldn't have tried to fight me, Rafe,'' Gould said softly. "Other, stronger men have tried and lost. I'm sorry it came to this. I was always quite fond of you, you know. It really hurts to see my protégé fall so low.''

"It's taken me a long time to realize what things in life are truly priceless,'' Rafe said, his voice edged with contempt and disgust. "Wealth, power, fame—the things you took from me today are worthless.''

"Worthless! See how far you get as a bankrupt! And don't try to tell me you weren't caught short.''

Rafe shook his head. "It's gone, or most of it, anyway. But because you gave us time to plan, Huntington didn't lose. Smitherson was able to enlist reserves in time. When the accounting's done, I may have lost, but you didn't win.''

"Rubbish! You'll be the laughing stock of Wall Street in the morning—your fortune gone, your reputation in shreds. Don't tell me it doesn't matter!'' Gould's pale hands clenched in frustration, an empty victory slipping between his fingers.

"Not to me. Not anymore. The real pity of it is that you'll never understand why. I sacrificed my honor, my good name, and my loyalty for success because I had nothing else—no father's love, no wife's devotion. But I wasn't trying to prove my worth to the world. I was trying to prove it to myself! Well, no more. The world may laugh or condemn or applaud and I care not. Family, health, work, and love—these things give a man's life purpose. No, you can have everything you took today— except those. But covet them, and you'll pay with your life.''

Rafe clasped Brenna's shoulders and he drew her close, under his heart where he'd never lose her again. She trembled against him, her green gaze full of pride and the love they shared. Then a shadow clouded her eyes.

"Rafe,'' she whispered. "The children.''

Rafe pinned Gould with a look. "Where are my sons?'' he demanded.

The little man shriveled visibly, and his pale face took on a pasty hue. "I don't know.''

"What! Search the house!'' Rafe ordered angrily.

"It won't do any good.'' Gould's gaze rested on Larosse. "They're gone—somewhere. Only he knew.''

"No!'' Brenna's shrill cry was fraught with hysteria. She blinked back tears of fright, grasping at the frayed edges of her tattered composure. "They have to be here! Where are they?''

Rafe jumped at Gould, grabbing his collar and shaking him like a cat with a mouse. "Tell me where they are, or by heaven I'll strangle you with my bare hands!'' he roared.

"Rafe! Stop it!'' Giovanni vainly tried to pull Rafe away from the sick, cowering little man. "For God's sake, son! His blood on your hands won't do any good!''

The haze of red faded from before Rafe's eyes, and he opened his hands, dropping Gould back down in his chair as though he'd touched something vile and leperous.

"I swear I don't know where they are.'' Gould gasped, struggling for breath. All the fight and arrogant defiance left him and he nearly whimpered. "Larosse took them into the city for safekeeping when he delivered the letter. That's all I know."

"Rafe, my babies!" Brenna wailed, her anguish terrible to behold. He reached for her.

"Shh. We'll find them." His eyes fell on Larosse. Even in death, the killer seemed to grin evilly, taking a final revenge. He gestured and two of his men came forward to remove the corpse.

Giovanni grabbed Gould's arm, his face grim with purpose. "Come with me, Mr. Gould. There are people who will search, if given the right incentive. We'll send telegrams immediately. Your signature will be the guarantee we need, unless you want the press informed of this dastardly scheme. Not even Wall Street will forgive this, and I'm certain your children don't want to learn the details in the morning newspapers."

"Yes, yes. Scour the city, leave no stone unturned." Gould coughed violently and he appeared dazed, allowing Giovanni to lead him away. He paused uncertainly on the threshold and looked back at Rafe. "We're not so very different, you know. We both love our sons."

Brenna felt Rafe jerk as Gould's words shot home, and she pressed her cheek against the damp wool of his jacket, clinging to him. "You're not like him. You're not!" she whispered fiercely.

"I came close." Rafe's voice was strangely hoarse. His large hands trembled as they cupped her face, lifting it to his. "But a red-haired angel was my salvation. I've never been so scared in all my life as today when I thought I'd lost you."

They were words to gladden her heart, but her eyes filled with tears. Her chest was so tight she could hardly breathe. "Oh, Rafe! Sean and Peter. What will we do? They're so tiny. I can't bear it."

His forehead touched hers, and he drew a shaky breath. "I know, but we'll find them."

"But what if . . . what if—" A sob of terror caught her in her throat, preventing her from voicing the fear that was uppermost in her mind. Could even Larosse have brought himself to murder two helpless infants in cold blood?

"Don't even think it," Rafe said roughly. "They're all right, and we'll find them if we have to turn the city inside out."

"I can't stay here another minute. Take me home, Rafe."

He winced. "All right, for as long as it is home."

Brenna pulled back slightly. "It's true, then? You lost—everything?"

Rafe's jaw worked and he nodded shortly. "There's nothing left, although my creditors probably won't evict me tomorrow."

"It's all my fault. If I'd told you about Thomas Black making threats, maybe it wouldn't have happened this way." She briefly sketched the unfortunate Mr. Black's untimely demise. "I should have trusted you to know what to do. I'm so sorry."

"No one's to blame. The wheels were turning long before you had to deal with this Black."

"I feel so guilty that I was the reason you were forced to sacrifice everything."

"It was my idea to put myself in a vulnerable position," Rafe said, his mouth set in a grim line. "You tried to reason with me, but I wouldn't have it. Rest assured, you won't suffer from my foolhardiness. I'll be starting from scratch, but I'll see you and the boys settled comfortably while the legalities are straightened out. I realize this wasn't part of our bargain, so I'll understand if you want to separate immediately until the divorce is final. I won't keep you tied to a failure."

Brenna's soft, incredulous laugh startled him into silence.

"What a magnanimous gesture, Mr. Sinclair! And how totally wasted!" Her eyes were gentle, her tones dulcet with tenderness. She touched his lean cheek and sighed. "Oh, my love! Were all your fine speeches for Mr. Gould's benefit alone? No longer can you boast your court success at any price. You gave your all for me. What better proof of a man's worthiness can a woman ask? What finer proof of his love? And you do love me," she said with certainty.

Rafe's arms closed around her and he shuddered, his

lips moving against her temple. "Yes, I love you! My brave, valiant Red. With all my heart!"

"Then, penniless cowboy or millionaire railroader—my place, my home, is with you. I love you so much. Don't ever try to send me away from you again. Not unless you want the fight of your life!"

"No, Red, I won't." His lips covered hers in a tender joining, an emotional renewal of the vows that bound them. There was much more to be said, confidences to share and pledges to make, but those would have to wait. He lifted his head, gently nuzzling the salty slant of her cheekbone. His arm clasped her shoulder, and he turned her toward the door. "Come, my darling. We must go."

They paused in the hall, Rafe supporting Brenna as he ordered a carriage brought around. She was content to rely on his strength, at least for the moment. Her thoughts tumbled and she gave a sudden, startled gasp.

"What is it?" Rafe demanded, seeing her go white again.

"Annie! Oh, Rafe, I nearly forgot her! She's—"

"She's all right. She had to walk several miles for help, but our Annie's a tough Texan gal! She's waiting at home right now, with a shiner you won't believe."

"Oh, thank God she's safe!" Brenna breathed.

"Rafe." Giovanni appeared, carrying a leather portfolio. "Word has gone out. The police are being notified. What shall we tell them?"

Rafe met his father's eyes and knew that the desire for further revenge was as dead as Edgar Larosse. All that mattered was the twins. Exposure of Gould's part in the plot would only hurt innocent members of the family.

"No further good can come of this night's work. Tell them as little as possible. Tell them Larosse made an attempt on Gould's life and I killed him because he kidnapped my sons. They'll buy it."

"It takes a man of honor and character to know that 'mercy seasons justice,' " Brenna murmured. "Portia said it is twice blessed, by 'him that gives and him that takes.' "

"I'll need that blessing to stay my hand if harm befalls our sons," Rafe said grimly. He nodded to Giovanni. "Tell them that, and I'll answer questions later."

"As you wish," Giovanni agreed. "Take a look at these."

Rafe glanced into the portfolio, then studied the contents with greater interest. "The Southern Pacific securities."

"It's not a great deal, but they're yours by right," his father said. "You've got a stake again."

"That'll be something to think about—after we've found the twins," Rafe replied, his expression stony. The jingle of harnesses and muffled *clop-clop* of hooves drifted to their ears. "Come, Brenna. Giovanni, send any word to the townhouse, and I'll do the same."

"Rafe." Giovanni grabbed his son's arm to draw him back, and his face had lost its usual blandness. Instead, it reflected the agony of fear that shone on Rafe's and Brenna's expressions. "The men say Larosse knew the Five Points like the back of his hand. Remember that, and find my grandsons."

"I will, Papa." Rafe clasped the older man in a clumsy hug, then hurried Brenna out into the snowy night.

The trip back into the city was an ordeal of cold and treacherous roads. The horses fought for footing, and the driver cursed the near-invisibility of the path and the blinding flurries of snow that hindered their progress. Brenna clung to Rafe, seeking the solace of his warm embrace, wordlessly drawing on his strength and fighting the chill dread that clawed at her vitals. She dropped into an uneasy doze, but woke when they finally reached the townhouse.

Rafe would have left her then, but she forestalled him. She had hot food brought for them both, and while he telephoned instructions to employees he roused from warm beds, she tended the knife wound in his arm, cleaning and bandaging it. The servants were in a state, flitting here and there, some in their night clothes, all equally upset and disturbed over the fate of the twins. Brenna visited Annie, hugging her bruised and battered friend, then had to sternly order her to remain in her bed when the feisty Texan insisted on going out to look for her charges herself. Rafe was equally stern with Brenna when it became clear she intended to join in the search.

"You cannot deny me," Brenna said, adamant.

Rafe broke off from giving Carlisle detailed orders to frown at her. "Darling, be reasonable. You'll only wear yourself out. I'll send word."

"I'm going with you," she repeated stubbornly. "I couldn't rest, knowing they're lost and frightened and hungry and cold. . . ." Her lower lip trembled and she bit it hard to control the tremor.

"I only want to spare you the strain. If . . . if it comes to the worst—"

"Don't say it!" she shrilled, teetering on the brink of despair.

"Hush, Red." Rafe held her against him, feeling her pain almost more than his own. "You've got to trust me."

"I do, with my love and my life." She clutched at his lapels, trying to make him understand. "Oh, Rafe, don't you see? I have to be with you. I was so afraid that loving you would turn me into a pitiful, weak, downtrodden creature. But I do trust you to let me share in your life, the good and bad, as a partner and an equal. Don't shut me out or try to shield me. I'll go mad if you do!"

"No, you won't. That plucky, independent streak of yours makes you strong—stronger than I am," Rafe said slowly. "But I understand, or perhaps I will fully someday, with your help. We'll build a new life together, whatever comes. Together, then, my love—for always."

The city was lifeless under its blanket of snow, but the legions enlisted in the cause spread out through the thoroughfares, heedless of the hardship. Many residents were awakened from their hibernation that night, but the word that came back to the townhouse on 57th Street was the same: no one had seen Sean and Peter Sinclair.

Brenna and Rafe led the way, beginning in the dormitories for lost children at countless police precincts in upper and lower Manhattan, then to the Newsboy's Lodging Houses and other establishments of the Children's Aid Society, and then through the homes for abandoned children on Randall's Island established by the Commissioners of Charity. But though Brenna eagerly studied many sleepy babies, none were the two she so desperately wanted to find.

Grimly, Rafe took them farther into the nether reaches of the city. By dawn, a clear crisp morning of pristine glory that denied the darkness hovering in their souls, they had run the gamut of Bowery flophouses and Bottle Alley saloons. As the city residents dug themselves out of their crystalline carapace and the streets became marked with muddy ruts and black-on-white hoof prints, they took their search to the church sanctuaries, and to the sweatshops, and to the whorehouses, and finally, by mid-afternoon, to the only place Rafe could no longer ignore—the city morgue.

It was there that Brenna finally broke down. She sat tense and straight on the bench in the waiting room until Rafe reappeared from within the bowels of that hellish establishment. His face was deathly pale under his swarthy skin, and his eyes were red-rimmed, but he shook his head. No, neither Sean nor Peter were there. Relieved of the worst fear, yet growing ever more certain that she'd never see her children again, Brenna put her face in her hands and sobbed, unable to contain her anguish any longer.

"We'll go home now," Rafe whispered, cradling her in his arms and feeling the thickness of tears in his own throat.

"Oh, Rafe, my babies," she sobbed. "There are so many homeless children! You told me about it once. Will ours just disappear like so many others?"

"No, of course not. We're not giving up," he said firmly. "But you need to rest." In her grief, Brenna hardly knew when he lifted her into the coach. She leaned against him, weeping.

"I can't pray anymore. I prayed for their return, and then I prayed that someone would find them who'd take care of them and . . . love them, but I can't anymore. You'll have to do it for me. As you love me, pray for our sons."

"I will, sweetheart. Shh, Brenna, you'll make yourself ill," he soothed, rocking her. He pressed her cheek against his chest and held her tight.

Nothing he could do could spare her this pain, and the knowledge flayed him like a whip. He'd known little of God nor held much sway with the religion of his youth, but he could not deny her anything in her wretchedness, so he held her and prayed to God, exhorting Him, pleading with Him, and at last, when he carried a nearly unconsciousness Brenna into the house, humbling himself before Him with a cry from the heart.

Brenna came awake with a little gasp of gladness, her ears ringing with the lingering echo of childish babbling. The boys! She sat up, swinging her dressing-gowned legs off the bed.

"Brenna? Are you all right?" Rafe asked urgently, leaning forward in the rocker beside the bed. His dark face was haggard with weariness in the pale glow of the lamp. He caught her cool fingers in his.

"Oh, Rafe! Where are they?" she asked joyously.

"Who?"

"The boys. Sean. Peter." She faltered to a stop, stricken by Rafe's sorrowful expression. Her face crumbled and the light died in her eyes, her disappointment tearing at Rafe's lacerated heart. "Aren't they here?"

Rafe shook his head and looked at his toes. "No. We—there's nothing new."

"But I heard them!" Unconsciously she touched the silver medallion at her throat in supplication and reassurance.

"You must have been dreaming."

Her voice was a pitiful thread of sound. "But it seemed so real. . . ."

"Sometimes we dream what we want to be true," he said, rubbing her fingers. He bowed his head in an agony of defeat. "It's snowing again."

Hearing the pain in his choked voice, Brenna touched his hair. It felt silky, so much like his sons'. How she longed to comfort him! If only her dream were real, the laughter and happy voices. . . . Her gaze became faraway.

"I know where they are," she said softly.

Rafe's head jerked up. "What?"

Her smile was sweet, her face smooth and worry free. "I know where they are."

"Brenna, I don't want you to be devastated when they're not here, that's all," Rafe said, helping his wife down from the carriage. He pulled his collar higher against the wind that whistled down Mulberry Street. At the corner, golden light shone behind the window glasses of the local saloon, but no other life was moving. Even the pushcarts were gone, banished by the inclement weather.

"I won't be," Brenna replied confidently, tugging him toward the plain door near the alley opening.

"But we checked the Ward of Mercy several times." He sighed at her serene expression. Was the strain driving her insane? He could only humor her. Reluctantly, he knocked.

"Yes, my children?" the black-coifed nun inquired, ushering them inside the narrow foyer. "How may I help you?"

"Forgive us the lateness of the hour, Sister," Rafe began. "We're looking for our sons—twin boys, about six months old . . ."

Brenna stiffened at his side, her attitude listening. Suddenly a radiant smile parted her lips, and her glad cry was a hosanna of joy. "They're here!"

Brenna ran down the hall, and Rafe, concerned, hurried after her, apologies and explanations on his lips. "My wife is beside herself. She didn't believe . . . I had to prove to her . . ."

He jerked to a halt on the threshold of the small nun's cell, his words drying up at the sight before him. On her knees before old Sister Magdalene, Brenna laughed and cried and hugged and kissed a lapful of squirming, squealing babies!

"Oh, Rafe, they're safe! They're safe!" she cried, her face radiant. She lifted bright-eyed Sean and whirled him around, shoving him into Rafe's astonished, trembling hands.

Sean chortled loudly, twining his tiny fingers into his father's thick mustache. "Da!" he announced proudly.

"Isn't it wonderful?" Brenna twirled Peter in merry circles. She kissed the chubby folds of his neck, and he giggled wildly.

Sister Magdalene smiled benignly and folded her wrinkled hands. "Such fine boys you have, Raphael."

"But how? I don't understand," Rafe muttered. He grimaced and hastily untwisted Sean's busy fingers.

Grinning, he dropped a kiss on his son's unrepentant head. "Watch it, my boy!"

"A lady brought them to us, just a short time ago," the other nun said. "We were going to send word to you first thing in the morning."

Rafe held Sean in one arm and with his other captured Brenna and Peter and squeezed them tight. His chest felt full and he swallowed on a suspicious thickness. His family was intact again and he knew a full measure of happiness. What did it matter that he had little in the way of material wealth? He had a good strong back and the will to work. The future was an open door. Nothing would be impossible for him with Brenna and his sons at his side.

He cleared his throat. "Did you know this lady? We're extremely grateful. I'd like to reward her if I can."

"No, I'd never seen her before," the nun replied. "She wouldn't stay. She only smiled. There was something odd about her though, wasn't there, Sister Magdalene?"

Sister Magdalene smiled vaguely. "Her name was Ingrid."

Brenna blinked. Her lips parted on a whisper. "Ingrid?"

Then a most amazing thing occurred. Rafe stared at the cross on the wall behind Sister Magdalene, his lips moving in silent gratitude. And from his silver eyes flowed purifying, unashamed tears of reconciliation that banished past hatreds and hurt forevermore.

Sister Magdalene gave a satisfied sigh and smiled once more. "Go with God, my children," she said. "Go with God."

Epilogue

One Year Later

The horseman drew his mount to a halt on the little rise of ground and surveyed the scene below. A deep sense of pride in the accomplishments of a year's time filled him with contentment. The new ranch house, with its wide Texan porches and native stone chimneys, stretched like a lazy cat in the mild December sunshine. A new barn and corrals shone with bright paint, and the nucleus of a herd of beef cattle wintered below the ridge. The yard was still patchy, but Brenna had set out shrubs and saplings in preparation for her sisters' Christmas visit, and there'd be a garden in the spring and roses blooming before next summer.

Rafe Sinclair smiled. Not a bad job, building the place up from ashes, making it rise again and take on new life like a phoenix of old. But it wasn't so much this place, although the kindred feeling was there, especially in the newly fenced cemetery with its simple marker for Pete Hooke and the smiling angel memorial for Ingrid Rossini. No, it was the people who were important to him, in ways he was only beginning to understand. Rafe's hand closed on the rolled-up newspaper he carried. There was a need in him now to seek the reassurance of those he loved. He kicked his horse into a canter.

Brenna heard the clatter of horse's hooves and hurried to the front porch, tugging her shawl over her shoulders. She recognized the tall rider, and a radiant smile of welcome lit her face. Rafe. How she'd missed him!

Although he'd only been gone a few days, it was the first time they'd been separated since leaving New York.

"Rafe, darling!" She was beside him as he dismounted, claiming her place in his arms as her right. His mouth was sweet against hers and, oh, so welcome, but there was something else, something that strummed through him. Puzzled, she searched his face with wide green eyes, gently touching his cheek and smoothing his mustache with her fingertip. "Rafe? What is it?"

"Gould is dead."

Brenna shivered. "How?"

"He died at home, in his own bed, with his children around him. It was consumption. And no one guessed. All this time, even to the very last, he fooled the world."

Rafe flipped open the newspaper, and the black headlines of the *New York World* blared the news for all to read. Slowly, Brenna took the paper and scanned the report.

"How very cruel they are," she said. "And how self-righteous. Listen. 'When an utterly sordid life, pursuing its selfish ends through broken laws, corrupted legislatures, and wrecked railroads, comes to its end, an honest press and pulpit should hold it up to the light of day as a stupendous failure. . . . It is not a death that will cause any public sorrow.' " She set the paper aside and shook her head sadly. "How hard this must be for Helen and George."

"Other editorials lauded him as a mastermind of foresight, courage, coolness, and energy, a man whose purpose matched a period of growth in this country that we'll never see again." Rafe shrugged. "Maybe the *Recorder*'s quote from Byron said it best: 'Neither the greatest nor the worst of men.' "

"Well, God rest his soul. Perhaps he's at peace now, at last," Brenna murmured. She studied her husband with some concern. "Are you all right?"

"It—startled me. He was an important part of my life for a long time."

She glanced at him, biting her lip hesitantly. "Do you regret giving up that life?"

Rafe's silver eyes were smoky with tenderness, and he

touched her cheek. "Never. It was empty and barren, but I never knew that until I found you."

She smiled. "And your new enterprise with Giovanni and Mr. Smitherson and the Santa Fe line?"

"Is something entirely different. I'll be able to actually see the progress we make, see the good the railroad can bring to Texas and the southwest. Owning the stock and directing a company from New York was one thing, but here I'll be building something with my own two hands."

"Like the ranch?"

"Yes. The ranch is for us, but the railroad's for the future."

"A man like you needs a challenge," she said simply, accepting him as he was. "I think Mr. Gould would have understood that need."

Rafe nodded. "There'll never be another like him."

"Some would say that's a blessing, I'm sure. He was driven by things I could never understand. Poor man."

"What a strange thing to say about the richest man in America, Red," Rafe said, his hands on her shoulders and his lips faintly smiling.

"He lived in poverty, for all his wealth. We're rich in so many other ways."

Rafe bent, gently kissing her, feeling her response and knowing himself blessed. "I love you very much, Brenna. Have I told you how glad I am you didn't become a schoolmarm?"

"Dreams change. Someday I might think about that one again, but now I have so much more than I ever hoped for." She dimpled and blushed. "Besides, with your help, I'm filling up a schoolroom in my own fashion."

"What . . . ?" As she guided his hand to rest low and intimately against her belly, delighted comprehension lit his dark face. "Really? Are you certain?"

She nodded, laughing, only to be pulled against him and kissed breathless.

Childish laughter interrupted them. Two black-haired toddlers raced around the corner of the house after a tiger-striped kitten, their chubby legs pumping furiously. A puffing, fussing Annie Barlow followed them. At the sight of their father, the boys forgot the cat and flung themselves at his legs. "Papa! Papa!"

Rafe scooped up his sons, tossing each in turn into the air, his deep laughter a counterpoint to their shrieks of delight.

"Now, Mr. Rafe," Annie chided, "you just stop that! Those two will never settle down for supper as it is!"

"Yes, ma'am!" Rafe grinned and allowed Annie to shoo her small charges into the house. He dropped an arm around his wife's shoulders as they followed them inside, and his voice was husky. "Yes, Red, we're very rich, indeed."

The front door closed, and on the porch, the forgotten newspaper fluttered in the breeze.

Author's Note

Although nothing in my research indicates that Jay Gould was a kidnaper of babies, it is clear that his contemporaries would not have found such behavior in any way astounding. The facts of his life indicate that he was a ruthless and innovative financial genius at a time in American history when no regulations existed to balance the public good with private ambition. In his own lifetime he was purported to have reached unheralded heights of villainy and justly earned the title of "most hated man in America" for his accomplishments. Yet it was also recognized that he was a tender and devoted husband and father, and a quiet, modest family man with simple tastes.

Maury Klein, in his scholarly work, *The Life and Legend of Jay Gould,* indicates that Gould was a victim of yellow journalism in his own time, and that his reputation as the arch villain of robber barons persists because of this, despite the facts of his life, even almost a century after his death. I have attempted to portray the diversity of the perception of Jay Gould's character by giving Brenna the prevailing opinion of her generation, while Rafe, as Gould's associate, is able to see the equally true picture of the hard-working, single-minded millionaire businessman.

Although Jay Gould made a very satisfactory villain for a work of fiction, his life story is as fascinating and exciting as any novel. He was a real man, with real hopes and dreams, and real disappointments. His greatest disappointment today would be the knowledge that the immense fortune he left to his children did not bring happiness, but instead caused bitterness and acrimony among his heirs.

—S.D.

SUZANNAH DAVIS

SUZANNAH DAVIS has lived in the same sleepy Louisiana town for most of her life and feels that the easy pace and old-fashioned values keep her feet on the ground while her head stays in the clouds dreaming up romances. The daughter of a newspaper family, Suzannah Davis was born with printer's ink in her veins, but she never thought her tendency to fantasize would lead to a career as an author. After college at Louisiana State University, she worked as a librarian and social worker, then "retired" to become a homemaker and mother. Now, her ecclectic tastes and passion for the written word keep her busy at her new vocation: exploring life's endless variety and love's many adventures through her novels. She's always believed in happy endings, and her attorney-husband and three lively children are a constant reminder that dreams do come true—sometimes in the most unexpected fashion!

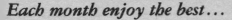

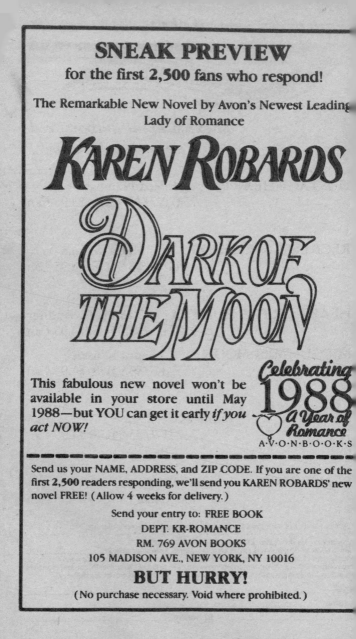